Classics

£ 3

James Matthew Barrie (1860–1937) was the ninth child and the youngest of three sons born in Kirriemuir, Angus, where his father was a linen-weaver. Brought up in the Free Kirk with its staunch sense of morals and duty, Barrie was educated at Kirriemuir and then at Glasgow, Forfar and Dumfries Academies, before going to Edinburgh University to study English, where he graduated in 1882. He worked for two years as a journalist for the *Nottingham Journal* before returning to Kirriemuir to produce a series of fictionalised sketches of local life and manners in 'Thrums', based on stories and events recounted by his mother. Published *in St James's Gazette* and *Cornhill Magazine* these tales were soon associated with what came to be known as the 'Kailyard School' of sentimental Scottish rural fiction, although this does not do justice to Barrie's complex relationship with his material. Encouraged by publication, the young writer moved to London in 1885, writing for *The British Weekly* and trying his hand with a self-published novel, *Better Dead* (1886) and, as 'Gavin Ogilvie', with *When a Man's Single* (1888). The Thrums stories were collected as *Auld Licht Idylls* (1888) and *A Window in Thrums* (1889), followed by the autobiographical memoir *An Edinburgh Eleven: Pen Portraits of College Life* (1889), sketches on the joys of smoking in *My Lady Nicotine* (1890), and his most successful novel yet, *The Little Minister* (1891).

Barrie married the actress Mary Ansell in 1894, but the marriage was not a success and indeed the author seems to have had a lifelong difficulty in sustaining an adult relationship with women – a difficulty often ascribed to the intensity of his emotional dependence on his mother whom he felt rejected his affections after the accidental death of her favourite second son. (A biographical version of this relationship was published as *Margaret Ogilvy* in 1896, the year after his mother died.) Barrie's wife eventually left him for another man and they were divorced in 1909. His last novels, *Sentimental Tommy* (1896) and *Tommy and Grizel* (1900), draw on the difficulties of his childhood and early married life. Shy, childless and yet drawn to children Barrie befriended the Llewelyn Davies family in 1896. The strange fantasy of *The Little White Bird* (1902) was written to entertain the Llewelyn Davies children, and it marks the first and most original exploration of a theme which was to make Barrie world famous when redeveloped as the play *Peter Pan, or The Boy Who Wouldn't Grow Up* (1904) and done again in prose as *Peter and Wendy* (1911).

The Little Minister was very successfully dramatised in 1897, and from 1900 onwards, Barrie wrote mostly for the London stage, making both his reputation and his fortune with over thirty-six plays in the next thirty years. Apart from *Peter Pan*, his most notable plays include *Quality Street* (1901), *The Admirable Crichton* (1902), *What Every Woman Knows* (1908), *Dear Brutus* (1917), *Mary Rose* (1920), *Shall We Join the Ladies?* (1921) and *The Boy David* (1936). A privately published collection of autobiographical studies appeared as *The Greenwood Hat* in 1930, and a late novella *Farewell Miss Julie Logan* (1932) returned to his fascination with the supernatural and a sense of romantic loss.

Barrie's success as a popular dramatist brought him into contact with most of the writers, society figures and politicians of his day. He became Sir James Barrie when granted a baronetcy in 1913, and received the Order of Merit in 1922. He was elected Rector of the University of St Andrews and later Chancellor of the University of Edinburgh.

ANDREW NASH received his doctorate from the University of St Andrews and has published several articles on Barrie's fiction as well as on other aspects of Scottish literature and Victorian publishing. He is currently a research fellow based jointly at the Univeristy of Reading and the Institute of English Studies in the Univeristy of London.

J.M. Barrie

FAREWELL MISS JULIE LOGAN:
A BARRIE OMNIBUS

The Little White Bird
The Twelve-Pound Look
Farewell Miss Julie Logan

Introduced and Edited by
ANDREW NASH

CANONGATE
CLASSICS
92

This edition first published as a Canongate Classic in 2000 by Canongate Books Ltd, 14 High Street, Edinburgh EH1 1TE. *The Little White Bird* first published by Hodder and Stoughton in 1902; *The Twelve-Pound Look* first published by Hodder and Stoughton in 1914; *Farewell Miss Julie Logan* first published by Hodder annd Stoughton in 1932. Copyright © the estate of J.M. Barrie. *The Little White Bird, The Twelve-Pound Look* and *Farewell Miss Julie Logan* are reproduced by permission of Samuel French Ltd on behalf of the Estate of J.M. Barrie. Introductions, notes and glossary copyright © Andrew Nash 2000.

The publishers gratefully acknowledge general subsidy from the Scottish Arts Council towards the publication of the Canongate Classics series and a specific grant towards the publication of this title.

Set in 10pt Plantin by Hewer Text Ltd, Edinburgh. Printed and bound in Scotland by Omnia Books Limited Bishopbriggs, Glasgow.

Canongate Classics
Series Editor: Roderick Watson
Editorial Board: J.B. Pick, Cairns Craig, Dorothy McMillan

British Library Cataloguing-in-Publication Data
A catalogue record for this book is available on request from the British Library.

ISBN 1 84195 003 3

www.canongate.net

Contents

Introduction

On afternoons in the Kensington Gardens in 1897 and 1898 a short, strange looking man with an enormous brown and white dog would often catch sight of two small boys in red berets, walking together with their nurse and their baby brother. The man was James Matthew Barrie, a successful novelist and fledgling playwright; the boys were George, Jack and Peter Llewelyn Davies, the grandsons of the novelist and *Punch* cartoonist George Du Maurier. Their meeting was to change the lives of everyone concerned as well as result in the creation of a fictional character who has attained mythic status – Peter Pan. Barrie had an astonishing affinity for children; he was able to capture their attention through adventure stories and conjuring tricks and he quickly became a great favourite of the Llewelyn Davies boys, particularly the eldest, George. When later he made the acquaintance of their mother, Sylvia, his entrance into the circle of their lives was complete and he soon came to monopolise the family, though his ubiquitous presence was always resented by the father, Arthur. When the boys were orphaned in 1910 Barrie assumed responsibility for them and became their guardian.

It is appropriate that the story of Barrie's relationship with the Llewelyn Davies family should have been made the subject of both a book and a television drama.[1] It means that the story exists for us in a number of artistic versions, because as a work of fiction *The Little White Bird* itself stands as an expression, or an artistic embodiment, of that relationship. Few writers have dramatised their own lives in art in such an explicit and searching a manner as Barrie, so much so that his work has often been seen as little more than a revelation of his complicated personality. The resort to autobiographical experience was, however, a necessary part of his artistic concerns, for Barrie was a writer obsessed with the question of what it means to create art: to play out roles, invent fantasies and live in the world of the imagination. The republication of *The Little White Bird* offers the chance to restore these themes to the discussion of Barrie's fiction as well as to situate him more appropriately in the canon of Scottish literature.

Barrie first achieved literary success in 1888 with *Auld Licht Idylls*, a humorous collection of sketches compiled from previously published newspaper articles. Based on the childhood memories of his mother, the sketches were set in a rural Scotland of the mid-nineteenth century and told of life in 'Thrums' – Barrie's fictional name for his native town of Kirriemuir. The work appealed to the contemporary vogue for regionalism and Thrums soon became as famous as Hardy's Wessex, prompting Barrie to embark on a similar volume that appeared the following year entitled *A Window in Thrums*. These two books have become the basis for the discussion of Barrie within the context of Scottish literature though in truth they are little more than apprentice works. That they should have remained in the cultural consciousness for so long is due not to their intrinsic quality but to the fact that they precipitated a host of imitations – works that with their largely nostalgic and sentimental tone earned the now legendary epithet 'kail-yard'. The result has been the comparative neglect of Barrie's later, more ambitious works of fiction, where he moved his attention away from the genres of local colour and social realism, towards a more reflexive concern with art, creativity and fantasy.

The representation of reality in fiction was one of the issues that preoccupied novelists and critics in the late-nineteenth century and in the work of Henry James in particular there was a movement away from the emphasis on an external reality towards a concern with how the individual mind apprehended, or tried to apprehend, reality. In Barrie's fiction this concern with the internal life took the form of a developing interest in the construction of reality by the artistic mind. The explicit contrast between the world of reality and the world of the story that we find explored in *The Little White Bird* was to emerge gradually through the novels that followed on from the Thrums collections. The narrator of *The Little Minister* (1891), for example, identifies himself as a conscious artist and continually draws attention to his struggle to persuade the reader of the reality and profundity of his fictional illusion. As a result, the novel moves away from the largely realistic portrayal of a community found in *Auld Licht Idylls* and presents a deliberately artificial world of myth, romance and fairy tale. With the publication of *Sentimental Tommy* (1896) and *Tommy and Grizel* (1900) – two novels that had an important effect on the young D.H. Lawrence – Barrie took the issue of the creative mind to the centre of his work. Tommy, the hero of these two largely autobiographical works, is a fantasist whose identity consists entirely in role-playing. He is able to believe so completely in any imaginary situation that he loses the boundary between reality and pretence and has no concrete self. In both works Tommy is presented as the archetypal artist, substituting reality with a world of his own making, but whereas in the first novel it is implied that art and fantasy are the legitimate domain of childhood, the later novel dramatises the debilitating effects Tommy's fantasies have on other people, and charts his struggle to reject them and embrace reality. Like Joyce's *Portrait of the Artist*, the Tommy novels are autobiographical not because they recount factual details of Barrie's life but because they define the author's vocation as an artist. Barrie saw this artistic vocation as forming his essential identity and he came to view his childhood role-playing games as the early products of his dramatic imagination. From an early stage in his adult life he kept a series of notebooks where he recorded the events and emotions of his life and began to shape them into works of art. The artist was thus fulfilling his vocation by responding to life in no other terms than as raw material for art, and it is for this reason that Barrie's works necessarily draw on the events of his life. For him life was, in a very real sense, fiction. All of his mature output turns on the question of the boundaries between fiction and reality and the implications of living inside self-made illusions.

Tommy and Grizel bears a further important relation to *The Little White Bird* in its preoccupation with male sexuality and sexual desire. Because everything Tommy does is pretence and all his emotions are fake, he is presented as incapable of genuine emotional desire and thus unable to return the affections of Grizel, the woman who loves him. The work is an extended analysis of the failure of male sexual desire and has recently been identified as groundbreaking in the way it treats the sexual warfare *within* a man.[2] The work was clearly written out of Barrie's emotions towards his own unhappy marriage with the actress Mary Ansell, which according to some reports was unconsummated and was to end in divorce in 1909. As Barrie transferred his time and affection to the Llewelyn Davies boys he found in that family an outlet for the fatherly emotions that, for whatever reason, he was unable to experience in his own life. When in 1899 Sylvia became pregnant with her fourth child, Barrie was able to join in with the tremendous excitement of the family and he started to jot down ideas for a story in his notebook. There were already a number of notes for fairy stories that were clearly suggested by the tales he was telling to George, but one note in particular proved the catalyst for a work: 'my white bird a book, hers a baby'.[3] Through his adventures with George, Barrie had found an idea for the exploration of the theme that had been slowly emerging through his writing. Life, expressed through its ultimate source of maternity, was to be contrasted to Art and its source: creative inspiration.

The contrast between the creative artist and the creative mother provides the frame within which the narrative of *The Little White Bird* is structured. The narrator, a retired soldier and London bachelor clubman, tells stories to a little boy in order to recreate him as a fictional character so that he can claim parental possession of him. The narrative thus turns on the act of narration itself and it is significant that the narrator's claim to ownership takes the form of a myth that seeks to transcend natal creation: the extended fantasy that he tells David – that children do not originate in the womb but have a previous life as birds in the Kensington Gardens – has the aim of disempowering the biological mother and laying claim to prior knowledge of her child. *The Little White Bird* is thus on one level a fantasy of self-fathering – a recurrent theme of *fin de siècle* works – where the asexual world of art is claimed as superior to the real world of sexuality and childbearing. It is no coincidence that the narrator often asks us to 'conceive' his imaginary situations; he views writing as a substitute for giving birth and he is able to indulge in his fantasies of self-fathering because of David's implicit belief in the stories that he is told. Barrie saw children as archetypal artists and fantasists, and David's capacity to take the story as reality enables the narrator to cast himself as the creator of the boy's identity.

Because the narrator is a fantasist, and because parts of the work consist of stories that he is telling to David, *The Little White Bird* has a complicated layering of address and a shifting narrative tone. Some passages are addressed solely to the reader and others principally to David; the Peter Pan chapters, however, are narrated in a tone that in its adopted child-speech is surely meant to be told *with* David, and in these chapters the narrator not only claims to understand children but casts himself as part of the world they inhabit – a world to which parents, nurses and schoolmasters are permitted no access. But it is not just the tone of the narration that makes the structure of the work both innovative and complicated. By making the narrator of his work a fantasist Barrie creates an unstable narrative where we can never be certain what is true and what is made up. As a result, fantasy operates on a number of levels: there is a contrast, for example, between the conscious illusion of the Peter Pan chapters and the magical transformation of the dog, Porthos, which is presented as something that actually happens. Some critics have taken Barrie to task for what they see as his devious narrative methods but this instability in the narrative is what marks out his distinctiveness as a fantasy writer. *The Little White Bird* is not a fantasy in the way that Lewis Carroll's *Alice* books are, for example; instead it plays out a reflexive debate on the values and drawbacks of fantasy.

As far as the Peter Pan story is concerned, this essential dynamic has become lost in the various prose versions of the myth that circulate today. When the Peter Pan chapters were lifted from *The Little White Bird* and published separately as *Peter Pan in Kensington Gardens* the work became divorced from its original context as a deliberately artificial story told by a middle-aged bachelor to a little boy inside a novel that we later learn the bachelor to be writing. The implications of this divorcing have been discussed at length by Jacqueline Rose who is able to show that much of the complexity of Peter Pan is lost if the work is read outside *The Little White Bird*.[4] When Barrie developed the story and produced the play *Peter Pan* in 1904 he was able to use his sophisticated command of staging to highlight the essential artifice of the work, but in the various prose retellings of 'Peter Pan' that have been circulated ever since the play was first performed the metafictional basis of the story has been eroded. With *The Little White Bird* we can see how the fantasy of *Peter Pan* was first written as part of an extended analysis of the act of fantasy itself.

The narrator has an ambivalent relationship with the fantasies he creates. As Lynette Hunter has argued, he is presented as 'continually slipping into fantasy and continually drawing back to destroy the illusion'.[5] In the chapter 'A Confirmed Spinster' he explains how he was once trapped within fantasy. He recounts his involvement with a mysterious 'she', whose identity (and even existence) is made deliberately vague. Some critics have seen her as a real person with whom the narrator was once in love, but the manuscript drafts suggest that she is supposed to be seen as the embodiment of an ideal woman that the narrator has created in his own mind. 'She' existed for him so long as he believed in her implicitly, but as soon as he stepped outside the 'magic circle' and left the 'enchanted fields' he lost her. 'She' is thus a metaphor for fantasy and the narrator's loss of her is an indication that he can now distinguish fantasy from reality. He remains, however, tempted by the lure of fantasy, as seen in the very next chapter when he considers changing the events of the story he is writing so that he did not drop the letter that reconciled David's parents but attempted to woo Mary himself. The temptation is to deny reality and live inside a purely imaginative world that he, as the author of the story, can control completely. The events of the book, however, show how reality is always intruding upon the narrator's fantasies, breaking them down and forcing him to recognise their limitations.

It is the contrast between fantasy and reality that illuminates the issue of sentimentality, which is central to all of Barrie's work. The narrator is a sentimentalist in Barrie's specific definition of the term because his displays of emotion and moments of feeling are prompted more by a love of emotion itself than a genuine interest in the situation at stake. He tries, for instance, to avoid becoming

emotionally involved with the very real experiences of the
family of his club waiter, and the voyeurism that accom-
panies his philanthropic interest in the life of Mary and her
husband turns his generosity into something near self-
indulgence. His determination to remain unknown to
the couple demonstrates Oscar Wilde's definition that a
'sentimentalist is simply one who desires to have the luxury
of an emotion without paying for it'.[6] The falsity of his
emotional attachment to them is captured in the imaginary
portrait that Mary's husband paints of their mystery bene-
factor: to them, he is only knowable as a work of art. When
Mary tracks him down and forces him to become real to
them, his sentimental attachment is broken and he is forced
to come out of the world of art into reality.

The narrator's sentimentalism means that his deepest
emotional experiences are always played-out at the level of
fantasy. Timothy, the imaginary child he invents on the
night that David is born, gives him the sublimated emotion
of paternity he so desires in real life. The dream child,
however, is eventually usurped by the real child when the
narrator kills Timothy off so that he can pretend to have lots
of toys and clothes to give David. But Timothy's death
allows the narrator to indulge his sentimentality. He
mourns the death of his imaginary son like Jack Worthing
does his imaginary brother in Wilde's *The Importance of
Being Earnest* but unlike Jack he does so not because he has
to but because he wants to, and not in public but in private.
The comparison that he is always drawing between
Timothy and David is thus part of a larger comparison
between the relative profundity to be found in invented
emotion and that within real experience, and for all his love
of sentimentality, the presence of David throughout the
work continually reminds the narrator of the superior
claims of reality. Every time that he calls him 'father' the
narrator is reminded of the falsity of his claims to ownership
of the boy, and the key episode where David spends the

night with him shows clearly that the narrator's desire for possession can only be realised within fantasy. At the very point when the two are at their closest – too close, some might argue, for the work to be free from the stigma of paedophilia – the narrator forgets David's name and calls him Timothy, a mistake that hits exactly at his struggle between fantasy and reality. David, the real child, can only 'slip from his arms like a trout'. The only way the narrator can truly possess him is if he is misrecognised as the dream child Timothy.

In the serial text it is suggested that Timothy and Peter Pan are one and the same, and the Peter Pan chapters, which at first glance appear to form an isolated story, relate carefully to the character of the man who is narrating them. The intertextuality and parodic style serves to make the artifice of the story visible and the chapters continue the metafictional debate on fantasy. Whereas in the play Peter is the boy who chooses not to grow up, in *The Little White Bird* he is presented as locked out of reality and forced to live in a world that he must interpret for himself. He thus becomes a metaphor for the ultimate fantasist, marooned on an island and locked in a park in the same way as the narrator explains that he was once entrapped within the magic circle of fantasy. But the drawback for Peter is that he is limited to the island and to himself; he is unable to penetrate beyond the iron bars to reality and always feels a sense of lack. It is significant, therefore, that this first telling of the Peter Pan story should be articulated with the sense of tragedy that Barrie always associated with it.

Both Timothy and Peter Pan have a further identity, however, and that is *The Little White Bird* itself. It is made clear at the end of the work that the narrator is not just telling the story but actively *writing* the book we are reading, and he is doing so explicitly to contrast his artistic creativity with the maternal creativity of the pregnant Mary. Both the book that the narrator writes and the story that is contained within it are thus identified as a substitute child and as part of a claim the narrator makes that art is superior to reality – the 'substance' as opposed to the 'shadow'. In the story that he tells inside the novel he tries to elevate his creative power over that of the mother firstly by allowing her child to be born without her physically giving birth and then, when his fantasy has been broken by the demands of David, pretending that the sex of the unborn child can be determined by the outcome of a cricket match. Throughout these closing chapters, however, there is an ironic detachment in the narrator's tone as he claims that there has never been so much at stake on the outcome of a cricket match, when he knows only too well that there is nothing at stake at all. What breaks the narrator's fantasy again is the reality of David, who really believes that if he loses the match his mother will not give birth to the girl she so desperately wants. It is his fear that breaks the omnipotence of the artist-narrator and undermines the force of his creative power, just as it is the mother who triumphs over the dishonest artistry that he purveys in the dedication.

After *The Little White Bird* Barrie turned his attention almost exclusively to the stage and produced some of the most popular and critically-acclaimed plays of his generation. His drama demonstrates a commitment to issues of myth and fantasy that contrast with the school of realism and social criticism typified by his contemporary, Shaw. The one-act piece *The Twelve-Pound Look* nevertheless shows him to be a perceptive social critic in his own right and represents his wit and subtlety at its sharpest. Barrie recognised that the 'text' of a play was always the text in performance and he constantly altered and revised his scripts with each production he oversaw. Whenever his plays were printed he added the elaborate commentary found in the stage directions, drawing attention to the differing perspectives generated by reading and viewing a play. The stage directions in *The Twelve-Pound Look* have a particular oddity in that parts are addressed to a male audience, asking the reader to identify with Harry. Barrie had been a supporter of women's suffrage during his time as a leader-writer on the *Nottingham Journal* and the feminist manifesto contained in *The Twelve-Pound Look* is remarkable for its conviction and the way that it identifies the existing social order as sterile and illusory. The play is characteristic of Barrie in that it turns on the question of roles and role-playing, revealing characters either living in illusions or escaping them. The 'spiritless' Lady Sims is on the point of recognising the illusion from which Kate has already broken free – that a woman's identity only exists in relation to her husband and that she should think herself amply provided for by him. Kate, by contrast, speaks and acts as she feels not as etiquette directs her and is revealed as an illusionist herself, having fooled Harry by living the double-life of a typist whilst still being Mrs Sims. An earlier play, *What Every Woman Knows* (1908), had advanced the theory that women are intellectually superior to men and the scene between Kate and Harry serves to ridicule him as he completely fails to follow her metaphors and continues in his misplaced confidence in his knowledge of women. For all the revelations that confront him, we are told that Harry is 'soon himself again', a self that we, however, know only to be a role: the proud, successful Sir Harry that he is, literally, acting out at the beginning of the play.

In 1931, forty years after he had published *The Little Minister*, Barrie returned to the Scottish setting of his early works and produced the novella *Farewell Miss Julie Logan*, a supernatural story that contains some of the author's richest prose. By making the work take the form of a diary, Barrie allows the character of Adam Yestreen to emerge from his own writing. The poetic phrases and sensual descriptions, together with the self-conscious mix of cultivated English and synthetic Scots, reveals the dissociation that exists between the minister's vivid, imaginative longings and the rational, puritanical demands of his calling. It is the struggle to repress these longings that brings about the loosening of Adam's grip on reality, but the figure of Julie Logan, and the minister's exultant emotions towards her, suggests that it is only in the imagination that he can truly express himself and fulfil his emotional needs. His repression of these needs is symbolised by the way his overtly feminised violin follows him around, tempting him, and exposing the self-denial upon which his sense of 'reality' is based. Reality emerges as a fiction that the minister has created and in trying to cling to it, it becomes damaging to him. In this sense the work offers a contrast to *The Little White Bird* by exploring the dangers of not permitting imaginative, sensuous or artistic elements to enter one's life. Taken together, the two works suggest the importance of having a place for both reality and the imagination.

As a symbol of the forbidden, the violin introduces the wider cultural reference raised by *Farewell Miss Julie Logan*: Jacobitism and the Scottish national past. The story appears to operate at the level of a national as well as individual psyche, presenting the now famous exposition of a Scotland dissociated between the romantic past and the rational present. That romantic past is seen to belong to the world of art and the imagination – to the Jacobite lilts that flow so freely from the violin and the spectre of Julie Logan herself that is created by the minister's imagination. The suggestion is that the Scottish past can only be brought back to the present in ghostly forms, and even then only when the glen is 'locked' and in 'stillness'; when reality is, momentarily, suspended. The isolated setting of the story and the recurring images of caging and imprisonment all add to the densely symbolic texture of the work.

Barrie has often been accused of being an insufficiently Scottish writer, yet the investigations into the relationship between illusion and reality that recur throughout his work place him at the centre of a visible tradition in Scottish fiction, traceable from James Hogg to Alasdair Gray, that has been produced by a culture engaged with the question of the apprehension of reality by the creative mind and of the limits of the artistic imagination. The works gathered together in this volume reveal him not as an author who evades or falsifies reality by retreating into a world of childhood, but one concerned with the relationship between the rational and the imaginative, the fantastic and the real. *A Barrie Omnibus* restores innovative texts by an innovative writer whose place in the canon of Scottish literature is still to be adequately mapped out.

Andrew Nash

1. Andrew Birkin wrote the series of television plays first broadcast in 1978 and a biographical account entitled *J.M. Barrie and the Lost Boys* (London, 1979).
2. See Eve Kosofsky Sedgwick, *Epistemology of the Closet* (London, 1990).
3. Beinecke Library MS A2/19.
4. Jacqueline Rose, *The Case of Peter Pan, or the Impossibility of Children's Fiction* (London and Basingstoke, 1984).
5. Lynette Hunter, 'J.M. Barrie: The Rejection of Fantasy', *Scottish Literary Journal*, 5, 1 (1978), 39–52, p. 46.
6. Oscar Wilde, *De Profundis*, 1905 (Harmondsworth, 1954), p. 196.

THE LITTLE WHITE BIRD

The Child's Map of Kensington Gardens

The Little White Bird was first published in *Scribner's Magazine* in four monthly instalments from August to November 1902. At the request of the editor, Edward Livermore Burlingame, three chapters were omitted in the serial version: chapter 17, 'The Little House', chapter 18, 'Peter's Goat' and chapter 20, 'David and Porthos Compared'. The omissions shortened the portion of the work devoted to Peter Pan and also darkened the atmosphere of that section, which in the serial closes with Peter confronted by the locked iron bars at the end of chapter 16. When revising the work for book publication Barrie made one significant change, removing a line in the final chapter where Mary A——— explicitly correlates Peter Pan with Timothy. He also dispensed with the alternative title and added the elaborate map which furnishes the frontispiece of the book.

In his negotiation with Burlingame, Barrie had suggested that the Peter Pan chapters might be given pictures and suggested the name of Henry Ford, who had illustrated Andrew Lang's fairy books. In the event, however, it was not until the Peter Pan chapters were published independently as *Peter Pan in Kensington Gardens* (1906) that any illustrations were published. The publication of that volume followed on from the success of the play *Peter Pan*, first performed in 1904.

The present text is taken from the first UK book edition published by Hodder and Stoughton in November 1902. The work was published simultaneously in New York by Charles Scribner's Sons. Apart from minor changes of spelling and punctuation the variants in the serialised version are listed below in the Notes at the end. Obvious printing errors have been silently corrected. Details from a manuscript of the work held in the Beinecke Rare Book and Manuscript Library, Yale University, are contained in the explanatory notes.

Contents

ONE

David and I Set Forth upon a Journey

SOMETIMES THE LITTLE boy who calls me father brings me an invitation from his mother: 'I shall be so pleased if you will come and see me,' and I always reply in some such words as these: 'Dear madam, I decline.' And if David asks why I decline, I explain that it is because I have no desire to meet the woman.

'Come this time, father,' he urged lately, 'for it is her birthday, and she is twenty-six,' which is so great an age to David, that I think he fears she cannot last much longer.

'Twenty-six, is she, David?' I replied. 'Tell her I said she looks more.'

I had my delicious dream that night. I dreamt that I too was twenty-six, which was a long time ago, and that I took train to a place called my home, whose whereabouts I see not in my waking hours; and when I alighted at the station a dear lost love was waiting for me, and we went away together. She met me in no ecstasy of emotion, nor was I surprised to find her there; it was as if we had been married for years and parted for a day. I like to think that I gave her some of the things to carry.

Were I to tell my delightful dream to David's mother, to whom I have never in my life addressed one word, she would droop her head and raise it bravely, to imply that I make her sad but proud, and she would be wishful to lend me her absurd little pocket handkerchief. And then, had I the heart, I might make a disclosure that would startle her, for it is not the face of David's mother that I see in my dreams.

Has it ever been your lot, reader, to be persecuted by a

pretty woman who thinks, without a tittle of reason, that you are bowed down under a hopeless partiality for her? It is thus that I have been pursued for several years now by the unwelcome sympathy of the tender-hearted and virtuous Mary A———. When we pass in the street the poor deluded soul subdues her buoyancy, as if it were shame to walk happy before one she has lamed, and at such times the rustle of her gown is whispered words of comfort to me, and her arms are kindly wings that wish I was a little boy like David. I also detect in her a fearful elation, which I am unaware of until she has passed, when it comes back to me like a faint note of challenge. Eyes that say you never must, nose that says why don't you? and a mouth that says I rather wish you could: such is the portrait of Mary A——— as she and I pass by.

Once she dared to address me, so that she could boast to David that I had spoken to her. I was in the Kensington Gardens, and she asked would I tell her the time please, just as children ask, and forget as they run back with it to their nurse. But I was prepared even for this, and raising my hat I pointed with my staff to a clock in the distance. She should have been overwhelmed, but as I walked on listening intently, I thought with displeasure that I heard her laughing.

Her laugh is very like David's, whom I could punch all day in order to hear him laugh. I dare say she put this laugh into him. She has been putting qualities into David, altering him, turning him for ever on a lathe since the day she first knew him, and indeed long before, and all so deftly that he is still called a child of nature. When you release David's hand he is immediately lost like an arrow from the bow. No sooner do you cast eyes on him than you are thinking of birds. It is difficult to believe that he walks to the Kensington Gardens; he always seems to have alighted there: and were I to scatter crumbs I opine he would come and peck. This is not what he set out to be; it is all the doing of that timid-looking lady who affects to be greatly surprised by it. He strikes a hundred gallant poses in a day; when he tumbles, which is often, he comes to the ground like a Greek god; so Mary A——— has willed it. But how she suffers that he may achieve! I have seen him climbing a tree while she stood beneath in unutterable anguish; she had to let him climb, for boys must be brave, but I am sure that, as she watched him, she fell from every branch.

David admires her prodigiously; he thinks her so good that she will be able to get him into heaven, however naughty he is. Otherwise he would trespass less light-heartedly. Perhaps she has discovered this; for, as I learn from him, she warned him lately that she is not such a dear as he thinks her.

'I am very sure of it,' I replied.

'Is she such a dear as you think her?' he asked me.

'Heaven help her,' I said, 'if she be not dearer than that.'

Heaven help all mothers if they be not really dears, for their boy will certainly know it in that strange short hour of the day when every mother stands revealed before her little son. That dread hour ticks between six and seven; when children go to bed later the revelation has ceased to come. He is lapt in for the night now and lies quietly there, madam, with great mysterious eyes fixed upon his mother. He is summing up your day. Nothing in the revelations that kept you together and yet apart in play-time can save you now; it is the boy's hour, and you have come up for judgment.

'Have I done well today, my son?' You have got to say it, and nothing may you hide from him; he knows all. How like your voice has grown to his, but more tremulous, and both so solemn, so unlike the voice of either of you by day.

'You were a little unjust to me today about the apple; were you not, mother?'

Stand there, woman, by the foot of the bed, and cross your hands and answer him.

'Yes, my son, I was. I thought—'

But what you thought will not affect the verdict.

'Was it fair, mother, to say that I could stay out till six, and then pretend it was six before it was quite six?'

'No, it was very unfair. I thought—'

'Would it have been a lie if *I* had said it was quite six?'

'O my son, my son! I shall never tell you a lie again.'

'No, mother, please don't.'

'My boy, have I done well today on the whole?'

Suppose he were unable to say yes?

These are the merest peccadilloes, you may say. Is it then a little thing to be false to the agreement you signed when you got the boy? There are mothers who avoid their children in that hour, but this will not save them. Why is it that so many women are afraid to be left alone with their thoughts between six and seven? I am not asking this of you, Mary. I believe that when you close David's door softly there is a gladness in your eyes, and the awe of one who knows that the God to whom little boys say their prayers has a face very like their mother's.

I may mention here that David is a stout believer in prayer, and has had his first fight with another young Christian who challenged him to the jump and prayed for victory, which David thought was taking an unfair advantage.

'So Mary is twenty-six! I say, David, she is getting on. Tell her that I am coming in to kiss her when she is fifty-two.'

He told her, and I understand that she pretended to be indignant. When I pass her in the street now she pouts. Clearly preparing for our meeting. She has also said, I learn, that I shall not think so much of her when she is fifty-two, meaning that she will not be so pretty then. So

little does the sex know of beauty. Surely a spirited old
lady may be the prettiest sight in the world. For my part,
I confess that it is they, and not the young ones, who have
ever been my undoing. Just as I was about to fall in love I
suddenly found that I preferred the mother. Indeed, I
cannot see a likely young creature without impatiently
considering her chances for, say, fifty-two. O you mysterious girls, when you are fifty-two we shall find you out;
you must come into the open then. If the mouth has
fallen sourly yours the blame: all the meannesses your
youth concealed have been gathering in your face. But the
pretty thoughts and sweet ways and dear, forgotten kind-
nesses linger there also, to bloom in your twilight like
evening primroses.

Is it not strange that, though I talk thus plainly to David
about his mother, he still seems to think me fond of her?
How now, I reflect, what sort of bumpkin is this? and
perhaps I say to him cruelly: 'Boy, you are uncommonly
like your mother.'

To which David: 'Is that why you are so kind to me?'

I suppose I am kind to him, but if so it is not for love of
his mother, but because he sometimes calls me father. On
my honour as a soldier, there is nothing more in it than
that. I must not let him know this, for it would make him
conscious, and so break the spell that binds him and me
together. Oftenest I am but Captain W——— to him,
and for the best of reasons. He addresses me as father
when he is in a hurry only, and never have I dared ask him
to use the name. He says, 'Come, father,' with an accursed
beautiful carelessness. So let it be, David, for a little while
longer.

I like to hear him say it before others, as in shops. When
in shops he asks the salesman how much money he makes
in a day, and which drawer he keeps it in, and why his hair is
red, and does he like Achilles, of whom David has lately
heard, and is so enamoured that he wants to die to meet

him. At such times the shopkeepers accept me as his father, and I cannot explain the peculiar pleasure this gives me. I am always in two minds then, to linger that we may have more of it, and to snatch him away before he volunteers the information, 'He is not really my father.'

When David meets Achilles I know what will happen. The little boy will take the hero by the hand, call him father, and drag him away to some Round Pond.

One day, when David was about five, I sent him the following letter: 'Dear David: If you really want to know how it began, will you come and have a chop with me to-day at the club?'

Mary, who, I have found out, opens all his letters, gave her consent, and, I doubt not, instructed him to pay heed to what happened so that he might repeat it to her, for despite her curiosity she knows not how it began herself. I chuckled, guessing that she expected something romantic.

He came to me arrayed as for a mighty journey, and looking unusually solemn, as little boys always do look when they are wearing a greatcoat. There was a shawl round his neck. 'You can take some of them off,' I said, 'when we come to summer.'

'Shall we come to summer?' he asked, properly awed.

'To many summers,' I replied, 'for we are going away back, David, to see your mother as she was in the days before there was you.'

We hailed a hansom. 'Drive back six years,' I said to the cabby, 'and stop at the Junior Old Fogies' Club.'

He was a stupid fellow, and I had to guide him with my umbrella.

The streets were not quite as they had been in the morning. For instance, the book-shop at the corner was now selling fish. I dropped David a hint of what was going on.

'It doesn't make me littler, does it?' he asked anxiously; and then, with a terrible misgiving: 'It won't make me too

little, will it, father?' by which he meant that he hoped it
would not do for him altogether. He slipped his hand
nervously into mine, and I put it in my pocket.

You can't think how little David looked as we entered the
portals of the club.

TWO

The Little Nursery Governess

AS I ENTER the club smoking-room you are to conceive David vanishing into nothingness, and that it is any day six years ago at two in the afternoon. I ring for coffee, cigarette, and cherry brandy, and take my chair by the window, just as the absurd little nursery governess comes tripping into the street. I always feel that I have rung for her.

While I am lifting the coffee-pot cautiously lest the lid fall into the cup, she is crossing to the post-office; as I select the one suitable lump of sugar she is taking six last looks at the letter; with the aid of William I light my cigarette, and now she is re-reading the delicious address. I lie back in my chair, and by this time she has dropped the letter down the slit. I toy with my liqueur, and she is listening to hear whether the postal authorities have come for her letter. I scowl at a fellow-member who has had the impudence to enter the smoking-room, and her two little charges are pulling her away from the post-office. When I look out at the window again she is gone, but I shall ring for her to-morrow at two sharp.

She must have passed the window many times before I noticed her. I know not where she lives, though I suppose it to be hard by. She is taking the little boy and girl, who bully her, to the St James's Park, as their hoops tell me, and she ought to look crushed and faded. No doubt her mistress overworks her. It must enrage the other servants to see her deporting herself as if she were quite the lady.

I noticed that she had sometimes other letters to post, but that the posting of the one only was a process. They shot down the slit, plebeians all, but it followed pom-

14

pously like royalty. I have even seen her blow a kiss after it.

Then there was her ring, of which she was as conscious as if it rather than she was what came gaily down the street. She felt it through her glove to make sure that it was still there. She took off the glove and raised the ring to her lips, though I doubt not it was the cheapest trinket. She viewed it from afar by stretching out her hand; she stooped to see how it looked near the ground; she considered its effect on the right of her and on the left of her and through one eye at a time. Even when you saw that she had made up her mind to think hard of something else, the little silly would take another look.

I give any one three chances to guess why Mary was so happy.

No and no and no. The reason was simply this, that a lout of a young man loved her. And so, instead of crying because she was the merest nobody, she must, forsooth, sail jauntily down Pall Mall, very trim as to her tackle, and ticketed with the insufferable air of an engaged woman. At first her complacency disturbed me, but gradually it became part of my life at two o'clock with the coffee, the cigarette, and the liqueur. Now comes the tragedy.

Thursday is her great day. She has from two to three every Thursday for her very own; just think of it: this girl, who is probably paid several pounds a year, gets a whole hour to herself once a week. And what does she with it? Attend classes for making her a more accomplished person? Not she. This is what she does: sets sail for Pall Mall, wearing all her pretty things, including the blue feathers, and with such a sparkle of expectation on her face that I stir my coffee quite fiercely. On ordinary days she at least tries to look demure, but on a Thursday she has had the impudence to use the glass door of the club as a mirror in which to see how she likes her engaging trifle of a figure today.

In the meantime a long-legged oaf is waiting for her outside the post-office, where they meet every Thursday, a fellow who always wears the same suit of clothes, but has a face that must ever make him free of the company of gentlemen. He is one of your lean, clean Englishmen, who strip so well, and I fear me he is handsome; I say fear, for your handsome men have always annoyed me, and had I lived in the duelling days I swear I would have called every one of them out. He seems to be quite unaware that he is a pretty fellow, but Lord, how obviously Mary knows it. I conclude that he belongs to the artistic classes, he is so easily elated and depressed; and because he carries his left thumb curiously, as if it were feeling for the hole of a palette, I have entered his name among the painters. I find pleasure in deciding that they are shocking bad pictures, for obviously no one buys them. I feel sure Mary says they are splendid; she is that sort of woman. Hence the rapture with which he greets her. Her first effect upon him is to make him shout with laughter. He laughs suddenly *haw* from an eager exulting face, and then *haw* again, and then, when you are thanking Heaven that it is at last over, comes a final *haw*, louder than the others. I take them to be roars of joy because Mary is his, and they have a ring of youth about them that is hard to bear. I could forgive him everything save his youth, but it is so aggressive that I have sometimes to order William testily to close the window.

How much more deceitful than her lover is the little nursery governess. The moment she comes into sight she looks at the post-office and sees him. Then she looks straight before her, and now she is observed, and he rushes across to her in a glory, and she starts – positively starts – as if he had taken her by surprise. Observe her hand rising suddenly to her wicked little heart. This is the moment when I stir my coffee violently. He gazes down at her in such rapture that he is in everybody's way, and as she takes his arm she gives it a little squeeze, and then away they strut, Mary doing nine-tenths of the talking. I fall to wondering what they will look like when they grow up.

What a ludicrous difference do these two nobodies make to each other. You can see that they are to be married when he has twopence.

Thus I have not an atom of sympathy with this girl, to whom London is famous only as the residence of a young man who mistakes her for some one else, but her happiness had become part of my repast at two p.m., and when one day she walked down Pall Mall without gradually posting a letter I was indignant. It was as if William had disobeyed orders. Her two charges were as surprised as I, and pointed questioningly to the slit, at which she shook her head. She put her finger to her eyes, exactly like a sad baby, and so passed from the street.

Next day the same thing happened, and I was so furious that I bit through my cigarette. Thursday came, when I prayed that there might be an end of this annoyance, but no, neither of them appeared on that acquainted ground. Had they changed their post-office? No, for her eyes were red every day, and heavy was her foolish little heart. Love had put out his lights, and the little nursery governess walked in darkness.

I felt I could complain to the committee.

O you selfish young zany of a man, after all you have said to her, won't you make it up and let me return to my coffee? Not he.

Little nursery governess, I appeal to you. Annoying girl, be joyous as of old during the five minutes of the day when you are anything to me, and for the rest of the time, so far as I am concerned, you may be as wretched as you list. Show some courage. I assure you he must be a very bad painter: only the other day I saw him looking longingly into the window of a cheap Italian restaurant, and in the end he had to crush down his aspirations with two penny scones.

You can do better than that. Come, Mary.

All in vain. She wants to be loved; can't do without love from morning till night; never knew how little a woman needs till she lost that little. They are all like this.

Zounds, madam, if you are resolved to be a drooping little figure till you die, you might at least do it in another street.

Not only does she maliciously depress me by walking past on ordinary days, but I have discovered that every Thursday from two to three she stands afar off, gazing hopelessly at the romantic post-office where she and he shall meet no more. On these windy days she is like a homeless leaf blown about by passers-by.

There is nothing I can do except thunder at William.

At last she accomplished her unworthy ambition. It was a wet Thursday, and from the window where I was writing letters I saw the forlorn soul taking up her position at the top of the street: in a blast of fury I rose with the one letter I had completed, meaning to write the others in my chambers. She had driven me from the club.

I had turned out of Pall Mall into a side street, when whom should I strike against but her false swain! It was my fault, but I hit out at him savagely, as I always do when I run into any one in the street. Then I looked at him. He was hollow-eyed; he was muddy; there was not a *haw* left in him. I never saw a more abject young man; he had not even the spirit to resent the testy stab I had given him with my umbrella. But this is the important thing: he was glaring wistfully at the post-office and thus in a twink I saw that he still adored my little governess. Whatever had been their quarrel he was as anxious to make it up as she, and perhaps he had been here every Thursday while she was round the corner in Pall Mall, each watching the post-office for an apparition. But from where they hovered neither could see the other.

I think what I did was quite clever. I dropped my letter unseen at his feet, and sauntered back to the club. Of course, a gentleman who finds a letter on the pavement feels bound to post it, and I presumed that he would naturally go to the nearest office.

With my hat on I strolled to the smoking-room window, and was just in time to see him posting my letter across the way. Then I looked for the little nursery governess. I saw her as woebegone as ever; then, suddenly – oh, you poor little soul, and has it really been as bad as that!

She was crying outright, and he was holding both her hands. It was a disgraceful exhibition. The young painter would evidently explode if he could not make use of his arms. She must die if she could not lay her head upon his breast. I must admit that he rose to the occasion; he hailed a hansom.

'William,' said I gaily, 'coffee, cigarette, and cherry brandy.'

As I sat there watching that old play David plucked my sleeve to ask what I was looking at so deedily; and when I told him he ran eagerly to the window, but he reached it just too late to see the lady who was to become his mother. What I told him of her doings, however, interested him greatly; and he intimated rather shyly that he was ac-quainted with the man who said, 'Haw-haw-*haw*.' On the other hand, he irritated me by betraying an idiotic interest in the two children, whom he seemed to regard as the hero and heroine of the story. What were their names? How old were they? Had they both hoops? Were they iron hoops, or just wooden hoops? Who gave them their hoops?

'You don't seem to understand, my boy,' I said tartly, 'that had I not dropped that letter, there would never have been a little boy called David A———.' But instead of being appalled by this he asked, sparkling, whether I meant that he would still be a bird flying about in the Kensington Gardens.

David knows that all children in our part of London were once birds in the Kensington Gardens; and that the reason there are bars on nursery windows and a tall fender by the fire is because very little people sometimes forget that they have no longer wings, and try to fly away through the window or up the chimney.

Children in the bird stage are difficult to catch. David knows that many people have none, and his delight on a summer afternoon is to go with me to some spot in the Gardens where these unfortunates may be seen trying to catch one with small pieces of cake.

That the birds know what would happen if they were caught, and are even a little undecided about which is the better life, is obvious to every student of them. Thus, if you leave your empty perambulator under the trees and watch from a distance, you will see the birds boarding it and hopping about from pillow to blanket in a twitter of excitement; they are trying to find out how babyhood would suit them.

Quite the prettiest sight in the Gardens is when the babies stray from the tree where the nurse is sitting and are seen feeding the birds, not a grown-up near them. It is first a bit to me then a bit to you, and all the time such a jabbering and laughing from both sides of the railing. They are comparing notes and inquiring for old friends, and so on; but what they say I cannot determine, for when I approach they all fly away.

The first time I ever saw David was on the sward behind the Baby's Walk. He was a missel-thrush, attracted thither that hot day by a hose which lay on the ground sending forth a gay trickle of water, and David was on his back in the water, kicking up his legs. He used to enjoy being told of this, having forgotten all about it, and gradually it all came back to him, with a number of other incidents that had escaped my memory, though I remember that he was eventually caught by the leg with a long string and a

cunning arrangement of twigs near the Round Pond. He
never tires of this story, but I notice that it is now he who
tells it to me rather than I to him, and when we come to the
string he rubs his little leg as if it still smarted.

So when David saw his chance of being a missel-thrush
again he called out to me quickly: 'Don't drop the letter!'
and there were tree-tops in his eyes.

'Think of your mother,' I said severely.

He said he would often fly in to see her. The first thing he
would do would be to hug her. No, he would alight on the
water-jug first, and have a drink.

'Tell her, father,' he said with horrid heartlessness, 'always to have plenty of water in it, 'cos if I had to lean down
too far I might fall in and be drownded.'

'Am I not to drop the letter, David? Think of your poor
mother without her boy!'

It affected him, but he bore up. When she was asleep, he
said, he would hop on to the frilly things of her night-gown
and peck at her mouth.

'And then she would wake up, David, and find that she
had only a bird instead of a boy.'

This shock to Mary was more than he could endure.
'You can drop it,' he said with a sigh. So I dropped the
letter, as I think I have already mentioned; and that is how it
all began.

THREE

Her Marriage, Her Clothes, Her Appetite, and an Inventory of Her Furniture

A WEEK OR two after I dropped the letter I was in a hansom on my way to certain barracks, when loud above the city's roar I heard that accursed haw-haw-*haw*, and there they were, the two of them, just coming out of a shop where you may obtain pianos on the hire system. I had the merest glimpse of them, but there was an extraordinary rapture on her face, and his head was thrown proudly back, and all because they had been ordering a piano on the hire system.

So they were to be married directly. It was all rather contemptible, but I passed on tolerantly, for it is only when she is unhappy that this woman disturbs me, owing to a clever way she has at such times of looking more fragile than she really is.

When next I saw them, they were gazing greedily into the window of the sixpenny-halfpenny shop, which is one of the most deliciously dramatic spots in London. Mary was taking notes feverishly on a slip of paper while he did the adding up, and in the end they went away gloomily without buying anything. I was in high feather. 'Match abandoned, ma'am,' I said to myself; 'outlook hopeless; another visit to the Governesses' Agency inevitable; can't marry for want of a kitchen shovel.'

But I was imperfectly acquainted with the lady.

A few days afterwards I found myself walking behind her. There is something artful about her skirts by which I always know her, though I can't say what it is. She was carrying an enormous parcel that might have been a bird-cage wrapped in brown paper, and she took it into a bric-a-brac shop and came out without it. She then ran rather than walked in the direction of the sixpenny-halfpenny shop. Now mystery of any kind is detestable to me, and I went into the bric-a-brac shop, ostensibly to look at the cracked china; and there, still on the counter, with the wrapping torn off it, was the article Mary had sold in order to furnish on the proceeds. What do you think it was? It was a wonderful doll's house, with dolls at tea downstairs and dolls going to bed upstairs, and a doll showing a doll out at the front door. Loving lips had long ago licked most of the paint off, but otherwise the thing was in admirable preservation; obviously the joy of Mary's child-hood, it had now been sold by her that she might get married.

'Lately purchased by us,' said the shopwoman, seeing me look at the toy, 'from a lady who has no further use for it.'

I think I have seldom been more indignant with Mary. I bought the doll's house, and as they knew the lady's address (it was at this shop that I first learned her name) I instructed them to send it back to her with the following letter, which I wrote in the shop: 'Dear madam, don't be ridiculous. You will certainly have further use for this. – I am etc., the Man Who Dropped the Letter.'

It pained me afterwards, but too late to rescind the order, to reflect that I had sent her a wedding present; and when next I saw her she had been married for some months. The time was nine o'clock of a November evening, and we were in a street of shops that has not in twenty years decided whether to be genteel or frankly vulgar; here it minces in the fashion, but take a step onward and its tongue is in the cup of the ice-cream man. I usually rush this street, which is not far from my rooms, with the glass down, but tonight I was walking. Mary was in front of me, leaning in a somewhat foolish way on the haw-er, and they were chatting excitedly. She seemed to be remonstrating with him for going forward, yet more than half admiring him for not turning back, and I wondered why.

And after all, what was it that Mary and her painter had come out to do? To buy two pork chops. On my honour. She had been trying to persuade him, I decided, that they were living too lavishly. That was why she sought to draw him back. But in her heart she loves audacity, and that is why she admired him for pressing forward.

No sooner had they bought the chops than they scurried away like two gleeful children to cook them. I followed, hoping to trace them to their home, but they soon out-distanced me, and that night I composed the following aphorism: It is idle to attempt to overtake a pretty young woman carrying pork chops. I was now determined to be done with her. First, however, to find out their abode, which was probably within easy distance of the shop. I even conceived them lured into taking their house by the adver-tisement, 'Conveniently situated for the Pork Emporium.'

Well, one day – now this really is romantic, and I am rather proud of it. My chambers are on the second floor, and are backed by an anxiously polite street between which and mine are little yards called, I think, gardens. They are so small that if you have the tree your neighbour has the shade from it. I was looking out at my back window on the day we have come to when whom did I see but the whilom nursery governess sitting on a chair in one of these gardens. I put up my eyeglass to make sure, and undoubtedly it was she. But she sat there doing nothing, which was by no means my conception of the jade, so I brought a field-glass to bear and discovered that the object was merely a lady's jacket. It hung on the back of a kitchen chair, seemed to be a furry thing, and, I must suppose, was suspended there for an airing.

I was chagrined, and then I insisted stoutly with myself that, as it was not Mary, it must be Mary's jacket. I had never seen her wear such a jacket, mind you, yet I was confident, I can't tell why. Do clothes absorb a little of the character of their wearer, so that I recognised this jacket by a certain coquetry? If she has a way with her skirts that always advertises me of her presence, quite possibly she is as cunning with jackets. Or perhaps she is her own seamstress, and puts in little tucks of herself.

Figure it what you please; but I beg to inform you that I put on my hat, and five minutes afterwards saw Mary and her husband emerge from the house to which I had calculated that garden belonged. Now, am I clever, or am I not?

When they had left the street I examined the house leisurely, and a droll house it is. Seen from the front it appears to consist of a door and a window, though above them the trained eye may detect another window, the airhole of some apartment which it would be just like Mary's grandiloquence to call her bedroom. The houses on each side of the bandbox are tall, and I discovered later that it had once been an open passage to the back gardens. The storey and a half of which it consists had been knocked up cheaply, by carpenters I should say rather than masons, and the general effect is of a brightly coloured van that has stuck for ever on its way through the passage.

The low houses of London look so much more homely than the tall ones, that I never pass them without dropping a blessing on their builders, but this house was ridiculous; indeed it did not call itself a house, for over the door was a board with the inscription 'This space to be sold,' and I remembered, as I rang the bell, that this notice had been up for years. On avowing that I wanted a space, I was admitted by an elderly, somewhat dejected-looking female, whose fine figure was not on scale with her surroundings. Perhaps my face said so, for her first remark was explanatory.

'They get me cheap,' she said, 'because I drink.'

I bowed, and we passed on to the drawing-room. I forget whether I have described Mary's personal appearance, but if so you have a picture of that sunny drawing-room. My first reflection was, How can she have found the money to pay for it all! which is always your first reflection when you see Mary herself a-tripping down the street.

I have no space (in that little room) to catalogue all the whim-whams with which she had made it beautiful, from the hand-sewn bell-rope which pulled no bell to the hand-painted cigar-box that contained no cigars. The floor was of a delicious green with exquisite oriental rugs; green and white, I think, was the lady's scheme of colour, something cool, you observe, to keep the sun under. The window-curtains were of some rare material and the colour of the purple clematis; they swept the floor grandly and suggested a picture of Mary receiving visitors. The piano we may ignore, for I knew it to be hired, but there were many dainty pieces, mostly in green wood, a sofa, a corner cupboard, and a most captivating desk, which was so like its owner that it could have sat down at her and dashed off a note. The writing-paper on this desk had the word Mary printed on it, implying that if there were other Marys they didn't count. There were many oil-paintings on the walls, mostly without frames, and I must mention the chandelier, which was obviously of fabulous worth, for she had encased it in a holland bag.

'I perceive, ma'am,' said I to the stout maid, 'that your master is in affluent circumstances.'

She shook her head emphatically, and said something that I failed to catch.

'You wish to indicate,' I hazarded, 'that he married a fortune.'

This time I caught the words. They were 'Tinned meats,' and having uttered them she lapsed into gloomy silence.

'Nevertheless,' I said, 'this room must have cost a pretty penny.'

'She done it all herself,' replied my new friend, with concentrated scorn.

'But this green floor, so beautifully stained—'

'Boiling oil,' said she, with a flush of honest shame, 'and a shillingsworth o' paint.'

'Those rugs—'

'Remnants,' she sighed, and showed me how artfully they had been pieced together.

'The curtains—'

'Remnants.'

'At all events the sofa—'

She raised its drapery, and I saw that the sofa was built of packing-cases.

'The desk—'

I really thought that I was safe this time, for could I not see the drawers with their brass handles, the charming shelf for books, the pigeon-holes with their coverings of silk?

'She made it out of three orange-boxes,' said the lady, at last a little awed herself.

I looked around me despairingly, and my eye alighted on the holland covering. 'There is a fine chandelier in that holland bag,' I said coaxingly.

She sniffed, and was raising an untender hand, when I checked her. 'Forbear, ma'am,' I cried with authority, 'I prefer to believe in that bag. How much to be pitied, ma'am, are those who have lost faith in everything.' I think all the pretty things that the little nursery governess had made out of nothing squeezed my hand for letting the chandelier off.

'But, good God, ma'am,' said I to madam, 'what an exposure!'

She intimated that there were other exposures upstairs.

'So there is a stair,' said I, and then, suspiciously, 'did she make it?'

No, but how she had altered it.

The stair led to Mary's bedroom, and I said I would not look at that, nor at the studio, which was a shed in the garden.

'Did she build the studio with her own hands?'

No, but how she had altered it.

'How she alters everything,' I said. 'Do you think you are safe, ma'am?'

She thawed a little under my obvious sympathy, and honoured me with some of her views and confidences. The rental paid by Mary and her husband was not, it appeared, one on which any self-respecting domestic could reflect with pride. They got the house very cheap on the understanding that they were to vacate it promptly if any one bought it for building purposes, and because they paid so little they had to submit to the indignity of the noticeboard. Mary A——— detested the words: 'This space to be sold,' and had been known to shake her fist at them. She was as elated about her house as if it were a real house, and always trembled when any possible purchaser of spaces called.

As I have told you my own aphorism I feel I ought in fairness to record that of this aggrieved servant. It was on the subject of art. 'The difficulty,' she said, 'is not to paint pictures, but to get frames for them.' A home-thrust this.

She could not honestly say that she thought much of her master's work. Nor, apparently, did any other person. Result, tinned meats.

Yes, one person thought a deal of it, or pretended to do so; was constantly flinging up her hands in delight over it; had even been caught whispering fiercely to a friend, 'Praise it, praise it, praise it!' This was when the painter was sunk in gloom. Never, as I could well believe, was such a one as Mary for luring a man back to cheerfulness.

'A dangerous woman,' I said, with a shudder, and fell to examining a painting over the mantelshelf. It was a portrait of a man, and had impressed me favourably because it was framed.

'A friend of hers,' my guide informed me, 'but I never seed him.'

I would have turned away from it, had not an inscription on the picture drawn me nearer. It was in a lady's hand-writing, and these were the words: 'Fancy portrait of our dear unknown.' Could it be meant for me? I cannot tell you how interested I suddenly became.

It represented a very fine-looking fellow, indeed, and not a day more than thirty.

'A friend of hers, ma'am, did you say?' I asked quite shakily. 'How do you know that, if you have never seen him?'

'When master was painting of it,' she said, 'in the studio, he used to come running in here to say to her such like as, "What colour would you make his eyes?" '

'And her reply, ma'am?' I asked eagerly.

'She said, "Beautiful blue eyes." And he said, "You wouldn't make it a handsome face, would you?" and she says, "A very handsome face." And says he, "Middle-aged?" and says she, "Twenty-nine." And I mind him saying, "A little bald on the top?" and she says, says she, "Not at all." '

The dear, grateful girl, not to make me bald on the top.

'I have seed her kiss her hand to that picture,' said the maid.

Fancy Mary kissing her hand to me! O the pretty love! Pooh!

I was staring at the picture, cogitating what insulting message I could write on it, when I heard the woman's voice again. 'I think she has known him since she were a babby,' she was saying, 'for this here was a present he gave her.'

She was on her knees drawing the doll's house from beneath the sofa, where it had been hidden away; and immediately I thought, 'I shall slip the insulting message into this.' But I did not, and I shall tell you why. It was because the engaging toy had been redecorated by loving hands; there were fresh gowns for all the inhabitants, and the paint on the furniture was scarcely dry. The little doll's house was almost ready for further use.

I looked at the maid, but her face was expressionless. 'Put it back,' I said, ashamed to have surprised Mary's pretty secret, and I left the house dejectedly, with a profound conviction that the little nursery governess had hooked on to me again.

FOUR

A Night-piece

THERE CAME a night when the husband was alone in that street waiting. He can do nothing for you now, little nursery governess, you must fight it out by yourself; when there are great things to do in the house the man must leave. O man, selfish, indelicate, coarse-grained at the best, thy woman's hour has come; get thee gone.

He slouches from the house, always her true lover I do believe, chivalrous, brave, a boy until tonight; but was he ever unkind to her? It is the unpardonable sin now; is there the memory of an unkindness to stalk the street with him tonight? And if not an unkindness, still might he not sometimes have been a little kinder?

Shall we make a new rule of life from tonight: always to try to be a little kinder than is necessary?

Poor youth, she would come to the window if she were able, I am sure, to sign that the one little unkindness is long forgotten, to send you a reassuring smile till you and she meet again; and, if you are not to meet again, still to send you a reassuring, trembling smile.

Ah no, that was for yesterday: it is too late now. He wanders the streets thinking of her tonight, but she has forgotten him. In her great hour the man is nothing to the woman; their love is trivial now.

He and I were on opposite sides of the street, now become familiar ground to both of us, and divers pictures rose before me in which Mary A——— walked. Here was the morning after my only entry into her house. The agent had promised me to have the obnoxious notice-board removed, but I apprehended that as soon as the letter announcing his intention reached her she would remove it herself, and when I passed by in the morning there she was on a chair and a footstool pounding lustily at it with a hammer. When it fell she gave it such a vicious little kick.

There were the nights when her husband came out to watch for the postman. I suppose he was awaiting some letter big with the fate of a picture. He dogged the postman from door to door like an assassin or a guardian angel; never had he the courage to ask if there was a letter for him, but almost as it fell into the box he had it out and tore it open, and then if the door closed despairingly the woman who had been at the window all this time pressed her hand to her heart. But if the news was good they might emerge presently and strut off arm in arm in the direction of the pork emporium.

One last picture. On summer evenings I had caught glimpses of them through the open window, when she sat at the piano singing and playing to him. Or while she played with one hand, she flung out the other for him to grasp. She was so joyously happy, and she had such a romantic mind. I conceived her so sympathetic that she always laughed before he came to the joke, and I am sure she had filmy eyes from the very start of a pathetic story.

And so, laughing and crying, and haunted by whispers, the little nursery governess had gradually become another woman, glorified, mysterious. I suppose a man soon becomes used to the great change, and cannot recall a time when there were no babes sprawling in his Mary's face.

I am trying to conceive what were the thoughts of the young husband on the other side of the street. 'If the barrier is to be crossed tonight, may I not go with her? She is not so brave as you think her. When she talked so gaily a few hours ago, O my God, did she deceive even you?'

Plain questions tonight. 'Why should it all fall on her? What is the man that he should be flung out into the street in this terrible hour? You have not been fair to the man.'

Poor boy, his wife has quite forgotten him and his trumpery love. If she lives she will come back to him, but if she dies she will die triumphant and serene. Life and death, the child and the mother, are ever meeting as the one draws into harbour and the other sets sail. They exchange a bright 'All's well,' and pass on.

But afterwards?

The only ghosts, I believe, who creep into this world, are dead young mothers, returned to see how their children fare. There is no other inducement great enough to bring the departed back. They glide into the acquainted room when day and night, their jailers, are in the grip, and whisper, 'How is it with you, my child?' but always, lest a strange face should frighten him, they whisper it so low that he may not hear. They bend over him to see that he sleeps peacefully, and replace his sweet arm beneath the coverlet, and they open the drawers to count how many little vests he has. They love to do these things.

What is saddest about ghosts is that they may not know their child. They expect him to be just as he was when they left him, and they are easily bewildered, and search for him from room to room, and hate the unknown boy he has become. Poor, passionate souls, they may even do him an injury. These are the ghosts that go wailing about old houses, and foolish wild stories are invented to explain what is all so pathetic and simple. I know of a man who, after wandering far, returned to his early home to pass the evening of his days in it, and sometimes from his chair by the fire he saw the door open softly and a woman's face appear. She always looked at him very vindictively, and then vanished. Strange things happened in this house. Windows were opened in the night. The curtains of his bed were set fire to. A step on the stair was loosened. The covering of an old well in a corridor where he walked was cunningly removed. And when he fell ill the wrong potion was put in the glass by his bedside, and he died. How could the pretty young mother know that this grizzled interloper was the child of whom she was in search?

All our notions about ghosts are wrong. It is nothing so petty as lost wills or deeds of violence that brings them back, and we are not nearly so afraid of them as they are of us.

One by one the lights of the streets went out, but still a lamp burned steadily in the little window across the way. I know not how it happened, whether I had crossed first to him or he to me, but, after being for a long time as the echo of each other's steps, we were together now. I can have had no desire to deceive him, but some reason was needed to account for my vigil, and I may have said something that he misconstrued, for above my words he was always listening for other sounds. But however it came about, he had conceived the idea that I was an outcast for a reason similar to his own, and I let his mistake pass, it seemed to matter so little and to draw us together so naturally. We talked together of many things, such as worldly ambition. For long ambition has been like an ancient memory to me, some glorious day recalled from my springtime, so much a thing of the past that I must make a railway journey to revisit it as to look upon the pleasant fields in which that scene was laid. But he had been ambitious yesterday.

I mentioned worldly ambition. 'Good God!' he said with a shudder.

There was a clock hard by that struck the quarters, and one o'clock passed and two. What time is it now? Twenty past two. And now? It is still twenty past two.

I asked him about his relatives, and neither he nor she had any. 'We have a friend—' he began and paused, and then rambled into a not very understandable story about a letter and a doll's house and some unknown man who had bought one of his pictures, or was supposed to have done so, in a curiously clandestine manner. I could not quite follow the story.

'It is she who insists that it is always the same person,' he said. 'She thinks he will make himself known to me if anything happens to her.' His voice suddenly went husky. 'She told me,' he said, 'if she died and I discovered him, to give him her love.'

At this we parted abruptly, as we did at intervals throughout the night, to drift together again presently. He tried to tell me of some things she had asked him to do should she not get over this, but what they were I know not, for they engulfed him at the first step. He would draw back from them as ill-omened things, and next moment he was going over them to himself like a child at lessons. A child! In that short year she had made him entirely dependent on her. It is ever thus with women: their first deliberate act is to make their husband helpless. There are few men happily married who can knock in a nail.

But it was not of this that I was thinking. I was wishing I had not degenerated so much.

Well, as you know, the little nursery governess did not die. At eighteen minutes to four we heard the rustle of David's wings. He boasts about it to this day, and has the hour to a syllable, as if the first thing he ever did was to look at the clock.

An oldish gentleman had opened the door and waved congratulations to my companion, who immediately butted at me, drove me against a wall, hesitated for a second with his head down as if in doubt whether to toss me, and then rushed away. I followed slowly. I shook him by the hand, but by this time he was haw-haw-*haw*ing so abominably that a disgust of him swelled up within me, and with it a passionate desire to jeer once more at Mary A———'.

'It is little she will care for you now,' I said to the fellow; 'I know the sort of woman; her intellectuals (which are all she has to distinguish her from the brutes) are so imperfectly developed that she will be a crazy thing about that boy for the next three years. She has no longer occasion for you, my dear sir; you are like a picture painted out.'

But I question whether he heard me. I returned to my home. Home! As if one alone can build a nest. How often as I have ascended the stairs that lead to my lonely, sumptuous rooms, have I paused to listen to the hilarity of the servants below. That morning I could not rest: I wandered from chamber to chamber, followed by my great dog, and all were alike empty and desolate. I had nearly finished a cigar when I thought I heard a pebble strike the window, and looking out I saw David's father standing beneath. I had told him that I lived in this street, and I suppose my lights had guided him to my window.

'I could not lie down,' he called up hoarsely, 'until I heard your news. Is it all right?'

For a moment I failed to understand him. Then I said sourly: 'Yes, all is right.'

'Both doing well?' he inquired.

'Both,' I answered, and all the time I was trying to shut the window. It was undoubtedly a kindly impulse that had brought him out, but I was nevertheless in a passion with him.

'Boy or girl?' persisted the dodderer with ungentleman-like curiosity.

'Boy,' I said, very furiously.

'Splendid,' he called out, and I think he added something else, but by that time I had closed the window with a slam.

FIVE

The Fight for Timothy

MARY'S POOR PRETENTIOUS babe screamed continually, with a note of exultation in his din, as if he thought he was devoting himself to a life of pleasure, and often the last sound I heard as I got me out of the street was his haw-haw-*haw*, delivered triumphantly as if it were some entirely new thing, though he must have learned it like a parrot. I had not one tear for the woman, but Poor father! thought I; to know that every time your son is happy you are betrayed. Phew! a nauseous draught.

I have the acquaintance of a deliciously pretty girl, who is always sulky, and the thoughtless beseech her to be bright, not witting wherein lies her heroism. She was born the merriest of maids, but, being a student of her face, learned anon that sulkiness best becomes it, and so she has struggled and prevailed. A woman's history. Brave Margaret, when night falls and thy hair is down, dost thou return, I wonder, to thy natural state, or, dreading the shadow of indulgence, sleepest thou even sulkily?

But will a male child do as much for his father? This remains to be seen, and so, after waiting several months, I decided to buy David a rocking-horse. My St Bernard dog accompanied me, though I have always been diffident of taking him to toy-shops, which over-excite him. Hitherto the toys I had bought had always been for him, and as we durst not admit this to the saleswoman we were both horribly self-conscious when in the shop. A score of times I have told him that he had much better not come; I have announced fiercely that he is not to come. He then lets go of his legs, which is how a St Bernard sits down, making the noise of a sack of coals suddenly deposited, and, laying his head between his front paws, stares at me through the red haws that make his eyes so mournful. He will do this for an hour without blinking, for he knows that in time it will unman me. My dog knows very little, but what little he does know he knows extraordinarily well. One can get out of my chambers by a back way, and I sometimes steal softly – but I can't help looking back, and there he is, and there are those haws asking sorrowfully, 'Is this worthy of you?'

'Curse you,' I say, 'get your hat,' or words to that effect.

He has even been to the club, where he waddles up the stairs so exactly like some respected member that he makes everybody most uncomfortable. I forget how I became possessor of him. I think I cut him out of an old number of *Punch*. He costs me as much as an eight-roomed cottage in the country.

He was a full-grown dog when I first, most foolishly, introduced him to toys. I had bought a toy in the street for my own amusement. It represented a woman, a young mother, flinging her little son over her head with one hand and catching him in the other, and I was entertaining myself on the hearthrug with this pretty domestic scene when I heard an unwonted sound from Porthos, and looking up, I saw that noble and melancholic countenance on the broad grin. I shuddered and was for putting the toy away at once, but he sternly struck down my arm with his, and signed that I was to continue. The unmanly chuckle always came, I found, when the poor lady dropped her babe, but the whole thing entranced him; he tried to keep his excitement down by taking huge draughts of water; he forgot all his niceties of conduct; he sat in holy rapture with the toy between his paws, took it to bed with him, ate it in the night, and searched for it so longingly next day that I had to go out and buy him the man with the scythe. After that we had everything of note, the bootblack boy, the toper with bottle, the woolly rabbit that squeaks when you hold it in your mouth; they all vanished as inexplicably as the lady, but I dared not tell him my suspicions, for he suspected also, and his gentle heart would have mourned had I confirmed his fears.

The dame in the temple of toys which we frequent thinks I want them for a little boy and calls him 'the precious' and 'the lamb,' the while Porthos is standing gravely by my side. She is a motherly soul, but over-talkative.

'And how is the dear lamb today?' she begins, beaming.

'Well, ma'am, well,' I say, keeping tight grip of his collar.

'This blighty weather is not affecting his darling appetite?'

'No, ma'am, not at all.' (She would be considerably surprised if informed that he dined today on a sheepshead, a loaf, and three cabbages, and is suspected of a leg of mutton.)

'I hope he loves his toys.'

'He carries them about with him everywhere, ma'am.' (Has the one we bought yesterday with him now, though you might not think it to look at him.)

'What do you say to a box of tools this time?'

'I think not, ma'am.'

'Is the deary fond of digging?'

'Very partial to digging.' (We shall find the leg of mutton some day.)

'Then perhaps a weeny spade and a pail?'

She got me to buy a model of Canterbury Cathedral once, she was so insistent, and Porthos gave me his mind about it when we got home. He detests the kindergarten system, and as she is absurdly prejudiced in its favour we have had to try other shops. We went to the Lowther Arcade for the rocking-horse. Dear Lowther Arcade! Ofttimes have we wandered agape among thy enchanted palaces – Porthos and I, David and I, David and Porthos and I. I have heard that thou art vulgar, but I cannot see how, unless it be that tattered children haunt thy portals, those awful yet smiling entrances to so much joy. To the arcade there are two entrances, and with much to be sung in laudation of that which opens from the Strand, I yet on the whole prefer the other as the more truly romantic, because it is there the tattered ones congregate, waiting to see the Davids emerge with the magic lamp. We have always a penny for them, and I have known them, before entering the Arcade with it, retire (but whither?) to wash; surely the prettiest of all the compliments that are paid to the home of toys.

And now, O Arcade, so much fairer than thy West End brother, we are told that thou art doomed, anon to be turned into an eating-house or a hive for usurers, something rankly useful. All thy delights are under notice to quit. The Noah's arks are packed one within another, with clockwork horses harnessed to them; the soldiers, knapsack on back, are kissing their hands to the dear foolish girls, who, however, will not be left behind them; all the four-footed things gather around the elephant, who is overfull of drawing-room furniture; the birds flutter their wings; the man with the scythe mows his way through the crowd; the balloons tug at their strings; the ships rock under a swell of sail, everything is getting ready for the mighty exodus into the Strand. Tears will be shed.

So we bought the horse in the Lowther Arcade, Porthos, who thought it was for him, looking proud but uneasy, and it was sent to the band-box house anonymously. About a week afterward I had the ill-luck to meet Mary's husband in Kensington, so I asked him what he had called his little girl.

'It is a boy,' he replied, with intolerable good-humour; 'we call him David.'

And then with a singular lack of taste he wanted the name of my boy.

I flicked my glove. 'Timothy,' said I.

I saw a suppressed smile on his face, and said hotly that Timothy was as good a name as David. 'I like it,' he assured me, and expressed a hope that they would become friends. I boiled to say that I really could not allow Timothy to mix with boys of the David class, but I refrained, and listened coldly while he told me what David did when you said his toes were pigs going to market or returning from it, I forget which. He also boasted of David's weight (a subject about which we are uncommonly touchy at the club), as if children were for throwing forth for a wager.

But no more about Timothy. Gradually this vexed me. I felt what a forlorn little chap Timothy was, with no one to say a word for him, and I became his champion and hinted something about teething, but withdrew it when it seemed too surprising, and tried to get on to safer ground, such as bibs and general intelligence, but the painter fellow was so willing to let me have my say, and knew so much more about babies than is fitting for men to know, that I paled before him and wondered why the deuce he was listening to me so attentively.

You may remember a story he had told me about some anonymous friend. 'His latest,' said he now, 'is to send David a rocking-horse!'

I must say I could see no reason for his mirth. 'Picture it,' said he, 'a rocking-horse for a child not three months old!'

I was about to say fiercely, 'The stirrups are adjustable,' but thought it best to laugh with him. But I was pained to hear that Mary had laughed, though Heaven knows I have often laughed at her.

'But women are odd,' he said unexpectedly, and explained. It appears that in the middle of her merriment Mary had become grave, and said to him quite haughtily, 'I see nothing to laugh at.' Then she had kissed the horse solemnly on the nose, and said, 'I wish he was here to see me do it.' There are moments when one cannot help feeling a drawing to Mary.

But moments only, for the next thing he said put her in a

particularly odious light. He informed me that she had sworn to hunt Mr Anon down.

'She won't succeed,' I said, sneering but nervous.

'Then it will be her first failure,' said he.

'But she knows nothing about the man.'

'You would not say that if you heard her talking of him. She says he is a gentle, whimsical, lonely old bachelor.'

'Old?' I cried.

'Well, what she says is that he will soon be old if he doesn't take care. He is a bachelor, at all events, and is very fond of children, but has never had one to play with.'

'Could not play with a child though there was one,' I said brusquely; 'has forgotten the way; could stand and stare only?'

'Yes, if the parents were present. But she thinks that if he were alone with the child he could come out strong.'

'How the deuce—' I began.

'That is what she says,' he explained, apologetically. 'I think she will prove to be too clever for him.'

'Pooh!' I said, but undoubtedly I felt a dizziness, and the next time I met him he quite frightened me. 'Do you happen to know any one,' he said, 'who has a St Bernard dog?'

'No,' said I, picking up my stick.

'He has a St Bernard dog.'

'How have you found that out?'

'She has found it out.'

'But how?'

'I don't know.'

I left him at once, for Porthos was but a little way behind me. The mystery of it scared me, but I armed promptly for battle. I engaged a boy to walk Porthos in Kensington Gardens, and gave him these instructions: 'Should you find yourself followed by a young woman wheeling a second-hand perambulator, instantly hand her over to the police on the charge of attempting to steal the dog.'

Now then, Mary.

'By the way,' her husband said at our next meeting, 'that rocking-horse I told you of cost three guineas.'

'She has gone to the shop to ask?'

'No, not to ask that, but for a description of the purchaser's appearance.'

O Mary, Mary!

Here is the appearance of purchaser as supplied at the Arcade: Looked like a military gentleman; tall, dark, and rather dressy; fine Roman nose (quite so); carefully trimmed moustache going grey (not at all); hair thin and thoughtfully distributed over the head like fiddlestrings, as if to make the most of it (pah!); dusted chair with handkerchief before sitting down on it, and had other old-maidish ways (I should like to know what they are); tediously polite, but no talker; bored face; age forty-five if a day (a lie); was accompanied by an enormous yellow dog with sore eyes. (They always think the haws are sore eyes.)

'Do you know any one who is like that?' Mary's husband asked me innocently.

'My dear man,' I said, 'I know almost no one who is not like that,' and it was true, so like each other do we grow at the club. I was pleased, on the whole, with this talk, for it at least showed me how she had come to know of the St Bernard, but anxiety returned when one day from behind my curtains I saw Mary in my street with an inquiring eye on the windows. She stopped a nurse who was carrying a baby and went into pretended ecstasies over it. I was sure she also asked whether by any chance it was called Timothy. And if not, whether that nurse knew any other nurse who had charge of a Timothy.

Obviously Mary suspicioned me, but nevertheless, I clung to Timothy, though I wished fervently that I knew more about him; for I still met that other father occasionally, and he always stopped to compare notes about the boys. And the questions he asked were so intimate, how Timothy slept, how he woke up, how he fell off again, what we put in his bath. It is well that dogs and little boys have so much in common, for it was really of Porthos I told him; how he slept (peacefully), how he woke up (supposed to be subject to dreams), how he fell off again (with one little hand on his nose), but I glided past what we put in his bath (carbolic and a mop).

The man had not the least suspicion of me, and I thought it reasonable to hope that Mary would prove as generous. Yet was I straitened in my mind. For it might be that she was only biding her time to strike suddenly, and this attached me the more to Timothy, as if I feared she might soon snatch him from me. As was indeed to be the case.

SIX

A Shock

IT WAS ON a May day, and I saw Mary accompany her husband as far as the first crossing, whence she waved him out of sight as if he had boarded an Atlantic liner. All this time she bore the face of a woman happily married who meant to go straight home, there to await her lord's glorious return; and the military-looking gentleman watching her with a bored smile saw nothing better before him than a chapter on the Domestic Felicities. O Mary, can you not provide me with the tiniest little plot?

Halloa!

No sooner was she hid from him than she changed into another woman; she was now become a calculating, purposeful madam, who looked around her covertly and, having shrunk in size in order to appear less noticeable, set off nervously on some mysterious adventure.

'The deuce!' thought I, and followed her.

Like one anxious to keep an appointment she frequently consulted her watch, looking long at it, as if it were one of those watches that do not give up their secret until you have made a mental calculation. Once she kissed it. I had always known that she was fond of her cheap little watch, which he gave her, I think, on the day I dropped the letter, but why kiss it in the street? Ah, and why then replace it so hurriedly in your leather belt, Mary, as if it were guilt to you to kiss today, or any day, the watch your husband gave you?

It will be seen that I had made a very rapid journey from light thoughts to uneasiness. I wanted no plot by the time she reached her destination, a street of tawdry shops. She entered none of them, but paced slowly, and shrinking

from observation, up and down the street, a very figure of
shame; and never had I thought to read shame in the sweet
face of Mary A———. Had I crossed to her and pronounced her name I think it would have felled her, and
yet she remained there, waiting. I, too, was waiting for him,
wondering if this was the man, or this, or this, and I believe
I clutched my stick.

Did I suspect Mary? Oh, surely not for a moment of
time. But there was some foolishness here; she was come
without the knowledge of her husband, as her furtive
manner indicated, to a meeting she dreaded and was
ashamed to tell him of; she was come into danger; then
it must be to save, not herself but him; the folly to be
concealed could never have been Mary's. Yet what could
have happened in the past of that honest boy from the
consequences of which she might shield him by skulking
here? Could that laugh of his have survived a dishonour?
The open forehead, the curly locks, the pleasant smile, the
hundred ingratiating ways which we carry with us out of
childhood, they may all remain when the innocence has
fled, but surely the laugh of the morning of life must go. I
have never known the devil retain his grip on that.

But Mary was still waiting. She was no longer beautiful;
shame had possession of her face, she was an ugly woman.
Then the entanglement was her husband's, and I cursed
him for it. But without conviction, for, after all, what did I
know of women? I have some distant memories of them,
some vain inventions. But of men – I have known one man
indifferent well for over forty years, have exulted in him
(odd to think of it), shuddered at him, wearied of him, been
willing (God forgive me!) to jog along with him tolerantly
long after I have found him out; I know something of men,
and, on my soul, boy, I believe I am wronging you.

Then Mary is here for some innocent purpose, to do a
good deed that were better undone, as it so scares her.
Turn back, you foolish, soft heart, and I shall say no more

about it. Obstinate one, you saw the look on your husband's face as he left you. It is the studio light by which he paints and still sees to hope, despite all the disappointments of his not ignoble ambitions. That light is the dower you brought him, and he is a wealthy man if it does not flicker.

So anxious to be gone, and yet she would not go. Several times she made little darts, as if at last resolved to escape from the detestable street, and faltered and returned like a bird to the weasel. Again she looked at her watch and kissed it.

O Mary, take flight! What madness is this? Woman, be gone!

Suddenly she was gone. With one mighty effort and a last terrified look round, she popped into a pawnshop.

Long before she emerged I understood it all, I think even as the door rang and closed on her; why the timid soul had sought a street where she was unknown, why she crept so many times past that abhorred shop before desperately venturing in, why she looked so often at the watch she might never see again. So desperately cumbered was Mary to keep her little house over her head, and yet the brave heart was retaining a smiling face for her husband, who must not even know where her little treasures were going.

It must seem monstrously cruel of me, but I was now quite light-hearted again. Even when Mary fled from the shop where she had left her watch, and I had peace of mind to note how thin and worn she had become, as if her baby was grown too big for her slight arms, even then I was light-hearted. Without attempting to follow her, I sauntered homeward humming a snatch of song with a great deal of fal-de-ral-de-riddle-o in it, for I can never remember words. I saw her enter another shop, baby-linen shop or some nonsense of that sort, so it was plain for what she had popped her watch; but what cared I? I continued to sing most beautifully. I lunged gaily with my stick at a lamp-post, and missed it, whereat a street-urchin grinned, and I winked at him and slipped twopence down his back.

I presume I would have chosen the easy way had time been given me, but fate willed that I should meet the husband on his homeward journey, and his first remark inspired me to a folly.

'How is Timothy?' he asked; and the question opened a way so attractive that I think no one whose dull life craves for colour could have resisted it.

'He is no more,' I replied impulsively.

The painter was so startled that he gave utterance to a very oath of pity, and I felt a sinking myself, for in these hasty words my little boy was gone indeed; all my bright dreams of Timothy, all my efforts to shelter him from Mary's scorn, went whistling down the wind.

SEVEN

The Last of Timothy

SO ACCOMPLISHED a person as the reader must have seen at once that I made away with Timothy in order to give his little vests and pinafores and shoes to David, and, therefore, dear sir or madam, rail not overmuch at me for causing our painter pain. Know, too, that though his sympathy ran free I soon discovered many of his inquiries to be prompted by a mere selfish desire to save his boy from the fate of mine. Such are parents.

He asked compassionately if there was anything he could do for me, and, of course, there was something he could do, but were I to propose it I doubted not he would be on his stilts at once, for already I had reason to know him for a haughty, sensitive dog, who ever became high at the first hint of help. So the proposal must come from him. I spoke of the many little things in the house that were now hurtful to me to look upon, and he clutched my hand, deeply moved, though it was another house with its little things he saw. I was ashamed to harass him thus, but he had not a sufficiency of the little things, and besides, my impulsiveness had plunged me into a deuce of a mess, so I went on distastefully. Was there no profession in this age of specialism for taking away children's garments from houses where they were suddenly become a pain? Could I sell them? Could I give them to the needy, who would probably dispose of them for gin? I told him of a friend with a young child who had already refused them because it would be unpleasant to him to be reminded of Timothy, and I think this was what touched him to the quick, so that he made the offer I was waiting for.

49

I had done it with a heavy foot, and by this time was in a rage with both him and myself; but I always was a bungler, and, having adopted this means in a hurry, I could at the time see no other easy way out. Timothy's hold on life, as you may have apprehended, was ever of the slightest, and I suppose I always knew that he must soon revert to the obscure. He could never have penetrated into the open. It was no life for a boy.

Yet now that his time had come, I was loth to see him go. I seem to remember carrying him that evening to the window with uncommon tenderness (following the setting sun that was to take him away), and telling him with not unnatural bitterness that he had got to leave me because another child was in need of all his pretty things; and as the sun, his true father, lapt him in its dancing arms, he sent his love to a lady of long ago whom he called by the sweetest of names, not knowing in his innocence that the little white birds are the birds that never have a mother. I wished (so had the phantasy of Timothy taken possession of me) that before he went he could have played once in the Kensington Gardens, and have ridden on the fallen trees, calling gloriously to me to look; that he could have sailed one paper galleon on the Round Pond; fain would I have had him chase one hoop a little way down the laughing avenues of childhood, where memory tells us we run but once, on a long summer day, emerging at the other end as men and women with all the fun to pay for; and I think (thus fancy wantons with me in these desolate chambers) he knew my longings, and said with a boy-like flush that the reason he never did these things was not that he was afraid, for he would have loved to do them all, but because he was not quite like other boys; and, so saying, he let go my finger and faded from before my eyes into another and golden ether; but I shall ever hold that had he been quite like other boys there would have been none braver than my Timothy.

I fear I am not truly brave myself, for though when under

fire, so far as I can recollect, I behaved as others, morally I seem to be deficient. So I discovered next day when I attempted to buy David's outfit, and found myself as shy of entering the shop as any Mary at the pawnbroker's. The shop for little garments seems very alarming when you reach the door; a man abruptly become a parent, and thus lost to a finer sense of the proprieties, may be able to stalk in unprotected, but apparently I could not. Indeed, I have allowed a repugnance to entering shops of any kind, save my tailor's, to grow on me, and to my tailor's I fear I go too frequently.

So I skulked near the shop of the little garments, jeering at myself, and it was strange to me to reflect at, say, three o'clock that if I had been brazen at half-past two all would now be over.

To show what was my state, take the case of the very gentleman-like man whom I detected gazing fixedly at me, or so I thought, just as I had drawn valiantly near the door. I sauntered away, but when I returned he was still there, which seemed conclusive proof that he had smoked my purpose. Sternly controlling my temper I bowed, and said with icy politeness, 'You have the advantage of me, sir.'

'I beg your pardon,' said he, and I am now persuaded that my words turned his attention to me for the first time, but at the moment I was sure some impertinent meaning lurked behind his answer.

'I have not the pleasure of your acquaintance,' I barked.

'No one regrets it more than I do,' he replied, laughing.

'I mean, sir,' said I, 'that I shall wait here until you retire,' and with that I put my back to a shop-window.

By this time he was grown angry, and said he, 'I have no engagement,' and he put his back to the shop-window. Each of us was doggedly determined to tire the other out, and we must have looked ridiculous. We also felt it, for ten minutes afterwards, our passions having died away, we shook hands cordially and agreed to call hansoms.

Must I abandon the enterprise? Certainly I knew divers ladies who would make the purchases for me, but first I must explain, and, rather than explain it has ever been my custom to do without. I was in this despondency when a sudden recollection of Irene and Mrs Hicking heartened me like a cordial, for I saw in them at once the engine and decoy by which David should procure his outfit.

You must be told who they were.

EIGHT

The Inconsiderate Waiter

THEY WERE THE the family of William, one of our club waiters who had been disappointing me grievously of late. Many a time have I deferred dining several minutes that I might have the attendance of this ingrate. His efforts to reserve the window-table for me were satisfactory, and I used to allow him privileges, as to suggest dishes; I have given him information, as that some one had startled me in the reading-room by slamming a door; I have shown him how I cut my finger with a piece of string. William was none of your assertive waiters. We could have plotted a murder safely before him. It was one member who said to him that Saucy Sarah would win the Derby and another who said that Saucy Sarah had no chance, but it was William who agreed with both. The excellent fellow (as I thought him) was like a cheroot which may be smoked from either end.

I date his lapse from one evening when I was dining by the window. I had to repeat my order, 'Devilled kidney,' and instead of answering brightly, 'Yes, sir,' as if my selection of devilled kidney was a personal gratification to him, which is the manner one expects of a waiter, he gazed eagerly out at the window, and then, starting, asked, 'Did you say devilled kidney, sir?' A few minutes afterwards I became aware that some one was leaning over the back of my chair, and you may conceive my indignation on discovering that this rude person was William. Let me tell, in the measured words of one describing a past incident, what next took place. To get nearer the window he pressed heavily on my shoulder. 'William,' I said, 'you are not attending to me!'

To be fair to him, he shook, but never shall I forget his audacious apology, 'Beg pardon, sir, but I was thinking of something else.'

And immediately his eyes resought the window, and this burst from him passionately, 'For God's sake, sir, as we are man and man, tell me if you have seen a little girl looking up at the club windows.'

Man and man! But he had been a good waiter once, so I pointed out the girl to him. As soon as she saw William she ran into the middle of Pall Mall, regardless of hansoms (many of which seemed to pass over her), nodded her head significantly three times, and then disappeared (probably on a stretcher). She was the tawdriest little Arab of about ten years, but seemed to have brought relief to William. 'Thank God!' said he fervently, and in the worst taste.

I was as much horrified as if he had dropped a plate on my toes. 'Bread, William,' I said sharply.

'You are not vexed with me, sir?' he had the hardihood to whisper.

'It was a liberty,' I said.

'I know, sir, but I was beside myself.

'That was a liberty again.'

'It is my wife, sir, she—'

So William, whom I had favoured in so many ways, was a married man. I felt that this was the greatest liberty of all.

I gathered that the troublesome woman was ailing, and as one who likes after dinner to believe that there is no distress in the world, I desired to be told by William that the signals meant her return to health. He answered inconsiderately, however, that the doctor feared the worst.

'Bah, the doctor!' I said in a rage.

'Yes, sir,' said William.

'What is her confounded ailment?'

'She was allus one of the delicate kind, but full of spirit, and you see, sir, she has had a baby-girl lately—'

'William, how dare you!' I said, but in the same moment I saw that this father might be useful to me. 'How does your baby sleep, William?' I asked in a low voice, 'how does she wake up? what do you put in her bath?'

I saw surprise in his face, so I hurried on without waiting for an answer. 'That little girl comes here with a message from your wife?'

'Yes, sir, every evening; she's my eldest, and three nods from her means that the missus is a little better.'

'There were three nods to-day?'

'Yes, sir.'

'I suppose you live in some low part, William?'

The impudent fellow looked as if he could have struck me. 'Off Drury Lane,' he said, flushing, 'but it isn't low. And now,' he groaned, 'she's afeard she will die without my being there to hold her hand.'

'She should not say such things.'

'She never says them, sir. She allus pretends to be feeling stronger. But I knows what is in her mind when I am leaving the house in the morning, for then she looks at me from her bed, and I looks at her from the door – O my God, sir!'

'William!'

At last he saw that I was angry, and it was characteristic of him to beg my pardon and withdraw his wife as if she were some unsuccessful dish. I tried to forget his vulgar story in billiards, but he had spoiled my game, and next day to punish him I gave my orders through another waiter. As I had the window-seat, however, I could not but see that the little girl was late, and though this mattered nothing to me and I had finished my dinner, I lingered till she came. She not only nodded three times but waved her hat, and I arose, having now finished my dinner.

William came stealthily toward me. 'Her temperature has gone down, sir,' he said, rubbing his hands together.

'To whom are you referring?' I asked coldly, and retired to the billiard-room, where I played a capital game.

I took pains to show William that I had forgotten his maunderings, but I observed the girl nightly, and once, instead of nodding, she shook her head, and that evening I could not get into a pocket. Next evening there was no William in the dining-room, and I thought I knew what had happened. But, chancing to enter the library rather miserably, I was surprised to see him on a ladder dusting books. We had the room practically to ourselves, for though several members sat on chairs holding books in their hands they were all asleep, and William descended the ladder to tell me his blasting tale. He had sworn at a member!

'I hardly knew what I was doing all day, sir, for I had left her so weakly that—'

I stamped my foot.

'I beg your pardon for speaking of her,' he had the grace to say. 'But Irene had promised to come every two hours; and when she came about four o'clock and I saw she was crying, it sort of blinded me, sir, and I stumbled against a member, Mr B———, and he said, "Damn you?" Well, sir, I had but touched him after all, and I was so broken it sort of stung me to be treated so, and I lost my senses, and I said, "Damn *you!*" '

His shamed head sank on his chest, and I think some of the readers shuddered in their sleep.

'I was turned out of the dining-room at once, and sent here until the committee have decided what to do with me. O sir, I am willing to go on my knees to Mr B———'

How could I but despise a fellow who would be thus abject for a pound a week?

'For if I have to tell her I have lost my place she will just fall back and die.'

'I forbid your speaking to me of that woman,' I cried wryly, 'unless you can speak pleasantly,' and I left him to his fate and went off to look for B———. 'What is this story about your swearing at one of the waiters?' I asked him.

'You mean about his swearing at me,' said B———, reddening.

'I am glad that was it,' I said, 'for I could not believe you guilty of such bad form. The version which reached me was that you swore at each other, and that he was to be dismissed and you reprimanded.'

'Who told you that?' asked B———, who is a timid man.

'I am on the committee,' I replied lightly, and proceeded to talk of other matters, but presently B———, who had been reflecting, said: 'Do you know I fancy I was wrong in thinking that the waiter swore at me, and I shall withdraw the charge tomorrow.'

I was pleased to find that William's troubles were near an end without my having to interfere in his behalf, and I then remembered that he would not be able to see the girl Irene from the library windows, which are at the back of the club. I was looking down at her, but she refrained from signalling, because she could not see William, and, irritated by her stupidity, I went out and asked her how her mother was.

'My,' she ejaculated, after a long scrutiny of me, 'I b'lieve you are one of them!' and she gazed at me with delighted awe. I suppose William tells them of our splendid doings.

The invalid, it appeared, was a bit better, and this annoying child wanted to inform William that she had took all the tapioca. She was to indicate this by licking an imaginary plate in the middle of Pall Mall. I gave the little vulgarian a shilling, and returned to the club disgusted.

'By the way, William,' I said, 'Mr B——— is to inform the committee that he was mistaken in thinking you used improper language to him, so you will doubtless be restored to the dining-room tomorrow.'

I had to add immediately, 'Remember your place, William.'

'But Mr B——— knows I swore,' he insisted.

'A gentleman,' I replied stiffly, 'cannot remember for many hours what a waiter has said to him.'

'No, sir, but—'

To stop him I had to say, 'And – ah – William, your wife is decidedly better. She has eaten the tapioca – all of it.'

'How can you know, sir?'

'By an accident.'

'Irene signed to the window?'

'No.'

'Then you saw her and went out and—'

'How dare you, William!'

'O sir, to do that for me! May God bl—'

'William.'

He was reinstated in the dining-room, but often when I looked at him I seemed to see a dying wife in his face, and so the relations between us were still strained. But I watched the girl, and her pantomime was so illuminating that I knew the sufferer had again cleaned the platter on Tuesday, had attempted a boiled egg on Wednesday (you should have seen Irene chipping it in Pall Mall, and putting in the salt), but was in a woeful state of relapse on Thursday.

'Is your mother very ill today, Miss Irene?' I asked, as soon as I had drawn her out of range of the club windows.

'My!' she exclaimed again, and I saw an ecstatic look pass between her and a still smaller girl with her, whom she referred to as a neighbour.

I waited coldly. William's wife, I was informed, had looked like nothing but a dead one till she got the brandy.

'Hush, child!' I said, shocked. 'You don't know how the dead look.'

'Bless yer!' she replied.

Assisted by her friend, who was evidently enormously impressed by Irene's intimacy with me, she gave me a good deal of miscellaneous information, as that William's real name was Mr Hicking, but that he was known in their street, because of the number of his shirts, as Toff Hicking. That the street held that he should get away from the club before two in the morning, for his missus needed him more than the club needed him. That William replied (very sensibly) that if the club was short of waiters at supper-time some of the gentlemen might be kept waiting for their marrow-bone. That he sat up with his missus most of the night, and pretended to her that he got some nice long naps at the club. That what she talked to him about mostly was the kid. That the kid was in another part of London (in charge of a person called the old woman), because there was an epidemic in Irene's street.

'And what does the doctor say about your mother?'

'He sometimes says she would have a chance if she could get her kid back.'

'Nonsense.'

'And if she was took to the country.'

'Then why does not William take her?'

'My! And if she drank porty wine.'

'Doesn't she?'

'No. But father, he tells her 'bout how the gentlemen drinks it.'

I turned form her with relief, but she came after me.

'Ain't yer going to do it this time?' she demanded with a falling face. 'You done it last time. I tell her you done it' –

she pointed to her friend, who was looking wistfully at me – 'ain't you to let her see you doing of it?'

For a moment I thought that her desire was another shilling, but by a piece of pantomime she showed that she wanted me to lift my hat to her. So I lifted it, and when I looked behind she had her head in the air and her neighbour was gazing at her awestruck. Those little creatures are really not without merit.

About a week afterwards I was in a hired landau, holding a newspaper before my face lest any one should see me in company of a waiter and his wife. William was taking her into Surrey to stay with an old nurse of mine, and Irene was with us, wearing the most outrageous bonnet.

I formed a mean opinion of Mrs Hicking's intelligence from her pride in the baby, which was a very ordinary one. She created a regrettable scene when it was brought to her, because 'she had been feared it would not know her again.' I could have told her that they know no one for years had I not been in terror of Irene, who dandled the child on her knees and talked to it all the way. I have never known a bolder little hussy than this Irene. She asked the infant improper questions, such as, 'Oo know who gave me this bonnet?' and answered them herself, 'It was the pretty gentleman there'; and several times I had to affect sleep, because she announced, 'Kiddy wants to kiss the pretty gentleman.'

Irksome as all this necessarily was to a man of taste, I suffered still more acutely when we reached our destination, where disagreeable circumstances compelled me to drink tea with a waiter's family. William knew that I regarded thanks from persons of his class as an outrage, yet he looked them though he dared not speak them. Hardly had he sat down at the table by my orders than he remembered that I was a member of the club and jumped up. Nothing is in worse form than whispering, yet again and again he whispered to his poor foolish wife, 'How are you now? You don't feel faint?' And when she said she felt like another woman already, his face charged me with the change. I could not but conclude from the way she let the baby pound her that she was stronger than she pretended.

I remained longer than was necessary because I had something to say to William which I feared he would misunderstand, but when he announced that it was time for him to catch a train back to London, at which his wife paled, I delivered the message.

'William,' I said, backing away from him, 'the head-waiter asked me to say that you could take a fortnight's holiday. Your wages will be paid as usual.'

Confound him.

'William,' I cried furiously, 'go away.'

Then I saw his wife signing to him, and I knew she wanted to be left alone with me.

'William,' I cried in a panic, 'stay where you are.'

But he was gone, and I was alone with a woman whose eyes were filmy. Her class are fond of scenes. 'If you please, ma'am!' I said imploringly.

But she kissed my hand; she was like a little dog.

'It can be only the memory of some woman,' said she, 'that makes you so kind to me and mine.'

Memory was the word she used, as if all my youth were fled. I suppose I really am quite elderly.

'I should like to know her name, sir,' she said, 'that I may mention her with loving respect in my prayers.'

I raised the woman and told her the name. It was not Mary. 'But she has a home,' I said, 'as you have, and I have none. Perhaps, ma'am, it would be better worth your while to mention me.'

It was this woman, now in health, whom I intrusted with the purchase of the outfits, 'one for a boy of six months,' I explained to her, 'and one for a boy of a year,' for the painter had boasted to me of David's rapid growth. I think she was a little surprised to find that both outfits were for the same house; and she certainly betrayed an ignoble curiosity about the mother's Christian name, but she was much easier to browbeat than a fine lady would have been, and I am sure she and her daughter enjoyed themselves hugely in the shops, from one of which I shall never forget Irene emerging proudly with a commissionaire, who conducted her under an umbrella to the cab where I was lying in wait. I think that was the most celestial walk of Irene's life.

I told Mrs Hicking to give the articles a little active ill-treatment that they might not look quite new, at which she exclaimed, not being in my secret, and then to forward them to me. I then sent them to Mary and rejoiced in my devilish cunning all the evening, but chagrin came in the morning with a letter from her which showed she knew all, that I was her Mr Anon, and that there never had been a Timothy. I think I was never so gravelled. Even now I don't know how she had contrived it.

Her cleverness raised such a demon in me that I locked away her letter at once and have seldom read it since. No married lady should have indited such an epistle to a single man. It said, with other things which I decline to repeat, that I was her good fairy. As a sample of the deliberate falsehoods in it, I may mention that she said David loved me already. She hoped that I would come in often to see her husband, who was very proud of my friendship, and suggested that I should pay him my first visit today at three o'clock, an hour at which, as I happened to know, he is always away giving a painting-lesson. In short, she wanted first to meet me alone, so that she might draw the delicious, respectful romance out of me, and afterwards repeat it to him, with sighs and little peeps at him over her pocket-handkerchief.

She had dropped what were meant to look like two tears for me upon the paper, but I should not wonder though they were only artful drops of water.

I sent her a stiff and tart reply, declining to hold any communication with her.

NINE

A Confirmed Spinster

I AM IN danger, I see, of being included among the whimsical fellows, which I so little desire that I have got me into my writing-chair to combat the charge, but, having sat for an unconscionable time with pen poised, I am come agitatedly to the fear that there may be something in it.

So long a time has elapsed, you must know, since I abated of the ardours of self-inquiry that I revert in vain (through many rusty doors) for the beginning of this change in me, if changed I am; I seem ever to see this same man until I am back in those wonderful months which were half of my life, when, indeed, I know that I was otherwise than I am now; no whimsical fellow then, for that was one of the possibilities I put to myself while seeking for the explanation of things, and found to be inadmissible. Having failed in those days to discover why I was driven from the garden, I suppose I ceased to be enamoured of myself, as of some dull puzzle, and then perhaps the whimsicalities began to collect unnoticed.

It is a painful thought to me tonight, that he could wake up glorious once, this man in the elbow-chair by the fire, who is humorously known at the club as a 'confirmed spinster.' I remember him well when his years told four-and-twenty; on my soul the proudest subaltern of my acquaintance, and with the most reason to be proud. There was nothing he might not do in the future, having already done the biggest thing, this toddler up club steps today.

Not, indeed, that I am a knave; I am tolerably kind, I believe, and most inoffensive, a gentleman, I trust, even in the eyes of the ladies who smile at me as we converse; they

are an ever-increasing number, or so its seems to me tonight. Ah, ladies! I forget when I first began to notice that
smile and to be made uneasy by it. I think I understand it
now, and in some vague way it hurts me. I find that I watch
for it nowadays, but I hope I am still your loyal, obedient
servant.

You will scarcely credit it, but I have just remembered
that I once had a fascinating smile of my own. What has
become of my smile? I swear I have not noticed that it was
gone till now; I am like one who, revisiting his school, feels
suddenly for his old knife. I first heard of my smile from
another boy, whose sisters had considered all the smiles
they knew and placed mine on top. My friend was scornful,
and I bribed him to mention the plebiscite to no one, but
secretly I was elated and amazed. I feel lost tonight without
my smile. I rose a moment ago to look for it in my mirror.

I like to believe that she has it now. I think she may have
some other forgotten trifles of mine with it that make the
difference between that man and this. I remember her
speaking of my smile, telling me it was my one adornment,
and taking it from me, so to speak, for a moment to let me
see how she looked in it; she delighted to make sport of me
when she was in a wayward mood, and to show me all my
ungainly tricks of voice and gesture, exaggerated and
glorified in her entrancing self, like a star calling to the
earth: 'See, I will show you how you hobble round,' and
always there was a challenge to me in her eyes to stop her if I
dared, and upon them, when she was most audacious, lay a
sweet mist.

They all came to her court, as is the business of young
fellows, to tell her what love is, and she listened with a noble
frankness, having, indeed, the friendliest face for all engaged in this pursuit that can ever have sat on woman. I
have heard ladies call her coquette, not understanding that
she shone softly upon all who entered the lists, because with
the rarest intuition she foresaw that they must go away

broken men and already sympathised with their dear wounds. All wounds incurred for love were dear to her; at every true utterance about love she exulted with grave approval, or it might be with a little 'ah!' or 'oh!' like one drinking deliciously. Nothing could have been more fair, for she was for the first comer who could hit the target, which was her heart.

She adored all beautiful things in their every curve and fragrance, so that they became part of her. Day by day, she gathered beauty; had she had no heart (she who was the bosom of womanhood) her thoughts would still have been as lilies, because the good is the beautiful.

And they all forgave her; I never knew of one who did not forgive her; I think had there been one it would have proved that there was a flaw in her. Perhaps, when good-bye came she was weeping because all the pretty things were said and done with, or she was making doleful confessions about herself, so impulsive and generous and confidential, and so devoid of humour, that they compelled even a tragic swain to laugh. She made a looking-glass of his face to seek woefully in it whether she was at all to blame, and when his arms went out for her, and she stepped back so that they fell empty, she mourned, with dear sympathy, his lack of skill to seize her. For what her soft eyes said was that she was always waiting tremulously to be won. They all forgave her, because there was nothing to forgive, or very little, just the little that makes a dear girl dearer, and often afterwards, I believe, they have laughed fondly when thinking of her, like boys brought back. You ladies who are everything to your husbands save a girl from the dream of youth, have you never known that double-chinned industrious man laugh suddenly in a reverie and start up, as if he fancied he were being hailed from far away?

I hear her hailing me now. She was so light-hearted that her laugh is what comes first across the years; so high-spirited that she would have wept like Mary of Scots because she could not lie on the bare plains like the men. I hear her, but it is only as an echo; I see her, but it is as a light among distant trees, and the middle-aged man can draw no nearer; she was only for the boys. There was a month when I could have shown her to you in all her bravery, but then the veil fell, and from that moment I understood her not. For long I watched her, but she was never clear to me again, and for long she hovered round me, like a dear heart willing to give me a thousand chances to regain her love. She was so picturesque that she was the last word of art, but she was as young as if she were the first woman. The world must have rung with gallant deeds and grown lovely thoughts for numberless centuries before she could be; she was the child of all the brave and wistful imaginings of men. She was as mysterious as night when it fell for the first time upon the earth. She was the thing we call romance, which lives in the little hut beyond the blue haze of the pine-woods.

No one could have looked less elfish. She was all on a noble scale, her attributes were so generous, her manner unconquerably gracious, her movements indolently active, her face so candid that you must swear her every thought lived always in the open. Yet, with it all, she was a wild thing, alert, suspicious of the lasso, nosing it in every man's hand, more curious about it than aught else in the world; her quivering delight was to see it cast for her, her game to elude it; so mettlesome was she that she loved it to be cast fair that she might escape as it was closing round her; she scorned, however her heart might be beating, to run from her pursuers; she took only the one step backward, which still left her near them but always out of reach; her head on high now, but her face as friendly, her manner as gracious as before, she is yours for the catching. That was ever the unspoken compact between her and the huntsmen.

It may be but an old trick come back to me with these memories, but again I clasp my hands to my brows in amaze at the thought that all this was for me could I retain her love. For I won it, wonder of the gods, but I won it. I found myself with one foot across the magic circle wherein she moved, and which none but I had entered; and so, I think, I saw her in revelation, not as the wild thing they had all conceived her, but as she really was. I saw no tameless creature, nothing wild or strange. I saw my sweet love placid as a young cow browsing. As I brushed aside the haze and she was truly seen for the first time, she raised her head, like one caught, and gazed at me with meek affrighted eyes. I told her what had been revealed to me as I looked upon her, and she trembled, knowing she was at last found, and fain would she have fled away, but that her fear was less than her gladness. She came to me slowly; no incomprehensible thing to me now, but transparent as a pool, and so restful to look upon that she was a bath to the eyes, like banks of moss.

Because I knew the maid, she was mine. Every maid, I say, is for him who can know her. The others had but followed the glamour in which she walked, but I had pierced it and found the woman. I could anticipate her every thought and gesture, I could have flashed and rippled and mocked for her, and melted for her and been dear disdain for her. She would forget this and be suddenly conscious of it as she began to speak, when she gave me a look with a shy smile in it which meant that she knew I was already waiting at the end of what she had to say. I call this the blush of the eye. She had a look and a voice that were for me alone; her very finger-tips were charged with caresses for me. And I loved even her naughtinesses, as when she stamped her foot at me, which she could not do without also gnashing her teeth, like a child trying to look fearsome. How pretty was that gnashing of her teeth! All her tormentings of me turned suddenly into sweetnesses, and who could torment like this exquisite fury, wondering in sudden flame why she could give herself to any one, while I wondered only why she could give herself to me. It may be that I wondered overmuch. Perhaps that was why I lost her.

It was in the full of the moon that she was most restive, but I brought her back, and at first she could have bit my hand, but then she came willingly. Never, I thought, shall she be wholly tamed, but he who knows her will always be able to bring her back.

I am not the man, for, mystery of mysteries, I lost her. I know not how it was, though in the twilight of my life that then began I groped for reasons until I wearied of myself; all I know is that she had ceased to love me; I had won her love, but I could not keep it. The discovery came to me slowly, as if I were a most dull-witted man; at first I knew only that I no longer understood her as of old. I found myself wondering what she had meant by this and that; I did not see that when she began to puzzle me she was already lost to me. It was as if, unknowing, I had strayed outside the magic circle.

When I did understand, I tried to cheat myself into the belief that there was no change, and the dear heart bleeding for me assisted in that poor pretence. She sought to glide to me with swimming eyes as before, but it showed only that this caressing movement was still within her compass, but never again for me. With the hands she had pressed to her breast she touched mine, but no longer could they convey the message. The current was broken, and soon we had to desist miserably from our pretences. She could tell no more than I why she had ceased to love me; she was scarcely less anxious than I that I should make her love me again, and, as I have said, she waited with a wonderful tolerance while I strove futilely to discover in what I was lacking and to remedy it. And when, at last, she had to leave me, it was with compassionate cries and little backward flights.

The failure was mine alone, but I think I should not have been so altered by it had I known what was the defect in me through which I let her love escape. This puzzle has done me more harm than the loss of her. Nevertheless, you must know (if I am to speak honestly to you) that I do not repent me those dallyings in enchanted fields. It may not have been so always, for I remember a black night when a poor lieutenant lay down in an oarless boat and let it drift toward the weir. But his distant moans do not greatly pain me now; rather am I elated to find (as the waters bring him nearer) that this boy is I, for it is something to know that, once upon a time, a woman could draw blood from me as from another.

I saw her again, years afterwards, when she was a married woman playing with her children. She stamped her foot at a naughty one, and I saw the gleam of her teeth as she gnashed them in the dear pretty way I can't forget; and then a boy and girl, fighting for her shoulders, brought the whole group joyously to the ground. She picked herself up in the old leisurely manner, lazily active, and looked around her benignantly, like a cow: our dear wild one safely tethered at last with a rope of children. I meant to make her my devoirs, but, as I stepped forward, the old wound broke out afresh, and I had to turn away. They were but a few poor drops, which fell because I found that she was even a little sweeter than I had thought.

TEN

Sporting Reflections

I HAVE NOW told you (I presume) how I became whimsical, and I fear it would please Mary not at all. But speaking of her, and, as the cat's light keeps me in a ruminating mood, suppose, instead of returning Mary to her lover by means of the letter, I had presented a certain clubman to her consideration? Certainly no such whimsical idea crossed my mind when I dropped the letter, but between you and me and my night-socks, which have all this time been airing by the fire because I am subject to cold feet, I have sometimes toyed with it since.

Why did I not think of this in time? Was it because I must ever remain true to the unattainable she?

I am reminded of a passage in the life of a sweet lady, a friend of mine, whose daughter was on the eve of marriage, when suddenly her lover died. It then became pitiful to watch that trembling old face trying to point the way of courage to the young one. In time, however, there came another youth, as true, I dare say, as the first, but not so well known to me, and I shrugged my shoulders cynically to see my old friend once more a matchmaker. She took him to her heart and boasted of him; like one made young herself by the great event, she joyously dressed her pale daughter in her bridal gown, and, with smiles upon her face, she cast rice after the departing carriage. But soon after it had gone, I chanced upon her in her room, and she was on her knees in tears before the spirit of the dead lover. 'Forgive me,' she besought him, 'for I am old, and life is gray to friendless girls.' The pardon she wanted was for pretending to her daughter that women should act thus.

I am sure she felt herself soiled.

But men are of a coarser clay. At least I am, and nearly twenty years had elapsed, and here was I burdened under a load of affection, like a sack of returned love-letters, with no lap into which to dump them.

'They were all written to another woman, ma'am, and yet I am in hopes that you will find something in them about yourself.' It would have sounded oddly to Mary, but life is gray to friendless girls, and something might have come of it.

On the other hand, it would have brought her for ever out of the wood of the little hut, and I had but to drop the letter to send them both back there. The easiness of it tempted me.

Besides, she would tire of me when I was really known to her. They all do, you see.

And, after all, why should he lose his laugh because I had lost my smile?

And then, again, the whole thing was merely a whimsical idea.

I dropped the letter, and shouldered my burden.

ELEVEN

The Runaway Perambulator

I SOMETIMES MET David in public places such as the Kensington Gardens, where he lorded it surrounded by his suite and wearing the blank face and glass eyes of all carriage people. On these occasions I always stalked by, meditating on higher things, though Mary seemed to think me very hard-hearted, and Irene, who had become his nurse (I forget how, but fear I had something to do with it), ran after me with messages, as, would I not call and see him in his home at twelve o'clock, at which moment, it seemed, he was at his best.

No, I would not.

'He says tick-tack to the clock,' Irene said, trying to snare me.

'Pooh!' said I.

'Other little 'uns jest says "tick-tick," ' she told me, with a flush of pride.

'I prefer "tick-tick," ' I said, whereat she departed in dudgeon.

Had they had the sense to wheel him behind a tree and leave him, I would have looked; but as they lacked it, I decided to wait until he cold walk, when it would be more easy to waylay him. However, he was a cautious little gorbal who, after many threats to rise, always seemed to come to the conclusion that he might do worse than remain where he was, and when he had completed his first year I lost patience with him.

'When I was his age,' I said to Irene, 'I was running about.' I consulted them casually about this matter at the club, and they had all been running about at a year old.

I made this nurse the following offer: If she would bring the dilatory boy to my rooms, and leave him there for half an hour, I would look at him. At first Mary, to whom the offer was passed on, rejected it with hauteur; but presently she wavered, and the upshot was that Irene, looking scornful and anxious, arrived one day with the perambulator. Without casting eyes on its occupant, I pointed Irene to the door: 'In half an hour,' I said.

She begged permission to remain, and promised to turn her back, and so on; but I was obdurate, and she then delivered herself of a passionately affectionate farewell to her charge, which was really all directed against me, and ended with these powerful words: 'And if he takes off your socks, my pretty, may he be blasted for evermore.'

'I shall probably take off her socks,' I said carelessly to this.

Her socks. Do you see what made Irene scream?

'It is a girl, is it not?' I asked, thus neatly depriving her of coherent speech as I pushed her to the door. I then turned round to— to begin, and, after reflecting, I began by sitting down behind the hood of his carriage. My plan was to accustom him to his new surroundings before bursting on the scene myself.

I had various thoughts. Was he awake? If not, better let him wake naturally. Half an hour was a long time. Why had I not said quarter of an hour? Anon, I saw that if I was to sit there much longer I should have said an hour, so I whistled softly; but he took no notice. I remember trying to persuade myself that if I never budged till Irene's return, it would be an amusing triumph over Mary. I coughed, but still there was no response. Abruptly the fear smote me. Perhaps he is not there.

I rose hastily, and was striding forward, when I distinctly noticed a covert movement somewhere near the middle of the carriage, and heard a low gurgle, which was instantly suppressed. I stopped dead at this sharp reminder that I was probably not the only curious person in the room, and for a long moment we both lay low, after which, I am glad to remember, I made the first advance. Earlier in the day I had arranged some likely articles on a side-table: my watch and chain, my bunch of keys, and two war-medals for plodding merit, and with a glance at these (as something to fall back upon), I stepped forward doggedly, looking (I fear now) a little like a professor of legerdemain. David was sitting up, and he immediately fixed his eyes on me.

It would ill become me to attempt to describe this dear boy to you, for of course I know really nothing about children, so I shall say only this, that I thought him very like what Timothy would have been had he ever had a chance.

I, to whom David had been brought for judgment, now found myself being judged by him, and this rearrangement of the pieces seemed so natural that I felt no surprise; I felt only a humble craving to hear him signify that I would do. I have stood up before other keen judges and deceived them all, but I made no effort to deceive David; I wanted to, but dared not. Those unblinking eyes were too new to the world to be hooded by any of its tricks. In them I saw my true self. They opened for me that peddler's pack of which I have made so much ado, and I found that it was weighted less with pretty little sad love-tokens than with ignoble thoughts and deeds and an unguided life. I looked dejectedly at David, not so much, I think, because I had such a sorry display for him, as because I feared he would not have me in his service. I seemed to know that he was making up his mind once and for all.

And in the end he smiled; perhaps only because I looked so frightened, but the reason scarcely mattered to me. I felt myself a fine fellow at once. It was a long smile, too, opening slowly to its fullest extent (as if to let me in), and then as slowly shutting.

Then, to divert me from sad thoughts, or to rivet our

friendship, or because the time had come for each of us to show the other what he could do, he immediately held one foot high in the air. This made him slide down the perambulator, and I saw at once that it was very necessary to replace him. But never before had I come into such close contact with a child; the most I had ever done was, when they were held up to me, to shut my eyes and kiss a vacuum. David, of course, though no doubt he was eternally being replaced, could tell as little as myself how it was contrived, and yet we managed it between us quite easily. His body instinctively assumed a certain position as I touched him, which compelled my arms to fall into place, and the thing was done. I felt absurdly pleased, but he was already considering what he should do next.

He again held up his foot, which had a gouty appearance owing to its being contained in a dumpy little worsted sock, and I thought he proposed to repeat his first performance; but in this I did him an injustice, for, unlike Porthos, he was one who scorned to do the same feat twice; perhaps, like the conjurers, he knew that the audience were more on the alert the second time.

I discovered that he wanted me to take off his sock!

Remembering Irene's dread warnings on this subject, I must say that I felt uneasy. Had he heard her, and was he daring me? And what dire thing could happen if the sock was removed? I sought to reason with him, but he signed to me to look sharp, and I removed the sock. The part of him thus revealed gave David considerable pleasure, but I noticed, as a curious thing, that he seemed to have no interest in the other foot.

However, it was not there merely to be looked at, for after giving me a glance which said 'Now observe!' he raised his bare foot and ran his mouth along the toes, like one playing on a barbaric instrument. He then tossed his foot aside, smiled his long triumphant smile, and intimated that it was now my turn to do something. I thought the best thing I could do would be to put his sock on him again, but as soon as I tried to do so I discovered why Irene had warned me so portentously against taking it off. I should say that she had trouble in socking him every morning.

Nevertheless I managed to slip it on while he was debating what to do with my watch. I bitterly regretted that I could do nothing with it myself – put it under a wine-glass, for instance, and make it turn into a rabbit, which so many people can do. In the meantime David, occupied with similar thoughts, very nearly made it disappear altogether, and I was thankful to be able to pull it back by the chain.

'Haw-haw-*haw*!'

Thus he commented on his new feat, but it was also a reminder to me, a trifle cruel, that he was not my boy. After all, you see, Mary had not given him the whole of his laugh. The watch said that five-and-twenty minutes had passed, and looking out I saw Irene at one end of the street staring up at my window, and at the other end Mary's husband staring up at my window, and beneath me Mary staring up at my window. They had all broken their promise.

I returned to David, and asked him in a low voice whether he would give me a kiss. He shook his head about six times, and I was in despair. Then the smile came, and I knew that he was teasing me only. He now nodded his head about six times.

This was the prettiest of all his exploits. It was so pretty, that, contrary to his rule, he repeated it. I had held out my arms to him, and first he shook his head, and then after a long pause (to frighten me), he nodded it.

But no sooner was he in my arms than I seemed to see Mary and her husband and Irene bearing down upon my chambers to take him from me, and acting under an impulse I whipped him into the perambulator and was off with it without a licence down the back staircase. To the Kensington Gardens we went; it may have been Manitoba we started for, but we arrived at the Kensington Gardens, and it had all been so unpremeditated and smartly carried out that I remember clapping my hand to my head in the street, to make sure that I was wearing a hat.

I watched David to see what he thought of it, and he had not yet made up his mind. Strange to say, I no longer felt shy. I was grown suddenly indifferent to public comment, and my elation increased when I discovered that I was being pursued. They drew a cordon round me near Margot Meredith's tree, but I broke through it by a strategic movement to the south, and was next heard of in the Baby's Walk. They held both ends of this passage, and then thought to close on me, but I slipped through their fingers by doubling up Bunting's Thumb into Picnic Street. Cowering at St Govor's Well, we saw them rush distractedly up the Hump, and when they had crossed to the Round Pond we paraded gaily in the Broad Walk, not feeling the tiniest bit sorry for anybody.

Here, however, it gradually came into David's eyes that, after all, I was a strange man, and they opened wider and wider, until they were the size of my medals, and then, with the deliberation that distinguishes his smile, he slowly prepared to howl. I saw all his forces gathering in his face, and I had nothing to oppose to them; it was an unarmed man against a regiment.

Even then I did not chide him. He could not know that it was I who had dropped the letter.

I think I must have stepped over a grateful fairy at that moment, for who else could have reminded me so opportunely of my famous manipulation of the eyebrows, forgotten since I was in the fifth form? I alone of boys had been able to elevate and lower my eyebrows separately; when the one was climbing my forehead the other descended it, like the two buckets in the well.

Most diffidently did I call this accomplishment to my aid now, and immediately David checked his forces and considered my unexpected movement without prejudice. His face remained as it was, his mouth open to emit the howl if I did not surpass expectation. I saw that, like the fair-minded boy he has always been, he was giving me my chance, and I worked feverishly, my chief fear being that, owing to his youth, he might not know how marvellous was this thing I was doing. It is an appeal to the intellect, as well as to the senses, and no one on earth can do it except myself.

When I paused for a moment exhausted he signed gravely, with unchanged face, that though it was undeniably funny, he had not yet decided whether it was funny enough, and taking this for encouragement, at it I went once more, till I saw his forces wavering, when I sent my left eyebrow up almost farther than I could bring it back: and with that I had him – the smile broke through the clouds.

In the midst of my hard-won triumph I heard cheering.

I had been vaguely conscious that we were not quite alone, but had not dared to look away from David. I looked now, and found to my annoyance that I was the centre of a deeply interesting gathering of children. There was in particular one vulgar little street boy—

However, if that damped me in the moment of victory, I was soon to triumph gloriously in what began like defeat. I had sat me down on one of the garden seats in the Figs, with one hand resting carelessly on the perambulator, in imitation of the nurses – it was so pleasant to assume the air of one who walked with David daily, – when to my chagrin I saw Mary approaching with quick, stealthy steps, and already so near me that flight would have been ignominy. Porthos, of whom she had hold, bounded toward me, waving his traitorous tail, but she slowed on seeing that I had observed her. She had run me down with my own dog.

I have not mentioned that Porthos had for some time now been a visitor at her house, though never can I forget the shock I got the first time I saw him strolling out of it like an afternoon caller. Of late he has avoided it, crossing to the other side when I go that way, and rejoining me farther on, so I conclude that Mary's husband is painting him.

I waited her coming stiffly, in great depression of spirits, and noted that her first attentions were for David, who, somewhat shabbily, gave her the end of a smile which had been begun for me. It seemed to relieve her, for what one may call the wild maternal look left her face, and trying to check little gasps of breath, the result of unseemly running, she signed to her confederates to remain in the background, and turned curious eyes on me. Had she spoken as she approached, I am sure her words would have been as flushed as her face, but now her mouth puckered as David's does before he sets forth upon his smile, and I saw that she thought she had me in a parley at last.

'I could not help being a little anxious,' she said craftily, but I must own, with some sweetness.

I merely raised my hat, and at that she turned quickly to David – I cannot understand why the movement was so hasty – and lowered her face to his. O little trump of a boy! Instead of kissing her, he seized her face with one hand and tried to work her eyebrows up and down with the other. He failed, and his obvious disappointment in his mother was as nectar to me.

'I don't understand what you want, darling,' said she in distress, and looked at me inquiringly, and I understood what he wanted, and let her see that I understood. Had I been prepared to converse with her, I should have said elatedly that, had she known what he wanted, still she could not have done it, though she had practised for twenty years.

I tried to express all this by another movement of my hat.

It caught David's eye, and at once he appealed to me with the most perfect confidence. She failed to see what I did, for I shyly gave her my back, but the effect on David was miraculous; he signed to her to go, for he was engaged for the afternoon.

What would you have done then, reader? I didn't. In my great moment I had strength of character to raise my hat for the third time and walk away, leaving the child to judge between us. I walked slowly, for I knew I must give him time to get it out, and I listened eagerly; but that was unnecessary, for when it did come it was a very roar of anguish. I turned my head, and saw David fiercely pushing the woman aside, that he might have one last long look at me. He held out his wistful arms and nodded repeatedly, and I faltered, but my glorious scheme saved me, and I walked on. It was a scheme conceived in a flash, and ever since relentlessly pursued – to burrow under Mary's influence with the boy, expose her to him in all her vagaries, take him utterly from her and make him mine.

TWELVE

The Pleasantest Club in London

ALL PERAMBULATORS lead to the Kensington Gardens.

Not, however, that you will see David in his perambulator much longer, for soon after I first shook his faith in his mother, it came to him to be up and doing, and he up and did in the Broad Walk itself, where he would stand alone most elaborately poised, signing imperiously to the British public to time him, and looking his most heavenly just before he fell. He fell with a dump, and as they always laughed then, he pretended that this was his funny way of finishing.

That was on a Monday. On Tuesday he climbed the stone stair of the Gold King, looking over his shoulder gloriously at each step, and on Wednesday he struck three and went into knickerbockers. For the Kensington Gardens, you must know, are full of short cuts, familiar to all who play there; and the shortest leads from the baby in long clothes to the little boy of three riding on the fence. It is called the Mother's Tragedy.

If you are a burgess of the gardens (which have a vocabulary of their own), the faces of these quaint mothers are a clock to you, in which you may read the ages of their young. When he is three they are said to wear the knickerbocker face, and you may take it from me that Mary assumed that face with a sigh; fain would she have kept her boy a baby longer, but he insisted on his rights, and I encouraged him that I might notch another point against her. I was now seeing David once at least every week, his mother, who remained culpably obtuse to my sinister design, having instructed Irene that I was to be allowed to

82

share him with her, and we had become close friends, though the little nurse was ever a threatening shadow in the background. Irene, in short, did not improve with acquaintance. I found her to be high and mighty, chiefly, I think, because she now wore a nurse's cap with streamers, of which the little creature was ludicrously proud. She assumed the airs of an official person, and always talked as if generations of babies had passed through her hands. She was also extremely jealous, and had a way of signifying disapproval of my methods that led to many coldnesses and even bickerings between us, which I now see to have been undignified. I brought the following accusations against her:–

That she prated too much about right and wrong.

That she was a martinet.

That she pretended it was a real cap, with real streamers, when she knew Mary had made the whole thing out of a muslin blind. I regret having used this argument, but it was the only one that really damped her.

On the other hand, she accused me of spoiling him.

Of not thinking of his future.

Of never asking him where he expected to go to if he did such things.

Of telling him tales that had no moral application.

Of saying that the handkerchief disappeared into nothingness, when it really disappeared into a small tin cup attached to my person by a piece of elastic.

To this last charge I plead guilty, for in those days I had a pathetic faith in legerdemain, and the eyebrow feat (which, however, is entirely an affair of skill) having yielded such good results, I naturally cast about for similar diversions when it ceased to attract. It lost its hold on David suddenly, as I was to discover was the fate of all of them; twenty times would he call for my latest, and exult in it, and the twenty-first time (and ever afterwards) he would stare blankly, as if wondering what the man meant. He was like the child queen who, when the great joke was explained to her, said coldly, 'We are not amused,' and, I assure you, it is a humiliating thing to perform before an infant who intimates, after giving you ample time to make your points, that he is not amused. I hoped that when David was able to talk – and not merely to stare at me for five minutes and then say 'hat' – his spoken verdict, however damning, would be less expressive than his verdict without words, but I was disillusioned. I remember once in those later years, when he could keep up such spirited conversations with himself that he had little need for any of us, promising him to do something exceedingly funny with a box and two marbles, and after he had watched for a long time he said gravely, 'Tell me when it begins to be funny.'

I confess to having received a few simple lessons in conjuring, in a dimly-lighted chamber beneath a shop, from a gifted young man with a long neck and a pimply face, who as I entered took a barber's pole from my pocket, saying at the same time, 'Come, come, sir, this will never do.' Whether because he knew too much, or because he wore a trick shirt, he was the most depressing person I ever encountered; he felt none of the artist's joy, and it was sad to see one so well calculated to give pleasure to thousands not caring a dump about it.

The barber's pole I successfully extracted from David's mouth, but the difficulty (not foreseen) of knowing how to dispose of a barber's pole in the Kensington Gardens is considerable, there always being polite children hovering near who run after you and restore it to you. The young man, again, had said that any one would lend me a bottle or a lemon; but though these were articles on which he seemed ever able to lay his hand, I found (what I never had noticed before) that there is a curious dearth of them in the Gardens. The magic egg-cup I usually carried about with me, and with its connivance I did some astonishing things with pennies; but even the penny that costs sixpence is uncertain, and just when you are saying triumphantly that it will be found in the egg-cup, it may clatter to the ground, whereon some ungenerous spectator, such as Irene, accuses you of fibbing and corrupting youthful minds. It was useless to tell her, through clenched teeth, that the whole thing was a joke, for she understood no jokes except her own, of which she had the most immoderately high opinion, and that would have mattered little to me had not David liked them also. There were times when I could not but think less of the boy, seeing him rock convulsed over antics of Irene that have been known to every nurse-maid since the year One. While I stood by, sneering, he would give me the ecstatic look that meant, 'Irene is really very entertaining, isn't she?'

We were rivals, but I desire to treat her with scrupulous fairness, and I admit that she had one good thing, to wit, her gutta-percha tooth. In earlier days one of her front teeth, as she told me, had fallen out; but instead of then parting with it, the resourceful child had hammered it in again with a hair-brush, which she offered to show me, with the dents on it. This tooth, having in time passed away, its place was supplied by one of gutta-percha, made by herself, which seldom came out except when she sneezed, and if it merely fell at her feet this was a sign that the cold was to be a slight one, but if it shot across the room she knew she was in for something notable. Irene's tooth was very favourably known in the Gardens, where the perambulators used to gather round her to hear whether it had been doing any-thing today, and I would not have grudged David his proprietary pride in it, had he seemed to understand that Irene's one poor little accomplishment, though undeniably showy, was without intellectual merit. I have sometimes stalked away from him, intimating that if his regard was to be got so cheaply I begged to retire from the competition, but the Gardens are the pleasantest club in London, and I soon returned. How I scoured the Gardens looking for

him, and how skilful I became at picking him out far away
among the trees, though other mothers imitated the picturesque attire of him, to Mary's indignation. I also cut
Irene's wings (so to speak) by taking her to a dentist.

And David did some adorable things. For instance, he
used my pockets as receptacles into which he put any article
he might not happen to want at the moment. He shoved it
in, quite as if they were his own pockets, without saying, By
your leave, and perhaps I discovered it on reaching home –
a tin-soldier, or a pistol – when I put it on my mantelshelf
and sighed. And here is another pleasant memory. One day
I had been over-friendly to another boy, and, after enduring
it for some time David up and struck him. It was exactly as
Porthos does when I favour other dogs (he knocks them
down with his foot and stands over them, looking very
noble and stern), so I knew its meaning at once; it was
David's first public intimation that he knew I belonged to
him.

Irene scolded him for striking that boy, and made him
stand in disgrace at the corner of a seat in the Broad Walk.
The seat at the corner of which David stood suffering for
love of me is the one nearest to the Round Pond to persons
coming from the north.

You may be sure that she and I had words over this
fiendish cruelty. When next we met I treated her as one
who no longer existed, and at first she bridled and then was
depressed, and as I was going away she burst into tears. She
cried because at neither meeting nor parting had I lifted my
hat to her, a foolish custom of mine, of which, as I now
learned to my surprise, she was very proud. She and I still
have our tiffs, but I have never since then forgotten to lift
my hat to Irene. I also made her promise to bow to me, at
which she affected to scoff, saying I was taking my fun off
her, but she was really pleased, and I tell you, Irene has one
of the prettiest and most touching little bows imaginable; it
is half to the side (if I may so express myself), which has

always been my favourite bow, and, I doubt not, she acquired it by watching Mary.

I should be sorry to have it thought, as you may now be thinking, that I look on children as on puppy-dogs, who care only for play. Perhaps that was my idea when first I tried to lure David to my unaccustomed arms, and even for some time after, for if I am to be candid, I must own that until he was three years old I sought merely to amuse him. God forgive me, but I had only one day a week in which to capture him, and I was very raw at the business.

I was about to say that David opened my eyes to the folly of it, but really I think this was Irene's doing. Watching her with children, I learned that partial as they are to fun they are moved almost more profoundly by moral excellence. So fond of babes was this little mother that she had always room near her for one more, and often have I seen her in the Gardens the centre of a dozen mites, who gazed awestruck at her while she told them severely how little ladies and gentlemen behave. They were children of the well-to-pass, and she was from Drury Lane, but they believed in her as the greatest of all authorities on little ladies and gentlemen, and the more they heard of how these romantic creatures keep themselves tidy and avoid pools and wait till they come to a gate, the more they admired them, though their faces showed how profoundly they felt that to be little ladies and gentlemen was not for them. You can't think what hopeless little faces they were.

Children are not at all like puppies, I have said. But do puppies care only for play? That wistful look, which the merriest of them sometimes wear, I wonder whether it means that they would like to hear about the good puppies?

As you shall see, I invented many stories for David, practising the telling of them by my fireside as if they were conjuring feats, while Irene knew only one, but she told it as never has any other fairy-tale been told in my hearing. It was the prettiest of them all, and was recited by the heroine.

'Why were the king and queen not at home?' David would ask her breathlessly.

'I suppose,' said Irene, thinking it out, 'they was away buying the victuals.'

She always told the story gazing into vacancy, so that David thought it was really happening somewhere up the Broad Walk, and when she came to its great moments her little bosom heaved. Never shall I forget the concentrated scorn with which the prince said to the sisters, 'Neither of you ain't the one what wore the glass slipper.'

'And then— and then— and then—,' said Irene, not artistically to increase the suspense, but because it was all so glorious to her.

'Tell me – tell me quick,' cried David, though he knew the tale by heart.

'She sits down like,' said Irene, trembling in second-sight, 'and she tries on the glass slipper, and it fits her to a T; and then the prince, he cries in a ringing voice, "This here is my true love, Cinderella, what now I makes my lawful wedded wife." '

Then she would come out of her dream, and look round at the grandees of the Gardens with an extraordinary elation. 'Her, as was only a kitchen drudge,' she would say in a strange soft voice and with shining eyes, 'but was true and faithful in word and deed, such was her reward.'

I am sure that had the fairy godmother appeared just then and touched Irene with her wand, David would have been interested rather than astonished. As for myself, I believe I have surprised this little girl's secret. She knows there are no fairy godmothers nowadays, but she hopes that if she is always true and faithful she may some day turn into a lady in word and deed, like the mistress whom she adores.

It is a dead secret, a Drury Lane child's romance; but

what an amount of heavy artillery will be brought to bear against it in this sad London of ours. Not much chance for her, I suppose.

Good luck to you, Irene.

THIRTEEN

The Grand Tour of the Gardens

YOU MUST SEE for yourselves that it will be difficult to follow our adventures unless you are familiar with the Kensington Gardens, as they now became known to David. They are in London, where the King lives, and you go to them every day unless you are looking decidedly flushed, but no one has ever been in the whole of the Gardens, because it is so soon time to turn back. The reason it is soon time to turn back is that you sleep from twelve to one. If your mother was not so sure that you sleep from twelve to one, you could most likely see the whole of them.

The Gardens are bounded on one side by a never-ending line of omnibuses, over which Irene has such authority that if she holds up her finger to any one of them it stops immediately. She then crosses with you in safety to the other side. There are more gates to the Gardens than one gate, but that is the one you go in at, and before you go in you speak to the lady with the balloons, who sits just outside. This is as near to being inside as she may venture, because, if she were to let go her hold of the railings for one moment, the balloons would lift her up, and she would be flown away. She sits very squat, for the balloons are always tugging at her, and the strain has given her quite a red face. Once she was a new one, because the old one had let go, and David was very sorry for the old one, but as she did let go, he wished he had been there to see.

The Gardens are a tremendous big place, with millions and hundreds of trees; and first you come to the Figs, but you scorn to loiter there, for the Figs is the resort of superior little persons, who are forbidden to mix with the commonalty, and is so named, according to legend, because they dress in full fig. These dainty ones are themselves contemptuously called Figs by David and other heroes, and you have a key to the manners and customs of this dandiacal section of the Gardens when I tell you that cricket is called crickets here. Occasionally a rebel Fig climbs over the fence into the world, and such a one was Miss Mabel Grey, of whom I shall tell you when we come to Miss Mabel Grey's gate. She was the only really celebrated Fig.

We are now in the Broad Walk, and it is as much bigger than the other walks as your father is bigger than you. David wondered if it began little, and grew and grew, until it was quite grown up, and whether the other walks are its babies, and he drew a picture, which diverted him very much, of the Broad Walk giving a tiny walk an airing in a perambulator. In the Broad Walk you meet all the people who are worth knowing, and there is usually a grown-up with them to prevent their going on the damp grass, and to make them stand disgraced at the corner of a seat if they have been mad-dog or Mary-Annish. To be Mary-Annish is to behave like a girl, whimpering because nurse won't carry you, or simpering with your thumb in your mouth, and it is a hateful quality; but to be mad-dog is to kick out at everything, and there is some satisfaction in that.

If I were to point out all the notable places as we pass up the Broad Walk, it would be time to turn back before we reach them, and I simply wave my stick at Cecco Hewlett's Tree, that memorable spot where a boy called Cecco lost his penny, and, looking for it, found twopence. There has been a good deal of excavation going on there ever since. Farther up the walk is the little wooden house in which Marmaduke Perry hid. There is no more awful story of the Gardens than this of Marmaduke Perry, who had been Mary-Annish three days in succession, and was sentenced to appear in the Broad Walk dressed in his sister's clothes.

He hid in the little wooden house, and refused to emerge until they brought him knickerbockers with pockets.

You now try to go to the Round Pond, but nurses hate it, because they are not really manly, and they make you look the other way, at the Big Penny and the Baby's Palace. She was the most celebrated baby of the Gardens, and lived in the palace all alone, with ever so many dolls, so people rang the bell, and up she got out of her bed, though it was past six o'clock, and she lighted a candle and opened the door in her nighty, and then they all cried with great rejoicings, 'Hail, Queen of England!' What puzzled David most was how she knew where the matches were kept. The Big Penny is a statue about her.

Next we come to the Hump, which is the part of the Broad Walk where all the big races are run; and even though you had no intention of running you do run when you come to the Hump, it is such a fascinating, slide-down kind of place. Often you stop when you have run about half-way down it, and then you are lost; but there is another little wooden house near here, called the Lost House, and so you tell the man that you are lost and then he finds you. It is glorious fun racing down the Hump, but you can't do it on windy days because then you are not there, but the fallen leaves do it instead of you. There is almost nothing that has such a keen sense of fun as a fallen leaf.

From the Hump we can see the gate that is called after Miss Mabel Grey, the Fig I promised to tell you about. There were always two nurses with her, or else one mother and one nurse, and for a long time she was a pattern-child who always coughed off the table and said, 'How do you do?' to the other Figs, and the only game she played at was flinging a ball gracefully and letting the nurse bring it back to her. Then one day she tired of it all and went mad-dog, and, first, to show that she really was mad-dog, she unloosened both her bootlaces and put out her tongue east, west, north, and south. She then flung her sash into a puddle and danced on it till dirty water was squirted over her frock, after which she climbed the fence and had a series of incredible adventures, one of the least of which was that she kicked off both her boots. At last she came to the gate that is now called after her, out of which she ran into streets David and I have never been in though we have heard them roaring, and still she ran on and would never again have been heard of had not her mother jumped into a 'bus and thus overtaken her. It all happened, I should say, long ago, and this is not the Mabel Grey whom David knows.

Returning up the Broad Walk we have on our right the Baby Walk, which is so full of perambulators that you could cross from side to side stepping on babies, but the nurses won't let you do it. From this walk a passage called Bunting's Thumb, because it is that length, leads into Picnic Street, where there are real kettles, and chestnut-blossom falls into your mug as you are drinking. Quite common children picnic here also, and the blossom falls into their mugs just the same.

Next comes St Govor's Well, which was full of water when Malcolm the Bold fell into it. He was his mother's favourite, and he let her put her arm round his neck in public because she was a widow; but he was also partial to adventures, and liked to play with a chimney-sweep who had killed a good many bears. The sweep's name was Sooty, and one day, when they were playing near the well, Malcolm fell in and would have been drowned had not Sooty dived in and rescued him; and the water had washed Sooty clean, and he now stood revealed as Malcolm's long-lost father. So Malcolm would not let his mother put her arm round his neck any more.

Between the well and the Round Pond are the cricket-pitches, and frequently the choosing of sides exhausts so much time that there is scarcely any cricket. Everybody wants to bat first, and as soon as he is out he bowls unless you are the better wrestler, and while you are wrestling with him the fielders have scattered to play at something else. The Gardens are noted for two kinds of cricket: boy cricket, which is real cricket with a bat, and girl cricket, which is with a racquet and the governess. Girls can't really play cricket, and when you are watching their futile efforts you make funny sounds at them. Nevertheless, there was a very disagreeable incident one day when some forward girls challenged David's team, and a disturbing creature called Angela Clare sent down so many yorkers that— However, instead of telling you the result of that regrettable match I shall pass on hurriedly to the Round Pond, which is the wheel that keeps all the Gardens going.

It is round because it is in the very middle of the Gardens, and when you are come to it you never want to go any farther. You can't be good all the time at the Round Pond, however much you try. You can be good in the Broad Walk all the time, but not at the Round Pond, and the reason is that you forget, and, when you remember, you are so wet that you may as well be wetter. There are men who sail boats on the Round Pond, such big boats that they bring them in barrows, and sometimes in perambulators, and then the baby has to walk. The bow-legged children in the Gardens are those who had to walk too soon because their father needed the perambulator.

You always want to have a yacht to sail on the Round Pond, and in the end your uncle gives you one; and to carry it to the Pond the first day is splendid, also to talk about it to boys who have no uncle is splendid, but soon you like to leave it at home. For the sweetest craft that slips her moorings in the Round Pond is what is called a stick-boat, because she is rather like a stick until she is in the water and you are holding the string. Then as you walk round, pulling her, you see little men running about her deck, and sails rise magically and catch the breeze, and you put in on dirty nights at snug harbours which are unknown to the lordly yachts. Night passes in a twink, and again your rakish craft

noses for the wind, whales spout, you glide over buried
cities, and have brushes with pirates, and cast anchor on
coral isles. You are a solitary boy while all this is taking
place, for two boys together cannot adventure far upon the
Round Pond, and though you may talk to yourself throughout the voyage, giving orders and executing them with
dispatch, you know not, when it is time to go home, where
you have been or what swelled your sails; your treasure-
trove is all locked away in your hold, so to speak, which will
be opened, perhaps, by another little boy many years
afterwards.

But those yachts have nothing in their hold. Does any
one return to this haunt of his youth because of the yachts
that used to sail it? Oh no. It is the stick-boat that is
freighted with memories. The yachts are toys, their owner
a fresh-water mariner; they can cross and recross a pond
only while the stick-boat goes to sea. You yachtsmen with
your wands, who think we are all there to gaze on you, your
ships are only accidents of this place, and were they all to be
boarded and sunk by the ducks, the real business of the
Round Pond would be carried on as usual.

Paths from everywhere crowd like children to the pond.
Some of them are ordinary paths, which have a rail on each
side, and are made by men with their coats off, but others
are vagrants, wide at one spot, and at another so narrow
that you can stand astride them. They are called Paths that
have Made Themselves, and David did wish he could see
them doing it. But, like all the most wonderful things that
happen in the Gardens, it is done, we concluded, at night
after the gates are closed. We have also decided that the
paths make themselves because it is their only chance of
getting to the Round Pond.

One of these gypsy paths comes from the place where the
sheep get their hair cut. When David shed his curls at the
hairdresser's, I am told, he said good-bye to them without a
tremor, though Mary has never been quite the same bright

creature since; so he despises the sheep as they run from their shearer, and calls out tauntingly, 'Cowardy, cowardy custard!' But when the man grips them between his legs David shakes a fist at him for using such big scissors. Another startling moment is when the man turns back the grimy wool from the sheeps' shoulders and they look suddenly like ladies in the stalls of a theatre. The sheep are so frightened by the shearing that it makes them quite white and thin, and as soon as they are set free they begin to nibble the grass at once, quite anxiously, as if they feared that they would never be worth eating. David wonders whether they know each other, now that they are so different, and if it makes them fight with the wrong ones. They are great fighters, and thus so unlike country sheep that every year they give Porthos a shock. He can make a field of country sheep fly by merely announcing his approach, but these town sheep come toward him with no promise of gentle entertainment, and then a light from last year breaks upon Porthos. He cannot with dignity retreat, but he stops and looks about him as if lost in admiration of the scenery, and presently he strolls away with a fine indifference and a glint at me from the corner of his eye.

The Serpentine begins near here. It is a lovely lake, and there is a drowned forest at the bottom of it. If you peer over the edge you can see the trees all growing upside down, and they say that at night there are also drowned stars in it. If so, Peter Pan sees them when he is sailing across the lake in the Thrush's Nest. A small part only of the Serpentine is in the Gardens, for soon it passes beneath a bridge to far away where the island is on which all the birds are born that become baby boys and girls. No one who is human, except Peter Pan (and he is only half human), can land on the island, but you may write what you want (boy or girl, dark or fair) on a piece of paper, and then twist it into the shape of a boat and slip it into the water, and it reaches Peter Pan's island after dark.

We are on the way home now, though of course, it is all pretence that we can go to so many of the places in one day. I should have had to be carrying David long ago, and resting on every seat like old Mr Salford. That was what we called him, because he always talked to us of a lovely place called Salford where he had been born. He was a crab-apple of an old gentleman who wandered all day in the Gardens from seat to seat trying to fall in with somebody who was acquainted with the town of Salford, and when we had known him for a year or more we actually did meet another aged solitary who had once spent Saturday to Monday in Salford. He was meek and timid, and carried his address inside his hat, and whatever part of London he was in search of he always went to Westminster Abbey first as a starting-point. Him we carried in triumph to our other friend, with the story of that Saturday to Monday, and never shall I forget the gloating joy with which Mr Salford leapt at him. They have been cronies ever since, and I notice that Mr Salford, who naturally does most of the talking, keeps tight grip of the other old man's coat.

The two last places before you come to our gate are the Dog's Cemetery and the chaffinch's nest, but we pretend not to know what the Dog's Cemetery is, as Porthos is always with us. The nest is very sad. It is quite white, and the way we found it was wonderful. We were having another look among the bushes for David's lost worsted ball, and instead of the ball we found a lovely nest made of the worsted, and containing four eggs, with scratches on them very like David's handwriting, so we think they must have been the mother's love-letters to the little ones inside. Every day we were in the Gardens we paid a call at the nest, taking care that no cruel boy should see us, and we dropped crumbs, and soon the bird knew us as friends, and sat in the nest looking at us kindly with her shoulders hunched up. But one day when we went there were only two eggs in the nest, and the next time there were none. The saddest part of it was that the poor little chaffinch fluttered about the bushes, looking so reproachfully at us that we knew she thought we had done it; and though David tried to explain to her, it was so long since he had spoken the bird language that I fear she did not understand. He and I left the Gardens that day with our knuckles in our eyes.

FOURTEEN

Peter Pan

IF YOU ASK your mother whether she knew about Peter Pan when she was a little girl, she will say, 'Why, of course I did, child'; and if you ask her whether he rode on a goat in those days, she will say, 'What a foolish question to ask; certainly he did.' Then if you ask your grandmother whether she knew about Peter Pan when she was a girl, she also says, 'Why, of course I did, child,' but if you ask her whether he rode on a goat in those days, she says she never heard of his having a goat. Perhaps she has forgotten, just as she sometimes forgets your name and calls you Mildred, which is your mother's name. Still, she could hardly forget such an important thing as the goat. Therefore there was no goat when your grandmother was a little girl. This shows that, in telling the story of Peter Pan, to begin with the goat (as most people do) is as silly as to put on your jacket before your vest.

Of course, it also shows that Peter is ever so old, but he is really always the same age, so that does not matter in the least. His age is one week, and though he was born so long ago he has never had a birthday, nor is there the slightest chance of his ever having one. The reason is that he escaped from being a human when he was seven days old; he escaped by the window and flew back to the Kensington Gardens.

If you think he was the only baby who ever wanted to escape, it shows how completely you have forgotten your own young days. When David heard this story first he was quite certain that he had never tried to escape, but I told him to think back hard, pressing his hands to his temples, and when he had done this hard, and even harder, he distinctly remembered a youthful desire to return to the tree-tops, and with that memory came others, as that he had lain in bed planning to escape as soon as his mother was asleep, and how she had once caught him half-way up the chimney. All children could have such recollections if they would press their hands hard to their temples, for, having been birds before they were human, they are naturally a little wild during the first few weeks, and very itchy at the shoulders, where their wings used to be. So David tells me.

I ought to mention here that the following is our way with a story: First I tell it to him, and then he tells it to me, the understanding being that it is quite a different story; and then I retell it with his additions, and so we go on until no one could say whether it is more his story or mine. In this story of Peter Pan, for instance, the bald narrative and most of the moral reflections are mine, though not all, for this boy can be a stern moralist; but the interesting bits about the ways and customs of babies in the bird-stage are mostly reminiscences of David's, recalled by pressing his hands to his temples and thinking hard.

Well, Peter Pan got out by the window, which had no bars. Standing on the ledge he could see trees far away, which were doubtless the Kensington Gardens, and the moment he saw them he entirely forgot that he was now a little boy in a nightgown, and away he flew, right over the houses to the Gardens. It is wonderful that he could fly without wings, but the place itched tremendously, and— and— perhaps we could all fly if we were as dead-confident-sure of our capacity to do it as was bold Peter Pan that evening.

He alighted gaily on the open sward, between the Baby's Palace and the Serpentine, and the first thing he did was to lie on his back and kick. He was quite unaware already that he had ever been human, and thought he was a bird, even in appearance, just the same as in his early days, and when he tried to catch a fly he did not understand that the reason he missed it was because he had attempted to seize it with his hand, which, of course, a bird never does. He saw, however, that it must be past Lock-out Time, for there were a good many fairies about, all too busy to notice him; they were getting breakfast ready, milking their cows, drawing water, and so on, and the sight of the water-pails made him thirsty, so he flew over to the Round Pond to have a drink. He stooped and dipped his beak in the pond; he thought it was his beak, but, of course, it was only his nose, and therefore, very little water came up, and that not so refreshing as usual, so next he tried a puddle, and he fell flop into it. When a real bird falls in flop, he spreads out his feathers and pecks them dry, but Peter could not remember what was the thing to do, and he decided rather sulkily to go to sleep on the weeping beech in the Baby Walk.

At first he found some difficulty in balancing himself on a branch, but presently he remembered the way, and fell asleep. He awoke long before morning, shivering, and saying to himself, 'I never was out on such a cold night'; he had really been out on colder nights when he was a bird, but, of course, as everybody knows, what seems a warm night to a bird is a cold night to a boy in a nightgown. Peter also felt strangely uncomfortable, as if his head was stuffy; he heard loud noises that made him look round sharply, though they were really himself sneezing. There was something he wanted very much, but, though he knew he wanted it, he could not think what it was. What he wanted so much was his mother to blow his nose, but that never struck him, so he decided to appeal to the fairies for enlightenment. They are reputed to know a good deal.

There were two of them strolling along the Baby Walk, with their arms round each other's waists, and he hopped down to address them. The fairies have their tiffs with the birds, but they usually give a civil answer to a civil question, and he was quite angry when these two ran away the moment they saw him. Another was lolling on a garden chair, reading a postage-stamp which some human had let fall, and when he heard Peter's voice he popped in alarm behind a tulip.

To Peter's bewilderment he discovered that every fairy he met fled from him. A band of workmen, who were sawing down a toadstool, rushed away, leaving their tools behind them. A milkmaid turned her pail upside down and hid in it. Soon the Gardens were in an uproar. Crowds of fairies were running this way and that, asking each other stoutly who was afraid; lights were extinguished, doors barricaded, and from the grounds of Queen Mab's palace came the rub-a-dub of drums, showing that the royal guard had been called out. A regiment of Lancers came charging down the Broad Walk, armed with holly-leaves, with which they jag the enemy horribly in passing. Peter heard the little people crying everywhere that there was a human in the Gardens after Lock-out Time, but he never thought for a moment that he was the human. He was feeling stuffier and stuffier, and more and more wistful to learn what he wanted done to his nose, but he pursued them with the vital question in vain; the timid creatures ran from him, and even the Lancers, when he approached them up the Hump, turned swiftly into a side-walk, on the pretence that they saw him there.

Despairing of the fairies, he resolved to consult the birds, but now he remembered, as an odd thing, that all the birds on the weeping-beech had flown away when he alighted on it, and though this had not troubled him at the time, he saw its meaning now. Every living thing was shunning him. Poor little Peter Pan! he sat down and cried, and even then he did not know that, for a bird, he was sitting on his wrong part. It is a blessing that he did not know, for otherwise he would have lost faith in his power to fly, and the moment you doubt whether you can fly, you cease for ever to be able to do it. The reason birds can fly and we can't is simply that they have perfect faith, for to have faith is to have wings.

Now, except by flying, no one can reach the island in the Serpentine, for the boats of humans are forbidden to land there, and there are stakes round it, standing up in the water, on each of which a bird-sentinel sits by day and night. It was to the island that Peter now flew to put his strange case before old Solomon Caw, and he alighted on it with relief, much heartened to find himself at last at home, as the birds call the island. All of them were asleep, including the sentinels, except Solomon, who was wide awake on one side, and he listened quietly to Peter's adventures, and then told him their true meaning.

'Look at your nightgown, if you don't believe me,' Solomon said; and with staring eyes Peter looked at his nightgown, and then at the sleeping birds. Not one of them wore anything.

'How many of your toes are thumbs?' said Solomon a little cruelly, and Peter saw to his consternation, that all his toes were fingers. The shock was so great that it drove away his cold.

'Ruffle your feathers,' said that grim old Solomon, and Peter tried most desperately hard to ruffle his feathers, but he had none. Then he rose up, quaking, and for the first time since he stood on the window ledge, he remembered a lady who had been very fond of him.

'I think I shall go back to mother,' he said timidly.

'Good-bye,' replied Solomon Caw with a queer look.

But Peter hesitated. 'Why don't you go?' the old one asked politely.

'I suppose,' said Peter huskily, 'I suppose I can still fly?'

You see, he had lost faith.

'Poor little half-and-half!' said Solomon, who was not really hard-hearted, 'you will never be able to fly again, not even on windy days. You must live here on the island always.'

'And never even go to the Kensington Gardens?' Peter asked tragically.

'How could you get across?' said Solomon. He promised very kindly, however, to teach Peter as many of the bird ways as could be learned by one of such an awkward shape.

'Then I shan't be exactly a human?' Peter asked.

'No.'

'Nor exactly a bird?'

'No.'

'What shall I be?'

'You will be a Betwixt-and-Between,' Solomon said, and certainly he was a wise old fellow, for that is exactly how it turned out.

The birds on the island never got used to him. His oddities tickled them every day, as if they were quite new, though it was really the birds that were new. They came out of the eggs daily, and laughed at him at once; then off they soon flew to be humans, and other birds came out of other eggs; and so it went on for ever. The crafty mother-birds, when they tired of sitting on their eggs, used to get the young ones to break their shells a day before the right time by whispering to them that now was their chance to see Peter washing or drinking or eating. Thousands gathered round him daily to watch him do these things, just as you watch the peacocks, and they screamed with delight when he lifted the crusts they flung him with his hands instead of in the usual way with the mouth. All his food was brought to him from the Gardens at Solomon's orders by the birds. He would not eat worms or insects (which they thought very silly of him), so they brought him bread in their beaks. Thus, when you cry out, 'Greedy! Greedy!' to the bird that flies away with the big crust, you know now that you ought not to do this, for he is very likely taking it to Peter Pan.

Peter wore no nightgown now. You see, the birds were always begging him for bits of it to line their nests with, and, being very good-natured, he could not refuse, so by Solomon's advice he had hidden what was left of it. But, though he was now quite naked, you must not think that he was cold or unhappy. He was usually very happy and gay, and the reason was that Solomon had kept his promise and taught him many of the bird ways. To be easily pleased, for instance, and always to be really doing something, and to think that whatever he was doing was a thing of vast importance. Peter became very clever at helping the birds to build their nests; soon he could build better than a wood-pigeon, and nearly as well as a blackbird, though never did he satisfy the finches, and he made nice little water-troughs near the nests and dug up worms for the young ones with his fingers. He also became very learned in bird-lore, and knew an east wind from a west wind by its smell, and he could see the grass growing and hear the insects walking about inside the tree-trunks. But the best thing Solomon had done was to teach him to have a glad heart. All birds have glad hearts unless you rob their nests, and so as they were the only kind of heart Solomon knew about, it was easy to him to teach Peter how to have one.

Peter's heart was so glad that he felt he must sing all day long, just as the birds sing for joy, but, being partly human, he needed an instrument, so he made a pipe of reeds, and he used to sit by the shore of the island of an evening, practising the sough of the wind and the ripple of the water, and catching handfuls of the shine of the moon, and he put them all in his pipe and played them so beautifully that even the birds were deceived, and they would say to each other, 'Was that a fish leaping in the water or was it Peter playing leaping fish on his pipe?' And sometimes he played the birth of birds, and then the mothers would turn round in their nests to see whether they had laid an egg. If you are a child of the Gardens you must know the chestnut-tree near the bridge, which comes out in flower first of all the chestnuts, but perhaps you have not heard why this tree leads the way. It is because Peter wearies for summer and plays that it has come, and the chestnut being so near, hears him and is cheated.

But as Peter sat by the shore tootling divinely on his pipe he sometimes fell into said thoughts, and then the music became sad also, and the reason of all this sadness was that he could not reach the Gardens, though he could see them through the arch of the bridge. He knew he could never be a real human again, and scarcely wanted to be one, but oh! how he longed to play as other children play, and of course there is no such lovely place to play in as the Gardens. The birds brought him news of how boys and girls play, and wistful tears started in Peter's eyes.

Perhaps you wonder why he did not swim across. The reason was that he could not swim. He wanted to know how to swim, but no one on the island knew the way except the ducks, and they are so stupid. They were quite willing to teach him, but all they could say about it was, 'You sit down on the top of the water in this way, and then you kick out like that.' Peter tried it often, but always before he could kick out he sank. What he really needed to know was how you sit on the water without sinking, and they said it was quite impossible to explain such an easy thing as that. Occasionally swans touched on the island, and he would give them all his day's food and then ask them how they sat on the water, but as soon as he had no more to give them the hateful things hissed at him and sailed away.

Once he really thought he had discovered a way of reaching the Gardens. A wonderful white thing, like a runaway newspaper, floated high over the island and then tumbled, rolling over and over after the manner of a bird that has broken its wing. Peter was so frightened that he hid, but the birds told him it was only a kite, and what a kite is, and that it must have tugged its string out of a boy's hand, and soared away. After that they laughed at Peter for being so fond of the kite; he loved it so much that he even slept with one hand on it, and I think this was pathetic and pretty, for the reason he loved it was because it had belonged to a real boy.

To the birds this was a very poor reason, but the older ones felt grateful to him at this time because he had nursed a number of fledglings through the German measles, and they offered to show him how birds fly a kite. So six of them took the end of the string in their beaks and flew away with it; and to his amazement it flew after them and went even higher than they.

Peter screamed out, 'Do it again!' and with great good-nature they did it several times, and always instead of thanking them he cried 'Do it again!' which shows that even now he had not quite forgotten what it was to be a boy.

At last, with a grand design burning within his brave heart, he begged them to do it once more with him clinging to the tail, and now a hundred flew off with the string, and Peter clung to the tail, meaning to drop off when he was over the Gardens. But the kite broke to pieces in the air, and he would have been drowned in the Serpentine had he not caught hold of two indignant swans and made them carry him to the island. After this the birds said that they would help him no more in his mad enterprise.

Nevertheless, Peter did reach the Gardens at last by the help of Shelley's boat, as I am now to tell you.

FIFTEEN

The Thrush's Nest

SHELLEY WAS a young gentleman and as grown-up as he need ever expect to be. He was a poet; and they are never exactly grown-up. They are people who despise money except what you need for today, and he had all that and five pounds over. So, when he was walking in the Kensington Gardens, he made a paper boat of his bank-note, and sent it sailing on the Serpentine.

It reached the island at night: and the look-out brought it to Solomon Caw, who thought at first that it was the usual thing, a message from a lady, saying she would be obliged if he could let her have a good one. They always ask for the best one he has, and if he likes the letter he sends one from Class A, but if it ruffles him he sends very funny ones indeed. Sometimes he sends none at all, and at another time he sends a nestful; it all depends on the mood you catch him in. He likes you to leave it all to him, and if you mention particularly that you hope he will see his way to making it *a boy this time*, he is almost sure to send another girl. And whether you are a lady or only a little boy who wants a baby-sister, always take pains to write your address clearly. You can't think what a lot of babies Solomon has sent to the wrong house.

Shelley's boat, when opened, completely puzzled Solomon, and he took counsel of his assistants, who having walked over it twice, first with their toes pointed out, and then with their toes pointed in, decided that it came from some greedy person who wanted five. They thought this because there was a large five printed on it. 'Preposterous!' cried Solomon in a rage, and he presented it to Peter;

anything useless which drifted upon the island was usually given to Peter as a plaything.

But he did not play with his precious bank-note, for he knew what it was at once, having been very observant during the week when he was an ordinary boy. With so much money, he reflected, he could surely at last contrive to reach the Gardens, and he considered all the possible ways, and decided (wisely, I think) to choose the best way. But, first, he had to tell the birds of the value of Shelley's boat; and though they were too honest to demand it back, he saw that they were galled, and they cast such black looks at Solomon, who was rather vain of his cleverness, that he flew away to the end of the island, and sat there very depressed with his head buried in his wings. Now Peter knew that unless Solomon was on your side, you never got anything done for you in the island, so he followed him and tried to hearten him.

Nor was this all that Peter did to gain the powerful old fellow's good-will. You must know that Solomon had no intention of remaining in office all his life. He looked forward to retiring by and by, and devoting his green old age to a life of pleasure on a certain yew-stump in the Figs which had taken his fancy, and for years he had been quietly filling his stocking. It was a stocking belonging to some bathing person which had been cast upon the island, and at the time I speak of it contained a hundred and eighty crumbs, thirty-four nuts, sixteen crusts, a pen-wiper, and a boot-lace. When his stocking was full, Solomon calculated that he would be able to retire on a competency. Peter now gave him a pound. He cut it off his bank-note with a sharp stick.

This made Solomon his friend for ever, and after the two had consulted together they called a meeting of the thrushes. You will see presently why thrushes only were invited.

The scheme to be put before them was really Peter's, but

Solomon did most of the talking, because he soon became irritable if other people talked. He began by saying that he had been much impressed by the superior ingenuity shown by the thrushes in nest-building, and this put them into good-humour at once, as it was meant to do; for all the quarrels between birds are about the best way of building nests. Other birds, said Solomon, omitted to line their nests with mud, and as a result they did not hold water. Here he cocked his head as if he had used an unanswerable argument; but, unfortunately, a Mrs Finch had come to the meeting uninvited, and she squeaked out, 'We don't build nests to hold water, but to hold eggs,' and then the thrushes stopped cheering, and Solomon was so perplexed that he took several sips of water.

'Consider,' he said at last, 'how warm the mud makes the nest.'

'Consider,' cried Mrs Finch, 'that when water gets into the nest it remains there and your little ones are drowned.'

The thrushes begged Solomon with a look to say something crushing in reply to this, but again he was perplexed.

'Try another drink,' suggested Mrs Finch pertly. Kate was her name, and all Kates are saucy.

Solomon did try another drink, and it inspired him. 'If,' said he, 'a finch's nest is placed on the Serpentine it fills and breaks to pieces, but a thrush's nest is still as dry as the cup of a swan's back.'

How the thrushes applauded! Now they knew why they lined their nests with mud, and when Mrs Finch called out, 'We don't place our nests on the Serpentine,' they did what they should have done at first – chased her from the meeting. After this it was most orderly. What they had been brought together to hear, said Solomon, was this: their young friend, Peter Pan, as they well knew, wanted very much to be able to cross to the Gardens, and he now proposed, with their help, to build a boat.

At this the thrushes began to fidget, which made Peter tremble for his scheme.

Solomon explained hastily that what he meant was not one of the cumbrous boats that humans use; the proposed boat was to be simply a thrush's nest large enough to hold Peter.

But still, to Peter's agony, the thrushes were sulky. 'We are very busy people,' they grumbled, 'and this would be a big job.'

'Quite so,' said Solomon, 'and, of course, Peter would not allow you to work for nothing. You must remember that he is now in comfortable circumstances, and he will pay you such wages as you have never been paid before. Peter Pan authorises me to say that you shall all be paid sixpence a day.'

Then all the thrushes hopped for joy, and that very day was begun the celebrated Building of the Boat. All their ordinary business fell into arrears. It was the time of the year when they should have been pairing, but not a thrush's nest was built except this big one, and so Solomon soon ran short of thrushes with which to supply the demand from the mainland. The stout, rather greedy children, who look so well in perambulators but get puffed easily when they walk, were all young thrushes once, and ladies often ask specially for them. What do you think Solomon did? He sent over to the housetops for a lot of sparrows and ordered them to lay their eggs in old thrushes' nests, and sent their young to the ladies and swore they were all thrushes! It was known afterwards on the island as the Sparrow's Year; and so, when you meet grown-up people in the Gardens who puff and blow as if they thought themselves bigger than they are, very likely they belong to that year. You ask them.

Peter was a just master, and paid his workpeople every evening. They stood in rows on the branches, waiting politely while he cut the paper sixpences out of his bank-note, and presently he called the roll, and then each bird, as the names were mentioned, flew down and got sixpence. It must have been a fine sight.

And at last, after months of labour, the boat was finished. O the deportment of Peter as he saw it growing more and more like a great thrush's nest! From the very beginning of the building of it he slept by its side, and often woke up to say sweet things to it, and after it was lined with mud and the mud had dried he always slept in it. He sleeps in his nest still, and has a fascinating way of curling round in it, for it is just large enough to hold him comfortably when he curls round like a kitten. It is brown inside, of course, but outside it is mostly green, being woven of grass and twigs, and when these wither or snap the walls are thatched afresh. There are also a few feathers here and there, which came off the thrushes while they were building.

The other birds were extremely jealous, and said that the boat would not balance on the water, but it lay most beautifully steady; they said the water would come into it, but no water came into it. Next they said that Peter had no oars, and this caused the thrushes to look at each other in dismay; but Peter replied that he had no need of oars, for he had a sail, and with such a proud, happy face he produced a sail which he had fashioned out of his nightgown, and though it was still rather like a nightgown it made a lovely sail. And that night, the moon being full, and all the birds asleep, he did enter his coracle (as Master Francis Pretty would have said) and depart out of the island. And first, he knew not why, he looked upward, with his hands clasped, and from that moment his eyes were pinned to the west.

He had promised the thrushes to begin by making short voyages, with them to his guides, but far away he saw the Kensington Gardens beckoning to him beneath the bridge, and he could not wait. His face was flushed, but he never looked back; there was an exultation in his little breast that drove out fear. Was Peter the least gallant of the English mariners who have sailed westward to meet the Unknown?

At first, his boat turned round and round, and he was driven back to the place of his starting, whereupon he shortened sail, by removing one of the sleeves, and was forthwith carried backwards by a contrary breeze, to his no small peril. He now let go the sail, with the result that he was drifted towards the far shore, where are black shadows he knew not the dangers of, but suspected them, and so once more hoisted his nightgown and went roomer of the shadows until he caught a favouring wind, which bore him westward, but at so great a speed that he was like to be broke against the bridge. Which, having avoided, he passed under the bridge and came, to his great rejoicing, within full sight of the delectable Gardens. But having tried to cast anchor, which was a stone at the end of a piece of the kite-string, he found no bottom, and was fain to hold off, seeking for moorage; and, feeling his way, he buffeted against a sunken reef that cast him overboard by the great-ness of the shock, and he was near to being drowned, but clambered back into the vessel. There now arose a mighty storm, accompanied by roaring of waters, such as he had never heard the like, and he was tossed this way and that, and his hands so numbed with the cold that he could not close them. Having escaped the danger of which, he was mercifully carried into a small bay, where his boat rode at peace.

Nevertheless, he was not yet in safety; for, on pretending to disembark, he found a multitude of small people drawn up on the shore to contest his landing, and shouting shrilly to him to be off, for it was long past Lock-out Time. This, with much brandishing of their holly-leaves, and also a company of them carried an arrow which some boy had left in the Gardens, and this they were prepared to use as a battering-ram.

Then Peter, who knew them for the fairies, called out

that he was not an ordinary human and had no desire to do them displeasure, but to be their friend; nevertheless, having found a jolly harbour, he was in no temper to draw off therefrom, and he warned them if they sought to mischief him to stand to their arms.

So saying, he boldly leapt ashore, and they gathered around him with intent to slay him, but there then arose a great cry among the women, and it was because they had now observed that his sail was a baby's nightgown. Whereupon, they straightaway loved him, and grieved that their laps were too small, the which I cannot explain, except by saying that such is the way of women. The men-fairies now sheathed their weapons on observing the behaviour of their women, on whose intelligence they set great store, and they led him civilly to their queen, who conferred upon him the courtesy of the Gardens after Lock-out Time, and henceforth Peter could go whither he chose, and the fairies had orders to put him in comfort.

Such was his first voyage to the Gardens, and you may gather from the antiquity of the language that it took place a long time ago. But Peter never grows any older, and if we could be watching for him under the bridge tonight (but, of course, we can't), I dare say we should see him hoisting his nightgown and sailing or paddling towards us in the Thrush's Nest. When he sails, he sits down, but he stands up to paddle. I shall tell you presently how he got his paddle.

Long before the time for the opening of the gates comes he steals back to the island, for people must not see him (he is not so human as all that), but this gives him hours for play, and he plays exactly as real children play. At least he thinks so, and it is one of the pathetic things about him that he often plays quite wrongly.

You see, he had no one to tell him how children really play, for the fairies are all more or less in hiding until dusk, and so know nothing, and though the birds pretended that they could tell him a great deal, when the time for telling came, it was wonderful how little they really knew. They told him the truth about hide-and-seek, and he often plays it by himself, but even the ducks on the Round Pond could not explain to him what it is that makes the pond so fascinating to boys. Every night the ducks have forgotten all the events of the day, except the number of pieces of cake thrown to them. They are gloomy creatures, and say that cake is not what it was in their young days.

So Peter had to find out many things for himself. He often played ships at the Round Pond, but his ship was only a hoop which he had found on the grass. Of course, he had never seen a hoop, and he wondered what you play at with them, and decided that you play at pretending they are boats. This hoop always sank at once, but he waded in for it, and sometimes he dragged it gleefully round the rim of the pond, and he was quite proud to think that he had discovered what boys do with hoops.

Another time, when he found a child's pail, he thought it was for sitting in, and he sat so hard in it that he could scarcely get out of it. Also he found a balloon. It was bobbing about on the Hump, quite as if it was having a game by itself, and he caught it after an exciting chase. But he thought it was a ball, and Jenny Wren had told him that boys kick balls, so he kicked it; and after that he could not find it anywhere.

Perhaps the most surprising thing he found was a perambulator. It was under a lime-tree, near the entrance to the Fairy Queen's Winter Palace (which is within the circle of the seven Spanish chestnuts), and Peter approached it warily, for the birds had never mentioned such things to him. Lest it was alive, he addressed it politely, and then, as it gave no answer, he went nearer and felt it cautiously. He gave it a little push, and it ran from him, which made him think it must be alive after all; but, as it had run from him, he was not afraid. So he stretched out his hand to pull it to him, but this time it ran at him, and he was so alarmed that he leapt the railing and scudded away to his boat. You must not think, however, that he was a coward, for he came back next night with a crust in one hand and a stick in the other, but the perambulator had gone, and he never saw another one. I have promised to tell you also about his paddle. It was a child's spade which he had found near St Govor's Well, and he thought it was a paddle.

Do you pity Peter Pan for making these mistakes? If so, I think it rather silly of you. What I mean is that, of course, one must pity him now and then, but to pity him all the time would be impertinence. He thought he had the most splendid time in the Gardens, and to think you have it is almost quite as good as really to have it. He played without ceasing, while you often waste time by being mad-dog or Mary-Annish. He could be neither of these things, for he had never heard of them, but do you think he is to be pitied for that?

Oh, he was merry! He was as much merrier than you, for instance, as you are merrier than your father. Sometimes he fell, like a spinning-top, from sheer merriment. Have you seen a greyhound leaping the fences of the Gardens? That is how Peter leaps them.

And think of the music of his pipe. Gentlemen who walk home at night write to the papers to say they heard a nightingale in the Gardens, but it is really Peter's pipe they hear. Of course, he had no mother – at least, what use was she to him? You can be sorry for him for that, but don't be too sorry, for the next thing I mean to tell you is how he revisited her. It was the fairies who gave him the chance.

SIXTEEN

Lock-out Time

IT IS FRIGHTFULLY difficult to know much about the fairies, and almost the only thing known for certain is that there are fairies wherever there are children. Long ago children were forbidden the Gardens, and at that time there was not a fairy in the place; then the children were admitted, and the fairies came trooping in that very evening. They can't resist following the children, but you seldom see them, partly because they live in the daytime behind the railings, where you are not allowed to go, and also partly because they are so cunning. They are not a bit cunning after Lock-out, but until Lock-out, my word!

When you were a bird you knew the fairies pretty well, and you remember a good deal about them in your babyhood, which it is a great pity you can't write down, for gradually you forget, and I have heard of children who declared that they had never once seen a fairy. Very likely if they said this in the Kensington Gardens, they were standing looking at a fairy all the time. The reason they were cheated was that she pretended to be something else. This is one of their best tricks. They usually pretend to be flowers, because the court sits in the Fairies' Basin, and there are so many flowers there, and all along the Baby Walk, that a flower is the thing least likely to attract attention. They dress exactly like flowers, and change with the seasons, putting on white when lilies are in and blue for bluebells, and so on. They like crocus and hyacinth time best of all, as they are partial to a bit of colour, but tulips (except white ones, which are the fairy cradles) they consider garish, and they sometimes put off dressing like tulips for days, so that the beginning of the tulip weeks is almost the best time to catch them.

When they think you are not looking they skip along pretty lively, but if you look, and they fear there is no time to hide, they stand quite still, pretending to be flowers. Then, after you have passed without knowing that they were fairies, they rush home and tell their mothers they have had such an adventure. The Fairy Basin, you re-member, is all covered with ground-ivy (from which they make their castor-oil), with flowers growing in it here and there. Most of them really are flowers, but some of them are fairies. You never can be sure of them, but a good plan is to walk by looking the other way, and then turn round sharply. Another good plan, which David and I sometimes follow, is to stare them down. After a long time they can't help winking, and then you know for certain that they are fairies.

There are also numbers of them along the Baby Walk, which is a famous gentle place, as spots frequented by fairies are called. Once twenty-four of them had an extra-ordinary adventure. They were a girls' school out for a walk with the governess, and all wearing hyacinth gowns, when she suddenly put her finger to her mouth, and then they all stood still on an empty bed and pretended to be hyacinths. Unfortunately what the governess had heard was two gardeners coming to plant new flowers in that very bed. They were wheeling a handcart with the flowers in it, and were quite surprised to find the bed occupied. 'Pity to lift them hyacinths,' said the one man. 'Duke's orders,' replied the other, and, having emptied the cart, they dug up the boarding-school and put the poor, terrified things in it in five rows. Of course, neither the governess nor the girls dare let on that they were fairies, so they were carted far away to a potting-shed, out of which they escaped in the night without their shoes, but there was a great row about it among the parents, and the school was ruined.

As for their houses, it is no use looking for them, because they are the exact opposite of our houses. You can see our houses by day but you can't see them by dark. Well, you can see their houses by dark, but you can't see them by day, for they are the colour of night, and I never heard of any one yet who could see night in the daytime. This does not mean that they are black, for night has its colours just as day has, but ever so much brighter. Their blues and reds and greens are like ours with a light behind them. The palace is entirely built of many-coloured glasses, and it is quite the loveliest of all royal residences, but the queen sometimes complains because the common people will peep in to see what she is doing. They are very inquisitive folk, and press quite hard against the glass, and that is why their noses are mostly snubby. The streets are miles long and very twisty, and have paths on each side made of bright worsted. The birds used to steal the worsted for their nests, but a policeman has been appointed to hold on at the other end.

One of the great differences between the fairies and us is that they never do anything useful. When the first baby laughed for the first time, his laugh broke into a million pieces, and they all went skipping about. That was the beginning of fairies. They look tremendously busy, you know, as if they had not a moment to spare, but if you were to ask them what they are doing, they could not tell you in the least. They are frightfully ignorant, and everything they do is make-believe. They have a postman, but he never calls except at Christmas with his little box, and though they have beautiful schools, nothing is taught in them; the youngest child being chief person is always elected mistress, and when she has called the roll, they all go out for a walk and never come back. It is a very noticeable thing that, in fairy families, the youngest is always chief person, and usually becomes a prince or princess; and children remember this, and think it must be so among humans also, and that is why they are often made uneasy when they come

upon their mother furtively putting new frills on the basin-
ette.

You have probably observed that your baby-sister wants
to do all sorts of things that your mother and her nurse want
her not to do – to stand up at sitting-down time, and to sit
down at stand-up time, for instance, or to wake up when
she should fall asleep, or to crawl on the floor when she is
wearing her best frock, and so on, and perhaps you put this
down to naughtiness. But it is not; it simply means that she
is doing as she has seen the fairies do; she begins by
following their ways, and it takes about two years to get
her into the human ways. Her fits of passion, which are
awful to behold, and are usually called teething, are no such
thing; they are her natural exasperation, because we don't
understand her, though she is talking an intelligible language. She is talking fairy. The reason mothers and nurses
know what her remarks mean, before other people know, as
that 'Guch' means 'Give it to me at once,' while 'Wa' is
'Why do you wear such a funny hat?' is because, mixing so
much with babies, they have picked up a little of the fairy
language.

Of late David has been thinking back hard about the fairy
tongue, with his hands clutching his temples, and he has
remembered a number of their phrases which I shall tell
you some day if I don't forget. He had heard them in the
days when he was a thrush, and though I suggested to him
that perhaps it is really bird language he is remembering, he
says not, for these phrases are about fun and adventures,
and the birds talked of nothing but nest-building. He
distinctly remembers that the birds used to go from spot
to spot like ladies at shop windows, looking at the different
nests and saying, 'Not my colour, my dear,' and 'How
would that do with a soft lining?' and 'But will it wear?' and
'What hideous trimming!' and so on.

The fairies are exquisite dancers, and that is why one of
the first things the baby does is to sign to you to dance to

him and then to cry when you do it. They hold their great balls in the open air, in what is called a fairy ring. For weeks afterwards you can see the ring on the grass. It is not there when they begin, but they make it by waltzing round and round. Sometimes you will find mushrooms inside the ring, and these are fairy chairs that the servants have forgotten to clear away. The chairs and the rings are the only tell-tale marks these little people leave behind them, and they would remove even these were they not so fond of dancing that they toe it till the very moment of the opening of the gates. David and I once found a fairy ring quite warm.

But there is also a way of finding out about the ball before it takes place. You know the boards which tell at what time the Gardens are to close today. Well, these tricky fairies sometimes slyly change the board on a ball night, so that it says the Gardens are to close at six-thirty, for instance, instead of at seven. This enables them to get begun half an hour earlier.

If on such a night we could remain behind in the Gardens, as the famous Maimie Mannering did, we might see delicious sights, hundreds of lovely fairies hastening to the ball, the married ones wearing their wedding rings round their waists, the gentlemen, all in uniform, holding up the ladies' trains, and linkmen running in front carrying winter cherries, which are the fairy-lanterns, the cloakroom where they put on their silver slippers and get a ticket for their wraps, the flowers streaming up from the Baby Walk to look on, and always welcome because they can lend a pin, the supper-table, with Queen Mab at the head of it, and behind her chair the Lord Chamberlain, who carries a dandelion on which he blows when her Majesty wants to know the time.

The tablecloth varies according to the seasons, and in May it is made of chestnut blossom. The way the fairy servants do this is: The men, scores of them, climb up the trees and shake the branches, and the blossom falls like snow. Then the lady servants sweep it together by whisking their skirts until it is exactly like a tablecloth, and that is how they get their tablecloth.

They have real glasses and real wine of three kinds, namely, blackthorn wine, berberris wine, and cowslip wine, and the Queen pours out, but the bottles are so heavy that she just pretends to pour out. There is bread-and-butter to begin with, of the size of a threepenny bit; and cakes to end with, and they are so small that they have no crumbs. The fairies sit round on mushrooms, and at first they are well-behaved and always cough off the table, and so on, but after a bit they are not so well-behaved and stick their fingers into the butter, which is got from the roots of old trees, and the really horrid ones crawl over the tablecloth chasing sugar or other delicacies with their tongues. When the Queen sees them doing this she signs to the servants to wash up and put away, and then every-body adjourns to the dance, the Queen walking in front while the Lord Chamberlain walks behind her, carrying two little pots, one of which contains the juice of wallflower and the other the juice of Solomon's seals. Wallflower juice is good for reviving dancers who fall to the ground in a fit, and Solomon's seals juice is for bruises. They bruise very easily, and when Peter plays faster and faster they foot it till they fall down in fits. For, as you know without my telling you, Peter Pan is the fairies' orchestra. He sits in the middle of the ring, and they would never dream of having a smart dance nowadays without him. 'P. P.' is written on the corner of the invitation-cards sent out by all really good families. They are grateful little people, too, and at the princess's coming-of-age ball (they come of age on their second birthday and have a birthday every month) they gave him the wish of his heart.

The way it was done was this. The Queen ordered him to kneel, and then said that for playing so beautifully she would give him the wish of his heart. Then they all gathered round Peter to hear what was the wish of his heart, but for a long time he hesitated, not being certain what it was himself.

'If I chose to go back to mother,' he asked at last, 'could you give me that wish?'

Now this question vexed them, for were he to return to his mother they should lose his music, so the Queen tilted her nose contemptuously and said, 'Pooh! ask for a much bigger wish than that.'

'Is that quite a little wish?' he inquired.

'As little as this,' the Queen answered, putting her hands near each other.

'What size is a big wish?' he asked.

She measured it off on her skirt and it was a very handsome length.

Then Peter reflected and said, 'Well, then, I think I shall have two little wishes instead of one big one.'

Of course, the fairies had to agree, though his cleverness rather shocked them, and he said that his first wish was to go to his mother, but with the right to return to the Gardens if he found her disappointing. His second wish he would hold in reserve.

They tried to dissuade him, and even put obstacles in the way.

'I can give you the power to fly to her house,' the Queen said, 'but I can't open the door for you.'

'The window I flew out at will be open,' Peter said confidently. 'Mother always keeps it open in the hope that I may fly back.'

'How do you know?' they asked, quite surprised, and, really, Peter could not explain how he knew.

'I just do know,' he said.

So as he persisted in his wish, they had to grant it. The way they gave him power to fly was this: They all tickled him on the shoulder, and soon he felt a funny itching in that part, and then up he rose higher and higher, and flew away out of the Gardens and over the housetops.

It was so delicious that instead of flying straight to his old home he skimmed away over St Paul's to the Crystal Palace and back by the river and Regent's Park, and by the time he reached his mother's window he had quite made up his mind that his second wish should be to become a bird.

The window was wide open, just as he knew it would be, and in he fluttered, and there was his mother lying asleep. Peter alighted softly on the wooden rail at the foot of the bed and had a good look at her. She lay with her head on her hand, and the hollow in the pillow was like a nest lined with her brown wavy hair. He remembered, though he had long forgotten it, that she always gave her hair a holiday at night. How sweet the frills of her nightgown were! He was very glad she was such a pretty mother.

But she looked sad, and he knew why she looked sad. One of her arms moved as if it wanted to go round something, and he knew what it wanted to go round.

'O mother!' said Peter to himself, 'if you just knew who is sitting on the rail at the foot of the bed.'

Very gently he patted the little mound that her feet made, and he could see by her face that she liked it. He knew he had but to say 'Mother' ever so softly, and she would wake up. They always wake up at once if it is you that says their name. Then she would give such a joyous cry and squeeze him tight. How nice that would be to him, but oh! how exquisitely delicious it would be to her. That, I am afraid, is how Peter regarded it. In returning to his mother he never doubted that he was giving her the greatest treat a woman can have. Nothing can be more splendid, he thought, than to have a little boy of your own. How proud of him they are! and very right and proper, too.

But why does Peter sit so long on the rail; why does he not tell his mother that he has come back?

I quite shrink from the truth, which is that he sat there in two minds. Sometimes he looked longingly at his mother, and sometimes he looked longingly at the window. Certainly it would be pleasant to be her boy again, but on the other hand, what times those had been in the Gardens! Was he so sure that he should enjoy wearing clothes again? He popped off the bed and opened some drawers to have a look at his old garments. They were still there, but he could not remember how you put them on. The socks, for instance, were they worn on the hands or on the feet? He was about to try one of them on his hand, when he had a great adventure. Perhaps the drawer had creaked; at any rate, his mother woke up, for he heard her say 'Peter,' as if it was the most lovely word in the language. He remained sitting on the floor and held his breath, wondering how she knew that he had come back. If she said 'Peter' again, he meant to cry 'Mother' and run to her. But she spoke no more, she made little moans only, and when he next peeped at her she was once more asleep, with tears on her face.

It made Peter very miserable, and what do you think was the first thing he did? Sitting on the rail at the foot of the bed, he played a beautiful lullaby to his mother on his pipe. He had made it up himself out of the way she said 'Peter,' and he never stopped playing until she looked happy.

He thought this so clever of him that he could scarcely resist wakening her to hear her say, 'O Peter, how exquisitely you play!' However, as she now seemed comfortable, he again cast looks at the window. You must not think that he meditated flying away and never coming back. He had quite decided to be his mother's boy, but hesitated about beginning tonight. It was the second wish which troubled him. He no longer meant to make it a wish to be a bird, but not to ask for a second wish seemed wasteful, and, of course, he could not ask for it without returning to the fairies. Also, if he put off asking for his wish too long it might go bad. He asked himself if he had not been hard-hearted to fly away without saying good-bye to Solomon. 'I should like awfully to sail in my boat just once more,' he said wistfully to his sleeping mother. He quite argued with her as if she could hear him. 'It would be so splendid to tell the birds of this adventure,' he said coaxingly. 'I promise to come back,' he said solemnly, and meant it, too.

And in the end, you know, he flew away. Twice he came back from the window, wanting to kiss his mother, but he feared the delight of it might waken her, so at last he played her a lovely kiss on his pipe, and then he flew back to the Gardens.

Many nights, and even months, passed before he asked the fairies for his second wish; and I am not sure that I quite know why he delayed so long. One reason was that he had so many good-byes to say, not only to his particular friends, but to a hundred favourite spots. Then he had his last sail, and his very last sail, and his last sail of all, and so on. Again, a number of farewell feasts were given in his honour; and another comfortable reason was that, after all, there was no hurry, for his mother would never weary of waiting for him. This last reason displeased old Solomon, for it was an encouragement to the birds to procrastinate. Solomon had several excellent mottoes for keeping them at their work, such as 'Never put off laying today, because you can lay tomorrow,' and 'In this world there are no second chances,' and yet here was Peter gaily putting off and none the worse for it. The birds pointed this out to each other, and fell into lazy habits.

But, mind you, though Peter was so slow in going back to his mother, he was quite decided to go back. The best proof of this was his caution with the fairies. They were most anxious that he should remain in the Gardens to play to them, and to bring this to pass they tried to trick him into making such a remark as 'I wish the grass was not so wet,' and some of them danced out of time in the hope that he might cry, 'I do wish you would keep time!' Then they

would have said that this was his second wish. But he
smoked their design, and though on occasions he began, 'I
wish—' he always stopped in time. So when at last he said
to them bravely, 'I wish now to go back to mother for ever
and always,' they had to tickle his shoulders and let him go.

He went in a hurry in the end, because he had dreamt
that his mother was crying, and he knew what was the great
thing she cried for, and that a hug from her splendid Peter
would quickly make her to smile. Oh! he felt sure of it, and
so eager was he to be nestling in her arms that this time he
flew straight to the window, which was always to be open
for him.

But the window was closed, and there were iron bars on
it, and peering inside he saw his mother sleeping peacefully
with her arm round another little boy.

Peter called, 'Mother! mother!' but she heard him not; in
vain he beat his little limbs against the iron bars. He had to
fly back, sobbing, to the Gardens, and he never saw his dear
again. What a glorious boy he had meant to be to her! Ah,
Peter! we who have made the great mistake, how differently
we should all act at the second chance. But Solomon was
right – there is no second chance, not for most of us. When
we reach the window it is Lock-out Time. The iron bars are
up for life.

SEVENTEEN

The Little House

EVERYBODY HAS HEARD of the Little House in the Kensington Gardens, which is the only house in the whole world that the fairies have built for humans. But no one has really seen it, except just three or four, and they have not only seen it but slept in it, and unless you sleep in it you never see it. This is because it is not there when you lie down, but it is there when you wake up and step outside.

In a kind of way every one may see it, but what you see is not really it, but only the light in the windows. You see the light after Lock-out Time. David, for instance, saw it quite distinctly far away among the trees as we were going home from the pantomime, and Oliver Bailey saw it the night he stayed so late at the Temple, which is the name of his father's office. Angela Clare, who loves to have a tooth extracted because then she is treated to tea in a shop, saw more than one light, she saw hundreds of them all together; and this must have been the fairies building the house, for they build it every night, and always in a different part of the Gardens. She thought one of the lights was bigger than the others, though she was not quite sure, for they jumped about so, and it might have been another one that was bigger. But if it was the same one, it was Peter Pan's light. Heaps of children have seen the light, so that is nothing. But Maimie Mannering was the famous one for whom the house was first built.

Maimie was always rather a strange girl, and it was at night that she was strange. She was four years of age, and in the daytime she was the ordinary kind. She was pleased when her brother Tony, who was a magnificent fellow of

six, took notice of her, and she looked up to him in the right
way, and tried in vain to imitate him, and was flattered
rather than annoyed when he shoved her about. Also, when
she was batting, she would pause though the ball was in the
air to point out to you that she was wearing new shoes. She
was quite the ordinary kind in the daytime.

But as the shades of night fell, Tony, the swaggerer, lost
his contempt for Maimie and eyed her fearfully; and no
wonder, for with dark there came into her face a look that I
can describe only as a leary look. It was also a serene look
that contrasted grandly with Tony's uneasy glances. Then
he would make her presents of his favourite toys (which he
always took away from her next morning), and she accepted
them with a disturbing smile. The reason he was now
become so wheedling and she so mysterious was (in brief)
that they knew they were about to be sent to bed. It was
then that Maimie was terrible. Tony entreated her not to do
it tonight, and the mother and their coloured nurse threatened her, but Maimie merely smiled her agitating smile.
And by and by when they were alone with their night-light
she would start up in bed crying 'Hsh! what was that?' Tony
beseeches her, 'It was nothing – don't, Maimie, don't!' and
pulls the sheet over his head. 'It is coming nearer!' she cries.
'Oh, look at it, Tony! It is feeling your bed with its horns – it
is boring for you, O Tony, oh!' and she desists not until he
rushes downstairs in his combinations, screeching. When
they came up to whip Maimie they usually found her
sleeping tranquilly – not shamming, you know, but really
sleeping, and looking like the sweetest little angel, which
seems to me to make it almost worse.

But of course it was daytime when they were in the
Gardens, and then Tony did most of the talking. You could
gather from his talk that he was a very brave boy, and no
one was so proud of it as Maimie. She would have loved to
have a ticket on her saying that she was his sister. And at no
time did she admire him more than when he told her, as he

often did with splendid firmness, that one day he meant to remain behind in the Gardens after the gates were closed.

'O Tony,' she would say with awful respect, 'but the fairies will be so angry!'

'I dare say,' replied Tony carelessly.

'Perhaps,' she said, thrilling, 'Peter Pan will give you a sail in his boat!'

'I shall make him,' replied Tony; no wonder she was proud of him.

But they should not have talked so loudly, for one day they were overheard by a fairy who had been gathering skeleton leaves, from which the little people weave their summer curtains, and after that Tony was a marked boy. They loosened the rails before he sat on them, so that down he came on the back of his head; they tripped him up by catching his bootlace and bribed the ducks to sink his boat. Nearly all the nasty accidents you meet with in the Gardens occur because the fairies have taken an ill-will to you, and so it behoves you to be careful what you say about them.

Maimie was one of the kind who like to fix a day for doing things, but Tony was not that kind, and when she asked him which day he was to remain behind in the Gardens after Lock-out he merely replied, 'Just some day'; he was quite vague about which day except when she asked, 'Will it be today?' and then he could always say for certain that it would not be today. So she saw that he was waiting for a real good chance.

This brings us to an afternoon when the Gardens were white with snow, and there was ice on the Round Pond; not thick enough to skate on, but at least you could spoil it for tomorrow by flinging stones, and many bright little boys and girls were doing that.

When Tony and his sister arrived they wanted to go straight to the pond, but their ayah said they must take a sharp walk first, and as she said this she glanced at the time-board to see when the Gardens closed that night. It read

half-past five. Poor ayah! she is the one who laughs con-
tinuously because there are so many white children in the
world, but she was not to laugh much more that day.

Well, they went up the Baby Walk and back, and when
they returned to the time-board she was surprised to see
that it now read five o'clock for closing-time. But she was
unacquainted with the tricky ways of the fairies, and so did
not see (as Maimie and Tony saw at once) that they had
changed the hour because there was to be a ball tonight.
She said there was only time now to walk to the top of the
Hump and back, and as they trotted along with her she little
guessed what was thrilling their little breasts. You see the
chance had come of seeing a fairy ball. Never, Tony felt,
could he hope for a better chance.

He had to feel this for Maimie so plainly felt it for him.
Her eager eyes asked the question, 'Is it today?' and he
gasped and then nodded. Maimie slipped her hand into
Tony's, and hers was hot, but his was cold. She did a very
kind thing; she took off her scarf and gave it to him. 'In case
you should feel cold,' she whispered. Her face was aglow,
but Tony's was very gloomy.

As they turned on the top of the Hump he whispered to
her, 'I'm afraid Nurse would see me, so I shan't be able to
do it.'

Maimie admired him more than ever for being afraid of
nothing but their ayah, when there were so many unknown
terrors to fear, and she said aloud, 'Tony, I shall race you to
the gate,' and in a whisper, 'Then you can hide,' and off
they ran.

Tony could always outdistance her easily, but never had
she known him speed away so quickly as now, and she was
sure he hurried that he might have more time to hide.
'Brave, brave!' her doting eyes were crying when she got a
dreadful shock; instead of hiding, her hero had run out at
the gate! At this bitter sight Maimie stopped blankly, as if all
her lapful of darling treasures were suddenly spilled, and

then for very disdain she could not sob; in a swell of protest against all puling cowards she ran to St Govor's Well and hid in Tony's stead.

When the ayah reached the gate and saw Tony far in front she thought her other charge was with him and passed out. Twilight crept over the Gardens, and hundreds of people passed out, including the last one, who always has to run for it, but Maimie saw them not. She had shut her eyes tight and glued them with passionate tears. When she opened them something very cold ran up her legs and up her arms and dropped into her heart. It was the stillness of the Gardens. Then she heard *clang*, then from another part *clang*, then *clang*, *clang* far away. It was the Closing of the Gates.

Immediately the last clang had died away Maimie distinctly heard a voice say, 'So that's all right.' It had a wooden sound and seemed to come from above, and she looked up in time to see an elm-tree stretching out its arms and yawning.

She was about to say, 'I never knew you could speak!' when a metallic voice that seemed to come from the ladle at the well remarked to the elm, 'I suppose it is a bit coldish up there?' and the elm replied, 'Not particularly, but you do get numb standing so long on one leg,' and he flapped his arms vigorously just as the cabmen do before they drive off. Maimie was quite surprised to see that a number of other tall trees were doing the same sort of thing, and she stole away to the Baby Walk and crouched observantly under a Minorca holly which shrugged its shoulders but did not seem to mind her.

She was not in the least cold. She was wearing a russet-coloured pelisse and had the hood over her head, so that nothing of her showed except her dear little face and her curls. The rest of her real self was hidden far away inside so many warm garments that in shape she seemed rather like a ball. She was about forty round the waist.

There was a good deal going on in the Baby Walk, where Maimie arrived in time to see a magnolia and a Persian lilac step over the railing and set off for a smart walk. They moved in a jerky sort of way certainly, but that was because they used crutches. An elderberry hobbled across the walk, and stood chatting with some young quinces, and they all had crutches. The crutches were the sticks that are tied to young trees and shrubs. They were quite familiar objects to Maimie, but she had never known what they were for until tonight.

She peeped up the walk and saw her first fairy. He was a street boy fairy who was running up the walk closing the weeping trees. The way he did it was this: he pressed a spring in the trunks and they shut like umbrellas, deluging the little plants beneath with snow. 'O you naughty, naughty child!' Maimie cried indignantly, for she knew what it was to have a dripping umbrella about your ears.

Fortunately the mischievous fellow was out of earshot, but a chrysanthemum heard her, and said so pointedly, 'Hoity-toity, what is this?' that she had to come out and show herself. Then the whole vegetable kingdom was rather puzzled what to do.

'Of course it is no affair of ours,' a spindle-tree said after they had whispered together, 'but you know quite well you ought not to be here, and perhaps our duty is to report you to the fairies; what do you think yourself?'

'I think you should not,' Maimie replied, which so perplexed them that they said petulantly there was no arguing with her. 'I wouldn't ask it of you,' she assured them, 'if I thought it was wrong,' and of course after this they could not well carry tales. They then said, 'Well-a-day,' and 'Such is life,' for they can be frightfully sarcastic; but she felt sorry for those of them who had no crutches, and she said good-naturedly, 'Before I go to the fairies' ball, I should like to take you for a walk one at a time; you can lean on me, you know.'

At this they clapped their hands, and she escorted them up the Baby Walk and back again, one at a time, putting an arm or a finger round the very frail, setting their leg right when it got too ridiculous, and treating the foreign ones quite as courteously as the English, though she could not understand a word they said.

They behaved well on the whole, though some whimpered that she had not taken them as far as she took Nancy or Grace or Dorothy, and others jagged her, but it was quite unintentional, and she was too much of a lady to cry out. So much walking tired her, and she was anxious to be off to the ball, but she no longer felt afraid. The reason she felt no more fear was that it was now night-time, and in the dark, you remember, Maimie was always rather strange.

They were now loth to let her go, for, 'If the fairies see you,' they warned her, 'they will mischief you – stab you to death, or compel you to nurse their children, or turn you into something tedious, like an evergreen oak.' As they said this they looked with affected pity at an evergreen oak, for in winter they are very envious of the evergreens.

'Oh, la!' replied the oak bitingly, 'how deliciously cosy it is to stand here buttoned to the neck and watch you poor naked creatures shivering.'

This made them sulky, though they had really brought it on themselves, and they drew for Maimie a very gloomy picture of the perils that would face her if she insisted on going to the ball.

She learned from a purple filbert that the court was not in its usual good temper at present, the cause being the tantalising heart of the Duke of Christmas Daisies. He was an Oriental fairy, very poorly of a dreadful complaint, namely, inability to love, and though he had tried many ladies in many lands he could not fall in love with one of them. Queen Mab, who rules in the Gardens, had been confident that her girls would bewitch him, but alas! his heart, the doctor said, remained cold. This rather irritating doctor, who was his private physician, felt the Duke's heart immediately after any lady was presented, and then always shook his bald head and murmured, 'Cold, quite cold.' Naturally Queen Mab felt disgraced, and first she tried the effect of ordering the court into tears for nine minutes, and then she blamed the Cupids and decreed that they should wear fools' caps until they thawed the Duke's frozen heart.

'How I should love to see the Cupids in their dear little fools' caps!' Maimie cried, and away she ran to look for them very recklessly, for the Cupids hate to be laughed at.

It is always easy to discover where a fairies' ball is being held, as ribbons are stretched between it and all the populous parts of the Gardens, on which those invited may walk to the dance without wetting their pumps. This night the ribbons were red, and looked very pretty on the snow.

Maimie walked alongside one of them for some distance without meeting anybody, but at last she saw a fairy cavalcade approaching. To her surprise they seemed to be returning from the ball, and she had just time to hide from them by bending her knees and holding out her arms and pretending to be a garden chair. There were six horsemen in front and six behind; in the middle walked a prim lady wearing a long train held up by two pages, and on the train, as if it were a couch, reclined a lovely girl, for in this way do aristocratic fairies travel about. She was dressed in golden rain, but the most enviable part of her was her neck, which was blue in colour and of a velvet texture, and of course showed off her diamond necklace as no white throat could have glorified it. The high-born fairies obtain this admired effect by pricking their skin, which lets the blue blood come through and dye them, and you cannot imagine anything so dazzling unless you have seen the ladies' busts in the jewellers' windows.

Maimie also noticed that the whole cavalcade seemed to be in a passion, tilting their noses higher than it can be safe for even fairies to tilt them, and she concluded that this must be another case in which the doctor had said, 'Cold, quite cold.'

Well, she followed the ribbon to a place where it became a bridge over a dry puddle into which another fairy had fallen and been unable to climb out. At first this little damsel was afraid of Maimie, who most kindly went to her aid, but soon she sat in her hand chatting gaily and explaining that her name was Brownie, and that though only a poor street singer she was on her way to the ball to see if the Duke would have her.

'Of course,' she said, 'I am rather plain,' and this made Maimie uncomfortable, for indeed the simple little creature was almost quite plain for a fairy.

It was difficult to know what to reply.

'I see you think I have no chance,' Brownie said falteringly.

'I don't say that,' Maimie answered politely; 'of course your face is just a tiny bit homely, but—' Really it was quite awkward for her.

Fortunately she remembered about her father and the bazaar. He had gone to a fashionable bazaar where all the most beautiful ladies in London were on view for half a crown the second day, but on his return home, instead of being dissatisfied with Maimie's mother, he had said, 'You can't think, my dear, what a relief it is to see a homely face again.'

Maimie repeated this story, and it fortified Brownie tremendously, indeed she had no longer the slightest doubt that the Duke would choose her. So she scudded away up the ribbon, calling out to Maimie not to follow lest the Queen should mischief her.

But Maimie's curiosity tugged her forward, and presently at the seven Spanish chestnuts she saw a wonderful light. She crept forward until she was quite near it, and then she peeped from behind a tree.

The light, which was as high as your head above the ground, was composed of myriads of glow-worms all holding on to each other, and so forming a dazzling canopy over the fairy ring. There were thousands of little people looking on, but they were in shadow and drab in colour compared to the glorious creatures within that luminous circle, who were so bewilderingly bright that Maimie had to wink hard all the time she looked at them.

It was amazing and even irritating to her that the Duke of Christmas Daisies should be able to keep out of love for a moment: yet out of love his dusky grace still was: you could see it by the shamed looks of the Queen and court (though they pretended not to care), by the way darling ladies brought forward for his approval burst into tears as they were told to pass on, and by his own most dreary face.

Maimie could also see the pompous doctor feeling the Duke's heart and hear him give utterance to his parrot cry, and she was particularly sorry for the Cupids, who stood in their fools' caps in obscure places and, every time they heard that 'Cold, quite cold,' bowed their disgraced little heads.

She was disappointed not to see Peter Pan, and I may as well tell you now why he was so late that night. It was because his boat had got wedged on the Serpentine between fields of floating ice, through which he had to break a perilous passage with his trusty paddle.

The fairies had as yet scarcely missed him, for they could not dance, so heavy were their hearts. They forget all the steps when they are sad, and remember them again when they are merry. David tells me that fairies never say, 'We feel happy': what they say is, 'We feel *dancey*.'

Well, they were looking very undancey indeed, when sudden laughter broke out among the onlookers, caused by Brownie, who had just arrived and was insisting on her right to be presented to the Duke.

Maimie craned forward eagerly to see how her friend

fared, though she had really no hope; no one seemed to have the least hope except Brownie herself, who, however, was absolutely confident. She was led before his grace, and the doctor putting a finger carelessly on the ducal heart, which for convenience' sake was reached by a little trap-door in his diamond shirt, had begun to say mechanically, 'Cold, qui—,' when he stopped abruptly.

'What's this?' he cried, and first he shook the heart like a watch, and then he put his ear to it.

'Bless my soul!' cried the doctor, and by this time of course the excitement among the spectators was tremen-dous, fairies fainting right and left.

Everybody stared breathlessly at the Duke, who was very much startled, and looked as if he would like to run away. 'Good gracious me!' the doctor was heard muttering, and now the heart was evidently on fire, for he had to jerk his fingers away from it and put them in his mouth.

The suspense was awful.

Then in a loud voice, and bowing low, 'My Lord Duke,' said the physician elatedly, 'I have the honour to inform your excellency that your grace is in love.'

You can't conceive the effect of it. Brownie held out her arms to the Duke and he flung himself into them, the Queen leapt into the arms of the Lord Chamberlain, and the ladies of the court leapt into the arms of her gentlemen, for it is etiquette to follow her example in everything. Thus in a single moment about fifty marriages took place, for if you leap into each other's arms it is a fairy wedding. Of course a clergyman has to be present.

How the crowd cheered and leapt! Trumpets brayed, the moon came out, and immediately a thousand couples seized hold of its rays as if they were ribbons in a May dance and waltzed in wild abandon round the fairy ring. Most gladsome sight of all, the Cupids plucked the hated fools' caps from their heads and cast them high in the air. And then Maimie went and spoiled everything.

She couldn't help it. She was crazy with delight over her little friend's good fortune, so she took several steps forward and cried in an ecstasy, 'O Brownie, how splendid!'

Everybody stood still, the music ceased, the lights went out, and all in the time you may take to say, 'Oh dear!' An awful sense of her peril came upon Maimie; too late she remembered that she was a lost child in a place where no human must be between the locking and the opening of the gates; she heard the murmur of an angry multitude; she saw a thousand swords flashing for her blood, and she uttered a cry of terror and fled.

How she ran! and all the time her eyes were starting out of her head. Many times she lay down, and then quickly jumped up and ran on again. Her little mind was so entangled in terrors that she no longer knew she was in the Gardens. The one thing she was sure of was that she must never cease to run, and she thought she was still running long after she had dropped in the Figs and gone to sleep. She thought the snowflakes falling on her face were her mother kissing her good-night. She thought her coverlet of snow was a warm blanket, and tried to pull it over her head. And when she heard talking through her dreams she thought it was mother bringing father to the nursery door to look at her as she slept. But it was the fairies.

I am very glad to be able to say that they no longer desired to mischief her. When she rushed away they had rent the air with such cries as 'Slay her!' 'Turn her into something extremely unpleasant!' and so on, but the pursuit was delayed while they discussed who should march in front, and this gave Duchess Brownie time to cast herself before the Queen and demand a boon.

Every bride has a right to a boon, and what she asked for was Maimie's life. 'Anything except that,' replied Queen Mab sternly, and all the fairies echoed, 'Anything except that.' But when they learned how Maimie had befriended Brownie and so enabled her to attend the ball to their great glory and renown, they gave three huzzas for the little human, and set off, like an army, to thank her, the court advancing in front and the canopy keeping step with it. They traced Maimie easily by her footprints in the snow.

But though they found her deep in snow in the Figs, it seemed impossible to thank Maimie, for they could not waken her. They went through the form of thanking her – that is to say, the new King stood on her body and read her a long address of welcome, but she heard not a word of it. They also cleared the snow off her, but soon she was covered again, and they saw she was in danger of perishing of cold.

'Turn her into something that does not mind the cold,' seemed a good suggestion of the doctor's, but the only thing they could think of that does not mind cold was a snowflake. 'And it might melt,' the Queen pointed out, so that idea had to be given up.

A magnificent attempt was made to carry her to a sheltered spot, but though there were so many of them she was too heavy. By this time all the ladies were crying in their handkerchiefs, but presently the Cupids had a lovely idea. 'Build a house round her,' they cried, and at once everybody perceived that this was the thing to do; in a moment a hundred fairy sawyers were among the branches, architects were running round Maimie, measuring her; a bricklayer's yard sprang up at her feet, seventy-five masons rushed up with the foundation-stone, and the Queen laid it, overseers were appointed to keep the boys off, scaffoldings were run up, the whole place rang with hammers and chisels and turning-lathes, and by this time the roof was on and the glaziers were putting in the windows.

The house was exactly the size of Maimie, and perfectly lovely. One of her arms was extended, and this had bothered them for a second, but they built a verandah round it, leading to the front door. The windows were the size of a coloured picture-book and the door rather smaller, but it would be easy for her to get out by taking off the roof. The fairies, as is their custom, clapped their hands with delight over their cleverness, and they were so madly in love with the little house that they could not bear to think they had finished it. So they gave it ever so many little extra touches, and even then they added more extra touches.

For instance, two of them ran up a ladder and put on a chimney.

'Now we fear it is quite finished,' they sighed.

But no, for another two ran up the ladder, and tied some smoke to the chimney.

'That certainly finishes it,' they said reluctantly.

'Not at all,' cried a glow-worm; 'if she were to wake without seeing a night-light she might be frightened, so I shall be her night-light.'

'Wait one moment,' said a china merchant, 'and I shall make you a saucer.'

Now, alas! it was absolutely finished.

Oh, dear no!

'Gracious me!' cried a brass manufacturer, 'there's no handle on the door,' and he put one on.

An ironmonger added a scraper, and an old lady ran up with a door-mat. Carpenters arrived with a water-butt, and the painters insisted on painting it.

Finished at last!

'Finished! how can it be finished,' the plumber demanded scornfully, 'before hot and cold are put in?' and he put in hot and cold. Then an army of gardeners arrived with fairy carts and spades and seeds and bulbs and forcing-houses, and soon they had a flower-garden to the right of the verandah, and a vegetable garden to the left, and roses and clematis on the walls of the house, and in less time than five minutes all these dear things were in full bloom.

Oh, how beautiful the little house was now! But it was at last finished true as true, and they had to leave it and return to the dance. They all kissed their hands to it as they went away, and the last to go was Brownie. She stayed a moment behind the others to drop a pleasant dream down the chimney.

All through the night the exquisite little house stood there in the Figs taking care of Maimie, and she never knew. She slept until the dream was quite finished, and woke feeling deliciously cosy just as morning was breaking from its egg, and then she almost fell asleep again, and then she called out, 'Tony,' for she thought she was at home in the nursery. As Tony made no answer, she sat up, where-upon her head hit the roof, and it opened like the lid of a box, and to her bewilderment she saw all around her the Kensington Gardens lying deep in snow. As she was not in the nursery she wondered whether this was really herself, so she pinched her cheeks, and then she knew it was herself, and this reminded her that she was in the middle of a great adventure. She remembered now everything that had happened to her from the closing of the gates up to her running away from the fairies, but however, she asked herself, had she got into this funny place? She stepped out by the roof, right over the garden, and then she saw the dear house in which she had passed the night. It so entranced her that she could think of nothing else.

'O you darling! O you sweet! O you love!' she cried.

Perhaps a human voice frightened the little house, or maybe it now knew than its work was done, for no sooner had Maimie spoken than it began to grow smaller; it shrank so slowly that she could scarce believe it was shrinking, yet she soon knew that it could not contain her now. It always remained as complete as ever, but it became smaller and smaller, and the garden dwindled at the same time, and the snow crept closer, lapping house and garden up. Now the house was the size of a little dog's kennel, and now of a Noah's Ark, but still you could see the smoke and the door-handle and the roses on the wall, every one complete. The glow-worm light was waning too, but it was still there.

'Darling, loveliest, don't go!' Maimie cried, falling on her knees, for the little house was now the size of a reel of thread, but still quite complete. But as she stretched out her arms imploringly the snow crept up on all sides until it met itself, and where the little house had been was now one unbroken expanse of snow.

Maimie stamped her foot naughtily, and was putting her fingers to her eyes, when she heard a kind voice say, 'Don't cry, pretty human, don't cry,' and then she turned round and saw a beautiful little naked boy regarding her wistfully. She knew at once that he must be Peter Pan.

EIGHTEEN

Peter's Goat

MAIMIE FELT QUITE shy, but Peter knew not what shy was.

'I hope you have had a good night,' he said earnestly.

'Thank you,' she replied, 'I was so cosy and warm. But you' – and she looked at his nakedness awkwardly – 'don't you feel the least bit cold?'

Now cold was another word Peter had forgotten, so he answered, 'I think not, but I may be wrong: you see I am rather ignorant. I am not exactly a boy; Solomon says I am a Betwixt-and-Between.'

'So that is what it is called,' said Maimie thoughtfully.

'That's not my name,' he explained, 'my name is Peter Pan.'

'Yes, of course,' she said, 'I know, everybody knows.'

You can't think how pleased Peter was to learn that all the people outside the gates knew about him. He begged Maimie to tell him what they knew and what they said, and she did so. They were sitting by this time on a fallen tree; Peter had cleared off the snow for Maimie, but he sat on a snowy bit himself.

'Squeeze closer,' Maimie said.

'What is that?' he asked, and she showed him, and then he did it. They talked together and he found that people knew a great deal about him, but not everything, not that he had gone back to his mother and been barred out, for instance, and he said nothing of this to Maimie, for it still humiliated him.

'Do they know that I play games exactly like real boys?' he asked very proudly. 'O Maimie, please tell them!' But when he revealed how he played, by sailing his hoop on the Round Pond, and so on, she was simply horrified.

'All your ways of playing,' she said with her big eyes on him, 'are quite, quite wrong, and not in the least like how boys play.'

Poor Peter uttered a little moan at this, and he cried for the first time for I know not how long. Maimie was extremely sorry for him, and lent him her handkerchief, but he didn't know in the least what to do with it, so she showed him, that is to say, she wiped her eyes, and then gave it back to him, saying, 'Now you do it,' but instead of wiping his own eyes he wiped hers, and she thought it best to pretend that this was what she had meant.

She said out of pity for him, 'I shall give you a kiss if you like,' but though he once knew, he had long forgotten what kisses are, and he replied, 'Thank you,' and held out his hand, thinking she had offered to put something into it. This was a great shock to her, but she felt she could not explain without shaming him, so with charming delicacy she gave Peter a thimble which happened to be in her pocket, and pretended that it was a kiss. Poor little boy! he quite believed her, and to this day he wears it on his finger, though there can be scarcely any one who needs a thimble so little. You see, though still a tiny child, it was really years and years since he had seen his mother, and I dare say the baby who had supplanted him was now a man with whiskers.

But you must not think that Peter Pan was a boy to pity rather than to admire; if Maimie began by thinking this, she soon found she was very much mistaken. Her eyes glistened with admiration when he told her of his adventures, especially of how he went to and fro between the island and the Gardens in the Thrush's Nest.

'How romantic!' Maimie exclaimed, but this was another unknown word, and he hung his head thinking she was despising him.

'I suppose Tony would not have done that?' he said very humbly.

'Never, never!' she answered with conviction, 'he would have been afraid.'

'What is afraid?' asked Peter longingly. He thought it must be some splendid thing. 'I do wish you would teach me how to be afraid, Maimie,' he said.

'I believe no one could teach that to you,' she answered adoringly, but Peter thought she meant that he was stupid. She had told him about Tony and of the wicked thing she did in the dark to frighten him (she knew quite well that it was wicked), but Peter misunderstood her meaning and said, 'Oh, how I wish I was as brave as Tony!'

It quite irritated her. 'You are twenty thousand times braver than Tony,' she said; 'you are ever so much the bravest boy I ever knew.'

He could scarcely believe she meant it, but when he did believe he screamed with joy.

'And if you want very much to give me a kiss,' Maimie said, 'you can do it.'

Very reluctantly Peter began to take the thimble off his finger. He thought she wanted it back.

'I don't mean a kiss,' she said hurriedly, 'I mean a thimble.'

'What's that?' Peter asked.

'It's like this,' she said, and kissed him.

'I should love to give you a thimble,' Peter said gravely, so he gave her one. He gave her quite a number of thimbles, and then a delightful idea came into his head. 'Maimie,' he said, 'will you marry me?'

Now, strange to tell, the same idea had come at exactly the same time into Maimie's head. 'I should like to,' she answered, 'but will there be room in your boat for two?'

'If you squeeze close,' he said eagerly.

'Perhaps the birds would be angry?'

He assured her that the birds would love to have her, though I am not so certain of it myself. Also that there were very few birds in winter. 'Of course they might want your clothes,' he had to admit rather falteringly.

She was somewhat indignant at this.

'They are always thinking of their nests,' he said apologetically, 'and there are some bits of you' – he stroked the fur on her pelisse – 'that would excite them very much.'

'They shan't have my fur,' she said sharply.

'No,' he said, still fondling it, however, 'no. O Maimie,' he said rapturously, 'do you know why I love you? It is because you are like a beautiful nest.'

Somehow this made her uneasy. 'I think you are speaking more like a bird than a boy now,' she said, holding back, and indeed he was even looking rather like a bird. 'After all,' she said, 'you are only a Betwixt-and-Between.' But it hurt him so much that she immediately added, 'It must be a delicious thing to be.'

'Come and be one, then, dear Maimie,' he implored her, and they set off for the boat, for it was now very near Open-Gate time. 'And you are not a bit like a nest,' he whispered to please her.

'But I think it is rather nice to be like one,' she said in a woman's contradictory way. 'And, Peter, dear, though I can't give them my fur, I wouldn't mind their building in it. Fancy a nest in my neck with little spotty eggs in it! O Peter, how perfectly lovely!'

But as they drew near the Serpentine, she shivered a little, and said, 'Of course I shall go and see mother often, quite often. It is not as if I was saying good-bye for ever to mother, it is not in the least like that.'

'Oh no,' answered Peter, but in his heart he knew it was very like that, and he would have told her so had he not been in a quaking fear of losing her. He was so fond of her, he felt he could not live without her. 'She will forget her mother in time, and be happy with me,' he kept saying to himself, and he hurried her on, giving her thimbles by the way.

But even when she had seen the boat and exclaimed ecstatically over its loveliness, she still talked tremblingly about her mother. 'You know quite well, Peter, don't you,' she said, 'that I wouldn't come unless I knew for certain I could go back to mother whenever I want to? Peter, say it.'

He said it, but he could no longer look her in the face.

'If you are sure your mother will always want you,' he added rather sourly.

'The idea of mother's not always wanting me!' Maimie cried, and her face glistened.

'If she doesn't bar you out,' said Peter huskily.

'The door,' replied Maimie, 'will always, always be open, and mother will always be waiting at it for me.'

'Then,' said Peter, not without grimness, 'step in, if you feel so sure of her,' and he helped Maimie into the Thrush's Nest.

'But why don't you look at me,' she asked, taking him by the arm.

Peter tried hard not to look, he tried to push off, then he gave a great gulp and jumped ashore and sat down miserably in the snow.

She went to him. 'What is it, dear, dear Peter?' she said, wondering.

'O Maimie,' he cried, 'it isn't fair to take you with me if you think you can go back! Your mother' – he gulped again – 'you don't know them as well as I do.'

And then he told her the woeful story of how he had been barred out, and she gasped all the time. 'But my mother,' she said, '*my* mother—'

'Yes, she would,' said Peter, 'they are all the same. I dare say she is looking for another one already.'

Maimie said aghast, 'I can't believe it. You see, when

you went away your mother had none, but my mother has Tony, and surely they are satisfied when they have one.'

Peter replied bitterly, 'You should see the letters Solomon gets from ladies who have six.'

Just then they heard a grating *creak*, followed by *creak, creak*, all round the Gardens. It was the Opening of the Gates, and Peter jumped nervously into his boat. He knew Maimie would not come with him now, and he was trying bravely not to cry. But Maimie was sobbing painfully.

'If I should be too late,' she said in agony, 'O Peter, if she has got another one already!'

Again he sprang ashore as if she had called him back. 'I shall come and look for you tonight,' he said, squeezing close, 'but if you hurry away I think you will be in time.'

Then he pressed a last thimble on her sweet little mouth, and covered his face with his hands so that he might not see her go.

'Dear Peter!' she cried.

'Dear Maimie!' cried the tragic boy.

She leapt into his arms, so that it was a sort of fairy wedding, and then she hurried away. Oh, how she hastened to the gates! Peter, you may be sure, was back in the Gardens that night as soon as Lock-out sounded, but he found no Maimie, and so he knew she had been in time. For long he hoped that some night she would come back to him; often he thought he saw her waiting for him by the shore of the Serpentine as his bark drew to land, but Maimie never went back. She wanted to, but she was afraid that if she saw her dear Betwixt-and-Between again she would linger with him too long, and besides the ayah now kept a sharp eye on her. But she often talked lovingly of Peter, and she knitted a kettle-holder for him, and one day when she was wondering what Easter present he would like, her mother made a suggestion.

'Nothing,' she said thoughtfully, 'would be so useful to him as a goat.'

'He could ride on it,' cried Maimie, 'and play on his pipe at the same time.'

'Then,' her mother asked, 'won't you give him your goat, the one you frighten Tony with at night?'

'But it isn't a real goat,' Maimie said.

'It seems very real to Tony,' replied her mother.

'It seems frightfully real to me too,' Maimie admitted, 'but how could I give it to Peter?'

Her mother knew a way, and next day, accompanied by Tony (who was really quite a nice boy, though of course he could not compare), they went to the Gardens, and Maimie stood alone within a fairy ring, and then her mother, who was a rather gifted lady, said:

> My daughter, tell me, if you can,
> What have you got for Peter Pan?

To which Maimie replied:

> I have a goat for him to ride,
> Observe me cast it far and wide.

She then flung her arms about as if she were sowing seed, and turned round three times.

Next Tony said:

> If P. doth find it waiting here,
> Wilt ne'er again make me to fear?

And Maimie answered:

> By dark or light I fondly swear
> Never to see goats anywhere.

She also left a letter to Peter in a likely place, explaining what she had done, and begging him to ask the fairies to turn the goat into one convenient for riding on. Well, it all happened just as she hoped, for Peter found the letter, and of course nothing could be easier for the fairies than to turn the goat into a real one, and so that is how Peter got the goat on which he now rides round the Gardens every night playing sublimely on his pipe. And Maimie kept her promise, and never frightened Tony with a goat again, though I have heard that she created another animal. Until she was quite a big girl she continued to leave presents for Peter in the Gardens (with letters explaining how humans play with them), and she is not the only one who has done this. David does it, for instance, and he and I know the likeliest place for leaving them in, and we shall tell you if you like, but for mercy's sake don't ask us before Porthos, for were he to find out the place he would take every one of them.

Though Peter still remembers Maimie he is become as gay as ever, and often in sheer happiness he jumps off his goat and lies kicking merrily on the grass. Oh, he has a joyful time! But he has still a vague memory that he was a human once, and it makes him especially kind to the house-swallows when they visit the island, for house-swallows are the spirits of little children who have died. They always build in the eaves of the houses where they lived when they were humans, and sometimes they try to fly in at a nursery window, and perhaps that is why Peter loves them best of all the birds.

And the little house? Every lawful night (that is to say, every night except ball nights) the fairies now build the little house lest there should be a human child lost in the Gardens, and Peter rides the marches looking for lost ones, and if he finds them he carries them on his goat to the little house, and when they wake up they are in it, and when they step out they see it. The fairies build the house merely because it is so pretty, but Peter rides round in memory of Maimie, and because he still loves to do just as he believes real boys would do.

But you must not think that, because somewhere among the trees the little house is twinkling, it is a safe thing to remain in the Gardens after Lock-out time. If the bad ones among the fairies happen to be out that night they will certainly mischief you, and even though they are not, you may perish of cold and dark before Peter Pan comes round. He has been too late several times, and when he sees he is too late he runs back to the Thrush's Nest for his paddle, of which Maimie had told him the true use, and he digs a grave for the child and erects a little tombstone, and carves the poor thing's initials on it. He does this at once because he thinks it is what real boys would do, and you must have noticed the little stones, and that there are always two together. He puts them in twos because they seem less lonely. I think that quite the most touching sight in the Gardens is the two tombstones of Walter Stephen Matthews and Phoebe Phelps. They stand together at the spot where the parish of Westminster St Mary's is said to meet the parish of Paddington. Here Peter found the two babes, who had fallen unnoticed from their perambulators, Phoebe aged thirteen months and Walter probably still younger, for Peter seems to have felt a delicacy about putting any age on his stone. They lie side by side, and the simple inscriptions read

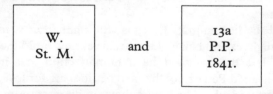

David sometimes places white flowers on these two innocent graves.

But how strange for parents, when they hurry into the Gardens at the opening of the gates looking for their lost one, to find the sweetest little tombstone instead. I do hope that Peter is not too ready with his spade. It is all rather sad.

NINETEEN

An Interloper

DAVID AND I had a tremendous adventure. It was this – he passed the night with me. We had often talked of it as a possible thing, and at last Mary consented to our having it.

The adventure began with David's coming to me at the unwonted hour of six p.m., carrying what looked like a packet of sandwiches, but proved to be his requisites for the night done up in a neat paper parcel. We were both so excited that, at the moment of greeting, neither of us could be apposite to the occasion in words, so we communicated our feelings by signs; as thus: David half sat down in a place where there was no chair, which is his favourite preparation for being emphatic, and is borrowed, I think, from the frogs, and we then made the extraordinary faces that mean, 'What a tremendous adventure!'

We were to do all the important things precisely as they are done every evening at his own home, and so I am in a puzzle to know how it was such an adventure to David. But I have now said enough to show you what an adventure it was to me.

For a little while we played with my two medals, and, with the delicacy of a sleeping companion, David abstained on this occasion from asking why one of them was not a Victoria Cross. He is very troubled because I never won the Victoria Cross, for it lowers his status in the Gardens. He never says in the Gardens that I won it, but he fights any boy of his year who says I didn't. Their fighting consists of challenging each other.

At twenty-five past six I turned on the hot water in the bath, and covertly swallowed a small glass of brandy. I then said, 'Half-past six; time for little boys to be in bed.' I said it in the matter-of-fact voice of one made free of the company of parents, as if I had said it often before, and would have to say it often again, and as if there was nothing particularly delicious to me in hearing myself say it. I tried to say it in that way.

And David was deceived. To my exceeding joy he stamped his little foot, and was so naughty that, in gratitude, I gave him five minutes with a match-box. Matches, which he drops on the floor when lighted, are the greatest treat you can give David; indeed, I think his private heaven is a place with a roaring bonfire.

Then I placed my hand carelessly on his shoulder, like one a trifle bored by the dull routine of putting my little boys to bed, and conducted him to the night nursery, which had lately been my private chamber. There was an extra bed in it tonight, very near my own, but differently shaped, and scarcely less conspicuous was the new mantelshelf ornament: a tumbler of milk, with a biscuit on top of it, and a chocolate riding on the biscuit. To enter the room without seeing the tumbler at once was impossible. I had tried it several times, and David saw and promptly did his frog business, the while, with an indescribable emotion, I produced a night-light from my pocket and planted it in a saucer on the washstand.

David watched my preparations with distasteful levity, but anon made a noble amend by abruptly offering me his foot as if he had no longer use for it, and I knew by intuition that he expected me to take off his boots. I took them off with all the coolness of an old hand, and then I placed him on my knee and removed his blouse. This was a delightful experience, but I think I remained wonderfully calm until I came somewhat too suddenly to his little braces, which agitated me profoundly.

I cannot proceed in public with the disrobing of David. Soon the night nursery was in darkness but for the glimmer from the night-light, and very still save when the door creaked as a man peered in at the little figure on the bed. However softly I opened the door, an inch at a time, his bright eyes turned to me at once, and he always made the face which means, 'What a tremendous adventure!'

'Are you never to fall asleep, David?' I always said.

'When are you coming to bed?' he always replied, very brave but in a whisper, as if he feared the bears and wolves might have him. When little boys are in bed there is nothing between them and bears and wolves but the night-light.

I returned to my chair to think, and at last he fell asleep with his face to the wall, but even then I stood many times at the door, listening.

Long after I had gone to bed a sudden silence filled the chamber, and I knew that David had awaked. I lay motionless, and, after what seemed a long time of waiting, a little far-away voice said in a cautious whisper, 'Irene!'

'You are sleeping with me tonight, you know, David,' I said.

'I didn't know,' he replied, a little troubled, but trying not to be a nuisance.

'You remember you are with me?' I asked.

After a moment's hesitation he replied, 'I nearly remember,' and presently he added very gratefully, as if to some angel who had whispered to him, 'I remember now.'

I think he had nigh fallen asleep again when he stirred and said, 'Is it going on now?'

'What?'

'The adventure.'

'Yes, David.'

Perhaps this disturbed him, for by and by I had to inquire, 'You are not frightened, are you?'

'Am I not?' he answered politely, and I knew his hand was groping in the darkness, so I put out mine and he held on tightly to one finger.

'I am not frightened now,' he whispered.

'And there is nothing else you want?'

'Is there not?' he again asked politely. 'Are you sure there's not?' he added.

'What can it be, David?'

'I don't take up very much room,' the far-away voice said.

'Why, David,' said I, sitting up, 'do you want to come into my bed?'

'Mother said I wasn't to want it unless you wanted it first,' he squeaked.

'It is what I have been wanting all the time,' said I, and then without more ado the little white figure rose and flung itself at me. For the rest of the night he lay on me and across me, and sometimes his feet were at the bottom of the bed and sometimes on the pillow, but he always retained possession of my finger, and occasionally he woke me to say that he was sleeping with me. I had not a good night. I lay thinking.

Of this little boy, who, in the midst of his play while I undressed him, had suddenly buried his head on my knees.

Of the woman who had been for him who could be sufficiently daring.

Of David's dripping little form in the bath, and how when I essayed to catch him he had slipped from my arms like a trout.

Of how I had stood by the open door listening to his sweet breathing, had stood so long that I forgot his name and called him Timothy.

TWENTY

David and Porthos Compared

BUT MARY SPOILT it all, when I sent David back to her in the morning, by inquiring too curiously into his person and discovering that I had put his combinations on him with the buttons to the front. For this I wrote her the following insulting letter. When Mary does anything that specially annoys me I send her an insulting letter. I once had a photograph taken of David being hanged on a tree. I sent her that. You can't think of all the subtle ways of grieving her I have. No woman with the spirit of a crow would stand it.

'Dear Madam,' I wrote, 'it has come to my knowledge that when you walk in the Gardens with the boy David you listen avidly for encomiums of him and of your fanciful dressing of him by passers-by, storing them in your heart the while you make vain pretence to regard them not: wherefore lest you be swollen by these very small things, I, who now know David both by day and by night, am minded to compare him and Porthos the one with the other, both in this matter and in other matters of graver account. And touching this matter of outward show, they are both very lordly, and neither of them likes it to be referred to, but they endure in different ways. For David says "Oh, bother!" and even at times hits out, but Porthos droops his tail and lets them have their say. Yet is he extolled as beautiful and a darling ten times for the once that David is extolled.

'The manners of Porthos are therefore prettier than the manners of David, who when he has sent me to hide from him behind a tree sometimes comes not in search, and on emerging tamely from my concealment I find him playing other games entirely forgetful of my existence. Whereas Porthos always comes in search. Also, if David wearies of you he scruples not to say so, but Porthos, in like circumstances, offers you his paw, meaning "Farewell," and to bearded men he does this all the time (I think because of a hereditary distaste for goats), so that they conceive him to be enamoured of them when he is only begging them courteously to go. Thus while the manners of Porthos are more polite, it may be argued that those of David are more efficacious.

'In gentleness David compares ill with Porthos, for whereas the one shoves, and has been known to kick, on slight provocation, the other, who is noisily hated of all small dogs by reason of his size, remonstrates not, even when they cling in froth and fury to his chest, but carries them along tolerantly until they drop off from fatigue. Again, David will not unbend when in the company of babies, expecting them unreasonably to rise to his level; but contrariwise Porthos, though terrible to tramps, suffers all things of babies, even to an exploration of his mouth in an attempt to discover what his tongue is like at the other end. The comings and goings of David are unnoticed by perambulators, which lie in wait for the advent of Porthos. The strong and wicked fear Porthos but no little creature fears him, not the hedgehogs he conveys from place to place in his mouth, nor the sparrows that steal his straw from under him.

'In proof of which gentleness I adduce his adventure with the rabbit. Having gone for a time to reside in a rabbit country, Porthos was elated to discover at last something small that ran from him, and developing at once into an ecstatic sportsman, he did pound hotly in pursuit, though always overshooting the mark by a hundred yards or so and wondering very much what had become of the rabbit. There was a steep path, from the top of which the rabbit suddenly came into view, and the practice of Porthos was to advance up it on tiptoe, turning near the summit to give me a knowing look and then bounding forward. The rabbit here did something tricky with a hole in the ground, but Porthos tore onwards in full faith that the game was being played fairly, and always returned panting and puzzled but glorious.

'I sometimes shuddered to think of his perplexity should he catch the rabbit, which, however, was extremely unlikely; nevertheless he did catch it, I know not how, but presume it to have been another than the one of which he was in chase. I found him with it, his brows furrowed in the deepest thought. The rabbit, terrified but uninjured, cowered between his paws. Porthos gave me a happy look, and again dropped into a weighty frame of mind. "What is the next thing one does?" was obviously the puzzle with him, and the position was scarcely less awkward for the rabbit, which several times made a move to end this intolerable suspense. Whereupon Porthos immediately gave it a warning tap with his foot, and again fell to pondering. The strain on me was very great.

'At last they seemed to hit upon a compromise. Porthos looked over his shoulder very self-consciously, and the rabbit, at first slowly, and then in a flash, withdrew. Porthos pretended to make a search for it, but you cannot think how relieved he looked. He even tried to brazen out his disgrace before me and waved his tail appealingly. But he could not look me in the face, and when he saw that this was what I insisted on he collapsed at my feet and moaned. There were real tears in his eyes, and I was touched, and swore to him that he had done everything a dog could do, and though he knew I was lying he became happy again. For so long as I am pleased with him, ma'am, nothing else greatly matters to Porthos. I told this story to David, having first extracted a promise from him that he would not think the less of Porthos. And now I must demand the same promise of you.

Also, an admission that in innocence of heart, for which David has been properly commended, he can nevertheless teach Porthos nothing, but on the contrary may learn much from him.

'And now to come to those qualities in which David excels over Porthos – the first is that he is no snob, but esteems the girl Irene (pretentiously called his nurse) more than any fine lady, and envies every ragged boy who can hit to leg. Whereas Porthos would have every class keep its place, and though fond of going down into the kitchen, always barks at the top of the stairs for a servile invitation before he graciously descends. Most of the servants in our street have had the loan of him to be photographed with, and I have but now seen him stalking off for that purpose with a proud little housemaid who is looking up to him as if he were a warrior for whom she had paid a shilling.

'Again, when David and Porthos are in their bath, praise is due to the one and must be withheld from the other. For David, as I have noticed, loves to splash in his bath and to slip back into it from the hands that would transfer him to a towel. But Porthos stands in his bath drooping abjectly like a shamed figure cut out of some limp material.

'Furthermore, the inventiveness of David is beyond that of Porthos, who cannot play by himself, and knows not even how to take a solitary walk, while David invents playfully all day long. Lastly, when David is discovered of some offence and expresses sorrow therefor, he does that thing no more for a time, but looks about him for other offences, whereas Porthos incontinently repeats his offence – in other words, he again buries his bone in the backyard, and marvels greatly that I know it, although his nose be crusted with earth.

'Touching these matters, therefore, let it be granted that David excels Porthos; and in divers similar qualities the one is no more than a match for the other, as in the quality of curiosity; for, if a parcel comes into my chambers Porthos is miserable until it is opened, and I have noticed the same thing of David.

'Also there is the taking of medicine. For at production of the vial all gaiety suddenly departs from Porthos and he looks the other way; but if I say I have forgotten to have the vial refilled he skips joyfully, yet thinks he still has a right to a chocolate; and when I remarked disparagingly on this to David, he looked so shy that there was revealed to me a picture of a certain lady treating him for youthful maladies.

'A thing to be considered of in both is their receiving of punishments, and I am now reminded that the girl Irene (whom I take in this matter to be your mouthpiece) complains that I am not sufficiently severe with David, and do leave the chiding of him for offences against myself to her in the hope that he will love her less and me more thereby. Which we have hotly argued in the Gardens to the detriment of our dignity. And I here say that if I am slow to be severe to David, the reason thereof is that I dare not be severe to Porthos, and I have ever sought to treat the one the same with the other.

'Now I refrain from raising hand or voice to Porthos because his great heart is nigh to breaking if he so much as suspects that all is not well between him and me, and having struck him once some years ago never can I forget the shudder which passed through him when he saw it was I who had struck; and I shall strike him, ma'am, no more. But when he is detected in any unseemly act now, it is my stern practice to cane my writing-table in his presence, and even this punishment is almost more than he can bear. Wherefore if such chastisement inflicted on David encourages him but to enter upon fresh trespasses (as the girl Irene avers), the reason must be that his heart is not like unto that of the noble Porthos.

'And if you retort that David is naturally a depraved little boy, and so demands harsher measure, I have still my answer, to wit, what is the manner of severity meted out to him at home? And lest you should shuffle in your reply, I shall mention a notable passage that has come to my ears.

'As thus, that David having heard a horrid word in the street, uttered it with unction in the home. That the mother threatened corporal punishment, whereat the father tremblingly intervened. That David continuing to rejoice exceedingly in his word, the father spoke darkly of a cane, but the mother rushed between the combatants. That the problematical chastisement became to David an object of romantic interest. That this darkened the happy home. That casting from his path a weeping mother, the goaded father at last dashed from the house yelling that he was away to buy a cane. That he merely walked the streets white to the lips because of the terror David must now be feeling. And that when he returned, it was David radiant with hope who opened the door and then burst into tears because there was no cane. Truly, ma'am, you are a fitting person to tax me with want of severity. Rather should you be giving thanks that it is not you I am comparing with Porthos.

'But to make an end of this comparison, I mention that Porthos is ever wishful to express gratitude for my kindness to him, so that looking up from my book I see his mournful eyes fixed upon me with a passionate attachment, and then I know that the well-nigh unbearable sadness which comes into the face of dogs is because they cannot say 'Thank you' to their masters. Whereas David takes my kindness as his right. But for this, while I should chide him I cannot do so, for of all the ways David has of making me to love him the most poignant is that he expects it of me as a matter of course. David is all for fun, but none may plumb the depths of Porthos. Nevertheless I am most nearly doing so when I lie down beside him on the floor and he puts an arm about my neck. On my soul, ma'am, a protecting arm. At such times it is as if each of us knew what was the want of the other.

'Thus weighing Porthos with David, it were hard to tell which is the worthier. Wherefore, do you keep your boy while I keep my dog, and so we shall both be pleased.'

TWENTY-ONE

William Paterson

WE HAD BEEN together, we three, in my rooms, David telling me about the fairy language and Porthos lolling on the sofa listening, as one may say. It is his favourite place of a dull day, and under him were some sheets of newspaper, which I spread there at such times to deceive my house-keeper, who thinks dogs should lie on the floor.

Fairy me tribber is what you say to the fairies when you want them to give you a cup of tea, but it is not so easy as it looks, for all the *r's* should be pronounced as *w's*, and I forget this so often that David believes I should find difficulty in making myself understood.

'What would you say,' he asked me, 'if you wanted them to turn you into a hollyhock?' He thinks the ease with which they can turn you into things is their most engaging quality.

The answer is *Fairy me lukka*, but though he had often told me this I again forgot the *lukka*.

'I should never dream,' I said (to cover my discomfiture), 'of asking them to turn me into anything. If I was a hollyhock I should soon wither, David.'

He himself had provided me with this objection not long before, but now he seemed to think it merely silly. 'Just before the time to wither begins,' he said airily, 'you say to them "*Fairy me bola.*"'

Fairy me bola means 'Turn me back again,' and David's discovery made me uncomfortable, for I knew he had hitherto kept his distance of the fairies mainly because of a feeling that their conversions are permanent.

So I returned him to his home. I send him home from my rooms under the care of Porthos. I may walk on the other side unknown to them, but they have no need of me, for at such times nothing would induce Porthos to depart from the care of David. If any one addresses them he growls softly and shows the teeth that crunch bones as if they were biscuits. Thus amicably the two pass on to Mary's house, where Porthos barks his knock-and-ring bark till the door is opened. Sometimes he goes in with David, but on this occasion he said good-bye on the step. Nothing remarkable in this, but he did not return to me, not that day nor next day, nor in weeks and months. I was a man distraught; and David wore his knuckles in his eyes. Conceive it, we had lost our dear Porthos – at least – well – something disquieting happened. I don't quite know what to think of it even now. I know what David thinks. However, you shall think as you choose.

My first hope was that Porthos had strolled to the Gardens and got locked in for the night, and almost as soon as Lock-out was over I was there to make inquiries. But there was no news of Porthos, though I learned that some one was believed to have spent the night in the Gardens, a young gentleman who walked out hastily the moment the gates were opened. He had said nothing, however, of having seen a dog. I feared an accident now, for I knew no thief could steal him; yet even an accident seemed incredible, he was always so cautious at crossings; also there could not possibly have been an accident to Porthos without there being an accident to something else.

David in the middle of his games would suddenly remember the great blank and step aside to cry. It was one of his qualities that when he knew he was about to cry he turned aside to do it, and I always respected his privacy and waited for him. Of course being but a little boy he was soon playing again, but his sudden floods of feeling, of which we never spoke, were dear to me in those desolate days.

We had a favourite haunt, called the Story-seat, and we went back to that, meaning not to look at the grass near it where Porthos used to squat; but we could not help looking at it sideways, and to our distress a man was sitting on the acquainted spot. He rose at our approach and took two steps toward us, so quick that they were almost jumps, then as he saw that we were passing indignantly I thought I heard him give a little cry.

I put him down for one of your garrulous fellows who try to lure strangers into talk, but next day, when we found him sitting on the Story-seat itself, I had a longer scrutiny of him. He was dandiacally dressed, seemed to tell something under twenty years, and had a handsome wistful face atop of a heavy lumbering, almost corpulent figure, which however did not betoken inactivity; for David's purple hat (a conceit of his mother's of which we were both heartily ashamed) blowing off as we neared him, he leapt the railings without touching them and was back with it in three seconds; only instead of delivering it straightway he seemed to expect David to chase him for it.

You have introduced yourself to David when you jump the railings without touching them, and William Paterson (as proved to be his name) was at once our friend. We often found him waiting for us at the Story-seat, and the great stout fellow laughed and wept over our tales like a three-year-old. Often he said with extraordinary pride, 'You are telling the story to me quite as much as to David, aren't you?' He was of an innocence such as you shall seldom encounter, and believed stories at which even David blinked. Often he looked at me in quick alarm if David said that of course these things did not really happen, and unable to resist that appeal I would reply that they really did. I never saw him irate except when David was still sceptical, but then he would say quite warningly '*He* says it is true, so it must be true.' This brings me to that one of his qualities, which at once gratified and pained me, his admiration for myself. His eyes, which at times had a rim of red, were ever fixed upon me fondly, except perhaps when I told him of Porthos, and said that death alone could have kept him so long from my side. Then Paterson's sympathy was such that he had to look away. He was shy of speaking of himself, so I asked him no personal questions, but concluded that his upbringing must have been lonely, to account for his ignorance of affairs, and loveless, else how could he have felt such a drawing to me?

I remember very well the day when the strange, and surely monstrous, suspicion first made my head tingle. We had been blown, the three of us, to my rooms by a gust of rain; it was also, I think, the first time Paterson had entered them. 'Take the sofa, Mr Paterson,' I said, as I drew a chair nearer to the fire, and for the moment my eyes were off him. Then I saw that, before sitting down on the sofa, he was spreading the day's paper over it. 'Whatever makes you do that?' I asked, and he started like one bewildered by the question, then went white, and pushed the paper aside.

David had noticed nothing, but I was strangely uncomfortable, and, despite my efforts at talk, often lapsed into silence, to be roused from it by a feeling that Paterson was looking at me covertly. Pooh! what vapours of the imagination were these; I blew them from me, and to prove to myself, so to speak, that they were dissipated, I asked him to see David home. As soon as I was alone, I flung me down on the floor laughing, then as quickly jumped up and was after them; and very sober too, for it was come to me abruptly as an odd thing that Paterson had set off without asking where David lived.

Seeing them in front of me, I crossed the street and followed. They were walking side by side rather solemnly, and perhaps nothing remarkable happened until they reached David's door. I say perhaps, for something did occur. A lady, who has several pretty reasons for frequenting the Gardens, recognised David in the street, and was stooping to address him, when Paterson did something that alarmed her. I was too far off to see what it was, but had he growled 'Hands off!' she could not have scurried away more precipitately. He then ponderously marched his charge to the door, where, assuredly, he did a strange thing. Instead of knocking or ringing, he stood on the step and called out sharply, 'Hie, hie, hie!' until the door was opened.

The whimsy, for it could be nothing more, curtailed me of my sleep that night, and you may picture me trying both sides of the pillow.

I recalled other queer things of Paterson, and they came back to me charged with new meanings. There was his way of shaking hands. He now did it in the ordinary way, but when first we knew him his arm had described a circle, and the hand had sometimes missed mine and come heavily upon my chest instead. His walk, again, might more correctly have been called a waddle.

There were his perfervid thanks. He seldom departed without thanking me with an intensity that was out of proportion to the little I had done for him. In the Gardens, too, he seemed ever to take the sward rather than the seats; perhaps a wise preference, but he had an unusual way of sitting down. I can describe it only by saying that he let go of himself and went down with a thud.

I reverted to the occasion when he lunched with me at the Club. We had cutlets, and I noticed that he ate his in a somewhat finicking manner; yet having left the table for a moment to consult the sweets-card, I saw, when I returned, that there was now no bone on his plate. The waiters were looking at him rather curiously.

David was very partial to him, but showed it in a somewhat singular manner – used to pat his head, for instance. I remembered, also, that while David shouted to me or Irene to attract our attention, he usually whistled to Paterson, he could not explain why.

These ghosts made me to sweat in bed; not merely that night, but often when some new shock brought them back in force, yet, unsupported, they would have disturbed me little by day. Day, however, had its reflections, and they came to me while I was shaving – that ten minutes when, brought face to face with the harsher realities of life, we see things most clearly as they are. Then the beautiful nature of Paterson loomed offensively, and his honest eyes insulted over me. No one come to nigh twenty years had a right to such faith in his fellow-creatures. He could not backbite, nor envy, nor prevaricate, nor jump at mean motives for generous acts. He had not a single base story about women. It all seemed inhuman.

What creatures we be! I was more than half ashamed of Paterson's faith in me, but when I saw it begin to shrink I fought for it. An easy task, you may say, but it was a hard one, for gradually a change had come over the youth. I am now arrived at a time when the light-heartedness had gone out of him; he had lost his zest for fun, and dubiety sat in the eyes that were once so certain. He was not doubtful of me, not then, but of human nature in general; that whilom noble edifice was tottering. He mixed with boys in the Gardens; ah, mothers! it is hard to say, but how could he retain his innocence when he had mixed with boys? He heard you talk of yourselves, and so, ladies, that part of the edifice went down. I have not the heart to follow him in all his discoveries. Sometimes he went in flame at them, but for the most part he stood looking on, bewildered and numbed, like one moaning inwardly.

He saw all, as one fresh to the world, before he had time to breathe upon the glass. So would your child be, madam, if born with a man's powers; and when disillusioned of all else, he would cling for a moment longer to you, the woman of whom, before he saw you, he had heard so much. How you would strive to cheat him, even as I strove to hide my real self from Paterson, and still you would strive as I strove after you knew the game was up.

The sorrowful eyes of Paterson stripped me bare. There

were days when I could not endure looking at him, though surely I have long ceased to be a vain man. He still met us in the Gardens, but for hours he and I would be together without speaking. It was so upon the last day, one of those innumerable dreary days when David, having sneezed the night before, was kept at home in flannel, and I sat alone with Paterson on the Story-seat. At last I turned to address him. Never had we spoken of what chained our tongues, and I meant only to say now that we must go, for soon the gates would close, but when I looked at him I saw that he was more mournful than ever before; he shut his eyes so tightly that a drop of blood fell from them.

'It was all over, Paterson, long ago,' I broke out harshly, 'why do we linger?'

He beat his hands together miserably, and yet cast me appealing looks that had much affection in them.

'You expected too much of me,' I told him, and he bowed his head. 'I don't know where you brought your grand ideas of men and women from. I don't want to know,' I added hastily.

'But it must have been from a prettier world than this,' I said: 'are you quite sure that you were wise in leaving it?'

He rose and sat down again. 'I wanted to know you,' he replied slowly, 'I wanted to be like you.'

'And now you know me,' I said, 'do you want to be like me still? I am a curious person to attach oneself to, Paterson; don't you see that even David often smiles at me when he thinks he is unobserved. I work very hard to retain that little boy's love; but I shall lose him soon; even now I am not what I was to him; in a year or two at longest, Paterson, David will grow out of me.'

The poor fellow shot out his hand to me, but 'No,' said I, 'you have found me out. Everybody finds me out except my dog, and that is why the loss of him makes such a difference to me. Shall we go, Paterson?'

He would not come with me, and I left him on the seat;

when I was far away I looked back, and he was still sitting there forlornly.

For long I could not close my ears that night: I lay listening, I knew what for. A scare was on me that made me dislike the dark, and I switched on the light and slept at last. I was roused by a great to-do in the early morning, servants knocking excitedly, and my door opened, and the dear Porthos I had mourned so long tore in. They had heard his bark, but whence he came no one knew. He was in excellent condition, and after he had leaped upon me from all points I flung him on the floor by a trick I know, and lay down beside him, while he put his protecting arm round me, and looked at me with the old adoring eyes.

But we never saw Paterson again. You may think as you choose.

TWENTY-TWO

Joey

WISE CHILDREN ALWAYS choose a mother who was a shocking flirt in her maiden days, and so had several offers before she accepted their fortunate papa. The reason they do this is because every offer refused by their mother means another pantomime to them. You see you can't trust to your father's taking you to the pantomime, but you can trust to every one of the poor frenzied gentlemen for whom that lady has wept a delicious little tear on her lovely little cambric handkerchief. It is pretty (but dreadfully affecting) to see them on Boxing Night gathering together the babies of their old loves. Some knock at but one door and bring a hansom, but others go from street to street in private 'buses, and even wear false noses to conceal the sufferings you inflict upon them as you grow more and more like your sweet, cruel mamma.

So I took David to the pantomime, and I hope you follow my reasoning, for I don't. He went with the fairest anticipations, pausing on the threshold to peer through the hole in the little house called 'Pay Here,' which he thought was Red Riding Hood's residence, and asked politely whether he might see her, but they said she had gone to the wood; and it was quite true, for there she was in the wood gathering a stick for her grandmother's fire. She sang a beautiful song about the Boys and their dashing ways, which flattered David considerably, but she forgot to take away the stick after all. Other parts of the play were not so nice, but David thought it all lovely, he really did.

Yet he left the place in tears. All the way home he sobbed

in the darkest corner of the growler, and if I tried to comfort him he struck me.

The clown had done it, that man of whom he expected things so fair. He had asked in a loud voice of the middling funny gentleman (then in the middle of a song) whether he thought Joey would be long in coming, and when at last Joey did come he screamed out, 'How do you do, Joey!' and went into convulsions of mirth.

Joey and his father were shadowing a pork-butcher's shop, pocketing the sausages for which their family has such a fatal weakness, and so when the butcher engaged Joey as his assistant there was soon not a sausage left. However, this did not matter, for there was a box rather like an ice-cream machine, and you put chunks of pork in at one end and turned a handle, and they came out as sausages at the other end. Joey quite enjoyed doing this, and you could see that the sausages were excellent by the way he licked his fingers after touching them, but soon there were no more pieces of pork; and just then a dear little Irish terrier-dog came trotting down the street, so what did Joey do but pop it into the machine, and it came out at the other end as sausages.

It was this callous act that turned all David's mirth to woe, and drove us weeping to our growler.

Heaven knows I have no wish to defend this cruel deed, but as Joey told me afterwards, it is very difficult to say what they will think funny and what barbarous. I was forced to admit to him that David had perceived only the joyous in the pokering of the policeman's legs, and had called out heartily 'Do it again!' every time Joey knocked the pantaloon down with one kick and helped him up with another.

'It hurts the poor chap,' I was told by Joey, whom I was agreeably surprised to find by no means wanting in the more humane feelings, 'and he wouldn't stand it if there wasn't the laugh to encourage him.'

He maintained that the dog got that laugh to encourage him also.

However, he had not got it from David, whose mother and father and nurse combined could not comfort him, though they swore that the dog was still alive and kicking, which might all have been very well had not David seen the sausages. It was to inquire whether anything could be done to atone that in considerable trepidation I sent in my card to the clown, and the result of our talk was that he invited me and David to have tea with him on Thursday next at his lodgings.

'I shan't laugh,' David said, nobly true to the memory of the little dog, 'I shan't laugh once,' and he closed his jaws very tightly as we drew near the house in Soho where Joey lodged. But he also gripped my hand, like one who knew that it would be an ordeal not to laugh.

The house was rather like the ordinary kind, but there was a convenient sausage-shop exactly opposite (trust Joey for that), and we saw a policeman in the street looking the other way, as they always do look just before you rub them. A woman wearing the same kind of clothes as people in other houses wear told us to go up to the second floor, and she grinned at David, as if she had heard about him. So up we went, David muttering through his clenched teeth, 'I shan't laugh'; and as soon as we knocked a voice called out, 'Here we are again!' at which a shudder passed through David as if he feared that he had set himself an impossible task. In we went, however, and though the voice had certainly come from this room we found nobody there. I looked in bewilderment at David, and he quickly put his hand over his mouth.

It was a funny room, of course, but not so funny as you might expect; there were droll things in it, but they did nothing funny – you could see that they were just waiting for Joey. There were padded chairs with friendly-looking rents down the middle of them, and a table and a horse-hair sofa, and we sat down very cautiously on the sofa but nothing happened to us.

The biggest piece of furniture was an enormous wicker trunk, with a very lively-coloured stocking dangling out at a hole in it, and a notice on the top that Joey was the funniest man on earth. David tried to pull the stocking out of the hole, but it was so long that it never came to an end, and when it measured six times the length of the room he had to cover his mouth again.

'I'm not laughing,' he said to me, quite fiercely. He even managed not to laugh (though he did gulp) when we discovered on the mantelpiece a photograph of Joey in ordinary clothes, the garments he wore before he became a clown. You can't think how absurd he looked in them. But David didn't laugh.

Suddenly Joey was standing beside us; it could not have been more sudden though he had come from beneath the table; and he was wearing his pantomime clothes (which he told us afterwards were the only clothes he had), and his red-and-white face was so funny that David made gurgling sounds, which were his laugh trying to force a passage.

I introduced David, who offered his hand stiffly; but Joey, instead of taking it, put out his tongue and waggled it, and this was so droll that David had again to save himself by clapping his hand over his mouth. Joey thought he had toothache, so I explained what it really meant, and then Joey said, 'Oh, I shall soon make him laugh,' whereupon the following conversation took place between them:

'No, you shan't,' said David doggedly.

'Yes, I shall.'

'No, you shan't not.'

'Yes, I shall so.'

'Shan't, shan't, shan't.'

'Shall, shall, shall.'

'You shut up.'

'You're another.'

By this time Joey was in a frightful wax (because he saw he was getting the worst of it); and he boasted that he had David's laugh in his pocket, and David challenged him to produce it, and Joey searched his pockets and brought out the most unexpected articles, including a duck and a bunch of carrots; and you could see by his manner that the simple soul thought these were things which all boys carried loose in their pockets.

I dare say David would have had to laugh in the end, had there not been a half-gnawed sausage in one of the pockets, and the sight of it reminded him so cruelly of the poor dog's fate that he howled; and Joey's heart was touched at last, and he also wept, but he wiped his eyes with the duck.

It was at this touching moment that the pantaloon hobbled in, also dressed as we had seen him last, and carrying, unfortunately, a trayful of sausages, which at once increased the general gloom, for he announced, in his squeaky voice, that they were the very sausages that had lately been the dog.

Then Joey seemed to have a great idea, and his excitement was so impressive that we stood gazing at him. First, he counted the sausages, and said that they were two short, and he found the missing two up the pantaloon's sleeve. Then he ran out of the room and came back with the sausage-machine; and what do you think he did? He put all the sausages into the end of the machine that they had issued from, and turned the handle backwards, and then out came the dog at the other end!

Can you picture the joy of David?

He clasped the dear little terrier in his arms; and then we noticed that there was a sausage adhering to its tail. The pantaloon said we must have put in a sausage too many, but Joey said the machine had not worked quite smoothly, and that he feared this sausage was the dog's bark, which distressed David, for he saw how awkward it must be to a dog to have its bark outside; and we were considering what should be done when the dog closed the discussion by swallowing the sausage.

After that, David had the most hilarious hour of his life, entering into the childish pleasures of this family as heartily as if he had been brought up on sausages, and knocking the pantaloon down repeatedly. You must not think that he did this viciously; he did it to please the old gentleman, who begged him to do it, and always shook hands warmly and said, 'Thank you,' when he had done it. They are quite a simple people.

Joey called David and me 'Sonny,' and asked David, who addressed him as 'Mr Clown,' to call him Joey. He also told us that the pantaloon's name was old Joey, and the co-lumbine's Josy, and the harlequin's Joeykin.

We were sorry to hear that old Joey gave him a good deal of trouble. This was because his memory is so bad that he often forgets whether it is your head or your feet you should stand on, and he usually begins the day by standing on the end that happens to get out of bed first. Thus he requires constant watching; and the worst of it is, you dare not draw attention to his mistake, he is so shrinkingly sensitive about it. No sooner had Joey told us this than the poor old fellow began to turn upside down and stood on his head; but we pretended not to notice, and talked about the weather till he came to.

Josy and Joeykin, all skirts and spangles, were with us by this time, for they had been invited to tea. They came in dancing, and danced off and on most of the time. Even in the middle of what they were saying they would begin to flutter; it was not so much that they meant to dance as that the slightest thing set them going, such as sitting in a draught; and David found he could blow them about the room like pieces of paper. You could see by the shortness of Josy's dress that she was very young indeed; and at first this made him shy, as he always is when introduced formally to little girls, and he stood sucking his thumb, and so did she;

but soon the stiffness wore off, and they sat together on the sofa holding each other's hands.

All this time the harlequin was rotating like a beautiful fish, and David requested him to jump through the wall, at which he is such an adept; and first he said he would, and then he said better not, for the last time he did it the people in the next house had made such a fuss. David had to admit that it must be rather startling to the people on the other side of the wall, but he was sorry.

By this time tea was ready, and Josy, who poured out, remembered to ask if you took milk with just one drop of tea in it, exactly as her mother would have asked. There was nothing to eat, of course, except sausages, but what a number of them there were! hundreds at least, strings of sausages, and every now and then Joey jumped up and played skipping-rope with them. David had been taught not to look greedy, even though he felt greedy, and he was shocked to see the way in which Joey and old Joey and even Josy eyed the sausages they had given him. Soon Josy developed nobler feelings, for she and Joeykin suddenly fell madly in love with each other across the table; but, unaffected by this pretty picture, Joey continued to put whole sausages in his mouth at a time, and then rubbed himself a little lower down, while old Joey secreted them about his person; and when David wasn't looking they both pounced on his sausages, and yet as they gobbled they were constantly running to the top of the stair, and screaming to the servant to bring up more sausages.

You could see that Joey (if you caught him with his hand in your plate) was a bit ashamed of himself, and he admitted to us that sausages were a passion with him.

He said he had never once in his life had a sufficient number of sausages. They had maddened him since he was the smallest boy. He told us how, even in those days, his mother had feared for him, though fond of a sausage herself; how he had bought a sausage with his first penny, and hoped to buy one with his last (if they could not be got in any other way), and that he always slept with a string of them beneath his pillow.

While he was giving us these confidences, unfortunately, his eyes came to rest, at first accidentally, then wistfully, then with a horrid gleam in them, on the little dog, which was fooling about on the top of the sausage-machine, and his hands went out towards it convulsively; whereat David, in sudden fear, seized the dog in one arm and gallantly clenched his other fist, and then Joey begged his pardon and burst into tears, each one of which he flung against the wall, where it exploded with a bang.

David refused to pardon him unless he promised on wood never to look in that way at the dog again, but Joey said promises were nothing to him when he was short of sausages, and so his wisest course would be to present the dog to David. O the joy of David when he understood that the little dog he had saved was his very own! I can tell you he was now in a hurry to be off before Joey had time to change his mind.

'All I ask of you,' Joey said with a break in his voice, 'is to call him after me, and always to give him a sausage, sonny, of a Saturday night.'

There was a quiet dignity about Joey at the end, which showed that he might have risen to high distinction but for his fatal passion.

The last we saw of him was from the street. He was waving his tongue at us in his attractive, foolish way, and Josy was poised on Joeykin's hand like a butterfly that had alighted on a flower. We could not exactly see old Joey, but we saw his feet, and so feared the worst. Of course they are not everything they should be, but one can't help liking them.

TWENTY-THREE

Pilkington's

ON ATTAINING THE age of eight, or thereabout, children fly away from the Gardens, and never come back. When next you meet them they are ladies and gentlemen holding up their umbrellas to hail a hansom.

Where the girls go to I know not – to some private place, I suppose, to put up their hair, – but the boys have gone to Pilkington's. He is a man with a cane. You may not go to Pilkington's in knickerbockers made by your mother, make she ever so artfully. They must be real knickerbockers. It is his stern rule. Hence the fearful fascination of Pilkington's.

He may be conceived as one who, baiting his hook with real knickerbockers, fishes all day in the Gardens, which are to him but a pool swarming with small fry.

Abhorred shade! I know not what manner of man thou art in the flesh, sir, but figure thee bearded and blackavised, and of a lean, tortuous habit of body, that moves ever with a swish. Every morning, I swear, thou readest avidly the list of male births in thy paper, and then are thy hands rubbed gloatingly the one upon the other. 'Tis fear of thee and thy gown and thy cane, which are part of thee, that makes the fairies to hide by day; wert thou to linger but once among their haunts between the hours of Lock-out and Open Gates there would be left not one single gentle place in all the Gardens. The little people would flit. How much wiser they than the small boys who swim glamoured to thy crafty hook. Thou devastator of the Gardens, I know thee, Pilkington.

I first heard of Pilkington from David, who had it from Oliver Bailey.

This Oliver Bailey was one of the most dashing figures in the Gardens, and without apparent effort was daily drawing nearer the completion of his seventh year at a time when David seemed unable to get beyond half-past five. I have to speak of him in the past tense, for gone is Oliver from the Gardens (gone to Pilkington's), but he is still a name among us, and some lordly deeds are remembered of him, as that his father shaved twice a day. Oliver himself was all on that scale.

His not ignoble ambition seems always to have been to be wrecked upon an island – indeed I am told that he mentioned it insinuatingly in his prayers, – and it was perhaps inevitable that a boy with such an outlook should fascinate David. I am proud therefore to be able to state on wood that it was Oliver himself who made the overture.

On first hearing, from some satellite of Oliver's, of Wrecked Islands, as they are called in the Gardens, David said wistfully that he supposed you needed to be very, very good before you had any chance of being wrecked, and the remark was conveyed to Oliver, on whom it made an uncomfortable impression. For a time he tried to evade it, but ultimately David was presented to him and invited gloomily to say it again. The upshot was that Oliver advertised the Gardens of his intention to be good until he was eight, and if he had not been wrecked by that time, to be as jolly bad as a boy could be. He was naturally so bad that at the Kindergarten Academy, when the mistress ordered whoever had done the last naughty deed to step forward, Oliver's custom had been to step forward, not necessarily because he had done it, but because he presumed he very likely had.

The friendship of the two dated from this time, and at first I thought Oliver discovered generosity in hasting to David as to an equal; he also walked hand in hand with him, and even reproved him for delinquencies like a loving elder brother. But 'tis a grey world even in the Gardens, for I found that a new arrangement had been made which reduced Oliver to life-size. He had wearied of well-doing, and passed it on, so to speak, to his friend. In other words, on David now devolved the task of being good until he was eight, while Oliver clung to him so closely that the one could not be wrecked without the other.

When this was made known to me it was already too late to break the spell of Oliver, David was top-heavy with pride in him; and, faith, I began to find myself very much in the cold, for Oliver was frankly bored by me, and even David seemed to think it would be convenient if I went and sat with Irene. Am I affecting to laugh? I was really distressed and lonely, and rather bitter; and how humble I became. Sometimes when the dog Joey is unable, by frisking, to induce Porthos to play with him, he stands on his hind legs and begs it of him, and I do believe I was sometimes as humble as Joey. Then David would insist on my being suffered to join them, but it was plain that he had no real occasion for me.

It was an unheroic trouble, and I despised myself. For years I had been fighting Mary for David, and had not wholly failed, though she was advantaged by the accident of relationship; was I now to be knocked out so easily by a seven-year-old? I reconsidered my weapons, and I fought Oliver and beat him. Figure to yourself those two boys become as faithful to me as my coat-tails.

With wrecked islands I did it. I began in the most unpretentious way by telling them a story which might last an hour, and favoured by many an unexpected wind it lasted eighteen months. It started as the wreck of the simple Swiss family who looked up and saw the butter-tree, but soon a glorious inspiration of the night turned it into the wreck of David A—— and Oliver Bailey. At first it was what they were to do when they were wrecked, but imperceptibly it became what they had done. I spent much of my time staring reflectively at the titles of the boys' stories in the booksellers' windows, whistling for a breeze, so to say, for I found that the titles were even more helpful than the stories. We wrecked everybody of note, including all Homer's most taking characters and the hero of *Paradise Lost*. But we suffered them not to land. We stripped them of what we wanted, and left them to wander the high seas naked of adventure. And all this was merely the beginning.

By this time I had been cast upon the island. It was not my own proposal, but David knew my wishes, and he made it all right for me with Oliver. They found me among the breakers with a large dog, which had kept me afloat throughout that terrible night. I was the sole survivor of the ill-fated *Anna Pink*. So exhausted was I that they had to carry me to their hut, and great was my gratitude when on opening my eyes I found myself in that romantic edifice instead of in Davy Jones's locker. As we walked in the Gardens I told them of the hut they had built; and they were inflated but not surprised. On the other hand they looked for surprise from me.

'Did we tell you about the eggs we found in the sand?' asked Oliver, reverting to deeds of theirs of which I had previously told them.

'You did.'

'Who found them?' demanded David, not as one who needed information, but after the manner of a schoolmaster.

'They were found,' I said, 'by David A——, the younger of the two youths.'

'Who stabbed the wild pig?' asked the older of the two youths.

'Oliver Bailey,' I replied.

'Was it Oliver,' asked David sharply, 'that found the cocoa-nut tree first?'

'On the contrary,' I answered, 'it was first observed by David, who immediately climbed it, remarking, "This is certainly the *cocos nucifera*, for, see, dear Oliver, the slender columns supporting the crown of leaves, which fall with a grace that no art can imitate." '

'That's what I said,' remarked David with a wave of his hand.

'I said things like that too,' Oliver insisted.

'No, you didn't then,' said David.

'Yes, I did so.'

'No, you didn't so.'

'Shut up.'

'Well, then, let's hear one you said.'

Oliver looked appealingly at me. 'The following,' I announced, 'is one that Oliver said: "Truly, dear comrade, though the perils of these happenings are great, and our privations calculated to break the stoutest heart, yet to be rewarded by such fair sights I would endure still greater trials, and still rejoice even as the bird on yonder bough." '

'That's one I said!' crowed Oliver.

'I shot the bird,' said David instantly.

'What bird?'

'The yonder bird.'

'No, you didn't.'

'Did I not shoot the bird?'

'It was David who shot the bird,' I said, 'but it was Oliver who saw by its multi-coloured plumage that it was one of the *Psittacidæ*, an excellent substitute for partridge.'

'You didn't see that,' said Oliver, rather swollen.

'Yes, I did.'

'What did you see?'

'I saw that?'

'What?'

'You shut up.'

'David shot it,' I summed up, 'and Oliver knew its name, but I ate it. Do you remember how hungry I was?'

'Rather!' said David.

'I cooked it,' said Oliver.

'It was served up on toast,' I reminded them.

'I toasted it,' said David.

'Toast from the bread-fruit tree,' I said, 'which (as you both remarked simultaneously) bears two and sometimes three crops in a year, and also affords a serviceable gum for the pitching of canoes.'

'I pitched mine best,' said Oliver.

'I pitched mine farthest,' said David.

'And when I had finished my repast,' said I, 'you amazed me by handing me a cigar from the tobacco-plant.'

'I handed it,' said Oliver.

'I snicked off the end,' said David.

'And then,' said I, 'you gave me a light.'

'Which of us?' they cried together.

'Both of you,' I said. 'Never shall I forget my amazement when I saw you get that light by striking two stones together.'

At this they waggled their heads. 'You couldn't have done it!' said David.

'No, David,' I admitted, 'I can't do it, but of course I know that all wrecked boys do it quite easily. Show me how you did it.'

But after consulting apart they agreed not to show me. I was not shown everything.

David was now firmly convinced that he had once been wrecked on an island, while Oliver passed his days in dubiety. They used to argue it out together, and among their friends. As I unfolded the story Oliver listened with an open knife in his hand, and David, who was not allowed to have a knife, wore a pirate-string round his waist. Irene, in her usual interfering way, objected to this bauble, and dropped disparaging remarks about wrecked islands which were little to her credit. I was for defying her, but David, who had the knack of women, knew a better way; he craftily proposed that we 'should let Irene in,' in short, should wreck her, and though I objected, she proved a great success and recognised the *yucca filamentosa* by its long narrow leaves the very day she joined us. Thereafter we had no more scoffing from Irene, who listened to the story as hotly as anybody.

This encouraged us in time to let in David's father and mother, though they never knew it unless he told them, as I have no doubt he did. They were admitted primarily to gratify David, who was very soft-hearted, and knew that while he was on the island they must be missing him very much at home. So we let them in, and there was no part of the story he liked better than that which told of the joyous meeting. We were in need of another woman at any rate, some one more romantic-looking than Irene, and Mary, I can assure her now, had a busy time of it. She was constantly being carried off by cannibals, and David became quite an adept at plucking her from the very pot itself and springing from cliff to cliff with his lovely burden in his arms. There was seldom a Saturday in which David did not kill his man.

I shall now provide the proof that David believed it all to be as true as true. It was told me by Oliver, who had it from our hero himself. I had described to them how the savages had tattooed David's father, and Oliver informed me that one night shortly afterwards David was discovered softly lifting the blankets off his father's legs to have a look at the birds and reptiles etched thereon.

Thus many months passed with no word of Pilkington, and you may be asking where he was all this time. Ah, my friends, he was very busy fishing, though I was as yet unaware of his existence. Most suddenly I heard the whir of his hated reel, as he struck a fish. I remember that grim day with painful vividness; it was a wet day, indeed I think it has rained for me more or less ever since. As soon as they joined me I saw from the manner of the two boys that they had something to communicate. Oliver nudged David and retired a few paces, whereupon David said to me solemnly:

'Oliver is going to Pilkington's.'

I immediately perceived that it was some school, but so little did I understand the import of David's remark that I called out jocularly, 'I hope he won't swish you, Oliver.'

Evidently I had pained both of them, for they exchanged glances and retired for consultation behind a tree, whence David returned to say with emphasis:

'He has two jackets and two shirts and two knickerbockers, *all real ones.*'

'Well done, Oliver!' said I, but it was the wrong thing again, and once more they disappeared behind the tree. Evidently they decided that the time for plain speaking was come, for now David announced bluntly:

'He wants you not to call him Oliver any longer.'

'What shall I call him?'

'Bailey.'

'But why?'

'He's going to Pilkington's. And he can't play with us any more after next Saturday.'

'Why not?'

'He's going to Pilkington's.'

So now I knew the law about the thing, and we moved on together, Oliver stretching himself consciously, and methought that even David walked with a sedater air.

'David,' said I, with a sinking, 'are you going to Pilkington's?'

'When I am eight,' he replied.

'And shan't I call you David then, and won't you play with me in the Gardens any more?'

He looked at Bailey, and Bailey signalled him to be firm.

'Oh no,' said David cheerily.

Thus sharply did I learn how much longer I was to have of him. Strange that a little boy can give so much pain. I dropped his hand and walked on in silence, and presently I did my most churlish to hurt him by ending the story abruptly in a very cruel way. 'Ten years have elapsed,' said

I, 'since I last spoke, and our two heroes, now gay young men, are revisiting the wrecked island of their childhood. "Did we wreck ourselves," said one, "or was there some one to help us?" And the other, who was the younger, replied, "I think there was some one to help us, a man with a dog. I think he used to tell me stories in the Kensington Gardens, but I forget all about him; I don't remember even his name." '

This tame ending bored Bailey, and he drifted away from us, but David still walked by my side, and he was grown so quiet that I knew a storm was brewing. Suddenly he flashed lightning on me. 'It's not true,' he cried, 'it's a lie!' He gripped my hand. 'I shan't never forget you, father.'

Strange that a little boy can give so much pleasure.

Yet I could go on. 'You will forget, David, but there was once a boy who would have remembered.'

'Timothy?' said he at once. He thinks Timothy was a real boy, and he is very jealous of him. He turned his back to me, and stood alone and wept passionately, while I waited for him. You may be sure I begged his pardon, and made it all right with him, and had him laughing and happy again before I let him go. But nevertheless what I said was true. David is not my boy, and he will forget. But Timothy would have remembered.

TWENTY-FOUR

Barbara

ANOTHER SHOCK WAS waiting for me farther down the story.

For we had resumed our adventures, though we seldom saw Bailey now. At long intervals we met him on our way to or from the Gardens, and, if there was none from Pilkington's to mark him, methought he looked at us somewhat longingly, as if beneath his real knickerbockers a morsel of the egg-shell still adhered. Otherwise he gave David a not unfriendly kick in passing, and called him 'youngster.' That was about all.

When Oliver disappeared from the life of the Gardens we had lofted him out of the story, and did very well without him, extending our operations to the mainland, where they were on so vast a scale that we were rapidly depopulating the earth. And then said David one day:

'Shall we let Barbara in?'

We had occasionally considered the giving of Bailey's place to some other child of the Gardens, divers of David's year having sought election, even with bribes; but Barbara was new to me.

'Who is she?' I asked.

'She's my sister.'

You may imagine how I gaped.

'She hasn't come yet,' David said lightly, 'but she's coming.'

I was shocked, not perhaps so much shocked as disillusioned, for though I had always suspicioned Mary A——— as one who harboured the craziest ambitions when she looked most humble, of such presumption as this I had never thought her capable.

I wandered across the Broad Walk to have a look at Irene, and she was wearing an unmistakable air. It set me reflecting about Mary's husband and his manner the last time we met, for though I have had no opportunity to say so, we still meet now and again, and he has even dined with me at the club. On these occasions the subject of Timothy is barred, and if by any unfortunate accident Mary's name is mentioned, we immediately look opposite ways and a silence follows, in which I feel sure he is smiling, and wonder what the deuce he is smiling at. I remembered now that I had last seen him when I was dining with him at his club (for he is become member of a club of painter fellows, and Mary is so proud of this that she has had it printed on his card), when undoubtedly he had looked preoccupied. It had been the look, I saw now, of one who shared a guilty secret.

As all was thus suddenly revealed to me I laughed unpleasantly at myself, for, on my soul, I had been thinking well of Mary of late. Always foolishly inflated about David, she had been grudging him even to me during these last weeks, and I had forgiven her, putting it down to a mother's love. I knew from the poor boy of unwonted treats she had been giving him; I had seen her embrace him furtively in a public place; her every act, in so far as they were known to me, had been a challenge to whoever dared assert that she wanted any one but David. How could I, not being a woman, have guessed that she was really saying good-bye to him?

Reader, picture to yourself that simple little boy playing about the house at this time, on the understanding that everything was going on as usual. Have not his toys acquired a new pathos, especially the engine she bought him yesterday?

Did you look him in the face, Mary, as you gave him that

engine? I envy you not your feelings, ma'am, when with loving arms he wrapped you round for it. That childish confidence of his to me, in which unwittingly he betrayed you, indicates that at last you have been preparing him for the great change, and I suppose you are capable of replying to me that David is still happy, and even interested. But does he know from you what it really means to him? Rather, I do believe, you are one who would not scruple to give him to understand that B (which you may yet find stands for Benjamin) is primarily a gift for him. In your heart, ma'am, what do you think of this tricking of a little boy?

Suppose David had known what was to happen before he came to you, are you sure he would have come? Undoubtedly there is an unwritten compact in such matters between a mother and her first-born, and I desire to point out to you that he never breaks it. Again, what will the other boys say when they know? You are outside the criticism of the Gardens, but David is not. Faith, madam, I believe you would have been kinder to wait and let him run the gauntlet at Pilkington's.

You think your husband is a great man now because they are beginning to talk of his foregrounds and middle distances in the newspaper columns that nobody reads. I know you have bought him a velvet coat, and that he has taken a large, airy, and commodious studio in Mews Lane, where you are to be found in a soft material on first and third Wednesdays. Times are changing, but shall I tell you a story here, just to let you see that I am acquainted with it?

Three years ago a certain gallery accepted from a certain artist a picture which he and his wife knew to be monstrous fine. But no one spoke of the picture, no one wrote of it, and no one made an offer for it. Crushed was the artist, sorry for the denseness of connoisseurs was his wife, till the work was bought by a dealer for an anonymous client, and then elated were they both, and relieved also to discover that I was not the buyer. He came to me at once to make sure of this, and remained to walk the floor gloriously as he told me what recognition means to gentlemen of the artistic callings. O the happy boy!

But months afterwards, rummaging at his home in a closet that is usually kept locked, he discovered the picture, there hidden away. His wife backed into a corner and made trembling confession. How could she submit to see her dear's masterpiece ignored by the idiot public, and her dear himself plunged into gloom thereby? She knew as well as he (for had they not been married for years?) how the artistic instinct hungers for recognition, and so with her savings she bought the great work anonymously, and stored it away in a closet. At first, I believe, the man raved furiously, but by and by he was on his knees at the feet of this little darling. You know who she was, Mary, – but, bless me! I seem to be praising you, and that was not the enterprise on which I set out. What I intended to convey was that though you can now venture on small extravagances, you seem to be going too fast. Look at it how one may, this Barbara idea is undoubtedly a bad business.

How to be even with her? I cast about for a means, and on my lucky day I did conceive my final triumph over Mary, at which I have scarcely as yet dared to hint, lest by discovering it I should spoil my plot. For there has been a plot all the time.

For long I had known that Mary contemplated the writing of a book, my informant being David, who, because I have published a little volume on Military tactics, and am preparing a larger one on the same subject (which I shall never finish), likes to watch my methods of composition, how I dip, and so on, his desire being to help her. He may have done this on his own initiative, but it is also quite possible that in her desperation she urged him to it; he certainly implied that she had taken to book-writing because it must be easy if I could do it. She also informed him (very inconsiderately) that I did not print my books myself, and this lowered me in the eyes of David, for it was for the printing he had admired me and boasted of me in the Gardens.

'I suppose you didn't make the boxes neither, nor yet the labels,' he said to me in the voice of one shorn of belief in everything.

I should say here that my literary labours are abstruse, the token whereof is many rows of boxes nailed against my walls, each labelled with a letter of the alphabet. When I take a note in *A*, I drop it into the *A* box, and so on, much to the satisfaction of David, who likes to drop them in for me. I had now to admit that Wheeler & Gibb made the boxes.

'But I made the labels myself, David.'

'They are not so well made as the boxes,' he replied.

Thus I had reason to wish ill to Mary's work of imagination, as I presumed it to be, and I said to him with easy brutality, 'Tell her about the boxes, David, and that no one can begin a book until they are all full. That will frighten her.'

Soon thereafter he announced to me that she had got a box.

'One box!' I said with a sneer.

'She made it herself,' retorted David hotly.

I got little real information from him about the work, partly because David loses his footing when he descends to the practical, and perhaps still more because he found me unsympathetic. But when he blurted out the title, 'The Little White Bird,' I was like one who had read the book to its last page. I knew at once that the white bird was the little daughter Mary would fain have had. Somehow I had always known that she would like to have a little daughter; she was that kind of woman; and so long as she had the modesty to see that she could not have one, I sympathised with her deeply, whatever I may have said about her book to David.

In those days Mary had the loveliest ideas for her sad little book, and they came to her mostly in the morning when she was only three-parts awake, but as she stepped out of bed they all flew away like startled birds. I gathered from David that this depressed her exceedingly.

O Mary, your thoughts are much too pretty and holy to show themselves to any one but yourself! The shy things are hiding within you. If they could come into the open they would not be a book, they would be little Barbara.

But that was not the message I sent her. 'She will never be able to write it,' I explained to David. 'She has not the ability. Tell her I said that.'

I remembered now that for many months I had heard nothing of her ambitious project, so I questioned David and discovered that it was abandoned. He could not say why, nor was it necessary that he should, the trivial little reason was at once so plain to me. From that moment all my sympathy with Mary was spilled, and I searched for some means of exulting over her until I found it. It was this. I decided, unknown even to David, to write the book, 'The Little White Bird,' of which she had proved herself incapable, and then when, in the fulness of time, she held her baby on high, implying that she had done a big thing, I was to hold up the book. I venture to think that such a devilish revenge was never before planned and carried out.

Yes, carried out, for this is the book, rapidly approaching completion. She and I are running a neck-and-neck race.

I have also once more brought the story of David's adventures to an abrupt end. 'And it really is the end this time, David,' I said severely. (I always say that.)

It ended on the coast of Patagonia, whither we had gone to shoot the great Sloth, known to be the largest of animals, though we found his size to have been under-estimated. David, his father, and I had flung our limbs upon the beach and were having a last pipe before turning in, while Mary, attired in barbaric splendour, sang and danced before us. It was a lovely evening, and we lolled man-like, gazing, well content, at the pretty creature.

The night was absolutely still save for the roaring of the Sloths in the distance.

By and by Irene came to the entrance of our cave, where by the light of her torch we could see her exploring a shark that had been harpooned by David earlier in the day.

Everything conduced to repose, and a feeling of gentle peace crept over us, from which we were roused by a shrill cry. It was uttered by Irene, who came speeding to us, bearing certain articles, a watch, a pair of boots, a newspaper, which she had discovered in the interior of the shark. What was our surprise to find in the newspaper intelligence of the utmost importance to all of us. It was nothing less than this, the birth of a new baby in London to Mary.

How strange a method had Solomon chosen of sending us the news.

The bald announcement at once plunged us into a fever of excitement, and next morning we set sail for England. Soon we came within sight of the white cliffs of Albion. Mary could not sit down for a moment, so hot was she to see her child. She paced the deck in uncontrollable agitation.

'So did I!' cried David, when I had reached this point in the story.

On arriving at the docks we immediately hailed a cab.

'Never, David,' I said, 'shall I forget your mother's excitement. She kept putting her head out of the window and calling to the cabby to go quicker, quicker. How he lashed his horse! At last he drew up at your house, and then your mother, springing out, flew up the steps and beat with her hands upon the door.'

David was quite carried away by the reality of it. 'Father has the key!' he screamed.

'He opened the door,' I said grandly, 'and your mother rushed in, and next moment her Benjamin was in her arms.'

There was a pause.

'Barbara,' corrected David.

'Benjamin,' said I doggedly.

'Is that a girl's name?'

'No, it's a boy's name.'

'But mother wants a girl,' he said, very much shaken.

'Just like her presumption,' I replied testily. 'It is to be a boy, David, and you can tell her I said so.'

He was in a deplorable but most unselfish state of mind. A boy would have suited him quite well, but he put self aside altogether and was pertinaciously solicitous that Mary should be given her fancy.

'Barbara,' he repeatedly implored me.

'Benjamin,' I replied firmly.

For long I was obdurate, but the time was summer, and at last I agreed to play him for it, a two-innings match. If he won it was to be a girl, and if I won it was to be a boy.

TWENTY-FIVE

The Cricket Match

I THINK THERE has not been so much on a cricket match since the day when Sir Horace Mann walked about Broad Ha'penny agitatedly cutting down the daisies with his stick. And, be it remembered, the heroes of Hambledon played for money and renown only, while David was champion of a lady. A lady! May we not prettily say of two ladies? There were no spectators of our contest except now and again some loiterer in the Gardens who little thought what was the stake for which we played, but cannot we conceive Barbara standing at the ropes and agitatedly cutting down the daisies every time David missed the ball? I tell you, this was the historic match of the Gardens.

David wanted to play on a pitch near the Round Pond with which he is familiar, but this would have placed me at a disadvantage, so I insisted on unaccustomed ground, and we finally pitched stumps in the Figs. We could not exactly pitch stumps, for they are forbidden in the Gardens, but there are trees here and there which have chalkmarks on them throughout the summer, and when you take up your position with a bat near one of these you have really pitched stumps. The tree we selected is a ragged yew which consists of a broken trunk and one branch, and I viewed the ground with secret satisfaction, for it falls slightly at about four yards' distance from the tree, and this exactly suits my style of bowling.

I won the toss, and after examining the wicket decided to take first knock. As a rule when we play the wit at first flows free, but on this occasion I strode to the crease in an almost eerie silence. David had taken off his blouse and rolled up his shirt-sleeves, and his teeth were set, so I knew he would begin by sending me down some fast ones.

His delivery is under-arm and not inelegant, but he sometimes tries a round-arm ball, which I have seen double up the fielder at square leg. He has not a good length, but he varies his action bewilderingly, and has one especially teasing ball which falls from the branches just as you have stepped out of your ground to look for it. It was not, however, with his teaser that he bowled me that day. I had notched a three and two singles, when he sent me down a medium to fast, which got me in two minds, and I played back to it too late. Now, I am seldom out on a really grassy wicket for such a meagre score, and as David and I changed places without a word, there was a cheery look on his face that I found very galling. He ran in to my second ball and cut it neatly to the on for a single, and off my fifth and sixth he had two pretty drives for three, both behind the wicket. This, however, as I hoped, proved the undoing of him, for he now hit out confidently at everything, and with his score at nine I beat him with my shooter.

The look was now on my face.

I opened my second innings by treating him with uncommon respect, for I knew that his little arm soon tired if he was unsuccessful, and then when he sent me loose ones I banged him to the railings. What cared I though David's lips were twitching.

When he ultimately got past my defence, with a jumpy one which broke awkwardly from the off, I had fetched twenty-three, so that he needed twenty to win, a longer hand than he had ever yet made. As I gave him the bat he looked brave, but something wet fell on my hand, and then a sudden fear seized me lest David should not win.

At the very outset, however, he seemed to master the bowling, and soon fetched about ten runs in a classic manner. Then I tossed him a Yorker which he missed and it went off at a tangent as soon as it had reached the tree. 'Not out,' I cried hastily, for the face he turned to me was terrible.

Soon thereafter another incident happened, which I shall always recall with pleasure. He had caught the ball too high on the bat, and I just missed the catch. 'Dash it all!' said I irritably, and was about to resume bowling, when I noticed that he was unhappy. He hesitated, took up his position at the wicket, and then came to me manfully. 'I am a cad,' he said in distress, 'for when the ball was in the air I prayed.' He had prayed that I should miss the catch, and as I think I have already told you, it is considered unfair in the Gardens to pray for victory.

My splendid David! He has the faults of other little boys, but he has a noble sense of fairness. 'We shall call it a no-ball, David,' I said gravely.

I suppose the suspense of the reader is now painful, and therefore I shall say at once that David won the match with two lovely fours, the one over my head and the other to leg all along the ground. When I came back from fielding this last ball I found him embracing his bat, and to my sour congratulations he could at first reply only with hysterical sounds. But soon he was pelting home to his mother with the glorious news.

And that is how we let Barbara in.

TWENTY-SIX

The Dedication

IT WAS ONLY yesterday afternoon, dear reader, exactly three weeks after the birth of Barbara, that I finished the book, and even then it was not quite finished, for there remained the dedication, at which I set to elatedly. I think I have never enjoyed myself more; indeed, it is my opinion that I wrote the book as an excuse for writing the dedication.

'Madam,' I wrote wittily, 'I have no desire to exult over you, yet I should show a lamentable obtuseness to the irony of things were I not to dedicate this little work to you. For its inception was yours, and in your more ambitious days you thought to write the tale of the little white bird yourself. Why you so early deserted the nest is not for me to inquire. It now appears that you were otherwise occupied. In fine, madam, you chose the lower road, and contented yourself with obtaining the Bird. May I point out, by presenting you with this dedication, that in the meantime I am become the parent of the Book? To you the shadow, to me the substance. Trusting that you will accept my little offering in a Christian spirit, I am, dear madam,' etc.

It was heady work, for the saucy words showed their design plainly through the varnish, and I was re-reading in an ecstasy, when, without warning, the door burst open and a little boy entered, dragging in a faltering lady.

'Father,' said David, 'this is mother.'

Having thus briefly introduced us, he turned his attention to the electric light, and switched it on and off so rapidly that, as was very fitting, Mary and I may be said to have met for the first time to the accompaniment of flashes of lightning. I think she was arrayed in little blue feathers, but if such a costume is not seemly, I swear there were, at least, little blue feathers in her too coquettish cap, and that she was carrying a muff to match. No part of a woman is more dangerous than her muff, and as muffs are not worn in early autumn, even by invalids, I saw in a twink, that she had put on all her pretty things to wheedle me. I am also of opinion that she remembered she had worn blue in the days when I watched her from the club-window. Undoubtedly Mary is an engaging little creature, though not my style. She was paler than is her wont, and had the touching look of one whom it would be easy to break. I dare say this was a trick. Her skirts made music in my room, but perhaps this was only because no lady had ever rustled in it before. It was disquieting to me to reflect that despite her obvious uneasiness, she was a very artful woman.

With the quickness of David at the switch, I slipped a blotting-pad over the dedication, and then, 'Pray be seated,' I said coldly, but she remained standing, all in a twitter and very much afraid of me, and I know that her hands were pressed together within the muff. Had there been any dignified means of escape, I think we would both have taken it.

'I should not have come,' she said nervously, and then seemed to wait for some response, so I bowed.

'I was terrified to come, indeed I was,' she assured me with obvious sincerity.

'But I have come,' she finished rather baldly.

'It is an epitome, ma'am,' said I, seeing my chance, 'of your whole life,' and with that I put her into my elbow-chair.

She began to talk of my adventures with David in the Gardens, and of some little things I have not mentioned here, that I may have done for her when I was in a wayward mood, and her voice was as soft as her muff. She had also an affecting way of pronouncing all her *r*'s as *w*'s, just as the fairies do. 'And so,' she said, 'as you would not come to me to be thanked, I have come to you to thank you.' Whereupon she thanked me most abominably. She also slid one of her hands out of the muff, and though she was smiling her eyes were wet.

'Pooh, ma'am!' said I in desperation, but I did not take her hand.

'I am not very strong yet,' she said with low cunning. She said this to make me take her hand, so I took it, and perhaps I patted it a little. Then I walked brusquely to the window. The truth is, I was begun to think uncomfortably of the dedication.

I went to the window because, undoubtedly, it would be easier to address her severely from behind, and I wanted to say something that would sting her.

'When you have quite done, ma'am,' I said, after a long pause, 'perhaps you will allow me to say a word.'

I could see the back of her head only, but I knew from David's face that she had given him a quick look which did not imply that she was stung. Indeed I felt now, as I had felt before, that though she was agitated and in some fear of me, she was also enjoying herself considerably.

In such circumstances I might as well have tried to sting a sandbank, so I said, rather off my watch, 'If I have done all this for you, why did I do it?'

She made no answer in words, but seemed to grow taller in the chair, so that I could see her shoulders, and I knew from this that she was now holding herself conceitedly and trying to look modest. 'Not a bit of it, ma'am,' said I sharply, 'that was not the reason at all.'

I was pleased to see her whisk round, rather indignant at last.

'I never said it was,' she retorted with spirit, 'I never thought for a moment that it was.' She added, a trifle too late in the story, 'Besides, I don't know what you are talking of.'

I think I must have smiled here, for she turned from me quickly, and became quite little in the chair again.

'David,' said I mercilessly, 'did you ever see your mother blush?'

'What is blush?'

'She goes a beautiful pink colour.'

David, who had by this time broken my connection with the head office, crossed to his mother expectantly.

'I don't, David,' she cried.

'I think,' said I, 'she will do it now,' and with the instinct of a gentleman I looked away. Thus I cannot tell what happened, but presently David exclaimed admiringly, 'O mother, do it again!'

As she would not, he stood on the fender to see in the mantel-glass whether he could do it himself, and then Mary turned a most candid face on me, in which was maternity rather than reproach. Perhaps no look given by woman to man affects him quite so much. 'You see,' she said radiantly, and with a gesture that disclosed herself to me, 'I can forgive even that. You long ago earned the right to hurt me if you want to.'

It weaned me of all further desire to rail at Mary, and I felt an uncommon drawing to her.

'And if I did think *that* for a little while—,' she went on, with an unsteady smile.

'Think what?' I asked, but without the necessary snap.

'What we were talking of,' she replied wincing, but forgiving me again. 'If I once thought that, it was pretty to me while it lasted, and it lasted but a little time. I have long been sure that your kindness to me was due to some other reason.'

'Ma'am,' said I very honestly, 'I know not what was the reason. My concern for you was in the beginning a very fragile and even a selfish thing; yet not altogether selfish, for I think that what first stirred it was the joyous sway of the little nursery-governess as she walked down Pall Mall to meet her lover. It seemed such a mighty fine thing to you to be loved that I thought you had better continue to be loved for a little longer. And perhaps having helped you once by dropping a letter I was charmed by the ease with which you could be helped, for you must know that I am one who has chosen the easy way for more than twenty years.'

She shook her head and smiled. 'On my soul,' I assured her, 'I can think of no other reason.'

'A kind heart,' said she.

'More likely a whim,' said I.

'Or another woman,' said she.

I was very much taken aback.

'More than twenty years ago,' she said with a soft huskiness in her voice, and a tremor and a sweetness, as if she did not know that in twenty years all love-stories are grown mouldy.

On my honour as a soldier this explanation of my early solicitude for Mary was one that had never struck me, but the more I pondered it now – I raised her hand and touched it with my lips, as we whimsical old fellows do when some gracious girl makes us to hear the key in the lock of long ago. 'Why, ma'am,' I said, 'it is a pretty notion, and there may be something in it. Let us leave it at that.'

But there was still that accursed dedication, lying, you remember, beneath the blotting-pad. I had no longer any desire to crush her with it. I wished that she had succeeded in writing the book on which her longings had been so set.

'If only you had been less ambitious,' I said, much troubled that she should be disappointed in her heart's desire.

'I wanted all the dear delicious things,' she admitted contritely.

'It was unreasonable,' I said eagerly, appealing to her intellect. 'Especially this last thing.'

'Yes,' she agreed frankly, 'I know.' And then to my amazement she added triumphantly, 'But I got it.'

I suppose my look admonished her, for she continued apologetically, but still as if she really thought hers had been a romantic career, 'I know I have not deserved it, but I got it.'

'O ma'am!' I cried reproachfully, 'reflect. You have not got the great thing.' I saw her counting the great things in her mind, her wondrous husband and his obscure success, David, Barbara, and the other trifling contents of her jewel-box.

'I think I have,' said she.

'Come, madam,' I cried a little nettled, 'you know that there is lacking the one thing you craved for most of all.'

Will you believe me that I had to tell her what it was? And when I had told her, she exclaimed with extraordinary callousness, 'The book? I had forgotten all about the book!' And then after reflection she added, 'Pooh!' Had she not added Pooh! I might have spared her, but as it was I raised the blotting-pad rather haughtily and presented her with the sheet beneath it.

'What is this?' she asked.

'Ma'am,' said I, swelling, 'it is a Dedication,' and I walked majestically to the window.

There is no doubt that presently I heard an unexpected sound. Yet if indeed it had been a laugh she clipped it short, for in almost the same moment she was looking large-eyed at me, and tapping my sleeve impulsively with her fingers, just as David does when he suddenly likes you.

'How characteristic of you,' she said at the window.

'Characteristic,' I echoed uneasily. 'Ha!'

'And how kind.'

'Did you say kind, ma'am?'

'But it is I who have the substance and you who have the shadow, as you know very well,' said she.

Yes, I had always known that this was the one flaw in my dedication, but how could I have expected her to have the wit to see it? I was very depressed.

'And there is another mistake,' said she.

'Excuse me, ma'am, but that is the only one.'

'It was never of my little white bird I wanted to write,' she said.

I looked politely incredulous, and then indeed she overwhelmed me. 'It was of your little white bird,' she said; 'it was of a little boy whose name was Timothy.'

She had a very pretty way of saying Timothy, so David and I went into another room to leave her alone with the manuscript of this poor little book, and when we returned she had the greatest surprise of the day for me. She was both laughing and crying, which was no surprise, for all of us would laugh and cry over a book about such an interesting subject as ourselves; but said she, 'How wrong you are in thinking this book is about me and mine, it is really all about Timothy.'

At first I deemed this to be uncommon nonsense, but as I considered I saw that she was probably right again, and I gazed crestfallen at this very clever woman.

'And so,' said she, clapping her hands after the manner of David when he makes a great discovery, 'it proves to be my book after all.'

'With all your pretty thoughts left out,' I answered, properly humbled.

She spoke in a lower voice, as if David must not hear. 'I had only one pretty thought for the book,' she said, 'I was to give it a happy ending.' She said this so timidly that I was about to melt to her when she added with extraordinary boldness, 'The little white bird was to bear an olive-leaf in its mouth.'

For a long time she talked to me earnestly of a grand scheme on which she had set her heart, and ever and anon she tapped on me as if to get admittance for her ideas. I listened respectfully, smiling at this young thing for carrying it so motherly to me, and in the end I had to remind her that I was forty-seven years of age.

'It is quite young for a man,' she said brazenly.

'My father,' said I, 'was not forty-seven when he died, and I remember thinking him an old man.'

'But you don't think so now, do you?' she persisted. 'You feel young occasionally, don't you? Sometimes when you are playing with David in the Gardens your youth comes swinging back, does it not?'

'Mary A———,' I cried, grown afraid of the woman, 'I forbid you to make any more discoveries today.'

But still she hugged her scheme, which I doubt not was what had brought her to my rooms. 'They are very dear women,' said she coaxingly.

'I am sure,' I said, 'they must be dear women if they are friends of yours.'

'They are not exactly young,' she faltered, 'and perhaps they are not very pretty—'

But she had been reading so recently about the darling of my youth that she halted abashed at last, feeling, I apprehend, a stop in her mind against proposing this thing to me, who, in those presumptuous days, had thought to be content with nothing less than the loveliest lady in all the land.

My thoughts had reverted also, and for the last time my eyes saw the little hut through the pine-wood haze. I met Mary there, and we came back to the present together.

I have already told you, reader, that this conversation took place no longer ago than yesterday.

'Very well, ma'am,' I said, trying to put a brave face on it, 'I will come to your tea-parties, and we shall see what we shall see.'

It was really all she had asked for, but now that she had got what she wanted of me the foolish soul's eyes became wet; she knew so well that the youthful romances are the best.

It was now my turn to comfort her. 'In twenty years,' I said, smiling at her tears, 'a man grows humble, Mary. I have stored within me a great fund of affection, with

nobody to give it to, and I swear to you, on the word of a
soldier, that if there is one of those ladies who can be got to
care for me I shall be very proud.' Despite her semblance of
delight I knew that she was wondering at me; and I
wondered at myself; but it was true.

p. 8   *Mary A———*: the name makes the autobiographical reference complicated. Mary A——— clearly suggests Barrie's wife Mary Ansell but as David's mother Mary A———is also a fictionalised Sylvia Llewelyn Davies. Mary and David are names that recur throughout Barrie's works and the Biblical allusions are deliberate. His final play, produced in 1936, was entitled *The Boy David*.

p. 12   *the peculiar pleasure this gives me*: in a notebook filled with records of his adventures with the Llewelyn Davies boys, Barrie wrote: 'The Boys disgrace one in shops by asking shopkeeper abt his most private affairs. Shopkeeper &c take me for their father (I affect rage).' Beinecke MS A2/19.

p. 14   *The Little Nursery Governess*: based on a story Barrie published in the *Speaker*, March 29, 1890.

p. 16   *louder than the others*: the laugh was based on that of Barrie's friend the novelist A.E.W. Mason, who re-emerges as one of the pirates in *Peter Pan*.

p. 33   *The only ghosts . . . their children fare*: the idea behind Barrie's play *Mary Rose* (1920), which features a mother who disappears on a Hebridean island and returns to her family as a ghost years later, not having aged, but unable to recognise her now fully-grown son.

p. 37   *Mary's poor pretentious babe*: originally 'Mary's brat' in the manuscript. The alteration to 'pretentious' emphasises the narrator's attempt to undermine Mary's creation.

p. 37   *But will a male child do as much for his father?* Autobiographically this is a rather callous joke at the expense of Arthur Llewelyn Davies who had wanted his fourth son, Michael, to be a girl. Michael was the first of the boys to be born after Barrie had become acquainted with the family and David is in part a fictionalised version of him as well as George.

       My St Bernard dog: Barrie's real St Bernard, also called Porthos, was purchased ostensibly for Mary Barrie in 1894. It was in exercising Porthos that Barrie first met the

Llewelyn Davies children in Kensington Gardens and the dog played a variety of roles in Barrie's dramas with the boys.

it will unman me: in the manuscript, Barrie's original version of this line reads: 'it will prove to be more than I can bear.' The alteration is of considerable importance in view of the transformation of Porthos in chapter 21.

p. 53   *The Inconsiderate Waiter*: this chapter is a condensed and slightly altered version of a short story Barrie published in the 1891 Christmas Number of the *Illustrated London News*. The original had been reprinted, against Barrie's wishes, in a number of unauthorised American editions of his work.

p. 64   *confirmed spinster*: a notebook entry records that Barrie planned to call the narrator Jocelyn, which would have made his femininity even more explicit. Jocelyn was also Sylvia Llewelyn Davies's middle name and the name by which Barrie always addressed her.

p. 65   *I first heard of my smile . . . placed mine on top*: this has an autobiographical basis. In a speech given at Dumfries Academy Barrie spoke of how he once won a prize from the girls of his school for the boy who had the sweetest smile in the school: 'The tragic thing was that my smile disappeared that day and has never been seen since.' See *McConnachie and J.M.B.* (1938), p.5.

p. 66   *lack of skill to seize her*: the manuscript has a deleted passage here which makes clear what the published version only implies, that the mysterious 'she' is an imaginary woman whom the narrator has created in his own mind: 'and then, I think, as your arms went out and fell without her you knew that she was to you as some dear girl imprisoned in a book who would come out of it to your arms if you could invent a way where only your lack of skill determined her.'

p. 71   *suddenly her lover died*: Barrie's sister, Maggie, had been engaged to a man in 1892 who died suddenly when he was thrown from a horse that Barrie had given to him as a gift. Maggie married her dead fiancé's brother a year later.

p. 72   *'They were all written to another woman . . . something in them about yourself'*: an echo of *Tommy and Grizel* (1900) where Tommy keeps a ready-made love-letter in his pocket should he ever need to use it.

p. 75   *legerdemain*: conjuring. David and the narrator's relationship is based on conjuring, tricks and story-telling.

p. 78   *famous manipulation of the eyebrows*: a trick with which Barrie regularly entertained George and his brothers.

p. 83   *Irene, in short, did not improve with acquaintance*: Mary Hodgson, the real nurse of the Llewelyn Davies family, resented Barrie's involvement with the boys.

p. 86   *I belonged to him*: The manuscript reads 'he belongs to me'.

p. 91   *Cecco Hewlett's Tree*: Cecco Hewlett was the son of the novelist Maurice Hewlett, and often accompanied Barrie on walks in the gardens. He re-emerges as the pirate Cecco in *Peter Pan*.

p. 92   *the Baby's Palace*: Kensington Palace, birthplace of Queen Victoria.

p. 94   *Angela Clare*: a possible allusion to Angel Clare, a character in Thomas Hardy's *Tess of the D'Urbervilles* (1891).
         yorkers: a yorker is a term for a ball in cricket that pitches at the batsman's feet.

p. 95   *cast anchor on coral isles*: an allusion to the most famous boys' story of the century, *The Coral Island* (1858) by R.M. Ballantyne.

p. 102   *Queen Mab's palace*: Queen Mab was midwife to the fairies and also their Queen.

p. 105   *a pipe of reeds*: along with his goat, Peter's pipes explicitly link him with the classical Pan, the Greek God of Nature.

p. 108   *He was a poet*: the reference to Shelley may have been prompted by the fact that the poet's first wife drowned herself in the Serpentine in December 1816.

p. 110   *all Kates are saucy*: probably prompted by the character in *The Taming of the Shrew*, a play that Barrie used as the basis for an unpublished play of his own called *The Ladies' Shakespeare* (1913) and a speech under the same name given to the Stationers' Company in 1925. Kate is also the name given to two characters who are both disruptive influences in two other plays: *The Wedding Guest* (1900) and *The Twelve-Pound Look* (1910).

p. 112   *Master Francis Pretty*: Francis Pretty wrote a number of accounts of sixteenth-century voyages by such notable seafarers as Drake and Cavendish. The description of Peter's voyage parodies Pretty's style.

p. 113   *roomer*: a sixteenth-century nautical term meaning to change direction of the ship.

p. 126   *In this world there are no second chances*: the idea behind Barrie's play *Dear Brutus* (1917), which features a group of people who are offered the chance to reshape their lives in an enchanted wood.

p. 129   *leary*: knowing.

p. 136   *Brownie*: A benevolent spirit or goblin native to Scotland. One of James Hogg's early works is entitled *The Brownie of Bodsbeck* (1818).

p. 140   *Build a house round her*: In *Peter Pan* this idea became the Wendy House.

p. 145   *a thimble*: Another episode transferred to *Peter Pan* where Wendy gives Peter the thimble.

p. 152   *the two tombstones of Walter Stephen Matthews and Phoebe Phelps*: these are actually boundary stones marking the parishes of Westminster St Mary and Paddington. The episode is based on one that took place between Barrie and George Llewelyn Davies.

p. 157   *do you want to come into my bed?*: the suggestion in this chapter of paedophiliac desire seems not to have been confronted until Graham Greene published a mock-satirical article in the *Spectator* entitled 'Regina v Sir James Barrie' (November 8, 1969), p.634.

p. 164   *What was the want of the other*: the manuscript continues with a deleted passage: 'But you cannot understand, for the little white bird has visited you and so you have no want.'

p. 165   *William Paterson*: the early notebooks are filled with variations on the fantasy contained in this chapter. It was probably originally planned as a separate short story.

p. 181   *Pilkington's*: a thin disguise for Wilkinson's preparatory school in Orme Square which George Llewelyn Davies attended from 1901. The school overlooked Kensington Gardens.
         hook: the image points to Captain Hook of *Peter Pan* whom Pilkington much resembles.

p. 183   *wrecked islands*: the narrator's stories draw upon the scenes Barrie acted out with George, Jack and Peter in the summer of 1901. The photographs that Barrie took of the boys in their roles as castaways were later printed and bound in an elaborately designed volume entitled *The Boy Castaways of Black Lake Island*. Only two copies of the book were made and the one given to Arthur Llewelyn Davies was lost.
         the simple Swiss Family: Johann David Wyss's *The Swiss Family Robinson* (1812–13) was first published in English translation in 1814.

p. 190   *she's coming*: Barrie began to note ideas for this section of the book when Sylvia Llewelyn Davies was expecting her fourth child, Michael.

p. 194   *'The Little White Bird'*: the title was probably suggested by
          George. A notebook entry records: 'Little White Bird
          book described to me by George.' Beinecke MS A 2/19.

p. 199   *the on*: the left half of the field to a right-handed batsman.
          broke awkwardly from the off: i.e. a ball which spins into a
          right-handed batsman.

p. 200   *And that is how we let Barbara in*: in an early manuscript
          draft the chapter continues with a passage about the real
          Barbara: 'But as she is now lying in a sweet cot, with
          Mary bending adoringly over her, I hope you feel a tiny
          bit sorry for Benjamin. He is another of the little white
          birds. Barbara was born a fortnight ago, and with this
          chapter I end the book. Now, Mary A———, you who
          think you have done such a clever thing, I am ready for
          you. Dare to bring your Barbara here, ma'am, and you
          shall see what you shall see. Tell her, David, that I said
          that.' By omitting this final paragraph Barrie allowed the
          narrator in some sense to retain his fantasy that Barbara
          had been created not by Mary but by the cricket match.

p. 205   *'If only you had been less ambitious . . . her heart's desire*:
          The manuscript for this section reads: ' "If you had only
          been less ambitious," I said with a sigh, for my triumph
          over her no longer heartened me.'

	HODDER AND STOUGHTON	SCRIBNER'S MAGAZINE
Title	*The Little White Bird*	*The Little White Bird: or, Adventures in Kensington Gardens*
p. 8	a faint note of challenge.	a faint note of challenge. This note, I remember, sits airily on her least estimable and indeed slightly tilted feature, to which, nevertheless, I feel the greatest drawing.
	such is the portrait	that is the portrait
p. 9	can save you now	can save you now; you two are of no age, no experience of life separates you
p. 14	who has had the impudence to enter the smoking-room	who has disturbed me by entering the smoking room
p. 45	Halloa!	Hallo!
p. 174	Irish terrier-dog	Scotch terrier dog
p. 184	'Did we tell you about the eggs we found in the sand?'	'Did we tell you about the turtle we turned on its back?'
	'Who found them?'	'Who turned it?'
	'They were found,'	'It was turned,'
	'Who stabbed the wild pig?'	'Who made the monkeys fling cocoanuts at him?'
p. 207	'The little white bird was to bear an olive-leaf in its mouth.'	'The little white bird was to bear an olive leaf in its mouth. Peter Pan, who is really Timothy, was not to find the window closed.'

THE
TWELVE-POUND LOOK

A NOTE ON THE TEXT

The Twelve-Pound Look was first performed together with another one-act play by Barrie, *Old Friends*, and a fragment by George Meredith entitled *The Sentimentalists* at the Duke of York's Theatre on 1 March 1910. Its first American performance was in New York on 13 February 1911 and it was given 3 performances by the Glasgow Scottish Repertory Theatre in the same year. It was made into a film by The Ideal Film Company in 1920 and screened as a BBC television drama on 23 September 1957.

The script was first published by Hodder and Stoughton in December 1914 in the volume *Half-Hours*, which also contained *Pantaloon*, *Rosalind* and *The Will*. The present text is taken from that edition which was also used in the *Definitive Edition of the Plays of J.M. Barrie* published in 1942.

The Twelve-Pound Look

If quite convenient (as they say about cheques) you are to conceive that the scene is laid in your own house, and that HARRY SIMS *is you. Perhaps the ornamentation of the house is a trifle ostentatious, but if you cavil at that we are willing to re-decorate: you don't get out of being* HARRY SIMS *on a mere matter of plush and dados. It pleases us to make him a city man, but (rather than lose you) he can be turned with a scrape of the pen into a* K.C., *fashionable doctor, Secretary of State, or what you will. We conceive him of a pleasant rotundity with a thick red neck, but we shall waive that point if you know him to be thin.*

It is that day in your career when everything went wrong just when everything seemed to be superlatively right.

In HARRY'S *case it was a woman who did the mischief. She came to him in his great hour and told him she did not admire him. Of course he turned her out of the house and was soon himself again, but it spoilt the morning for him. This is the subject of the play, and quite enough too.*

HARRY *is to receive the honour of knighthood in a few days, and we discover him in the sumptuous 'snuggery' of his home in Kensington (or is it Westminster?), rehearsing the ceremony with his wife. They have been at it all the morning, a pleasing occupation.* MRS SIMS *(as we may call her for the last time, as it were, and strictly as a good-natured joke) is wearing her presentation gown, and personates the august one who is about to dub her* HARRY *knight. She is seated regally. Her jewelled shoulders proclaim aloud her husband's generosity. She must be an extraordinarily proud and happy woman, yet she has a drawn face and shrinking ways as if there were some one near her of whom she is afraid. She claps her hands, as the signal to* HARRY. *He enters bowing, and with a graceful swerve of the leg. He is only partly in costume, the sword and the real stockings not having arrived yet. With a gliding motion that is only delayed while one leg makes up on the other, he reaches his wife, and, going on one knee, raises her hand superbly to his lips. She taps him on the shoulder with a paper-knife and says huskily, 'Rise, Sir Harry.' He rises, bows, and glides about the room, going on his knees to various articles of furniture, and rising from each a knight. It is a radiant domestic scene, and* HARRY *is as dignified as if he knew that royalty was rehearsing it at the other end.*

SIR HARRY (*complacently*). Did that seem all right, eh?

LADY SIMS (*much relieved*). I think perfect.

SIR HARRY. But was it dignified?

LADY SIMS. Oh, very. And it will be still more so when you have the sword.

SIR HARRY. The sword will lend it an air. There are really the five moments – (*suiting the action to the word*) – the glide – the dip – the kiss – the tap – and you back out a knight. It's short, but it's a very beautiful ceremony. (*Kindly*) Anything you can suggest?

LADY SIMS. No – oh no. (*Nervously, seeing him pause to kiss the tassel of a cushion*) You don't think you have practised till you know what to do almost too well? (*He has been in a blissful temper, but such niggling criticism would try any man.*)

SIR HARRY. I do not. Don't talk nonsense. Wait till your opinion is asked for.

LADY SIMS. (*abashed*). I'm sorry, Harry. (*A perfect butler appears and presents a card.*) 'The Flora Type-Writing Agency.'

SIR HARRY. Ah, yes. I telephoned them to send some one. A woman, I suppose, Tombes?

TOMBES. Yes, Sir Harry.

SIR HARRY. Show her in here. (*He has very lately become a stickler for etiquette.*) And, Tombes, strictly speaking, you know, I am not Sir Harry till Thursday.

TOMBES. Beg pardon, sir, but it is such a satisfaction to us.

SIR HARRY. (*good-naturedly*). Ah, they like it downstairs, do they?

TOMBES (*unbending*). Especially the females, Sir Harry.

SIR HARRY. Exactly. You can show her in, Tombes. (*The butler departs on his mighty task.*) You can tell the woman what she is wanted for, Emmy, while I change. (*He is too modest to boast about himself, and prefers to keep a wife in the house for that purpose.*) You can tell her the sort of things about me that will come better from you. (*Smiling happily*) You heard what Tombes said, 'Especially the females.' And he is right. Success! The women like it even better than the men. And rightly. For they share. *You* share, *Lady* Sims. Not a woman will see that gown without being sick with envy of it. I know them. Have all our lady friends in to see it. It will make them ill for a week.

(*These sentiments carry him off light-heartedly, and presently the disturbing element is shown in. She is a mere typist, dressed in uncommonly good taste, but at contemptibly small expense, and she is carrying her typewriter in a friendly way rather than as a badge of slavery, as of course it is. Her eye is clear; and in odd contrast to* LADY SIMS, *she is self-reliant and serene.*)

KATE (*respectfully, but she should have waited to be spoken to*). Good morning, madam.

LADY SIMS (*in her nervous way, and scarcely noticing that the typist is a little too ready with her tongue*). Good morning. (*As a first impression she rather likes the woman, and the woman, though it is scarcely worth mentioning, rather likes her.* LADY SIMS *has a maid for buttoning and unbuttoning her, and probably another for waiting on the maid, and she gazes with a little envy perhaps at a woman who does things for herself.*) Is that the type-writing machine?

KATE (*who is getting it ready for use*). Yes (*not 'Yes, madam,' as it ought to be*). I suppose if I am to work here I may take this off. I get on better without it. (*She is referring to her hat.*)

LADY SIMS. Certainly. (*But the hat is already off.*) I ought to apologise for my gown. I am to be presented this week, and I was trying it on. (*Her tone is not really apologetic. She is rather clinging to the glory of her gown, wistfully, as if not absolutely certain, you know, that it is a glory.*

KATE. It is beautiful, if I may presume to say so. (*She frankly admires it. She probably has a best, and a second best of her own: that sort of thing.*)

LADY SIMS (*with a flush of pride in the gown*). Yes, it is very beautiful. (*The beauty of it gives her courage.*) Sit down, please.

KATE (*the sort of woman who would have sat down in any case*). I suppose it is some copying you want done? I got no particulars. I was told to come to this address, but that was all.

LADY SIMS (*almost with the humility of a servant*). Oh, it is not work for me, it is for my husband, and what he needs is not exactly copying. (*Swelling, for she is proud of* HARRY.) He wants a number of letters answered – hundreds of them – letters and telegrams of congratulation.

KATE (*as if it were all in the day's work*). Yes?

LADY SIMS (*remembering that* HARRY *expects every wife to do her duty*). My husband is a remarkable man. He is about to be knighted. (*Pause, but* KATE *does not fall to the floor.*) He is to be knighted for his services to – (*on reflection*) – for his services. (*She is conscious that she is not doing* HARRY *justice.*) He can explain it so much better than I can.

KATE (*in her business-like way*). And I am to answer the congratulations?

LADY SIMS (*afraid that it will be a hard task*). Yes.

KATE (*blithely*). It is work I have had some experience of. (*She proceeds to type.*)

LADY SIMS. But you can't begin till you know what he wants to say.

KATE. Only a specimen letter. Won't it be the usual thing?

LADY SIMS (*to whom this is a new idea*). Is there a usual thing?

KATE. Oh, yes.

(*She continues to type, and* LADY SIMS, *half-mesmerised, gazes at her nimble fingers. The useless woman watches the useful one, and she sighs, she could not tell why.*)

LADY SIMS. How quickly you do it. It must be delightful to be able to do something, and to do it well.

KATE (*thankfully*). Yes, it is delightful.

LADY SIMS (*again remembering the source of all her greatness*). But, excuse me, I don't think that will be any use. My husband wants me to explain to you that his is an exceptional case. He did not try to get this honour in any way. It was a complete surprise to him—

KATE (*who is a practical Kate and no dealer in sarcasm*). That is what I have written.

LADY SIMS (*in whom sarcasm would meet a dead wall*). But how could you know?

KATE. I only guessed.

LADY SIMS. Is that the usual thing?

KATE. Oh, yes.

LADY SIMS. They don't try to get it?

KATE. I don't know. That is what we are told to say in the letters.

(*To her at present the only important thing about the letters is that they are ten shillings the hundred.*)

LADY SIMS (*returning to surer ground*). I should explain that my husband is not a man who cares for honours. So long as he does his duty—

KATE. Yes, I have been putting that in.

LADY SIMS. Have you? But he particularly wants it to be known that he would have declined a title were it not—

KATE. I have got it here.

LADY SIMS. What have you got?

KATE (*reading*). 'Indeed I would have asked to be allowed to decline had it not been that I want to please my wife.'

LADY SIMS (*heavily*). But how could you know it was that?

KATE. Is it?

LADY SIMS (*who after all is the one with the right to ask questions*). Do they all accept it for that reason?

KATE. That is what we are told to say in the letters.

LADY SIMS (*thoughtlessly*). It is quite as if you knew my husband.

KATE. I assure you, I don't even know his name.

LADY SIMS (*suddenly showing that she knows him*). Oh, he wouldn't like that.

(*And it is here that* HARRY *re-enters in his city garments, looking so gay, feeling so jolly that we bleed for him*). *However, the annoying* KATHERINE *is to get a shock also.*)

LADY SIMS. This is the lady, Harry.

SIR HARRY (*shooting his cuffs*). Yes, yes. Good morning, my dear.

(*Then they see each other, and their mouths open, but not for words. After the first surprise* KATE *seems to find some humour in the situation, but* HARRY *lowers like a thunder-cloud.*)

LADY SIMS (*who has seen nothing*). I have been trying to explain to her—

SIR HARRY. Eh – what? (*He controls himself.*) Leave it to me, Emmy; I'll attend to her.

(LADY SIMS *goes, with a dread fear that somehow she has vexed her lord, and then* HARRY *attends to the intruder.*)

SIR HARRY (*with concentrated scorn*). You!

KATE (*as if agreeing with him*). Yes, it's funny.

SIR HARRY. The shamelessness of your daring to come here.

KATE. Believe me, it is not less a surprise to me than it is to you. I was sent here in the ordinary way of business. I was given only the number of the house. I was not told the name.

SIR HARRY (*withering her*). The ordinary way of business! This is what you have fallen to – a typist!

KATE (*unwithered*). Think of it.

SIR HARRY. After going through worse straits, I'll be bound.

KATE (*with some grim memories*). Much worse straits.

SIR HARRY (*alas, laughing coarsely*). My congratulations.

KATE. Thank you, Harry.

SIR HARRY (*who is annoyed, as any man would be, not to find her abject*). Eh? What was that you called me, madam?

KATE. Isn't it Harry? On my soul, I almost forget.

SIR HARRY. It isn't Harry to you. My name is Sims, if you please.

KATE. Yes, I had not forgotten that. It was my name, too, you see.

SIR HARRY (*in his best manner*). It was your name till you forfeited the right to bear it.

KATE. Exactly.

SIR HARRY (*gloating*). I was furious to find you here, but on second thoughts it pleases me. (*From the depths of his moral nature*) There is a grim justice in this.

KATE (*sympathetically*). Tell me?

SIR HARRY. Do you know what you were brought here to do?

KATE. I have just been learning. You have been made a knight, and I was summoned to answer the messages of congratulation.

SIR HARRY. That's it, that's it. You come on this day as my servant!

KATE. I, who might have been Lady Sims.

SIR HARRY. And you are her typist instead. And she has

four men-servants. Oh, I am glad you saw her in her presentation gown.

KATE. I wonder if she would let me do her washing, Sir Harry?

(*Her want of taste disgusts him.*)

SIR HARRY (*with dignity*). You can go. The mere thought that only a few flights of stairs separates such as you from my innocent children—

(*He will never know why a new light has come into her face.*)

KATE (*slowly*). You have children?

SIR HARRY (*inflated*). Two.

(*He wonders why she is so long in answering.*)

KATE (*resorting to impertinence*). Such a nice number.

SIR HARRY (*with an extra turn of the screw*). Both boys.

KATE. Successful in everything. Are they like you, Sir Harry?

SIR HARRY (*expanding*). They are very like me.

KATE. That's nice.

(*Even on such a subject as this she can be ribald.*)

SIR HARRY. Will you please to go.

KATE. Heigho! What shall I say to my employer?

SIR HARRY. That is no affair of mine.

KATE. What will you say to Lady Sims?

SIR HARRY. I flatter myself that whatever I say, Lady Sims will accept without comment.

(*She smiles, heaven knows why, unless her next remark explains it.*)

KATE. Still the same Harry.

SIR HARRY. What do you mean?

KATE. Only that you have the old confidence in your profound knowledge of the sex.

SIR HARRY (*beginning to think as little of her intellect as of her morals*). I suppose I know my wife.

KATE (*hopelessly dense*). I suppose so. I was only remembering that you used to think you knew her in the days when

I was the lady. (*He is merely wasting his time on her, and he indicates the door. She is not sufficiently the lady to retire worsted.*) Well, good-bye, Sir Harry. Won't you ring, and the four men-servants will show me out?

(*But he hesitates.*)

SIR HARRY (*in spite of himself*). As you are here, there is something I want to get out of you. (*Wishing he could ask it less eagerly*) Tell me, who was the man?

(*The strange woman – it is evident now that she has always been strange to him – smiles tolerantly.*)

KATE. You never found out?

SIR HARRY. I could never be sure.

KATE (*reflectively*). I thought that would worry you.

SIR HARRY (*sneering*). It's plain that he soon left you.

KATE. Very soon.

SIR HARRY. As I could have told you.

(*But still she surveys him with the smile of Monna Lisa. The badgered man has to entreat*) Who was he? It was fourteen years ago, and cannot matter to any of us now. Kate, tell me who he was?

(*It is his first youthful moment, and perhaps because of that she does not wish to hurt him.*)

KATE (*shaking a motherly head*). Better not ask.

SIR HARRY. I do ask. Tell me.

KATE. It is kinder not to tell you.

SIR HARRY (*violently*). Then, by James, it was one of my own pals. Was it Bernard Roche? (*She shakes her head.*) It may have been some one who comes to my house still.

KATE. I think not. (*Reflecting*) Fourteen years! You found my letter that night when you went home?

SIR HARRY (*impatient*). Yes.

KATE. I propped it against the decanters. I thought you would be sure to see it there. It was a room not unlike this, and the furniture was arranged in the same attractive way. How it all comes back to me. Don't you see me, Harry, in hat and cloak, putting the letter there, taking a

last look round, and then stealing out into the night to
meet—

SIR HARRY. Whom?

KATE. Him. Hours pass, no sound in the room but the tick-
tack of the clock, and then about midnight you return
alone. You take—

SIR HARRY (*gruffly*). I wasn't alone.

KATE (*the picture spoilt*). No? oh. (*Plaintively*) Here have I all
these years been conceiving it wrongly. (*She studies his
face.*) I believe something interesting happened?

SIR HARRY (*growling*). Something confoundedly annoying.

KATE (*coaxing*). Do tell me.

SIR HARRY. We won't go into that. Who was the man?
Surely a husband has a right to know with whom his wife
bolted.

KATE (*who is detestably ready with her tongue*). Surely the
wife has a right to know how he took it. (*The woman's love
of bargaining comes to her aid.*) A fair exchange. You tell
me what happened, and I will tell you who he was.

SIR HARRY. You will? Very well. (*It is the first point on which
they have agreed, and, forgetting himself, he takes a place
beside her on the fire-seat. He is thinking only of what he is to
tell her, but she, woman-like, is conscious of their proximity.*)

KATE (*tastelessly*). Quite like old times. (*He moves away from
her indignantly.*) Go on, Harry.

SIR HARRY (*who has a manful shrinking from saying anything
that is to his disadvantage.*) Well, as you know, I was
dining at the club that night.

KATE. Yes.

SIR HARRY. Jack Lamb drove me home. Mabbett Green
was with us, and I asked them to come in for a few
minutes.

KATE. Jack Lamb, Mabbett Green? I think I remember
them. Jack was in Parliament.

SIR HARRY. No, that was Mabbett. They came into the
house with me and – (*with sudden horror*) – was it him?

KATE (*bewildered*). Who?

SIR HARRY. Mabbett?

KATE. What?

SIR HARRY. The man?

KATE. What man? (*understanding*) Oh no. I thought you said he came into the house with you.

SIR HARRY. It might have been a blind.

KATE. Well, it wasn't. Go on.

SIR HARRY. They came in to finish a talk we had been having at the club.

KATE. An interesting talk, evidently.

SIR HARRY. The papers had been full that evening of the elopement of some countess woman with a fiddler. What was her name?

KATE. Does it matter?

SIR HARRY. No. (*Thus ends the countess.*) We had been discussing the thing and – (*he pulls a wry face*) – and I had been rather warm—

KATE (*with horrid relish*). I begin to see. You had been saying it served the husband right, that the man who could not look after his wife deserved to lose her. It was one of your favourite subjects. Oh, Harry, say it was that!

SIR HARRY (*sourly*). It may have been something like that.

KATE. And all the time the letter was there, waiting; and none of you knew except the clock. Harry, it is sweet of you to tell me. (*His face is not sweet. The illiterate woman has used the wrong adjective.*) I forget what I said precisely in the letter.

SIR HARRY (*pulverising her*). So do I. But I have it still.

KATE (*not pulverised*). Do let me see it again. (*She has observed his eye wandering to the desk.*)

SIR HARRY. You are welcome to it as a gift. (*The fateful letter, a poor little dead thing, is brought to light from a locked drawer.*)

KATE (*taking it*). Yes, this is it. Harry, how you did crumple it! (*She reads, not without curiosity.*) 'Dear husband – I call

you that for the last time – I am off. I am what you call
making a bolt of it. I won't try to excuse myself nor to
explain, for you would not accept the excuses nor understand the explanation. It will be a little shock to you, but
only to your pride; what will astound you is that any
woman could be such a fool as to leave such a man as
you. I am taking nothing with me that belongs to you.
May you be very happy. – Your ungrateful KATE. *P.S.* –
You need not try to find out who he is. You will try, but
you won't succeed.' (*She folds the nasty little thing up.*) I
may really have it for my very own?

SIR HARRY. You really may.

KATE (*impudently*). If you would care for a typed copy—?

SIR HARRY (*in a voice with which he used to frighten his
grandmother*). None of your sauce. (*Wincing*) I had to let
them see it in the end.

KATE. I can picture Jack Lamb eating it.

SIR HARRY. A penniless parson's daughter.

KATE. That is all I was.

SIR HARRY. We searched for the two of you high and low.

KATE. Private detectives?

SIR HARRY. They couldn't get on the track of you.

KATE (*smiling*). No?

SIR HARRY. But at last the courts let me serve the papers by
advertisement on a man unknown, and I got my freedom.

KATE. So I saw. It was the last I heard of you.

SIR HARRY (*each word a blow for her*). And I married again
just as soon as ever I could.

KATE. They say that is always a compliment to the first wife.

SIR HARRY (*violently*). I showed them.

KATE. You soon let them see that if one woman was a fool,
you still had the pick of the basket to choose from.

SIR HARRY. By James, I did.

KATE (*bringing him to earth again*). But still, you wondered
who he was.

SIR HARRY. I suspected everybody – even my pals. I felt like jumping at their throats and crying, 'It's you!'

KATE. You had been so admirable to me, an instinct told you that I was sure to choose another of the same.

SIR HARRY. I thought, it can't be money, so it must be looks. Some dolly face. (*He stares at her in perplexity.*) He must have had something wonderful about him to make you willing to give up all that you had with me.

KATE (*as if he was the stupid one*). Poor Harry.

SIR HARRY. And it couldn't have been going on for long, for I would have noticed the change in you.

KATE. Would you?

SIR HARRY. I knew you so well.

KATE. You amazing man.

SIR HARRY. So who was he? Out with it.

KATE. You are determined to know?

SIR HARRY. Your promise. You gave your word.

KATE. If I must— (*She is the villain of the piece, but it must be conceded that in this matter she is reluctant to pain him.*) I am sorry I promised. (*Looking at him steadily.*) There was no one, Harry; no one at all.

SIR HARRY (*rising*). If you think you can play with me—

KATE. I told you that you wouldn't like it.

SIR HARRY (*rasping*). It is unbelievable.

KATE. I suppose it is; but it is true.

SIR HARRY. Your letter itself gives you the lie.

KATE. That was intentional. I saw that if the truth were known you might have a difficulty in getting your freedom; and as I was getting mine it seemed fair that you should have yours also. So I wrote my good-bye in words that would be taken to mean what you thought they meant, and I knew the law would back you in your opinion. For the law, like you, Harry, has a profound understanding of women.

SIR HARRY (*trying to straighten himself*). I don't believe you yet.

KATE (*looking not unkindly into the soul of this man*). Perhaps that is the best way to take it. It is less unflattering than the truth. But you were the only one. (*Summing up her life.*) You sufficed.

SIR HARRY. Then what mad impulse—

KATE. It was no impulse, Harry. I had thought it out for a year.

SIR HARRY. A year? (*dazed*). One would think to hear you that I hadn't been a good husband to you.

KATE (*with a sad smile*). You were a good husband according to your lights.

SIR HARRY (*stoutly*). *I* think so.

KATE. And a moral man, and chatty, and quite the philanthropist.

SIR HARRY (*on sure ground*). All women envied you.

KATE. How you loved me to be envied.

SIR HARRY. I swaddled you in luxury.

KATE (*making her great revelation*). That was it.

SIR HARRY (*blankly*). What?

KATE (*who can be serene because it is all over*). How you beamed at me when I sat at the head of your fat dinners in my fat jewellery, surrounded by our fat friends.

SIR HARRY (*aggrieved*). They weren't so fat.

KATE (*a side issue*). All except those who were so thin. Have you ever noticed, Harry, that many jewels make women either incredibly fat or incredibly thin?

SIR HARRY (*shouting*). I have not. (*Is it worth while to argue with her any longer?*) We had all the most interesting society of the day. It wasn't only business men. There were politicians, painters, writers—

KATE. Only the glorious, dazzling successes. Oh, the fat talk while we ate too much – about who had made a hit and who was slipping back, and what the noo house cost and the noo motor and the gold soup-plates, and who was to be the noo knight.

SIR HARRY (*who it will be observed is unanswerable from first to last*). Was anybody getting on better than me, and consequently you?

KATE. Consequently me! Oh, Harry, you and your sublime religion.

SIR HARRY (*honest heart*). My religion? I never was one to talk about religion, but—

KATE. Pooh, Harry, you don't even know what your religion was and is and will be till the day of your expensive funeral. (*And here is the lesson that life has taught her.*) One's religion is whatever he is most interested in, and yours is Success.

SIR HARRY (*quoting from his morning paper*). Ambition – it is the last infirmity of noble minds.

KATE. Noble minds!

SIR HARRY (*at last grasping what she is talking about*). You are not saying that you left me because of my success?

KATE. Yes, that was it. (*And now she stands revealed to him.*) I couldn't endure it. If a failure had come now and then – but your success was suffocating me. (*She is rigid with emotion.*) The passionate craving I had to be done with it, to find myself among people who had not got on.

SIR HARRY (*with proper spirit*). There are plenty of them.

KATE. There were none in our set. When they began to go downhill they rolled out of our sight.

SIR HARRY (*clinching it*). I tell you I am worth a quarter of a million.

KATE (*unabashed*). That is what you are worth to yourself. I'll tell you what you are worth to me: exactly twelve pounds. For I made up my mind that I could launch myself on the world alone if I first proved my mettle by earning twelve pounds; and as soon as I had earned it I left you.

SIR HARRY (*in the scales*). Twelve pounds!

KATE. That is your value to a woman. If she can't make it she has to stick to you.

SIR HARRY (*remembering perhaps a rectory garden*). You valued me at more than that when you married me.

KATE (*seeing it also*). Ah, I didn't know you then. If only you had been a man, Harry.

SIR HARRY. A man? What do you mean by a man?

KATE (*leaving the garden*). Haven't you heard of them? They are something fine; and every woman is loath to admit to herself that her husband is not one. When she marries, even though she has been a very trivial person, there is in her some vague stirring toward a worthy life, as well as a fear of her capacity for evil. She knows her chance lies in him. If there is something good in him, what is good in her finds it, and they join forces against the baser parts. So I didn't give you up willingly, Harry. I invented all sorts of theories to explain you. Your hardness – I said it was a fine want of mawkishness. Your coarseness – I said it goes with strength. Your contempt for the weak – I called it virility. Your want of ideals was clear-sightedness. Your ignoble views of women – I tried to think them funny. Oh, I clung to you to save myself. But I had to let go; you had only the one quality, Harry, success; you had it so strong that it swallowed all the others.

SIR HARRY (*not to be diverted from the main issue*). How did you earn that twelve pounds?

KATE. It took me nearly six months; but I earned it fairly. (*She presses her hand on the typewriter as lovingly as many a woman has pressed a rose.*) I learned this. I hired it and taught myself. I got some work through a friend, and with my first twelve pounds I paid for my machine. Then I considered that I was free to go, and I went.

SIR HARRY. All this going on in my house while you were living in the lap of luxury! (*She nods.*) By God, you were determined.

KATE (*briefly*). By God, I was.

SIR HARRY (*staring*). How you must have hated me.

KATE (*smiling at the childish word*). Not a bit – after I saw that there was a way out. From that hour you amused me, Harry; I was even sorry for you, for I saw that you couldn't help yourself. Success is just a fatal gift.

SIR HARRY. Oh, thank you.

KATE (*thinking, dear friends in front, of you and me perhaps*). Yes, and some of your most successful friends knew it. One or two of them used to look very sad at times, as if they thought they might have come to something if they hadn't got on.

SIR HARRY (*who has a horror of sacrilege*). The battered crew you live among now – what are they but folk who have tried to succeed and failed?

KATE. That's it; they try, but they fail.

SIR HARRY. And always will fail.

KATE. Always. Poor souls – I say of them. Poor soul – they say of me. It keeps us human. That is why I never tire of them.

SIR HARRY (*comprehensively*). Bah! Kate, I tell you I'll be worth half a million yet.

KATE. I'm sure you will. You're getting stout, Harry.

SIR HARRY. No, I'm not.

KATE. What was the name of that fat old fellow who used to fall asleep at our dinner-parties?

SIR HARRY. If you mean Sir William Crackley—

KATE. That was the man. Sir William was to me a perfect picture of the grand success. He had got on so well that he was very, very stout, and when he sat on a chair it was thus (*her hands meeting in front of her*) – as if he were holding his success together. That is what you are working for, Harry. You will have that and the half million about the same time.

SIR HARRY (*who has surely been very patient*). Will you please to leave my house.

KATE (*putting on her gloves, soiled things*). But don't let us part in anger. How do you think I am looking, Harry, compared to the dull, inert thing that used to roll round in your padded carriages?

SIR HARRY (*in masterly fashion*). I forget what you were like. I'm very sure you never could have held a candle to the present Lady Sims.

KATE. That is a picture of her, is it not?

SIR HARRY (*seizing his chance again*). In her wedding-gown. Painted by an R.A.

KATE (*wickedly*). A knight?

SIR HARRY (*deceived*). Yes.

KATE (*who likes* LADY SIMS: *a piece of presumption on her part*). It is a very pretty face.

SIR HARRY (*with the pride of possession*). Acknowledged to be a beauty everywhere.

KATE. There is a merry look in the eyes, and character in the chin.

SIR HARRY (*like an auctioneer*). Noted for her wit.

KATE. All her life before her when that was painted. It is a *spirituelle* face too. (*Suddenly she turns on him with anger, for the first and only time in the play.*) Oh, Harry, you brute!

SIR HARRY (*staggered*). Eh? What?

KATE. That dear creature capable of becoming a noble wife and mother – she is the spiritless woman of no account that I saw here a few minutes ago. I forgive you for myself, for I escaped, but that poor lost soul, oh, Harry, Harry.

SIR HARRY (*waving her to the door*). I'll thank you – If ever there was a woman proud of her husband and happy in her married life, that woman is Lady Sims.

KATE. I wonder.

SIR HARRY. Then you needn't wonder.

KATE (*slowly*). If I was a husband – it is my advice to all of them – I would often watch my wife quietly to see whether the twelve-pound look was not coming into her eyes. Two boys, did you say, and both like you?

SIR HARRY. What is that to you?

KATE (*with glistening eyes*). I was only thinking that somewhere there are two little girls who, when they grow up –
the dear, pretty girls who are all meant for the men that
don't get on! Well, goodbye, Sir Harry.

SIR HARRY (*showing a little human weakness, it is to be
feared*). Say first that you're sorry.

KATE. For what?

SIR HARRY. That you left me. Say you regret it bitterly.
You know you do. (*She smiles and shakes her head. He is
pettish. He makes a terrible announcement.*) You have spoilt
the day for me.

KATE (*to hearten him*). I am sorry for that; but it is only a
pin-prick, Harry. I suppose it is a little jarring in the
moment of your triumph to find that there is – one old
friend – who does not think you a success; but you will
soon forget it. Who cares what a typist thinks?

SIR HARRY (*heartened*). Nobody. A typist at eighteen
shillings a week!

KATE (*proudly*). Not a bit of it, Harry. I double that.

SIR HARRY (*neatly*). Magnificent!
    (*There is a timid knock at the door.*)

LADY SIMS. May I come in?

SIR HARRY (*rather appealingly*). It is Lady Sims.

KATE. I won't tell. She is afraid to come into her husband's
room without knocking!

SIR HARRY. She is not. (*Uxoriously*) Come in, dearest.
    (*Dearest enters carrying the sword. She might have had
    the sense not to bring it in while this annoying person is
    here.*)

LADY SIMS (*thinking she has brought her welcome with her*).
Harry, the sword has come.

SIR HARRY (*who will dote on it presently*). Oh, all right.

LADY SIMS. But I thought you were so eager to practise
with it.
    (*The person smiles at this. He wishes he had not looked to
    see if she was smiling.*)

SIR HARRY (*sharply*). Put it down.

(LADY SIMS *flushes a little as she lays the sword aside.*)

KATE (*with her confounded courtesy*). It is a beautiful sword, if I may say so.

LADY SIMS (*helped*). Yes.

(*The person thinks she can put him in the wrong, does she? He'll show her.*)

SIR HARRY (*with one eye on* KATE). Emmy, the one thing your neck needs is more jewels.

LADY SIMS (*faltering*). More!

SIR HARRY. Some ropes of pearls. I'll see to it. It's a bagatelle to me. (KATE *conceals her chagrin, so she had better be shown the door. He rings.*) I won't detain you any longer, miss.

KATE. Thank you.

LADY SIMS. Going already? You have been very quick.

SIR HARRY. The person doesn't suit, Emmy.

LADY SIMS. I'm sorry.

KATE. So am I, madam, but it can't be helped. Good-bye, your ladyship – goodbye, Sir Harry. (*There is a suspicion of an impertinent curtsy, and she is escorted off the premises by* TOMBES. *The air of the room is purified by her going.* SIR HARRY *notices it at once.*)

LADY SIMS (*whose tendency is to say the wrong thing*). She seemed such a capable woman.

SIR HARRY (*on his hearth*). I don't like her style at all.

LADY SIMS (*meekly*). Of course you know best. (*This is the right kind of woman.*)

SIR HARRY (*rather anxious for corroboration*). Lord, how she winced when I said I was to give you those ropes of pearls.

LADY SIMS. Did she? I didn't notice. I suppose so.

SIR HARRY (*frowning*). Suppose? Surely I know enough about women to know that.

LADY SIMS. Yes, oh yes.

SIR HARRY. (*Odd that so confident a man should ask this.*)

Emmy, I know you well, don't I? I can read you like a
book, eh?

LADY SIMS (*nervously*). Yes, Harry.

SIR HARRY (*jovially, but with an inquiring eye*). What a
different existence yours is from that poor lonely
wretch's.

LADY SIMS. Yes, but she has a very contented face.

SIR HARRY (*with a stamp of his foot*). All put on. What?

LADY SIMS (*timidly*). I didn't say anything.

SIR HARRY (*snapping*). One would think you envied her.

LADY SIMS. Envied? Oh no – but I thought she looked so
alive. It was while she was working the machine.

SIR HARRY. Alive! That's no life. It is you that are alive.
(*Curtly*) I'm busy, Emmy. (*He sits at his writing-table.*)

LADY SIMS (*dutifully*). I'm sorry; I'll go, Harry. (*Incon-
sequentially*) Are they very expensive?

SIR HARRY. What?

LADY SIMS. Those machines?

(*When she has gone the possible meaning of her question
startles him. The curtain hides him from us, but we may be
sure that he will soon be bland again. We have a comfortable
feeling, you and I, that there is nothing of* HARRY SIMS *in
us.*)

FAREWELL
MISS JULIE LOGAN
– A WINTRY TALE

The setting of *Farewell Miss Julie Logan* draws upon a series of sketches Barrie published in the *Edinburgh Evening Dispatch* between January and May 1890 entitled 'A Clachan in Winter'. Some of these were reprinted against Barrie's wishes under the title 'Life in a Country Manse' in a number of unauthorised American editions of his work. Although some of the characters reappear in *Farewell Miss Julie Logan* the ghost story itself was an entirely new idea.

The story has a complicated textual history. It was first published as a free supplement to *The Times* on Christmas Eve, 1931. As a response to numerous requests it was reissued, still in the format of a newspaper (in columns and in small print), but printed on special paper and priced at one shilling. When Barrie agreed to the republication of the work in book form he revised the text extensively, making a considerable number of stylistic changes and adding some passages of description. Most significantly, however, he changed the ending so as to make the final effect of the work quite different. In *The Times* version Adam does not claim to have found the basket by the burn and it is not implied, as it is in the book, that Julie Logan was anything other than a figment of his imagination. Other substantial additions were the description of the manse (pp.248–50), the account of the minister's gown (p.252) and the passage where Adam claims his diary entry has mysteriously disappeared (pp.268–9). Throughout *The Times* text 'Christily' is spelt 'Christilly'.

The present text is taken from the Uniform Edition – the

first UK book edition – published in October 1932. Apart from minor changes of spelling, punctuation and paragraphing, a list of the variant readings in *The Times* version is given in the notes at the end.

Contents

ONE

The English

THIS IS Dec. 1, 186–; I think it prudent to go no nearer to the date, in case what I am writing should take an ill turn or fall into curious hands. I need not be so guarded about the weather. It is a night of sudden blasts that half an hour ago threw my window at me. They went skirling from room to room, like officers of the law seeking to seize and deliver to justice the venturesome Scots minister who is sitting here ready to impeach all wraiths and warlocks. There was another blast the now. I believe I could rope the winds of the manse to my bidding tonight, and by running from door to door, opening and shutting, become the conductor of a gey sinister orchestra.

I am trying to make a start at the Diary the English have challenged me to write. There is no call to begin tonight, for as yet not a flake has fallen in this my first winter in the glen; and the Diary is to be a record of my life here during the weeks ('tis said it may be months) in which the glen is 'locked,' meaning it may be so happit in snow that no one who is in can get out of it, and no one who is out can get in. Then, according to the stories that crawl like mists among our hills, where the English must have picked them up, come forms called the 'Strangers.' You 'go queer' yourself without knowing it and walk and talk with these doolies, thinking they are of your world till maybe they have mischieved you.

It is all, of course, superstitious havers, bred of folk who are used to the travail of out of doors, and take ill with having to squat by the saut-bucket; but I have promised with a smile to keep my eyes and ears intent for tergiversations among my flock, and to record them for the benefit of the English when they come back next August.

My name is the Rev. Adam Yestreen; and to be candid I care not for the Adam with its unfortunate associations. I am twenty-six years of age and, though long in the legs, look maybe younger than is seemly in my sacred calling, being clean-shaven without any need to use an implement; indeed I may say I have desisted for two years back.

I took a fair degree at St Andrews, but my Intellectuals suffered from an addiction to putting away my books and playing on the fiddle. When I got my call to this place my proper course was to have got rid of the fiddle before I made my entry into the glen, which I did walking with affected humility behind three cart-loads of furniture all my own, and well aware, though I looked down, that I was being keeked at from every window, of which there are about two to the mile.

When the English discovered how ashamed I was of my old backsliding with the fiddle, they had the effrontery to prig with me to give them a tune, but I hope it is unnecessary for me to say that they had to retire discomfited. I have never once performed on the instrument here, though I may have taken it out of its case nows and nans to fondle the strings.

What I miss, when my unstable mind is on the things of this world, is less my own poor cajoling with the gut than not hearing the tunes from better hands; the more homely Scottish lilts, I mean, for of course the old reprehensible songs that kow-tow to the Stewarts find no asylum with me.

Though but half a Highlander, I have the Gaelic sufficiently to be able to preach in it once every Sabbath, as enjoined; but the attendances are small, as, except for stravaigers, there are not so many pure Hielandmen nowadays in the glen.

My manse and kirk are isolated on one side of the burn, and the English call them cold as paddocks, but methinks a noble look falls on them when the Sabbath bell is ringing. My predecessor, Mr Carluke, tore down the jargonelle tree, which used to cling to my gable-end, because he considered that, when in flourish (or as the English say, in blossom, a word with no gallantry intilt), it gave the manse the appearance of a light woman. The marks are still scarted on the wall. Round the manse, within a neat paling that encloses my demesne, there are grossart-bushes, rizers and rasps, a gean, bee-skeps and the like, that in former hands were called the yard, but I call it the garden, and have made other improvements.

The gean is my only tree, but close by is a small wood of fir and birch with a path through it that since long before my time has been called the Thinking Path because so many ministers have walked up and down it before the diets of worship with their hands behind their backs. I try to emulate them, but they were deeper men than I am, and many a time I forget to think, though such had been my intention. In other days a squirrel frequented this wood, and as you might say adopted one minister after another, taking nuts from their hands, though scorning all overtures from the laity; but I have never seen it, and my detractors, of whom there are a flow (though I think I am well likit as a whole), say that it deserted the wood as a protest when it heard that I preached in a gown.

There is a deal of character about the manse, particularly, of course, in the study, which is also my living-room. It and my dining-room are the only two rooms in the glen (except at the Grand House) without a bed in them, and I mention this, not with complacence to show how I live nowadays, but as evidence that we are a thrifty people, though on Sabbath well put on. Some are also well plenished within; and to have their porridge with porter instead of milk is not an uncommon occurrence.

The finest of my gear, all the chairs in horsehair, belong to the dining-room, which, however, is best fitted for stately occasions, and you would know it is seldom used by the way the fire smokes. I cannot say that I am at ease in it, while, on the other hand, I never enter my study up the stair without feeling we are sib; to which one might say it responds.

Never have I a greater drawing to my study than when the lamp is lit and the low from the fire plays on my red curtains and the blue camstane and my clouty rug. It is an open fireplace without a grate, and I used to be shamed of its wood and peat scattering such a mess of ashes till the English told me that piles of ashes are a great adornment, since when I have conflict with my bit maid, because she wants to carry them away daily, not having the wit to know that they are an acquisition.

Most of my wall space and especially two presses are sternly lined with mighty books, such as have made some of my congregation thankful that they have never learned to read. Yet it is a room that says to any one of spirit, 'Come in by and take a chair, and not only a chair but the best chair,' which is the high-backed grandy, agreeably riven in the seat. I seldom occupy it myself, except at a by-time on a Sabbath afternoon when the two diets have exhausted me a wee, but Dr John sinks into it as naturally as if he had bought it at the roup. This was the auction of such plenishing as Mr Carluke did not take away with him, and in the inventory there was mentioned as part of the study furniture, 'servant's chair,' which puzzled some of the bidders, but I saw through it at once. It meant, not to his glorification, that a kitchen chair was kept here for the servant to sit on, and this meant that he held both morning and evening family exercise in the study, which meant again that he breakfasted and supped there; for he wouldna have two fires. It made me smile in a tolerant way, for one would have thought, on the night I spent with him, that the dining-room was his common resort.

On the other side of the burn, but so close that I can keep

a vigilant eye on them, are the Five Houses in a Row, which the English say, incorrectly but with no evil design, contain all the congregation I can depend upon in a tack of wild weather. On the contrair, there is a hantle of small farms in the glen, forbye shepherds' shielings and bothies, and an occasional roadside bigging of clay and divot in which may be man or beast; truly, when I chap I am sometimes doubtful which will come to the door.

The English, who make play with many old words that even our Highlandmen have forgotten, call the Five Houses the 'clachan.' They are one-storey houses, white-washed and thacked, and every one of them (to the astonishment of the English) has a hallan to itself. We may be poor, say the Scottish, but we will not open into a room. The doors face the glen road, on which grows a coarse bent grass in lines as straight as potato drills, and carriage-folk who do not keep the ruts are shaken most terrible. One of the English told me that his machine sometimes threw him so high in the air that when he was up there he saw small lochs hitherto unknown to man, and stopped his beast and fished them. The English, however, who have many virtues, though not of a very solid kind, are great exaggerators.

The carriage-folk, except when she lets what is familiarly called the Grand House to the English, consist of Mistress Lindinnock alone, who is called (but never to her face) the Old Lady. She has two spirited ponies, but not so spirited as herself. She goes to Edinburgh while the Grand House is let, and, excepting myself (on account of my office), she is the chief person in the glen. She has been a fine friend to me, but I have sometimes to admonish her for a little coarseness in her language, which may escape from her even when she is most genteel. I grieve to say that this lady of many commendable parts plays cards, and I once saw her at it. Her adversary was a travelling watchmaker, one of those who traverse the whole land carrying a wooden box of watches on his back, with a dozen more ticking in his many waistcoat pockets. They were playing for high sums too, the Old Lady sitting inside one of her windows and the man outside it on his box. I think this is done to preserve the difference in rank; but when I called her before me for it she said the object was to make all right for her future, as the players being on different sides of the window took away the curse.

She is also at times overly sly for one so old and little, and I am now referring to my gown. Soon after my settlement the ladies of the congregation presented me with a gown, and she as the most well to pass was the monetary strength of the movement; but though I was proud to wear my gown (without vain glory), we had members who argued that it had a touch of Rome. One may say that the congregation was divided anent it, and some Sabbaths I was sore bested whether to put it on or not. Whiles the decision was even taken out of my hands, for the gown would disappear at the back-end of the week and be returned to its nail on the Monday morning, the work undoubtedly of the no-gown party. On those occasions, of course, I made shift without it, and feeling ran so high that I could not but be conscious as I ascended the pulpit that they were titting at one another's sleeves.

They invented the phrase 'a gown Sabbath.' I took to hiding it, but whoever were the miscreants (and well I knew they were in their pews in front of me, looking as if they had never heard the word gown), they usually found my hoddy place. I mind once sitting on it a long Saturday night when I was labouring at my sermon, the which incident got about among my people. The Old Lady was very sympathetic and pressed me to lay the trouble before the Session, which in fairness to her as the outstanding subscriber I ettled to do, until (could any one believe it?) I discovered that she was the miscreant herself. I sorted her for it.

She is back again now, for the English, of course, have departed long since, and will not be seen again in the glen till next year's shooting time comes round. On the day they left they crossed over to remind me that they were looking forward to the Diary, and when I protested that I did not even know how to begin they said in their audacious way, 'You could begin by writing about us.' I have taken them at their word, though they little understand that I may have been making a quiet study of them while they thought that I was the divert.

As I say, I have found them to be very pleasant persons, so long as you make allowances for them that one could not be expected to make for his own people. The bright array of their kilts is a pretty bit of colour to us, the trousered people of the glen. They have a happy knack of skimming life that has a sort of attraction for deeper but undoubtedly slower natures.

The way they riot with their pockets is beyond words; I am credibly informed by Posty that they even have worms sent to them by post in tins.

They are easy to exploit for gain, as Posty was quick to see, and many a glass of——— has he, to my grief (for I am a totaler), got from them by referring to himself as 'she.' I have written that word with a dash because, now I cast back, I believe I have never heard it spoken by the glen folk. One might say that it is thus,———, pronounced by them. They invite you to partake, and you are dull in the uptake if you don't understand of what you are being asked to partake.

They make a complete sentence by saying of a friend, 'He is one who on a market day,' and leaving the rest to the listener's common sense.

Similarly they say, 'He never unless he is in company,' or, 'He just at a time because he is lonely like.'

Now the English in this matter as in many others are different, and they give the thing its name and boldly say, with pride in knowing the word, Usquebaugh. In this I hold that they come out of the murky affair with greater honesty but more shamelessly than we do.

They were hospitable to me, and had me up at the Grand House once, giving me the most attractive lady to take in on my arm to dinner, and putting the most popular man on the other side of her to make up for me. They are so well-meaning that it would have vexed them to know I noticed this, and of course I gave it the go-by; but there are few things that escape my observation. On the Sabbath there were always some of them in the kirk, where they were very kindly to the plate but lazy at turning up the chapters. When they had new arrivals these were always brought to see the shepherds' dogs in the pews; in fact, I have decided that the one thing the English know for certain about Scottish religion is that there are shepherds' dogs in the pews.

The English, how quick they are compared to a cautious Scot like myself. He may be far deeper in the fundamentals when there is time to take soundings; but they are so ready.

That time I dined with them the talk might be on subjects I was better versed in than any of them, but they would away to another topic before I could steady myself and give utterance. My most pitiful posture was when I was unable not only to say a thing worth while but to say anything at all, however superficial. Is man ever more lonely than in company when all language forsakes him and he would be thankful if he could cry out 'Agamemnon'? At that dinner I sometimes wished I could have had a dictionary on my knee so as to get hold of any word whatever.

The man on the other side of the lady I was in charge of made a flattering remark to her about her looking very pretty tonight (they stick at nothing), and said to me across her did I not agree with him. It may just have been a considerateness in him to bring the dumb into the talk, a meritorious quality they have; but to be approached in such a direct manner about a lady's looks before her face threw me off my balance, and all I could reply was that I had not given the subject sufficient consideration to be able to make a definite statement about it. She stopped quickly at that, like one looking for her feet, but on reflection I had a suspicion she was anxious not to let me see her making a mouth, at which they are great adepts; and she will never know now that I can say a neat thing myself if they will give me time.

The thoughtlessness of them is something grievous, but their manners make me wae for my own.

When they said good-bye to me at the Five Houses their departure was like a flight of birds. As the poet says, they seemed to take away the sun in their pockets.

At the manse I had shown them my study, this room I am now sitting in (with the wind still on the rampage), and especially I drew their attention to what I have called the finest plenishing thereof, the two presses containing theological and classical tomes of great girth, somewhat warped in the binding. My friends cried out at this being all the reading I had to carry me through the time when the glen may be locked, and they sniffed (but in a polite way) at the closeness of my cosy room, not understanding, as any Presbyterian would have done, that what they mistook for mustiness was the noble smell of learning.

The ladies said that what I needed to madden me pleasantly was not a Diary but a wife. They were at the Five Houses by this time, getting into their machines, and I countered them with 'Who would have me?' I was not putting them to the question, but all the ladies cried out, 'I will,' and made pretence to want to leap from their carriages. I can see now they were just getting after me.

Such are this strange race, the English, whose light-heartedness, as in this extraordinary scene, can rise to a pitch called by the French abandon. I dare say they had forgotten all about me before they were out of the glen, and will never have another thought of the Diary; indeed, now as I look at my shelves of massive volumes, which were not of my collecting, I wish I had not agreed to call it a Diary, for that is a word of ill omen in this manse.

TWO

Someone who was with Him

Dec. 3. I have read the above more than once and then hid it away from Christily, because it is written on sermon paper.

Christily is a most faithful young woman with a face as red and lush as a rasp, who knows her carritches both ways, and has such a reverence for ministers that she looks upon me more as an edifice than a mortal. She has an almost equal pride in herself for being a minister's servant, and walks into the kirk in her cheeping lastic sides with an official genteelity that some consider offensive. She has also a provoking way of discussing me in my presence as if I was not there, telling visitors the most intimate things about me, such as the food I like but it does not like me, the while she stands in what is meant to be a respectful attitude, neither inside nor outside the door.

My visitors are likely to be few for some time to come; neighbours from the Five Houses whiles, and I hope Mistress Lindinnock and Dr John from Branders.

The smith at the Five Houses is my chief elder, and as his bairns are innumerable, the family in their two pews are a heartsome sight. A more cautious man in argument I have never known. About as far as he will go is, 'I agree with you to a certain extent,' or 'My answer to that is Yes and No.' Posty has a story that he made the second of these answers at his marriage when asked if he took this woman.

Posty is also at the Five Houses, and is the kind that bears ill-will to none, even if they catch him cheating at the dambrod, which he does with the elbow. He has the cheery face that so often goes with roguery and being good at orra jobs, but though I don't lippen to him in matters of import,

I like to fall in with him more than with some better men. I sometimes play at the teetotum with the smith's bairns, when there is a prize of cracknuts, and undoubtedly on such occasions Posty's pranks add to the festive scene. He will walk miles, too, to tell any ill news.

His most valued possession is a velocipede, which has so often come to bits when he was on it that near every man in the glen has been at the repairing of it, including myself, or at least has contributed twine or iron girds. He brings the letters from Branders on this machine, and as it often runs away with him, we all, dogs, hens and humans, loup the dyke when we see him bearing down on us. He carries telegrams too, but there are so few of these, now the English have gone, that when we see him waving one we ask, 'Who is dead?'

My great friend is Dr John, who is sometimes in the glen to succour us, though he lives at Branders, where he sits under Mr Watery, with whom I sometimes suffer niffer pulpits.

Branders is an overgrown place of five hundred inhabitants, and stands high near a loch, out of which two streams run in opposite directions, like parties to a family feud that can no longer be settled with the claymore. In a spate as many new burns come brawling into this loch as there are hairs on a woman's head, and then are gone before they can be counted. Branders is not in the glen but just at the head of it, and, according to Dr John, it stopped there because it said to itself, 'Those who go farther will fare worse.' It is jimply six miles from my manse in summer weather, but seventeen from the nearest railway station and electric telegraph. Dr John says that whether Branders is the beginning or end of desolation depends on your looking up or down the road.

A gnarled, perjink little figure of about fifty is Dr John, grandly bearded, but for a man of larger size. His blue eyes are hod away in holes, sunken into them, I suppose, because he has looked so long on snow. He wears a plaid in all weathers and sometimes even in the house, for, as he says, before he has time to wap it off and find it again somebody on a cart-horse will be clattering to his door to hurry him to my glen. I have seen him, too, sitting behind on that clattering horse. Repute says that for humane ends he will get through when the glen is locked to all others, though his sole recompense may be a ham at the killing, or a kebbock or a keg of that drink I have spelt————. Though I touch it not, I cannot deny that he partakes as if it were water, and is celebrated (and even condoled with) for never being the worse of it. He always takes it hot, which he calls never mixing his drinks, and I don't know a neater hand at squeezing down the sugar with the ladle.

If he is in the glen he sometimes puts up his shalt at the Five Houses and stays the night with me, when we have long cracks, the kettle-lid plopping while he smokes his pipe, grunting, which is the Scottish way of bringing out the flavour. Last night was such an occasion, and up here in the study as we sat into the fire we got on to the stories about 'Strangers,' of which he says humorously he has heard many clutters though he has never had the luck to encounter the carls themselves. He maintains that the origin of all the clavers and clecking of nowadays was that lamentable affair of the '45, which, among its misdeeds, for long gave an ill name to the tartan.

The glen had been a great hiding place of 'pretty men' of the period, and among its fearsome crags and waur cleughs, if ancient tales be true, those ill-gettit gentlemen had lurked for months and some of them for years.

It is said that forebears of folk still in the glen used to see them from below searching for roots atween the rocks, and so distraught with hunger that they went on searching openly while they were being shot at by the red-coats, who would not face the speel. When the glen was in a sink of snow, and pursuit for a time at an end, they sometimes lay at the Grand House (which was loyal to their dark cause), and held secret carouse there.

They were talked of with an intake of breath by the glen folk, who liked best to be of no party unless they were of both, would not betray them to an enemy that hunted them with bloodhounds, yet would hold no intercourse with them willingly, and looked the other way if they came upon one of the gaunt red-shanks unexpectedly, as sometimes happened, carrying braxy mutton or venison to his lurking place, or a salmon that the otters had left by the burn after taking one nip from its neck.

Those glen folk were too mouse to call the fugitives Jacobites. 'The Strangers,' they said.

In one case they said 'Someone Who Was With Him,' as if that was as far as it was canny to go. The Him was the Stranger who is believed by the simple to have been the Chevalier himself. He is said to have lain in the glen for a time in July month, fevered and so hard pressed that no friends dared go nigh him with nourishment lest it led to his capture. I have not seen his hoddy place, but the doctor tells me it is still there and is no more than a lair beneath what we call a bield, a shelter for sheep. Very like, it began by being a tod's hole, and was torn bigger with dirks. If it ever existed, the lair has been long filled up with stones, which are all that remain to mark the royal residence.

Sheep again shelter in the bield, but there were none there in the time of the Prince, if it was he, nor, as I say the story goes, could food be passed to him. In his extremity he was saved by the mysterious Someone Who Was With Him.

Of course the legend has it that she was young and fair and of high degree, and that she loved much.

She fed him with the unwilling help of the eagles. The Eagles Rock, which is not far from the bield, is a mighty mass, said by the ghillies of today to be unscaleable by man because of what is called the Logan stone. No eagles build there now; they have fallen to the guns of their modern enemy, the keepers, who swear that one pair of eagles will carry a hundred grouse or more to their nest to feed their young.

At that time there was an eagle's nest on the top of the rock. The climb is a perilous one, but now and again hardy folk get up as far as the Logan stone, where they turn back. There are Logan stones, I am told, throughout the world, and they are rocking stones. It is said they may be seen rocking in the wind, and yet hold on for centuries. Such a monster hangs out from our Eagles Rock, and you cannot reach the top save by climbing over it, nor can you get on to it without leaping. Twice men of the glen have leapt and it threw them off. Nathless, the story is that this Someone Who Was With Him got through the searchers in the dark, reached the top of the rock by way of the Logan stone, and after sometimes fighting the parent eagles for possession, brought down young grouse for her lord.

By all kind accounts she was a maiden, and in our glen she is remembered by the white heather, which, never seen here till then, is said, nonsensically, to be the marks of her pretty naked feet.

The white heather brought her little luck. In a hurried and maybe bloody flitting she was left behind. Nothing more is recorded of her except that when her lord and master embarked for France he enjoined his Highlanders 'to feed her and honour her as she had fed and honoured him.' They were faithful though misguided, and I dare say they would have done it if they could. Some think that she is in the bield in the hole beneath the stones, still waiting. They say, maybe there was a promise.

Such was the doctor's tale as we sat over the fire. 'A wayward woman,' was how he summed her up, with a shake of the head.

THREE

The Spectrum

Dec. 3 (Contd.). 'I am thinking,' Dr John was saying when I caught up with him again, for my mind had been left behind with this woman, and I was wondering if she was 'wayward,' and what was wrong with it, for I liked the word, 'I am thinking that all the clash about the folk of nowadays meeting 'Strangers' when the glen is locked comes out of that troubled past. In a white winter, as you have jaloused yourself, there is ower little darg for a hardy race, and they hark back by the hearth-stone to the forgotten, ay, and the forbidden. But I assure you, Mr Yestreen, despite the whispers, the very name of the '45 is now buried in its own stour. Even Posty, though he is so gleg with the pipes, gets by himself if you press him about what his old ballants mean. Neither good luck nor mischief, so far as I can discover, comes to the havrels of nowadays who think they have talked or walked with a Stranger; unless indeed, as some say, it was one of them who mairtered poor Mr H.; and I understand he, being a learned man, always called it a Spectrum.'

This set us talking of him of whom I may have already let out that he once kept a Diary in this manse. It was so far back as to be just hearsay even to Dr John, and belongs to the days when there were no seats in my kirk and all stood on their shanks. Though I say we talked about him we really said very little, unless an occasional furtive glance be speech. All in these parts become furtive when a word, falling as meaningless you would say as a cinder from the fire, brings a sough of the old man back to mind.

Mr H. was a distant predecessor of mine, and a scholar such as the manse is not likely to house again. It was he who collected the library of noble erudition that is in the presses of this room, many of the volumes bound by his own hands that may have dawted them as he bound. His Diary was written on the flyleaves of a number of them.

I believe he thought in Latin and Greek quicker than in his own tongue, for his hurried notes are often in those languages and the more deliberate ones in ours. I am in a dunce's cap with the Greek, but I can plod along with a Latin dictionary, and his entries in the Latin have made me so uneasy that I have torn out the pages and burned them. Mr. Carluke, whom I succeeded, had to confine himself, having no Latin, to the English bits, and he treated some of them similarly, for as he said to me they were about things that will not do at all.

They appear suddenly amidst matter grandly set forth, as if a rat had got at the pages. Minute examination has made me question their being in the same handwrite, though an imitation. This tampering, if such it was, had got by Carluke's attention. 'You mean,' Dr John said to me when I had let him study these bits of Diary (which he peered into with a magnifier the size of a thimble that he carries in his waist-coat pocket and is near as much dreaded by malingerers as he is himself), 'that it is the handwrite of the Spectrum?' If Dr John has a failing it is that he hankers too much to tie one down to a statement, and of course I would not accept this interpretation, for I do not believe in Spectrums.

It is not known even by the credulous when, in Mr H.'s distorted fancy, the Spectrum first came chapping softly at the manse door, and afterwards blattering on it, in a wicked desire to drive the lawful possessor out of the house and take his place. But it was while the glen was locked. Sometimes one of the twain was inside the house and sometimes the other. Sounds were heard, they say, coming from the study, of voices in conflict and blows struck. The dwellers of that time in the Five Houses, of whom two carlines are still alive, maintained that they had seen Mr H. sitting on his dyke at night, because the other was in possession. By this time no servant would bide in the manse after gloaming; and yet, though Mr H. was now the one chapping at the door, they said they could see a light being carried in the house from room to room, and hear something padding on the floors. He did not walk, they said, he padded.

'When they found the minister, according to the stories,' Dr John said, 'his face was in an awful mess.'

What had caused that, I asked, and he said shortly that he supposed Spectrums had teeth.

It was eerie to reflect that to those two carlines, as we call ancient women, my study must still be more his than mine, and that they would not be taken aback if they came into it at that moment and found the old man in the grandy chair.

'The wayward woman was a better visitor to the glen than this other at any rate,' I ventured, and the answer he made I would as soon he had kept to himself. 'According to some of the ranters,' he said, with a sort of leer at me, 'they are the same person.'

We tried to get on to more comfortable subjects, but it was as if the scholar's story would not leave the room. 'I feel as if there were three of us here tonight,' I said to the doctor.

'Ay,' said he, 'and a fourth keeking in at the window.'

As usual, the old-wife gossip in which we had been luxuriating (for what more was it?) was interrupted by Christily coming in to announce that our sederunt was at an end. She did this, not in words, but by carrying away the kettle. This garr'd us to our beds, fuming at her as being one of those women, than whom there are few more exasperating, who think all men should do their bidding. I had to be up betimes this morning to see him take the gate.

FOUR

The Locking of the Glen

Dec. 19. In this white wastrie of a world the dreariest moment is when custom makes you wind up your watch. Were it not for the Sabbath I would get lost in my dates. Not a word has gone into my Diary for a fortnight past. Now would be the time for it if there were anything to chronicle; but nothing happens, unless one counts as an event that I brought my hens into the manse on discovering that their toes were frozen to the perch (I had to bring the perch too). My two sheep are also in by, and yesterday my garden slithered off to the burn with me on it like a passenger. I have sat down at an antrin time to the Diary to try to fill up with an account such as this of the locking of the glen, and the result has been rather disquieting to me, as I will maybe tell farther on and maybe not.

The glen road, on which our intercourse with ourselves as well as with the world so largely depends, was among the first to disappear under the blankets. White hillocks of the shape of eggs have arisen here and there, and are dangerous too, for they wobble as though some great beast beneath were trying to turn round. The mountains are so bellied out that they have ceased to be landmarks. The farm-towns look to me to be smored. I pull down my blinds so that I may rest my eyes on my blues and reds indoors. Though the Five Houses are barely a hundred yards away I have to pick out signs of life with my spy-glass.

I am practically cut off from my kind. Even the few trees are bearing white ropes, thick as my wrist, instead of branches, and the only thing that is a bonny black is the burn, once a mere driblet but now deep, with a lash around at corners, and unchancey to risk. At times of ordinary wet they cross here to the kirk in two easy jumps on boulders placed there for the purpose, and called the brig, but the boulders are now like sunk boats, and of the sprinkling of members who reached the kirk on the 9th, one used a vaulting pole and lost it.

Last Sabbath I did not open the kirk but got down to the burn and preached to a handful standing on the other side. My heart melted for the smith's bairns, every one of whom was there, and I have cried a notice across the burn that next Sabbath the bell will ring as a solemn reminder, but the service will be in the smiddy, whether I find that man's pole or not.

Two or three times Posty, without his velocipede, has penetrated to Branders and delivered my letters and a newspaper to me by casting them over the burn tied to stones. There is no word of Dr John. For nearly a week, except for an occasional shout, I have heard no voice but Christily's. I sit up here o' nights trying to get meanings out of Mr H.'s Diary, and not so much finding them in the written books as thinking I hear them padding up the stair as a wayward woman might do. In the long days I go out and shule, and get dunted by slides from the roof.

Of an evening Posty struts up and down in front of the Five Houses, playing on his pipes. I can see him like a pendulum passing the glints of light. I can hear him from the manse, but still better from the burn-side, if I slue down to listen in the dark. On one of those nights I got a dirl in the breast of me. It was when I went back to the manse after hearing him finish that Border boast, 'My name it is little Jock Elliot.' The glen was deserted by all other sound now, but as I birzed open the manse door (for the snow had got into the staples) I heard my fiddle playing 'My name it is little Jock Elliot.' For a moment I thought that Christily was at it, but then I knew she must be bedded, and she has no ear, and it was grander playing than Posty's though he is a kittle hand. I suppose I did not stand still in my darkened hallan for more than half a minute, and when I struck a light to get at a candle the music stopped. There is no denying that the stories about the Spectrum flitted through me, and it needed a shove from myself to take me up the stair. Of course there was nobody. I had come back with the tune in my ears, or it was caused by some vibration in the air. I found my fiddle in the locked press just as I had left it, except that it must have been leaning against the door, for it fell into my arms as I opened the press, and I had the queer notion that it clung to me. I could not compose myself till I had gone through my manse with the candle, and even after that I let the instrument sleep with me.

More reasonable fancies came to me in the morning, as that it might be hard on a fiddle never to be let do the one thing it can do; also that maybe, like the performers, they have a swelling to cry out to rivals, 'I can do better than that.' Any allure I may have felt, to take advantage of this mere fancy and put the neck-rest beneath my chin again, I suppressed; but I let Posty know he could have the loan of my instrument on condition that he got it across the burn dry. By the smith's connivance this was accomplished in a cart. It is now my fiddle Posty plays instead of his pipes, which are not in much better condition than his velocipede and are repaired in a similar manner. I extracted just one promise from him, that he would abstain from the baneful Jacobite lilts he was so fond of; but he sometimes forgets or excuses himself across the burn by saying, 'She likes that kind best, and she is ill to control once she's off.' It is pretty to hear him in the gloaming, letting the songs loose like pigeons.

To write this account of the glen when it is locked has been an effort, for the reason that I have done it twice already and in the morning it was not there. I sat down by lamplight on both occasions to write it and thought I had completed my task, but next morning I found just a few broken lines on otherwise blank pages. Some of them were repeated again and again like a cry, such as 'God help me,' as if I were a bird caught in a trap. I am not in any way disturbed of mind or body, at any rate in the morning. Yet this was what I had written. I am none so sure but what it may prove to be all I have written again.

I will now go and say good-night to the Old Lady, for though it is barely half nine on the clock, we keep early hours in the wilderness. This is a moment I owe to her ingenuity. The Grand House, which has of course a statelier name of its own, is a steep climb from here and is at present inaccessible, the approach having thrown in its lot with the fields, but it is visible, and at half nine o'clock she shoots her blind up and down twice, and I reply with mine. Hers, I am thankful to say, is red, or the lamp behind it has a red shade, and this shooting of the blinds is our way of saying good-night to each other. When she shoots hers three times it means something personal about my gown, and I make no answer. There is a warmth, however, in saying good-night to a living being when the glen is so still that I am thinking you could hear a whit-rit on the move. Sometimes I stand by my window long after hers is dumb, and I have felt that night was waiting, as it must have done once, for the first day. It is the stillness that is so terrible. If only something would crack the stillness.

FIVE

The Stranger

Dec. 21. For the first time since the glen was locked Dr John 'threw in,' as we say, this morning.

He came straight to the study, where he found us at family exercise. I did not look up from my knees, but Christily whispered to me, 'Be short,' which I dare say made me in consequence a little longer. Yet I knew she would not have taken such a liberty unless there was something untoward with the man, and though I found when I rose that he was on his knees with us, I saw that he had gone to sleep on them. His face was so peaked that I sent Christily hurriedly for the bottle of brandy which has lain in the manse uncorked since I came here six months ago, and as soon as he had partaken she hauled off his boots and ran him on to the stair-head to wring and scrape him, for he was getting on to the carpet.

I saw he ettled to be rid of her before communicating something by-ordinar to me, and he took the best way to effect this by saying in a sentence that he had got through to Joanna Minch and it was a girl and both were doing well; whereupon Christily was off to cry the tidings across the burn.

He was nodding in the grandy with fatigue, so that it looked as if only by sudden jerks could he keep his head on, but he brought out the words, 'There is more in it than I told Christily. I have been to the shieling, but I did not get through in time. There were two lives saved in that bit house in the small hours; but don't be congratulating me, for I had naught to do with it.'

Having said this, he fell head foremost into sleep, and I

had ill rousing him, which I was sweer to do, but he had made it plain that he wanted to say more.

'It's such a camsterie tale,' he told me, 'as might banish sleep in any man; but I am dog-tired and unless you keep pulling my beard with all the strength that is in you I'll be dovering again.'

I may say here that I had to do as he instructed me several times. We must have looked a strange pair, the doctor yawning and going off in the middle of sentences while I tugged fiercely at the beard.

I will put his bewildering tale together as best I can. He had forced his way last evening to the farm of the Whammle, where a herd was lying with two broken legs. While he was there Fargie Routh, the husband of Joanna, had tracked him down to say that she was terrible near her reckoning. The doctor started off with him rather anxious, for Fargie was 'throughither,' and it was Joanna's first. Dr John had floundered into worse drifts, but a stour of snow was plastering his face and he lost Fargie at the sleugh crossing. He tumbled and rumbled down in a way at which he is a master-hand, and reached the shieling hours before the husband, who is a decent stock but very unusual in the legs. The distance is a short mile when the track is above-ground. Dr John was relieved to smell smoke, for he feared to find he was on a sleeveless errand, and that the woman would be found frozen.

I told him I knew the house, which is a lonesome one-roomed cot of double stone and divot, with but a bole window. I asked if he had found Joanna alone, but he had taken the opportunity of my making a remark to fall asleep again.

I got his eyes open in the manner recommended by him, and he said with one of his little leers at me, 'She was not quite alone; but maybe you are one of those who do not count an infant till it be christened.'

'If there is any haste for that—' I cried, looking for my boots.

'There is none,' he said.

'But who had been with her? Was she in such a bad condition that she could give you no information about that?'

'She was in fine condition and she could and she did,' he said. 'I was with her till Fargie, who had gone back to the Whammle, brought down the gude-wife, and I have no doubt Joanna is now giving the particulars to them. They are such uncommon particulars,' he went on, taking a chew at them, 'that I can fancy even the proud infant sitting up to listen.'

Then who was it that had acted in his place, I enquired, not daring to be more prolix lest he should again be overtaken.

That, he said, was what he was asking me.

'Dr John—'

'Be assured,' said he, 'that I am too dung owner with tire to be trifling with you; but this will become more your affair than mine. It is not to me they will look to be told who she was but to their minister.'

'I hope I shall not fail them,' I said loftily. Nevertheless I dreed what was coming, and I insisted on his keeping awake 'or I would lay a hot iron on the beard.'

He said he had found a kettle on a bright fire and Joanna in her bed with the child, who was fittingly swaddled in her best brot. He would not let her talk until he had satisfied himself that everything necessary had been done, and then (for the curiosity was mounting to his brain) he said with pretended casualness, 'I see you have been having a nice cup of tea.'

'And merry she was at the making of it,' replied Joanna, turning merry herself.

'I forget,' said he, 'if you mentioned who she was?'

'Of course it was one of the Strangers,' she said.

'Of course it would be one of those curiosities,' said he, 'but I never chanced to fall in with ane; what was she like?'

'Oh,' said Joanna, 'she was like the little gentleman that sits under his tail' – meaning a squirrel.

'I thought she would be something like that,' he said; 'but had you no fear of her?'

'Never,' said Joanna, 'till after the bairn was born, and then for just a short time, when she capered about mad-like with glee, holding it high in the air, and dressing and undressing it in the brot, so as to have another peep at it, and very proud of what she had done for me and it till a queer change came over her and I had a sinking that she was going to bite it. I nippit it from her.'

'To bite them is not my usual procedure at a birth,' the doctor had said, 'but we all have our different ways.'

Joanna gave him a fuller story of the night than, as he said, would be of any profit to a sumph of a bachelor like Adam Yestreen, but he told me some of its events.

The door had blown open soon after Fargie's departure, leaving naught but reek to heat her, and the bole closed, and when the fire went down she would have been glad to cry back the reek. She thought the cold candle of her life was at the flicker. The Stranger relit the fire, but there was no way she could conceive of heating that body on the box-bed. Then the thought came to her.

'She strippit herself naked,' Joanna said, 'and made me keep my feet on her, as if she was one of them pig bottles for toasting the feet of the gentry; and when my feet were warm, she lay close to me, first on one side and then on the other. She was as warm as a browning bannock when she began, but by the time the heat of her had passed into me I'se uphaud she was cold as a trout.'

As to the actual birth, though this was Joanna's first child, she knew more about the business than did her visitor, who seems to have been in a dither of importance over the novelty of the occasion. She was sometimes very daring and sometimes at such a loss that in Joanna's words, 'she could just pet me and kiss me and draw droll faces at me with the intent to help me through, and when she got me through she went skeer with triumph, crying out as she strutted up and down that we were the three wonders of the world.'

The whole affair, Dr John decided, must have been strange enough 'to put the wits of any medical onlooker in a bucket,' and if he let his mind rest on it he would forget how to sleep as well as how to practise surgery; so in the name of Charity would I leave him in the land of Nod for an hour while I thought out some simple explanation for my glen folk.

He got his hour, though sorely did I grudge it, for I was in a bucket myself.

When he woke refreshed I was by his side to say at once, as if there had not been a moment's interruption, 'Of course she was some neighbour.'

There was a glint in his blue eyes now, but he said decisively, 'There is no way out by that road, my man; Joanna is acquaint with every neighbour in the glen.'

'An outside woman of flesh and blood,' I prigged with him, 'must have contrived to force the glen; as, after all, you did yourself.'

That, he maintained, was even less possible than the other.

I was stout for there being some natural explanation, and he reminded me unnecessarily that there was the one Joanna gave. At this I told him sternly to get behind me.

I could not forbear asking him if he had any witting of such stories being common to other lonely glens, and he shook his head, which made me the more desperate.

He saw in what a stramash I was, and, dropping his banter, came kindly to my relief. 'Do you really think,' he said, in his helpful confident way, 'that I have any more belief in warlocks and "Strangers" than you have yourself? I'll tell you my conclusion, which my sleep makes clearer. It is that Joanna did the whole thing by herself, as many a woman has done before her. She must at some time, though, have been in a trance, which are things I cannot pretend to fathom, and have thought a woman was about her who was not there. It cows to think of a practical kimmer like Joanna having, even in her hour of genius, such an imagination; that bit about nearly biting the bairn is worthy of Mr H.'s Spectrum.'

'None of that,' I cried. 'She no doubt got that out of the old minister's story.'

'Ay,' he granted, 'let's say that accounts for it. I admit it is the one thing that has been worrying me. But at any rate it is of no importance, as we are both agreed that Joanna was by her lonesome. She had no joyous visitor, no. Heigh-ho, Mr Yestreen, it's almost a pity to have to let such a pleasantly wayward woman go down the wind.'

It was far from a pity to me. I was so thankful to him for getting rid of her that I pressed his hand repeatedly. I was done with wayward women.

SIX

Superstition and its Antidote

Dec. 26. I got as far as the shieling two days behind
Joanna's story and held a kirstening, this being the first
at which I have ever officiated.

The usual course is to have it in the kirk toward the end
of a service, but in urgent cases it may be on the day of
birth. There was maybe no reason for precipitancy in this
case, the child being lusty, but in the peculiar circumstances I considered it my duty to make her safe. When I
took her in my arms, by far the youngest I had ever
meddled with, I was suddenly aware of my youthful presumption. I should have been warned beforehand about the
beauty of their finger nails.

Yet I dared not let on that I was the most ignorant in the
room, for I was the minister, and therefore to be looked up
to. Also Joanna swore to her visit from the Stranger, with
side-looks at me as if she had given birth to a quandary as
well as to a litlun; and the lave of the party present were
already familiar with her story and were all agog.

So, knowing how ill it fares with a minister's usefulness if
he does not keep upside with his flock, I was bolder than I
felt, and told them in a short exposition that there had been
no 'Stranger' in the affair; otherwise some of them would
certainly have seen her.

They all nodded their agreement and thanked me for
making it so clear, but I knew in my bones that they did not
accept one word of my redding up, though they regarded it
as very proper for a minister, especially one who was new to
the glen.

This way they have, of heartily accepting what you tell

them and then going their own gate, is disheartening to me, and at one time I thought of making any dirdum about Strangers a subject of stern discipline from the pulpit. Fear did not enter into my reluctance, for I knew they would esteem me the more the harder I got at them, but I drew back from the ease of superiority toward men and women whose simple lives have been so often more grimly fought than my own. It relieves me, therefore, to have decided that I may get through their chinks more creditably in another manner.

The amelioration in the weather, which probably will not last, is what put the idea into my head. Some of us have been able to step about a little these last days. A curran herd, weary of bothy life, have made so bold as to find out where the glen road is. Of course they cannot shule down to it, but they have staked some of the worst bits, and several carts have passed along as if the proximity to it gave them courage. I saw from the manse the Old Lady's carriage trying for Branders. The smith's klink-klink from the smiddy, which is the most murie sound in a countryside next to a saw-mill, shows that he has had at least one to shod. Posty has ridden on his velocipede the length of the Five Houses and back, with the result that you can hardly see his face for the brown paper.

It is true that there is no possibility of opening the kirk on Sabbath, for though we have thrown planks across the burn, with a taut rope to hang on by, the place is too mortal cold for sitting in through a service. There is, however, the smiddy, which can be used for other purposes besides preaching.

All our large social events take place in the smiddy, and the grandest consist of Penny Weddings, when you are expected, if convenient, to bring, say, a hen or a small piece of plenishing to the happy pair. The actual marriage, of course, takes place in the bride's home, and not, in the queer English way, in the kirk. We have had no weddings since I came, but twice last month we had Friendlies, which we consider the next best thing.

Our Friendlies are always in two parts, the first part being devoted to a lecture by the minister or some other person of culture, who is usually another minister. This lecture is invariably of a bright, entertaining character, and some are greater adepts at unbending in this way than others, the best being Mr Watery of Branders, whose smile is of such expansion that you might say it spreads over the company like honey. Laughter and the clapping of hands in moderation are not only permissible during the lectures but encouraged.

The second part of a Friendly is mostly musical with songs, and is provided by local talent, in which Posty takes too great a lead. There is an understanding that I remain for the first song or so, whether I am lecturing or in the Chair. This is to give a tone to the second part, and then I slip away, sometimes wishing I could bide to enjoy the mirth, but I know my presence casts a shadow on their ease. The time in which Friendlies would be most prized is when the glen is locked, but the difficulty for all except the Five Houses lies in getting to the smiddy.

Nevertheless we are to attempt a Friendly on Thursday, though Mr Watery, who was to be the lecturer with a magic lantern, which of course is a great addition, has cried off on account of nervousness lest the weather should change before he gets home again. I have undertaken to fill his place to the best of my more limited ability, as indeed it is.

I am doing so the more readily because of this idea that came to me, which promises to be a felicitous one. It is to lecture to them on Superstition, with some sly and yet shattering references to a recent so-called event in the glen, all to be done with a light touch, yet of course with a moral, which is that a sense of humour is the best antidote to credulity. There are few of the smaller subjects to which I

have given greater thought than to Humour, its ramifications and idiosyncrasies, and I have a hope that I may not
do so badly at this. I wish Mr Watery could be present, for I
think I can say that I know more about Humour than he
does, though he is easier at it.

SEVEN

Miss Julie Logan

Dec. 28. Hours have passed since I finished my lecture. I know not how many times I have sat down to write about her, and then taken to wandering the study floor instead. My mind goes back in search of every crumb of her, and I am thinking I could pick her up better on my fiddle than in written words.

My eyes never fell on her till I got to my peroration. This is no reflection on my sight, for all the company in the smiddy, and there were more than thirty, had to sit in darkness so that they could better watch my face between the two candles. She was with Mistress Lindinnock, who presented me to her, and they came over to the manse while the shelties were being yoked. I held her hand to guide her across the planks. She is the Old Lady's grand-niece, and her name is Miss Julie Logan. I am glad of her Christian name, for it has always been my favourite.

In the past few years, up to this night, my lot had thrown me mostly among my seniors, and a glow that once I knew seemed to be just a memory warning me that ministers must be done quickly with the clutches of youth.

I am no hand at describing the garb of beauty, and the nearest I can get to her, after much communing, is that she is a long stalk of loveliness. She carried a muff of fur, and at times would raise it to her face as if she knew no better than to think it was a scent-bottle, or peep over it like a sitting bird in the bole of a tree.

The upper part of her attire was black and the rest green. There was a diverting mutch on her head which, for some reason I cannot as yet determine, you could have got

282

on smiling terms with though you had met it hanging on a nob.

She is from Edinburgh, and it was to get her that I saw the Grand House carriage fighting its way to Branders yesterday.

I have only seen her for twenty minutes. There is such a beloved huskiness in her voice that she should be made to say everything twice. She glides up a manse stair with what I take to be the lithesomeness of a panther. I like her well when she is haughty, and even better when she is melting, and best of all when she is the two together, which she often is.

I was all throughither when she sat down on the one of my chairs that I have hitherto held to be of the least account. She looked as meek at that moment as if a dove was brooding in her face.

It is not beauty of person that I heed but internal beauty, which in her is as plain to read as if she wore it outside.

What I would last part with is the way her face sparkles, not just her eyes but her whole face. This comes and goes, and when it has gone there is left the sweet homeliness that is woman's surest promise to man. Fine I knew for ever that I needed none but her.

Fain would I have made observations to her that put a minister in a favourable light. I am thinking that the Old Lady spoke at times, for she is a masterpiece at conversation, but all I remember of her is that she soon fell asleep in the grandy chair, which is a sudden way she has. This disregard of her company has sometimes annoyed me at kirk meetings (where we have to pause till she wakes up), but not on this occasion.

In my lecture I had spoken about humour which is profound and humour which is shallow, such as pulling away your chair. Miss Julie Logan said to me in the manse that she was only interested in the profound kind, with its ramifications and idiosyncrasies. She said she found it a hard kind to detect, and wished she could be so instructed as to recognise profound humour, whether written or spoken.

When she said this there was something so pleading in her shining eyes that, instead of replying in a capable manner, I offered to explain the thing with a bit of paper and a pencil.

I drew a note of exclamation, and showed her how they were put into books, at the end of sentences, to indicate that the remark was of a humorous character. She got the loan of the pencil and practised making notes of exclamation under my instruction.

She said she questioned whether profound humour would not still baffle her in the spoken word, and I agreed that here it was more difficult, but told her that if you watched the speaker's face narrowly you could generally tell by a glint in it; and if there was no glint his was the mistake and not yours.

She asked me to say something humorous to her, the while she would watch for the glint, which I did, and she saw it.

She said she feared it would be a long time before she could do my glint, and asked me to watch her face while she practised it; and I was very willing.

She said she would like to have my opinion on the statement of an Englishman about the bagpipes, namely that they sound best if you are far away from them, and the farther away the better. Other people present had laughed at that, and could I tell her why?

I said that no doubt what they laughed at was at the man's forgetting that if you were too far away from the pipes you would not hear them at all.

Even in those moments I was not such a gowk as to be unaware that I was making a deplorable exhibition of myself. Whatever she seemed to want me to say I just had to say it, for the power had gone from me to show her that I was not mentally deficient. However, when it came to this about the pipes I broke up and laid my face on the table, and she raised my head, and was woebegone when she saw the ruin she had made.

'Have I hurt you?' she asked, and I could just nod. 'Why did you let me?' she said with every bit of her, and I answered darkly, 'I cannot help saying or doing whatever Miss Julie Logan wants.'

The wet glittered on her eyes in a sort of contest as you can sometimes hear them do on the strings.

I said, 'It is bitter mortifying to me to be seen in such disadvantageous circumstances by Miss Julie Logan at the very time of all others when I should have liked to be better than my best.'

I stroked her muff and, somehow, the action made me say, 'This is a very unhomely manse,' though I had never thought that before.

She held out her hand to me, with the palm upwards like one begging for forgiveness, and I have been wondering ever since what she meant me precisely to do with it. I pressed it on my heart, and I filled at long last with what becomes a man in his hour and I said, 'I love you, Miss Julie Logan,' and she said as soft as a snowflake, 'Yes, I know.' Then Christily came in with the blackberry wine on a server, and when Miss Julie Logan drank it I could see her throat flushing as it went down, which they say also happened with Mary Stewart. Then the Old Lady woke up and said that the ponies must be yoked by this time, so I took the ladies across to the carriage, Christily going in front with the lamp. I could hear Miss Julie Logan talking sweetly to her, though it was the Old Lady who was on my arm.

It is now on the chap of midnight, and since I wrote the above I have been down to my kirk and unlocked the door and lit a candle and stood looking for a long time at the manse pew. It is in a modest position on the right of the pulpit, disdaining to call attention to itself. For my part, I could never walk down the aisle of any kirk without being as conscious of which was the manse pew as of which was the pulpit. I do not look, I just feel it.

Usually there is only Christily in my pew, and she sits at the far end. Not all manse pews have a door, but mine has, and I would sit next it if I were out of the pulpit, which can only be if another minister is officiating for me. When a minister is a married man, as all ministers ought to be, it is the lawful right of his wife to sit next the door, with a long empty space between her and the servant, unless they be blessed with children. I stood by my manse pew picturing Miss Julie Logan sitting next the door. She is a tall lady, and I wondered whether the seat was too low for her; and such is my condition that, if I had brought nails and a hammer with me, I would have raised it there and then.

EIGHT

Christily goes Queer

Dec. 30. In the midst of my exaltation come disquieting symptoms in Christily. I think, now I look back, that she has been unsettled these past few days and that occasionally she has glanced covertly at me as if she feared I suspected her of something. Whether this was so or not, she is in a bad state now, and I am very ravelled in my mind about her.

It showed itself this morning when I made a remark to her about Miss Julie Logan. I knew it would be more befitting not to bring that name into everyday conversation, but something within me hankered to hear how it sounded on other lips. Nothing could have been more carefully casual than the way I introduced the subject, and yet the dryness came into my mouth that makes it so desirable for a public speaker to have a glass of water handy.

'And so,' I said, 'there is a young lady at the Grand House now, Christily.'

'Is there?' said she, like one cheering up for a gossip.

'Did you not know,' I enquired, 'that it is there Miss Julie Logan is staying?'

'What Miss Julie Logan?' she asked.

'The young lady,' I said patiently, 'whom Mistress Lindinnock brought to the manse the night before last.'

'I saw no young lady,' she said; 'there was just the two of you came in, you and Mistress Lindinnock.'

'Is this temper, Christily,' I demanded, 'or what is it? You helped Miss Julie Logan to a glass of blackberry wine; also you carried the lantern when I escorted them back to the carriage, and you were in front conversing with her.'

Her eyes stood out as in some sudden affliction, and,

when I stepped toward her, asking if she was ill, she cried 'God help me!' and rushed out of the study.

What did it portend? Had I unwittingly opened the door to some secret the poor soul had been keeping from me? I was very riven and I followed on her heels to the kitchen, but she had locked the door and no answer could I get when I spoke through the keyhole to her. This was very disturbing from such an excellent woman, and I went on my knees, with the door between us, and called in a loud voice to the malevolent one to come out of her. I could hear her wailing sore.

In much perturbation I got across to the Five Houses on the chance of finding Dr John, as Posty's wife is down with a complaint that beats the skill of her neighbours; the silly tod has found out that she is four years older than she thought, and though until that moment in robust health she at once took to her bed.

Fortunately I got the doctor, and on our way across I told him of what had happened. I was relieved to find that he did not take the matter with my seriousness; indeed he was more interested in Miss Julie Logan, of whom he had not heard till now, than in Christily's case, which he foretold would turn out to be tantrums brought on by my writing so many love-letters. It seems, though news to me, that Christily is responsible for tattle about my sitting for hours writing love-letters, these being what she has made of my Diary. However meddlesome this is, it took a load from my mind, and I was feeling comfortable when he went off to the kitchen, grinning, and declaring that he would shake her like a doctor's bottle.

He was gone for a long time, and it was a very different Dr John who came back. I have seen him worry his way through some rasping ordeals, but never showing the least emotion. Now, however, he was in such a throb that at sight of him I cried out, 'Is it as bad as that?'

'It's bad,' he said. 'Man, it is so bad and so unexpected

that for the first time in my practice I cannot even pretend to know how to act; let me be for a minute.' He paced the floor, digging his gnarled fists into his eyes, a way he has when in pursuit of a problem, as if the blackness thus created helped him to see better.

'There is one of two things that must be done,' he said, 'and I have got to choose, but the responsibility is very terrible.'

I waited, thinking he was to take me into his confidence, but, instead, he just fell to staring in a kind of wonderment at me. I began to assure him that every help I could give would be forthcoming, and at that he gave a jarring laugh. I was offended, but he was at once contrite and asked for my advice.

'We could ask the young lady to come down with Mistress Lindinnock and show herself,' I suggested.

'No, we could not,' he said, so sharply that I got stiff again. He put the matter right, though, when he told me of the two courses he had to decide between, for, after all, what I had proposed was one of them; namely to confront the poor sufferer with the two ladies, which he called the kill or cure step. The second course was to go canny for a few days in the hope that the hallucination might pass of itself. She might even wake up on the morrow without it, which at the worst would be a more gentle wakening than the other.

He asked me, not like a consultant but as one who needed a stronger man to lean on, which line of action I would prefer to be taken if I was in Christily's place, and on consideration I admitted that the first one seemed to carry the more grievous shock.

After some discussion we decided to give the softer plan a short trial. I said there could be no harm in it at any rate.

He said, still very worried, indeed he was shaking, that there might be great harm in it, but that he would risk it.

We agreed that, as on all subjects save the one she was as right as I was, it would be best for me in our daily intercourse to be just my usual, but not to talk to her as if I knew she was possessed by an evil spirit.

As the doctor was anxious she should be kept from brooding I also agreed to a proposal from him that her brother, Laurie, who is at present at a loose end in Branders, should pay a visit to the manse for a few days, ostensibly to brighten her, but really of course to watch her on the quiet.

This gives small promise for the time being of a comfortable manse; but what is running in my head even now is that tomorrow afternoon I go, be the weather what it likes, to the Grand House to see Miss Julie Logan again. It will be the last day of the year, but Laurie should be here by then, and Christily will be safe in his care.

Today I am keeping an observant eye on her myself. She has brought up my meals in her old exemplary way and we have exchanged a few cautious words about household affairs, but her face is sore begrutten, and if I try to be specially kind to her she knows the reason and there is more than a threatening of a breakdown.

Poor woman, it is like to be a sad New Year's Eve to her, and a heavy one too for Dr John, who left the manse, very broken. As I let him out I said, 'It is as if the Spectrum had come back to this house.'

'Wheesht, man,' he said.

NINE

The End of a Song

Dec. 31. I will try to put down the events of this terrible night with clearness and precision.

It was in the early afternoon, the snow shimmering like mica, which is sheeps-silver, that I set out for the Grand House, buttoned very thick. Despite the darkness that encompassed Christily I was in an awful and sublime state of happiness.

This may have got into my very appearance and made it unusual, for I met some of the smith's bairns, who generally run to me, but they hinted back, and when I asked what fleyed them one said, 'Your face has come so queer.' I could have danced to them in the snow from sheer joy. I am not sure but what I did dance, though I never learned it.

Some of the windows in the Five Houses already showed a glime of light, not that it was needed yet, but my folk were practising precautions against my seeing them presently, for it is always a night of solemn gallanting. These precautions largely consisted in hanging heavy cloths, such as human habiliments, behind the blinds, so as to deaden the light to me should I be watching from the manse. There was no music as yet, and I was wondering where Posty and my fiddle were, when I fell in with them on the way. Though he has forgotten who the broken men were about whom he likes to play, I notice that one little bit from his forebears, as I take it, still clings to him; he walks up and down, while he is playing the fiddle, as if it were the pipes. On this occasion, however, I expect he was on the march for seasonable largess at the Grand House, which I am sure he always receives with complete surprise.

A thing commonly said about the Grand House is that it should be called the Grand Houses, there being in a manner two of them: though the one is but a reflection of the other in a round of water close by.

This lochy is only a kitten in size but deep; and I know not whether its unusual reflective properties are accidental, or, as some say, were a device of olden times to confuse the enemy when in liquor. At any rate one cannot easily tell in certain lights, unless you are particular about things being upside down, which is the house and which the reflection.

There is an unacceptable tale of the lord of the glen having been tracked to the house after Culloden, and of the red-coats being lured by a faithful retainer into the water, where they tried doors and windows till they drowned, the lord and his faithful retainer keeking over the edge at them and crying 'Bo.'

The house is of many periods, but its wonder is the banqueting hall, or rather a window therein.

They never banquet now in the hall, not even the English, and indeed it is nigh empty of gear except for tapestries on the walls, which the ignorant take to be carpets damaged in the '45. The great bowed window is said by travelled persons to stand alone among windows, for it is twenty-eight feet in height and more than half as wide. All who come to look at it count its little lozens, as we call the panes, which are to the number of two hundred and sixteen. These panes are made of some rare glass that has a tint of yellow in it, so that, whatever the weather is, to any one inside the hall it looks to be a sunny day. In the glen this glass is not thought much of and they say it should be renewed. The house is a bit old and weary, and I dare say these lozens are the only part of it that would shame renewal.

It was not here but in a bien little chamber where however indiscriminately you sit down you sit soft, that Mistress Lindinnock received me. She was tatting (but that cannot be the right word) at a new tapestry, or mending an old one, which was so voluminous that she rose out of it as from the snow. She is such a little old person that when she stands up you may think she has sat down; nevertheless she is so gleg at coming to the boil that contradictious men have stepped back hurriedly from the loof of her hand, and yet not been quick enough. She has always, as I have said, been a fine friend to me till this unhappy day.

She was the same woman though unusual quiet while we were talking of the ravel Christily was in, which I did not have to stress, as I found Dr John had obligingly gone straight to her with the story from the manse yesterday. I could not help enquiring, with all the look of its being an orra question, how he had taken to Miss Julie Logan.

Sharp I got the dreadful answer: 'He had no opportunity, for I had already packed the woman back to Edinburgh.'

I was to have worse blows than this tonight, though at the moment I could not have credited it; so I will only say that when I rallied I asked with cold politeness when the young lady was coming back.

Mistress Lindinnock, I could see, was eyeing me closely to find out how I stood the news, but she replied at once, like one prepared for war, 'Never, I hope; I don't like your Miss Julie Logan, my good sir.'

I will not say that even in that stern moment I got no gliff of pleasure out of hearing her called my Miss Julie Logan. Also it gave me an opportunity to reply with the thunderbolt, 'That is what I want her to be.'

She stamped her foot at me, but I never weakened. 'I demand her address,' I said. She refused it, and I replied loftily that it mattered not as I was confident she would write to me.

She raised her arms at that, like on appealing to a Higher Power, and said, 'If she writes to you I give the thing up.' Once she swung me round with a rage I could not construe and said on her tiptoes, 'I could tell you things about her any one of which would make you drop her in the burn, though you were standing in the middle of it with the jade in your arms.'

I replied in my stateliest, which has froze many, that I would stand defiant in the middle of the ocean with Miss Julie Logan on those terms; and I meant it too, though I am no swimmer.

I dare say I was a rather dignified spectacle towering there, very erect, with my arms folded: at any rate she shuddered like one cowed who had never been cowed before; or else she became cunning, for she prigged with me to do as she, my old friend, wanted, saying endearing things about how much she had liked me in the days when I was sensible, and that if I were not such a calf I would see she was now fonder of me in my imbecility. Her words were not all, as will be seen, fittingly chosen, nor did I like the pity with which she glowered at me, for she was the one in need of it.

Yet I had a melting for her at moments; especially as I was going away with but a scantling of courtesy. When she said that it would be the first time I had left her house (and she might have added any house in the glen) without calling for a benison on it, I stood rebuked. As we went on our knees she whispered rather tremulously, 'Pray, dear minister, for all who may be in trouble this night, and even danger,' and I did so, and it made the tangled woman greet.

Of course I presumed she meant Christily, but as I was shaking hands with her my mind took a shrewd turn and I said almost threateningly, 'You were not referring, were you, to Miss Julie Logan?' It spoilt the comparative friendliness of our parting, for she flared up again and said, ''Deed no; she is the only one that is in no need of those words tonight.'

Unfortunate being, she little knew, nor did I, the impiety of that remark.

When I got outside I was like one with no gate to go. The

tae half of me was warring with the other half. I sat down very melancholic by the little round of water I have spoken of. The night was forlorn, with the merest rim of the moon in sight, and no reflection on the water beyond some misty stars. I don't know why I sat there. It was not to keep vigil; I am sure I had no suspicion that Miss Julie Logan was still in the house.

I may have been there a considerable time before I saw or heard anything. What I heard came first: distant music. It may just have been Posty playing far away the most reprehensible but the loveliest of all the Jacobite cries, 'Will you no come back again?' Soon after he finished, if it was mortal man who played, all was as still again as if the death-cart my folk tell about was nearing the glen to cart away the old year.

Candles to a great number, and very sly, were beginning to get lit in the water. I spied on them interestedly. The full moon was now out of the clouds, and it was one of those nights when she wanders. The big window nearly filled the pond, and through it I saw a throng of people in the hall. So long as my eyes were fixed on the water of course it was only their reflections I saw. I saw them on their heads as in an inverted mirror, and they looked just as agreeable as the other way; maybe Nature herself does things with a disordered mind in the last gasp of the year.

They were in the Highland dress of lang syne. I never saw them all at once, because if they came nearer they were lost in the weeds and if they went back they had a neat way of going through the walls. The older ladies were in fine head-dresses and others in their ringlets; they were more richly attired than the men, and yet the men made the finer show. I could see the trews and an occasional flashing silver button or a gleam of steel; but near all colour had been washed out of them, as if they had been ower long among the caves and the eagles.

There was plenty of food on a table that sometimes came

forward, and they drank toasts thereat. I could not always put a meaning to what they did, but I saw them dancing and conversing, and though they were perhaps poor and desperate, they all, the gentlemen as much as the ladies, seemed to me to be of the great. They did rochly things as if they had forgotten the pretty ways, and next minute there would be a flourish in their manners that would have beat the pipes.

There was no music, though, and when this came to me I minded that I was not getting a sound across the water from the hall itself, though owing to the quietness of the night I heard in the open as infinitely small a thing as the letting-go of a twig. The company were as quiet as their reflections. This made me look across the pond at the window itself, which so far I had been jouking lest the company there should take tent of me. I had a mistrust they were up to ploys that were not for a minister to see, and would mischief me if they catched me spying. But that stealthy stillness garr'd me look up and I took a step or two to see better. They were all on the move, but at once stopped, hands on dirk, and I opined they suspected a watcher. I doukit, and after that, except for a wink now and again, I looked at nothing but the reflections. I knew I was in danger, but this did not greatly fash me so long as I was not catched.

I had never lost a feeling that there was an air of expectancy about them. I saw them backing against the walls to leave more space in the middle, and all eyes turned to the door, as if awaiting a great person. I suppose the tune was still swimming in my head, for I thought I knew who was coming in, he who was fed from the eagle's nest, and I had a sinking that it would be my duty to seize him and hand him over.

But it was a woman, it was Miss Julie Logan. She was not finely attired like the other ladies, but so poorly that her garments were in tatters. She would have made a braver

show if each of the ladies had torn off an oddment and
made a frock for her between them.

It was not, however, as one of little account that they
treated her or she treated them. She was the one presence
in the hall to them. They approached her only when she
signed to them that she could do with it, and as if over-
powered by the distinction that was befalling them. The
men made profound obeisance, and the ladies sank in that
lovely way to the floor. On some she smiled and let them
salute her hand, and others she looked at in a way I did not
see, but they backed from her as if she had put the fear of
Death into them. She gave the back of her hand to Mistress
Lindinnock, and I never saw an old woman look so gratified.

With a few she took a step or two in the dance, mayhap to
make others glower, and soon something was taking place
that I could not at first fathom.

It was clear she was about to leave them; for a ceremony
similar in most respects to that with which she had been
received was repeated and the doors thrown open for her
passing. But then they all gathered in the far end of the hall,
or sank through it, with their backs to her, which was
baffling to me; for up to that moment you could see
how carefully they gave her their faces. Yet they did it of
set purpose, or possibly at her command, for she was
watching them more haughtily than ever.

As soon as she was sure that every face was to the wall a
complete change came over her. She hastened – she almost
ran in her eagerness – to a corner of the window and lifted
from the floor a good-sized basket that I dare say they had
placed there for her. She lifted it like one who knew for
certain it would be there. She filled it with viands from the
table, picking and choosing them with affectionate interest.

I thought that, being in some way I had to grope for, the
one they held highest, she was too proud to let them know
how hungry she was, though that very knowledge was what

had made them place the basket so handily and look the other way while she filled it.

I thought that, reckless of correct behaviour, as all on that side were, they were Strangers, come trailing back into the present day under a command to honour and feed one who had long ago been left behind.

While she had been lording it so imperiously in the hall, she was belike thinking more about the basket than that she was the last sough of a song.

A moment after she was gone from the hall, with a withering look for any peeping face, I heard the first sound that had reached me from the house since I took to looking in the water. It was the closing of the front door. I hurried forward, and was in time to meet Miss Julie Logan, no longer a reflection, coming down the steps with the basket.

She said, 'Carry the basket, Adam,' and I carried it, but first I put my top-coat on her, and she slipped my hand into one of the pockets along with her own.

I think it was snowing again, or a tempest or something of the kind, but we were not heeding.

She took me to a small ruin of a bield for sheltering sheep in, and in a corner of it where was a pile of stones, maybe to mark some old grave, we sat down on them and opened the basket. She was very hungry, and I myself was also slow to desist from eating. For drinking we ate the snow, against which I have warned my Sabbath School scholars. The basket was so crammed with food of an engaging nature that when we paused, replete, there was still near a basketful left. Never in my life was I so merry as sitting on those stones, and she was also very droll. She had a way of shining her face close into mine and showing her pretty teeth like a child. It was the gaiety of her, but I did not quite like it. When we wandered on I wanted to bring the basket, but she said that was the place to leave it.

We said the kind of things a man and woman never say till they know each other through and through. It was all

about ourselves, and love was one of the words I did not
scruple to handle.

We were not bothering about far-back times or Mistress
Lindinnock; but when we came to the burn it minded me of
what the Old Lady had said I would do in a certain hap.
Miss Julie Logan demanded of me to repeat to her the exact
words, which I did, with one exception, namely, 'I could
tell you things about her any one of which would make you
drop her in the burn, though you were standing in the
middle of it with the jade in your arms.' I omitted the word
jade, so as not to lessen the Old Lady.

Miss Julie Logan was in a dance of delight and handed
me back my coat, crying, 'Adam, let us try it!'

I said there was danger in it, and she said, 'I like danger
fine,' and she coaxed me, saying, 'When you have got me
there I'll tell you what the Old Lady meant, and then, if you
don't drop me, belike I will be yours, Adam.' I lifted her in
my arms, and in the exultation of my man's strength she
was like one without weight. I carried her into the burn. It
was deep and sucking. She rubbed her head on my
shoulder in a way that would make a man think she liked
to be where she was. She peeped up at me, and hod. I am
thinking now she was wae for both of us, though she was
glittering too.

She said, 'Kiss me first, Adam, in case you have to drop
me.' I kissed her. 'Hold me closer,' she said, 'lest by some
dread undoing you should let me slip.' I held her closer.
'Adam dear,' she said, 'It is this, I am a Papist.' At that
awful word I dropped her in the burn. That she is still there
I do not doubt, though I suppose she will have been carried
farther down.

I have written this clear statement in the study, to be
shown by Laurie to Dr John and by him to the Branders
constabulary. I have put down everything exactly as it
happened, and I swear to its accuracy.

I have refused to go to my bed this night, and I know that

Laurie is sitting on a chair outside my door. I have told him none of the facts, but I can see that the man already suspects me.

I can remember nothing after I heard the splash, but he says he found me running up and down the water-side, and that he had to take a high hand with me to get me home. I would not change out of my wet things for all his blustering, but Christily, her face swollen with misery, came bursting in and tore them off me and put me into something dry. This is the last service she will ever render to me.

TEN

A Quarter of a Century

IT is a quarter of a century since I stopped writing this Diary and put the thing out of my sight.

Circumstances made me want to look through it again; and there it was in the garret, between the same two boards of waxcloth where I had kept it hidden from Christily in the days of my windy youth. I had forgotten that it was written on sermon paper, and such dereliction from propriety disturbs my conscience now even more than the vapours set down in it about the Roman woman.

Of course I am aware now that she never existed. I have been aware all these twenty-five years that I was the one who went queer, and not the self-sacrificing Christily, that it was to watch me that the man Laurie was brought to the manse, and that the story the Old Lady told me was invented for her by Dr John. My two good friends had to work their way through thorns to clear my disordered mind, but they managed it by the time the glen road had come up again like a spring flower.

I was long pithless and bedded with fevers, for which the doctor blamed the burn, and in that quiet time I got rid of all my delusions; though once in the middle of my rally I escaped everybody and made for the sheep bield to decide for certain that the basket was not still there. I was perfectly sane, and yet I did that. The result of my escapade was to retard my recovery for another month.

I left the glen for good early in August, just before the return of the English, with whom, though I liked them well, I had no desire to have further discourse about Diaries or what may seem to happen when that glen is locked. I have had two charges since I gave up my first, and for eighteen years I have been minister in this flourishing place in a mining district. Two years after my call I married a lady of the neighbourhood and it has been a blessed union, for my Mima is one in a thousand and the children grow in grace. I tell Mima everything except about the Roman, that being a passage in my life that never took place, nor have I sufficient intellect to be able to speak about it without doing so as if it were real.

I am thankful to say that the Roman is to me as if she never had been (and of course she never was, that just being a slip of the pen). A Scottish minister has few topcoats in his life, and when any old clothes will suffice I sometimes wear the one that is in the Diary. Many a night in this part where the rain turns black as it alights, I have been out in the old topcoat without remembering how pretty she looked in it; and this is natural, for she never was in it.

I have only once revisited my first charge, and it was a month ago. I stayed a night at Branders with Dr John, who has got a partner now. My old friend's hold on life has become little more than a bat's to a shutter, but he will still be at it, and some day I suppose he will be found among his own hills stiff and content.

I walked down the glen through the heather, a solitary, unless it may be said that in a sense the young Adam I had been walked with me. The English were on the hills, but they were not my English.

I lay for two nights in the old manse, and preached twice. They were not great sermons, but are held by some to be my two best, and I keep them for visits. The lad that once I was thought himself a gifted preacher, but the man he became knows better. That is nothing to boast of, for there is naught that houks the spirit from you so much as knowing better.

Mr Gallacher, who is the new minister, the second in succession to me, was preaching at Branders, and his wife, a genteel thick lady, sat in my old pew, nearest the door. It gave me, may I be forgiven, a sort of scunner of her. Gallacher was very civil, but he is not the kind of man, I think, that the Old Lady would have waved good-night to with her window-blind. She of course has been away with it this many a year.

There is a new postman, who, 'tis said, has trudged a distance equal to round the world since the days of my Posty. Christily is married on a provision merchant in Ireland, and once a year sends me a present of eggs, with a letter enquiring very guardedly about my health. Joanna Minch and the lass have gone to some other glen. The only faces I could give a name to in the Five Houses are the smith and two of his sons. The once lusty man is now an old carl sitting on his dyke, having reached that terrible time for a Scotsman of knowing that he will never be allowed by his well-intentioned offspring to do another day's work for ever and ever. Sometimes, to give him an hour's pride, they let him wheel a barrow. He will have to die gradual on a fine bed of straw, but he would rather be gotten with his hammer in his hands.

There have been great changes at the manse, inside and out. One hardly knows the study now, for there is a sofa fornent the fireplace. It has a grate. They burn coal. I had sold the grandy to Mr Gallacher, and one could see by the look of it that it had never missed me. There is an erection containing a foreign plant on the identical spot where the Roman sat; but she never sat there.

Outside, the chief change in the manse is that Mr Gallacher has lifted the henhouse to the gable-end, which I consider a great mistake. He has also cut down my gean tree.

The glen has not been what can be called locked for the last eight years, and Mr Gallacher knows very little about the old superstitions that plagued young Adam. He had heard something nonsensical about a red-shanked man on a horse whose hoofs made no marks, a poor affair though unaccountable. Mr Gallacher was very sound about the hallucinations all being clavers unworthy of investigation, and on that point at least we were in agreement. I asked him, just to keep the conversation going, if any Stranger woman had been seen, but he had heard of none, nor could he, for there never was one.

Of course I could not go for a walk on the Sabbath day; but as I was leaving for Branders on the Monday I got up betimes to have a last wander in the glen. I did not specially want to do this, and I prefer to put it that the fillip came from the Adam I had been. The sun soon got very masterly, though there was a nip in the air at first, and I made the mistake of wearing the old top-coat.

I sat for a time among the heather by the pond, where the reflection from the Grand House is still to be seen, but it is somewhat spoilt by a small windmill having been erected close by to provide the breeze in which, 'tis said, the trout rise best. I am told that this was Posty's last contrivance to make things easy for the English. I thought with little respect of the Jacobites and the '45, and a dog that may have been of old descent drove me away.

I went on to the bield, but nothing is left of it now except the pile of stones. I stood looking for a long time at the place where we had left the basket.

I went to Joanna's shieling, though I knew she was gone, and I found it gone too. I just went because I was sure that Joanna's visitor had been my visitor, though we were both in a dwam when we thought we saw her. I liked to mind the Roman's bonny act in making a pig of herself to heat the cold body of Joanna. I wished she had been given a chance to do this. She would have done it if she could.

I went to the Eagles Rock, and it looked the more sinister because there was a scarf of rime hiding the Logan stone. When the rime drifted I thought I could see the stone shogging.

I left my visit to the burn-side to the end. There is now a swinging bridge for the convenience of church-goers in the back-end of the year; but though little more than a wimple of water was running and sometimes coming to a standstill, I found the exact bend in the burn where I dropped her, if she had been there to drop. I stood, unruffled, keeping an iron grip on myself, my mind so rid of the old fash that I marvelled at my calm. It was not so, however, with my top-coat, which I found becoming clammy-cold, as if recalling another time by the burn and feeling we were again too near for safety. You might have said it tugged at me to come away, but that of course was just a vagary of my mind.

The young Adam in me must have had the upper hand, for looking back, I see it was to him rather than to me it happened. He thought he had catched into his arms some-thing padding by, whose husky voice said 'Adam' lovingly, the while her glamorous face snuggled into his neck, the way a fiddle does. Next moment he gave a cry because he thought he was running with blood; and even I had a sinking till I tried my throat with my handkerchief. What-ever had been there was gone now; and I hurried away myself, for I was as shaken as if it had been the Spectrum.

I bided the night at Branders with Dr John, to whom all my story was so familiar except just one happening that I had always sworn never to reveal even to him.

We sat long over his pipe talking about what he called the old dead-and-done affair. We were very intimate that night, the one of us an ancient and the other getting on.

'Let us be thankful,' the doctor said, 'that it can all be so easily construed, for the long and the short of it is that you were just away in your mind. Any other construing of it would be too uncomfortable to go to our beds on even now.'

I said, taking a higher line: 'It is not even allowable'; and yet we discussed the possibility of its having had any backing to it for, I suppose, the last time. This would have meant that the glen, instead of its minister, does sometimes go queer in the terrible stillness of the time when it is locked. 'We should have to think,' the doctor said, with the kettle in his hand, 'that it all depended on the stillness of the glen. If it got to be stiller than themselves it woke them up, and they were at their old ploys again.'

'I am not seeing,' I said, 'how even that could bring me into it.'

'Nor am I,' he agreed, pouring out cosily, 'but let us say that in such incredible circumstances you might by some untoward accident have got involved while the rest of us escaped.'

The word accident is not a friend of mine, and so, or for some other reason, I said, 'I would rather think she had picked me out.' He smiled at that, not grasping that I was speaking for young Adam.

'Maybe,' he said to make me laugh, but failing, 'it was her echo that was back in the glen, and by some mischance you got into the echo.'

Then he grew graver, and said he would have none of those superstitions; the affair could only be construed naturally so long as we accepted the experiences I once thought I had gone through as having been nothing but the fancies of a crazy man.

'All of them?' I could not help saying.

'Every one,' said he, clapping me confidently on the shoulder; 'do you not see, man, that if any one of them was arguable it would be less easy to dispose of the lave?'

'That day during my illness,' I said, 'when I was but three parts convinced by your construing, and slipped away from you all to the bield to make certain that the basket was not there—'

'Precisely,' said he, 'that would be a case in point. What strange ravels might we have got entangled in if you had found that basket!'

My many years' old resolution to keep the thing dark

from all, even from him, broke down, and I spoke out the truth. 'Dr John,' I told him, 'I did find the basket that day.'

For long he threepit with me that I was away in my mind again, but he had to listen to me while I let out the tale, which has ceased to perturb me, though I have a sort of a shiver at writing it down. I found the basket with its provender in the bield where we had left it, and at that the peace which had been coming to me threatened to go, and my soul was affrichted. I prayed long, and I took the basket down to the burn and coupit its sodden gear therein, and itself I tore to bits and scattered. It was far waur to me at that time to think that she had been than that she was just a figment of the brain.

I told all this to Dr John, and at first he was for spurning it, nor can I say for certain that he believes it now. I leave it at that, but fine I know it would be like forsaking the callant that once I was to cast doubt on what lies folded up in his breast.

I am back now, secure and serene, in my mining town which, in many ways, with its enterprise and modern improvements, including gas and carts to carry away any fluff of snow that falls, is far superior to my first charge. I have a wider sphere of usefulness and a grand family life. As I become duller in the uptake, time will no doubt efface every memory of Miss Julie of the Logan; and of mornings I may be waking up without the thought that I have dropped her in the burn. Of course it is harder on young Adam. I have a greater drawing to the foolish youth that once I was than I have pretended. When I am gone it may be that he will away back to that glen.

	HODDER AND STOUGHTON (1932)	THE TIMES (1931)
p. 249	these doolies	them
p. 251	next August.	next August. Possibly there will be very little snow, for 'tis said, the white winters sometimes jump a year or two, which must be vexatious to the strangers.
p. 250	for two years back.	for two years back. My congregation would naturally have liked me to have a beard.
	When I got my call to this place my proper course	My proper course
	which I did walking with affected humility behind three cart-loads of furniture all my own	walking for six miles with sinful pride.
	and well aware . . . to the mile.	But I had not the moral strength.
	the fiddle	this instrument
	is less my own poor cajoling . . . from better hands	is not so much my own poor performances as not hearing the songs themselves.
	Scottish lilts, I mean	Scottish lilts
	small, as, except for stravaigers,	small for

	HODDER AND STOUGHTON (1932)	*THE TIMES* (1931)
pp. 250–52	My manse and kirk are isolated on one side of the burn . . . On the one side of the burn, but so close	My manse and kirk are isolated on one side of the burn, but on the other side so close
p. 253	depend upon in a tack of wild weather	depend upon for a wet day
	contrair	contrary
	man or beast	both man or beast
	I am sometimes doubtful	I seldom know
	play with	use of
	white-washed and thacked . . . in lines as straight	white-washed and thacked, and they all open on to the Glen road, as if not to miss any diversion that may be passing by. A coarse green grass grows on the road in lines as straight
	beast	horse
	she is the chief	is the chief
p. 254	man outside it on his box	man, body outside it, on a stool
	called her before me	denounced her
	She is also at times overly sly . . . She is back again now, for the English	She is back again now. The English
	again in the glen	again
p. 255	crossed over	came up to the manse
	happy knack	knack
	now I cast back, I believe	now I come to think of it,
	Usquebaugh	Usquebach

	HODDER AND STOUGHTON (1932)	*THE TIMES* (1931)
p. 256	popular	pleasing
	gave it the go-by	never let on
	give utterance . . . any word whatever	give utterance.
	considerateness	niceness
	the dumb	me
	meritorious	melting
p. 257	reflection	consideration
	to what I have called the	to the
	My friends	They
	locked . . . smell of learning.	locked.
	madden	distract
	I was not putting them to the question, but all the ladies cried out	All the ladies cried out
p. 257	carriages. I can see now they were just getting after me.	carriages.
	light-heartedness, . . . can rise	light-heartedness, which on occasions, rises
pp. 259–61	walks into the kirk in her creeping lastic sides	walks into the kirk
	Posty is also at the Five Houses and is the kind . . . any ill news	Posty is also at the Five Houses.
p. 260	twine	chains
	Mr Watery, with whom I sometimes suffer niffer pulpits.	Mr Watery.
	overgrown	important
	claymore . . . can be counted.	claymore.
	perjink little	little
pp. 260–1	larger size . . . snow.	larger size.

	HODDER AND STOUGHTON (1932)	*THE TIMES* (1931)
p. 261	may be a ham	will be a ham
	worse of it . . . with the ladle.	worse of it.
	the kettle-lid plopping while	the while
	and up here in the study as we sat into the fire	and
	all the clavers and clecking	all the clutters
	lamentable	clankering
	tartan	pipes
	waur cleughs	caverns
	folk still in the glen used to see them from below searching for roots atween the rocks	folk still in the glen saw them from below
	speel	climb
	sink	blanket
p. 262	an intake of breath by the glen folk	cautiously by the glen-folk of those times
	salmon that	salmon
	fugitives	hunted ones
	In one case . . . canny to go.	In the queerest story that has ever come down to us they called the heroine 'Someone who was with Him.'
	the Stranger	a fugitive
	for a time in July	in July
	nigh him with nourishment	nigh him
	dirks	Ogilvy dirks
	nor, as I say the story goes,	nor as they say

	HODDER AND STOUGHTON (1932)	*THE TIMES* (1931)
	saved by the mysterious Someone Who Was With Him.	saved by Some One.
p. 263	At that time	But at that time
	and yet hold on for centuries.	and that they never lose this property though with the centuries they wear small.
	get on to it	get onto the stone
	is said, nonsensically, to be the marks	is called the marks
	The white heather	It
	lord and master	master
	Some think	Some think, according to the doctor.
	Such was the doctor's tale . . . shake of the head	To what clan she belonged is unknown, but in the glen they think it was probably the one that is little better than the rest.
p. 264	Dr John was saying . . . clash about the folk	Dr John went on, 'that all the daftness about folk
	there is ower little darg for a hardy race, and they hark back	folk hark back
	assure you, Mr Yestreen,	assure you,
	buried in its own stour	grass-grown in this glen
	so gleg	sib
	by himself	dunder headed
	havrels of nowadays	havrels
	I may have already let out	I have already hinted
	far back	long ago

HODDER AND STOUGHTON (1932)	THE TIMES (1931)
hearsay	a legend
and belongs to	in
from the fire	on the hearth
brings a sough of the	brings the
house	know
bound by his own hands	bound or rebound by his own fair hands
his entries	entries
himself, having no Latin,	himself
set forth	put
as if a rat	as if, you might say, a rat
tampering	trickery
bits of	queer
lawful possessor	him
Sometimes one of the twain	According to the stories, sometimes one of them
possession.	possession. They claimed they had seen the other also, and that he did not walk. 'He paddled,' they said.
room to room . . . he padded.	room to room.
the minister	him
Dr John	the doctor
the old man in the grandy chair . . . the same person.'	found him in this chair instead of me.
As usual . . . take the gate.	As usual our sitting ended with Christilly coming in to announce that she gave us ten minutes before she

The page margin labels: p. 265 (at "house"), p. 266 (at "possession."), pp. 266–7 (at "As usual . . . take the gate.")

HODDER AND STOUGHTON (1932)	THE TIMES (1931)
	carried away the lamp. She also mentioned, as a matter of small importance, that it was snowing.

p. 268	wastrie of a world	world
	fortnight past	fortnight
	time for it	time
	an event	events
	my hens . . . yesterday	my hens, whose toes I found frozen to the perch, and my two sheep into the manse, or that yesterday
	at an antrin time	whiles
	fill up . . . maybe not.	fill up with old matter, but the whiteness of the sheets gives me a scunner, and I put it away. The snow has choked my Diary as well as the glen.
	blankets	blanket
	White hillocks of the shape of eggs have arisen here and there	White hillocks, which we have been unacquainted with in any colour, are here and there,
	bellied out	rounded
pp. 268–9	now deep, with a lash around at corners, and unchancey to risk. At times of ordinary wet	now deep and boastful, and unchancey to cross. At ordinary times
p. 269	melted for	rose with pride in
	and I have cried	but I have cried
	I sit up . . . from the roof	It is a treat to me now, though formerly when I had company an

	HODDER AND STOUGHTON (1932)	*THE TIMES* (1931)
		invitation, to see her friendly foot keeping the study door open. I sit up here reading and nodding, or I go out and shovel, though all I shovel away, and more, may be back by morning.
	I can see him like a pendulum passing the glints of light. I can	I can just see him passing and re-passing the glints of light like a pendulum. But I can
	slue	slip
	that Border boast	with a merely amusing piece
	The glen was deserted . . . For a moment	For a moment
p. 270	hallan	passage
	light	match
	also that maybe, like the performers	and that, maybe, like the fiddlers
	allure	enticement
	mere fancy	fancy
p. 271	To write this account . . . I will now go	I will now go
	half nine on the clock	barely nine o'clock
	half nine	nine
	good-night to each other . . . a living being	good night. There is a warmth about it
	dumb	dark
p. 272	which has	that has
	ran him on to the stair-head to wring and scrape	rushed him into the lobby to scrape
	ettled	wanted

HODDER AND STOUGHTON (1932)	THE TIMES (1931)
the grandy	his chair
head foremost into sleep	into a torpor

<!-- p. 273 -->

	HODDER AND STOUGHTON (1932)	THE TIMES (1931)
p. 273	he told me	he said
	I'll be dovering again	we'll never come to the end of it
	in the middle of sentences	as if for the winter months
	the farm of Whammle	an outlying farm
	but a stour . . . sleugh crossing	but the wind was lashing his face and the visibility was so bad that they soon lost each other
	for he feared . . . found frozen.	for he dreaded that Fargie might not have had the sense to heap on the peat and that the woman might be found frozen.
	divot, with but a bole window	divot
	one of his little leers	even a little leer
p. 274	Whammle	farm
	gude-wife	wife
	went on, taking a chew at them	went on
	tire	sleep
	her best brot	a shawl
	you have	you and your friend have
p. 275	till after	till
	brot	shawl
	done for me and it	done
	nippit	snatched
	heat her, and the bole closed,	heat her,

HODDER AND STOUGHTON (1932)	*THE TIMES* (1931)
and made me keep	and lay at my feet and made me keep
p. 276	bucket	creel
	as how to	as to
	leave him in	let him sink into
	an hour	a few hours
	grudge it	grudge them
	bucket	creel
	I could not forbear . . . He saw in what	He saw in what
	a stramash	distress
	kindly	bravely
p. 277	was not there	never came in
	a practical kimmer like Joanna	Joanna
	'None of that . . . old minister's story.'	'She no doubt got it out of that old story' I said.
	'Ay', he granted . . . go down the wind.'	'That might account for it. At any rate it is of no importance as we are both agreed that she was by her lonesome self. But what a pity for us to have to let that joyous visitor go down the wind.'
	I was done with wayward women	I was feeling very young
p. 278	kirstening	christening
	suddenly	well
	swore to her visit from the Stranger	repeated her story
	given birth . . . the party present	put me in a quandary, and the half dozen present

	HODDER AND STOUGHTON (1932)	THE TIMES (1931)
	seen her	seen her in the glen
	redding up	exposition
p. 279	gate	gait
	any dirdum about Strangers	the folly about 'strangers'
	the harder I got	the more I hammered
	shule	shovel
	place	kirk
p. 280	smile	triumphant smile
	takes too great	takes
	bide to enjoy the mirth, but I know my presence casts a shadow on their ease	bide to let them be more at ease
	so-called event	event
p. 281	shelties were being yoked	ponies were being put in
	across	over
	past few years	past
	had thrown	has thrown
	and a glow . . . youth	and I have sometimes wished I was old, so as to be done with the clutches of youth. I am not afraid of them now
	muff	large muff
	The upper part . . . There was a diverting	There was a diverting
p. 283	get her	convey her to here
	twenty minutes	twenty minutes only
	chairs	horse hair chairs
	to be of the least	of small
	This comes	That comes
	for ever that	that for ever
	the grandy chair	my big chair

	HODDER AND STOUGHTON (1932)	*THE TIMES* (1931)
	sudden way	way
	disregard of her company	indifference to others
p. 284	shining eyes	eyes
	gowk	gawk
p. 285	broke up . . . woebegone	broke down in shame and hid my face on the table. She was taken aback and raised my head gently, and she was woebegone
	she said with every bit of her	she asked
	in a sort of contest . . . strings	as if laughter and a tear had met, just as they do on the strings
	a server, and when Miss Julie Logan . . . Then the Old Lady	a tray, and the Old Lady
p. 287	I am very ravelled in my mind	I am in a faking
	hankered	craved
	carefully casual	thought out
p. 288	the keyhole	it
	got	sped
	the silly tod	she
	tattle about my sitting	a report that I sit
	in such a throb	so agitated
p. 289	fell to	stood
	ask the young lady . . . herself	get Mistress Lindinnock and the young lady to come down
	got stiff	stiffened
	of the two	the two
	for, after all,	for

	HODDER AND STOUGHTON (1932)	*THE TIMES* (1931)
p. 290	and a heavy one too for Dr John, who left the manse	and, for Dr John, who has known her from youth, and left the manse
	come back	come padding back
p. 291	This may have got . . . Some of the windows	I forgot my cloth and flung snowballs at the smith's bairns, who will remember this New Year's Eve for that. The windows
	already showed	showed
	my folk	they
	presently . . . heavy cloths	presently at some New Year devilment. These consisted in their hanging cloths
	watching from the manse	on the watch
	which I am sure	which
p. 292	gear	plenishing
	not here	not, of course, here
	bien little chamber	cosy little room
p. 293	snow	foam
	little old	little
	gleg at coming to the boil	ready
	loof	palm
	She was the same . . . manse yesterday	All was well while we were talking of Christilly's case, into which I did not have to go into much detail as I found Dr John had obligingly gone straight to her with it from the manse yesterday.

HODDER AND STOUGHTON (1932)	THE TIMES (1931)
look of its being an orra question	Appearance of its being an ordinary question
dreadful	staggering
to Edinburgh.	to Edinburgh this morning.
was to have	have had
when I rallied	on rallying
got no gliff of pleasure out of hearing her	took no pleasure in hearing her
round with a rage I could not construe	round very raized

p. 294

any one of which	that
which has froze many, that I would stand defiant	that I would stand
shuddered	looked
prigged	cajoled
fonder of me	fonder of me still
fittingly	happily
glowered	obviously regarded
Yet I had a melting . . . left her house	Yet I had a drawing to her, and when I was going away but a scantling of courtesy, she said sadly enough that it would be the first time I had left her house
my mind took a shrewd turn	I had another thought

pp. 294–5

When I got outside . . . melancholic	When I got outside something made me reluctant to make straight for the manse. I sat down very melancholy.

	HODDER AND STOUGHTON (1932)	*THE TIMES* (1931)
p. 295	first: distant music.	first.
	It may	It must
	as still . . . the old year.	as still.
	Candles	I thought no more of him, for candles
	The full moon was now out of the clouds, and it was one of those nights when she wanders	It was now one of those nights when the moon wanders
	throng	concourse
	So long as my eyes were fixed on the water of course	Of course
	the other way; maybe . . . year.	the other way.
	ower	over
p. 296	I minded that I was not getting a sound across the water from the hall itself	I recalled that I had not heard a sound from behind me in the Hall itself
	company	real folk
	This made me look across . . . was not catched.	If I had been an imaginative man I might have thought that the real house, which was invisible to me where I sat, was not lit up at all, and that what I saw in the water was just a reflection come trailing back from other days. I took a step or two to make sure about this, and then all the men in the water suddenly stood still, with their hands on dirk or broadsword. I thought they had heard a dis-

	HODDER AND STOUGHTON (1932)	*THE TIMES* (1931)
		quieting sound, and then I knew that what they heard had been my own movement. After that I sat very mouse, looking at nothing but the reflection. I was sure now that, despite the dancing, it was a gathering of the hunted folk as stealthy as the night itself.
	swimming	dirling
	he who was fed from the eagle's nest	the captain of them all
p. 297	only when she signed to them that she could do with it	singly
	soon	by and by
pp. 297–8	what had made them . . . filled it.	what had brought them together.
p. 298	come trailing	come
	under a	by some royal
	long ago been	been
	last sough	end
	withering	last withering
	engaging	agreeable
	face close	face
	I did not quite like it	I joukit
p. 299	had said	said
	hap	emergency
	did, with one exception,	did,
	any one of which	that
	jade in your arms . . . Old Lady.	jade.

HODDER AND STOUGHTON (1932)	THE TIMES (1931)
delight and handed me back my coat, crying,	delight and cried
what the Old Lady meant	the thing
belike	aiblins
I lifted her . . . into the burn	There and then I up with her and carried her into the burn
and hod . . . glittering too.	and her face was of the sweet homeliness of a dove that I have mentioned, and so also were her words.
I kissed her . . . I held her closer.	I kissed her, and I held her the tighter lest by some dread undoing I should let her slip. Her face was all sparkling now, almost more than enough.

p. 300	render to me.	render to me. She says she has wrung my top coat and put it before the kitchen fire. They both say I came back in it, but I know where my top-coat is.
p. 301	pithless and bedded with fevers	bedded with colds and throats
	though once in the middle of my rally I escaped	except once in the middle of my convalescence, when I escaped
	I was perfectly sane . . . another month.	I dug for it with my hands as if there had once been a basket, and the only result of my senseless escapade was that it retarded my recovery for another month

	HODDER AND STOUGHTON (1932)	THE TIMES (1931)
	the glen	that glen
p. 302	the neighbourhood	this neighbourhood
	suffice	do
	wear	still wear
	Many a night . . . I have been out	Many a time I have been out
	among his own hills stiff and content	sitting twisted in a drift, which is how he would like his end to be.
	but are held	though are held
	best, and I keep them for visits.	best.
	better. That is	better, which is
p. 303	nearest the door . . . a sort of scunner of her	nearest the door.
	well-intentioned offspring	off-spring
	barrow . . . in his hands.	barrow of manure.
	It has a grate . . . never missed me.	They burn coal.
	the Roman sat; but she never sat there.	The Roman sat when she drew notes of exclamation, but she never sat there nor drew anything. It is not to myself that I need to tell she never was, for I know perfectly, but to him, the poor gomeril, my young self, whom I have to carry about with me.
	to the gable-end, which I consider a great mistake. He has also cut down my gean tree.	from the west-end to the gable-end, which I consider a great mistake.

	HODDER AND STOUGHTON (1932)	THE TIMES (1931)
p. 304	horse whose hoofs made no marks	horse
	Mr Gallacher	He
	The sun soon got very masterly	It soon became very hot
	among the heather by the pond	by the pond
	told that	told
	of old descent	of a different opinion
	for a long time at the place where we had left the basket.	at them for a long time and I felt sure she was not there.
	though we were both in a dwam when we thought we saw her	and so it brought us together
	sinister	lonesome
p. 305	burn-side	burn
	running	running at present
	come away, but that of course was just a vagary of my mind.	come away.
	The young Adam	I kept calm, but the young Adam
	handkerchief.	handkerchief. I had the upper hand again.
	hurried away myself, for I was as shaken as if it had been the Spectrum.	hurried away. It must just have been the paddling sound that made me think of the Spectrum.
pp. 305–7	I bided the night . . . figment of the brain.	I stayed the night at Branders with Dr John to whom I told everything except just not that. One sees how little significance either of us now gave to what

HODDER AND
STOUGHTON (1932)

had been perturbing at
the time, that we could
banter each other over
his toddy, about the
dead-and-done affair. It
was as if the two of us,
the one ancient and the
other getting on, had
got rid of young Adam
for the nonce and could
play with any wayward
solutions that chanced
to strike a spark.

Dr John said in his
dry way that, after all,
there was no reason
why doings of the past
should not rise up like
other ghosts and come
back to be re-enacted.
He thought it might all
depend on the stillness
of the glen. If it was
stiller than themselves
perhaps it woke them
up.

We yammered on
agreeably to our whim,
thinking all the time of
one stranger and yet
never mentioning her.

We were on the edge
of the serious when he
advised me to drop
conjecture, and just
think of her, if think I
must, as what I had
once called her, the end
of a song. It was ended,
he said, long before my
time, but maybe its

HODDER AND STOUGHTON (1932)	THE TIMES (1931)
	echo stirred in the stillness, and by some mischance I had got into the echo. I am thinking that is the nearest we shall ever come to it; but we agreed, as he tapped out his pipe, that the wisest of us all had been the top-coat, when it said with a shove that this glen was no place for me.

p. 307	fluff	trifle
	duller	feeble
	may	will
	her in the burn.	something

Glossary

affrichted, affrighted
ane, one
anent, alongside
antrin, occasional
ballants, ballads
bannock, oatcake
bee-skeps, beehives
begrutten, tear-stained, sorrowful
bield, shelter
bien, comfortable
birzed, pushed with force
bole window, small opening in a wall
bothies, rough hut, used as temporary accommodation for shepherds
braxy, an intestinal disease common to sheep
brot, apron
callant, youth
camstane, hearthstone
camsterie, perverse, unruly
carlines, old women
carls, men
carritches, catechisms
chap, knock, stroke
cheeping, chirping, whispering
clachan, village
clavers, gossip
clecking, gossiping
cleughs, precipices
clouty, cloth
clutters, noises
contrair, contrary
coupit, overturned
cracknut, hazelnut

curran, few
dambrod, draughts
darg, work
dawted, caressed
dirdum, tumultuous noise, uproar
dirk, short dagger worn by Highlanders
dirl, tingling sensation
divert, entertainment, amusement
doolies, spectres
doukit, ducked
dovering, dozing
dreed, suspected, feared
dung, beaten
dunted, knocked, beaten, struck
dwam, swoon
ettled, attempted
fash, trouble
fleyed, frightened
forbye, in addition to
fornent, in front of
garr'd, forced
gean, wild cherry
gey, wild
gleg, quick, keen
gliff, glimpse
glime, squint
gowk, fool
grandy, grandfather
greet, cry
grossart-bushes, gooseberry bushes
gude-wife, mistress, landlady
hallan, porch

329

hantle, large number
happit, covered
havers, nonsense
havrels, chatterings
hinted, crept
hod, hidden
hoddy, hiding
houks, digs
ill-gettit, badly-behaved, perverse
jaloused, suspected
jimply, barely
jouking, ducking
kebbock, cheese
keeking, peeping
kimmer, girl, more usually godmother or midwife
kittle, cunning, skilful
lave, rest
likit, liked
lippen, trust
loof, palm
loup, leap
mairtered, martyred
murie, unidentified. SND cites Barrie's use of the word as a misprint for merry
mutch, cap
nans, again
natheless, nevertheless
niffer, exchange
nippit, pinched
nob, knob
orra, odd
ower, over
perjink, trim, neat
prig, plead
rasps, raspberries
ravelled, confused, muddled
redding up, clearing up
reek, smoke
riven, torn
rizers, redcurrants
rochly, rough
roup, auction
saut-bucket, salt-box

scantling, scarcity
scart, scratch
scunner, dislike
sederunt, meeting
shielings, huts or sheds
shogging, swaying
shule, shovel
sib, akin
skeer, wild
skirling, blowing, shrieking
sleugh, slough, marsh, quagmire
slue, slip
smored, smothered
sough, sound, deep sigh or gasp
speel, climb
stour, struggle
stramash, commotion
stravaigers, wanderers
strippit, stripped
sumph, simpleton
sweer, unwilling
tae half, one half
tangled, tired, weary, harassed
tatting, tangling
tent, heed
tergiversations, backsliding
thacked, patched
threepit, argued
throughither, disorganised, muddled
titting, tugging
tod, fox
unchancey, unlucky, dangerous
uphaud, maintain
wae, woeful
wap, throw
wastrie, reckless, wasteful
waur, worse
wheesht, be quiet
whit-rit, weasel or stoat
wimple, tangle, twist, ripple
Yestreen, yesterday evening